The
Finger
and
the
Moon

Set in the heart of Somerset, in south-west England, and in sight of the mysterious Glastonbury Tor, the Allhallows centre is run by former psychiatrist Martin Ellis. At the centre, students research the ancient arts of Magic, and make discoveries that deeply impact their lives. Graduates of Allhallows come from all walks of life, but they have one thing in common: they return to their previous endeavours with a new vigour and success, and often catch the public eye.

Ellis has become deeply involved in the occult as a means of rediscovering old answers to the ancient questions and anxieties of humanity. His success arouses the interest and curiosity of Geoffrey, a freelance journalist and expert on Arthurian legend, who comes to study the Allhallows phenomenon for an article and to find out what makes Ellis - and his famous graduates - tick.

Instead, amidst the strange, timeless atmosphere in the old house, the baffling maze and the mysterious sculptures in the garden, Geoffrey encounters, then experiences for himself, the astonishing sense-enhancing technique that appears to lie at the heart of Martin Ellis's success - and discovers that the original questions he posed lead inexorably on to answers that raise ever more disturbing questions - questions with deeper meaning than he had ever dreamed...

This magnificent work - the only novel penned to date by leading Arthurian scholar and Glastonbury resident Geoffrey Ashe - has been out of print for over a quarter of a century. In it, after the manner of Platonic Dialogue, Ashe uses the form of fiction to present some fascinating and very real insights on ancient myths and traditions, on the Magical Arts, and on human existence itself: insights which are even more valid today than they were when this book was first published in 1973.

For this new edition, based on the second UK edition of 1975, but completely re-transcribed and re-edited, the author has written a new and revealing Introduction, extensive and detailed Notes to the Text and an Afterword that place *The Finger and the Moon* in the context of his own later works, giving the original text even more meaning than before.

Long sought-after by Geoffrey Ashe's fans all over the world, the Brideswell Press is proud to offer a new edition of this outstanding work: a book that steps beyond the boundaries of fiction versus non-fiction, into a world that is entirely its own.

'An unusually intelligent story'—*Oxford Mail*

'Mr Ashe's authoritative touch lends credence to much that this dramatic and shivery story implies'—*The Scotsman*

'A hauntingly memorable achievement... and all the more so because Mr Ashe sees clearly, and states at every point, the case for the opposition'—*Times Literary Supplement*

BOOKS BY
GEOFFREY ASHE

The Tale of the Tub: A Survey of the Art of Bathing Through the Ages,
Newman Neame, 1950
King Arthur's Avalon: The Story of Glastonbury, Collins, 1957
From Caesar to Arthur, Collins, 1960
Land to the West: St. Brendan's Voyage to America, Collins, 1962
The Land and the Book, Collins, 1965
The Carmelite Order, Carmelite Press, 1965
Gandhi: A Study in Revolution, Stein & Day, 1968
(Editor and contributor) *The Quest for Arthur's Britain*, Pall Mall, 1968
King Arthur in Fact and Legend, T. Nelson, 1971
Camelot and the Vision of Albion, Heinemann, 1971
(With others) *The Quest for America*, Pall Mall, 1971
The Art of Writing Made Simple, W. H. Allen, 1972
Do What You Will: A History of Anti-morality, W. H. Allen, 1974
The Virgin, Routledge & Kegan Paul, 1976
The Ancient Wisdom, Macmillan, 1977
Miracles, Routledge & Kegan Paul, 1978
A Guidebook to Arthurian Britain, Longman, 1980
Kings and Queens of Early Britain, Methuen, 1982
Avalonian Quest, Methuen, 1982
The Discovery of King Arthur, Doubleday, 1985
The Landscape of King Arthur, Webb & Bower, 1987
(With Norris Lacy) *The Arthurian Handbook*, Garland, 1988
Mythology of the British Isles, Methuen, 1990
King Arthur: The Dream of a Golden Age, Thames & Hudson, 1990
Dawn Behind The Dawn, Henry Holt, 1992
Atlantis, Thames & Hudson, 1992
The Traveller's Guide to Arthurian Britain, Gothic Image, 1997
The Book of Prophecy, Blandford, 1999; Orion, 2002
The Hell-Fire Clubs (a revised version of *Do What You Will*),
Sutton, 2000
Merlin, Wessex Books, 2001
Labyrinths and Mazes, Wessex Books, 2003
The Discovery of King Arthur, Revised Edition, Sutton, 2003

The
Finger
and
the
Moon

Geoffrey Ashe

THE BRIDESWELL PRESS

First published in Great Britain
by William Heinemann Ltd, 1973
First American Edition published
by The John Day Company, 1974
Second UK Edition published
by Panther Books Ltd, 1975

This edition published 2004 in the United Kingdom
by The Brideswell Press,
Somersham, Cambridgeshire
info@brideswell.com • http://www.brideswell.com/

ISBN 0-9649553-2-6

Third Edition

British Library Cataloguing in Publication Data
A catalogue record for this book is available from the British Library

Printed by Lightning Source

Designed and typeset in ITC Kennerley
by Richard Elen at The Brideswell Press.

Contents

Preface to the Annotated Edition

FIRST PUBLISHED IN 1973, *The Finger and the Moon* had a curious history. It was not originally meant to be fiction at all. For some years I had been taking an interest in the famous phenomena of the late Sixties and early Seventies, the so-called hippie time: "alternative" life-styles, non-violent protest, psychedelic experiences, revived belief in occultism and magic. From my own marginal standpoint I even made contributions, in connection, for instance, with the centenary of Mahatma Gandhi, and the launching of the pop-mystical Glastonbury Fayre – since repeated from time to time, vastly changed, as the Glastonbury Festival. My feelings as an older sympathizer were always mixed. I was more impressed by the basic impulsions than by the happenings that expressed them. Many of that junior generation seemed to be looking in promising directions. Far fewer knew what they were talking about, or where they were going. Yet without accepting "alternative" notions, I could often see that it was a mistake to reject them totally.

A related truth in another field had been dawning on me through acquaintance with legends. Take the tale of King Arthur, with which I have had a good deal to do. The romantic believes it literally, and is wrong. The iconoclast, having seen through the fiction, dismisses it... but is also wrong. The mythos arises out of something authentic in Britain's past, and the patient appraisal that can lead towards this must take account of all the data – fantasy and fable included. The proper approach to legends like this is to take them *seriously* without taking them *literally*. And the same applied to some of the notions of the Sixties counter-culture, among them the magical and mystical.

At that time I was attracted by Jung's attitude in the later part of his career, when he studied alchemy and Gnosticism and occultism and even flying saucers. He, likewise, took them seriously without taking them literally. He did not imagine that alchemists had

9

turned lead into gold. But he claimed that such mysteries, even such delusions, could lead to insights into the human psyche and its workings, insights that were illuminating, and could be therapeutic. Even the Philosopher's Stone could be given a psychological meaning.

I forget when I came across the Zen maxim that supplied the title for this book. "*Teaching is like pointing a finger at the moon. The inquirer must look at the moon, not the finger.*" Jung seemed to be saying that these fringe topics are like the finger. They offer nothing that anyone should dwell on with naïve credulity, but they may point the way towards something real, and help the mind to focus on it - a moon. In Jung's system of thought, any such moon was to be looked for in the Unconscious, on the deep level where, he held, it is constant for all human beings. To explore fringe topics in the right spirit is to find clues to its functioning.

My original idea for this book was to write a study of magic and myth in that spirit, though not in uncritical agreement with Jung, whom I was already seeing reason to question. (Thirty years later I see more reason.) I drafted an outline, which a publisher accepted. The book was contracted for as non-fiction: a straightforward, if speculative, discussion.

But when I tried to write it, something happened which has happened with other books of mine, and which I have learned to recognize as a sign of vitality. In defiance of the first conception, it insisted on changing. As a straightforward discussion it refused to take shape. The material was inert.

I began wondering whether I could bring it to life by putting it in the form of conversations, with speakers voicing different points of view; whether I could humbly follow the great precedent of Platonic dialogue. That, however, would raise a further issue. Plato had ready-made characters, not only his master Socrates but other Athenians, with a ready-made milieu where long philosophic conversations were credible. In the latter part of the twentieth century, things were different. I would have to invent a setting where people might gather and talk on the lines I wanted, for days on end; I would have to invent people doing it; and if I went as far as that, they would obviously do more than talk. The essay would become a story. I discussed matters with the publisher's editor and the change was agreed to. I have a dim recollection that I manoeuvred him into suggesting it himself, but perhaps that is only retroactive vanity.

The imagined setting was a resident school of magic called Allhallows, near Glastonbury in Somerset. Here let me dispel a misunderstanding, that Allhallows was based on Chalice Orchard, a house on the lower slope of Glastonbury Tor that became my home. It used to belong to Dion Fortune, an author who conducted it as a sort of esoteric hostel. The truth is that when I wrote *The Finger and the Moon* I was not living there and would never have expected to live there. To the best of my remembrance, I did not even know of it, or of Dion Fortune's presence and activities. I had passed the gate when climbing the Tor, but had never gone in, or turned aside to look.

My story was supposed to take place in what, from the standpoint of the time of writing, was a vague near-future. I made no serious attempts at prediction, but did avoid the misjudgement of one reviewer, who criticized me for depicting a scene that had already been superseded by saner ways. My belief that the wave of magic – in a very broad sense – was not exhausted, and that people like my characters would continue to flourish, has been justified by the rise of what is commonly called the New Age. Though far from being the Sixties over again, it has resurrected some of the issues.

Astrology is more popular than ever. Witchcraft, now called Wicca, is presented not only as a valid religion, but as the religion that is showing the fastest growth. Unorthodox therapies flourish; clairvoyance and parapsychology hold their own. Rituals supposedly make contact with terrestrial energies in "Earth Magic". Neo-paganism includes Goddess-worship with pronounced magical elements. To look farther afield in space, alien beings are contacted by methods unknown to science; and to look farther afield in time, accounts of Atlantis and other repositories of Ancient Wisdom are paraded as challenges to normal history. Periodic festivals of "body, mind and spirit" provide showcases. While it would be absurd to re-issue *The Finger and the Moon* just as it was, I believe that in this new annotated version it can still have something to say. Revisiting it, I am rather surprised to notice some of its anticipations of the New Age. I invented or discovered, for instance, the landscape-goddess who is now, for some, a respected resident of Glastonbury.

A sceptic might quote a prophetic saying attributed to G.K. Chesterton: "*When people cease to believe in God, they won't believe in nothing, they will believe in everything.*" And many now believe in... well, a lot of things. A vocal enemy of religion, Richard Dawkins, has expressed a surprising fear that it may be replaced by New Age fantasy rather than scientific atheism. To admit the possibility seems to hint at a singular lack of confidence in his own convictions. Personally, I wouldn't embrace either of his alternatives. But while I am content to leave atheism to Professor Dawkins, I think it worthwhile to revert to some of the topics in *The Finger and the Moon*... even, perhaps, to consider why there is enough vitality in them to excuse his apprehension. In the midst of much credulity, and modes of thinking for which "magical" may still be a fair term, it remains a valid exercise to pick out anything that may be acceptable, and, when faced with the unacceptable, to ask whether there may yet be "moons" which even the weirdest "fingers" point to.

In the course of the story, I incorporated portions of my once-intended discussion as excerpts from imaginary lectures by the head of Allhallows (not, I hasten to add, very lengthy excerpts). I presented him as expounding - and the story explores in various ways - a theoretical "model" of the human psyche that went beyond Jung. How far this - or anything else in the novel - was meant to be taken seriously, and how far I might repeat it today, I try to make clearer in the Notes.

However, one point that definitely is serious is implicit throughout. The book embodies - and still embodies, however waywardly - a plea for true rationality. Over the years I have observed, in various situations, that would-be rational sceptics can be just as closed-minded and, in consequence, just as mistaken, as their opponents. A partial illustration is ready to hand. In 1973, when *The Finger and the Moon* first came out, it was quite widely reviewed, with notices ranging from the gratifyingly generous to the almost incoherently hostile. The review in the *New Statesman*, on the intellectual Left, included the following:

"This is certainly the most interesting question posed by the novel:

"Why are the notions and attitudes embodied in the word magic gaining ground, particularly among the young?"

And the review in the *Economist*, on the intellectual Right, put the same question more crossly:

"This, of course, is the important issue raised by this otherwise unimportant book: why is there a revival of magic, witchcraft, druidism, satanism, all the irrational luggage of organised superstition that western man has been shrugging off these 300 years past?"

Neither reviewer thought I offered an answer. The odd thing is that I did. It is offered fully and carefully, almost at the beginning, in section 2 of the "First Day". But it didn't suit the reviewers' type of rationality, so they couldn't see it on the page in front of them, or recognize that it was an answer. They were straitjacketed by presuppositions.

Their complaints remind me of a long-ago review by A.L. Rowse of another book on magical topics, in which he made the amazing statement that people who think rationally are wrong more often than others, because they fail to understand the majority who don't. Well, reason is supposed to be a method of arriving at truth, of thinking right. If it is a method of *not* arriving at truth, of thinking wrong, what is the point of it? Such a rationality is surely in need of reappraisal.

I am not attacking reason, directly or by implication. But Dr. Rowse's admission that to "reason" in his sense means, in effect, to be wrong more often than other people, seems to me to speak for itself. I am suggesting (with real evidence, more than can be quoted here) that the "reason" of these academics and humanists is a reduced, falsified version of the real thing. William Blake symbolized the process in his poetic myth of a fatal descent of intellect into "single vision". Much of *The Finger and the Moon* sketches a quest for a vision that remains rational but is more than "single".

I must not anticipate the Notes by indicating how some of my views have shifted since the first publication. However, it may be as well to say a word about a feature of the story that may now be thought repellent and is certainly dated: the use of the fictitious drug SP5. It was conceived when Aldous Huxley's claims about mescaline had been current for some years, and disciples of Timothy Leary were still proclaiming the wonders of LSD. I was always cautious, and never experimented myself (a few readers, impressed by the authenticity of the SP5 passages, assumed that I must have). But I wanted some of the characters to attain a special insight into reality, and, for that purpose, felt justified in inventing a substance that did what hallucinogenic drugs were alleged to do... and more.

Since then, the real drug scene has turned hideously sour; and if I were to write such a story now, while I might introduce a visionary technique, I would not base it on a chemical concoction.

A good deal of *The Finger and the Moon* is light-hearted and mildly satirical. I don't regret that. Any suggestion that the Allhallows company could have worked serious and powerful magic would have been entirely wrong. While sinister exploitation enters the story, it reflects purely human propensities.

After thirty years, however, I am more dubious about matters that once appeared fairly neutral. Let me say, for instance, by way of warning, that the notorious "black magician" Aleister Crowley is cited briefly several times; it was only fair to recognize that he did have touches of wisdom. But he said and did a great deal that was unwise and much worse, and I might not mention him if I were writing *The Finger and the Moon* today. Apart from that special case, I have seen elements of the New Age take a regrettable turn, as drug-taking has, if not so disastrously. My semi-comic shrine of the Horned One, if it existed, might not be as semi-comic as I imagined it. I have appended an Afterword to place these later realizations in the context of the story's development.

Finally, the characters use words and expressions that may now be objected to as sexist or politically incorrect. At the time of writing, they carried no such implication. It was acceptable to say "Man" meaning humanity, or "he" for someone in general, of either sex. A few dated phrases also occur, such as "Women's Lib". But I think they might still have been current at the time when the story happens - which, I remind the reader, is fairly indefinite.

Geoffrey Ashe
Glastonbury

Author's Note*

A WORD about the form in which I have written this book. *The Finger and the Moon* is fiction. Its major theme, and its setting in the 'near future' or 'not-quite-now', may class it as science-fiction. However, it is not fictitious in the pure sense. Behind it are the fertile hybrids of television, the dramatized documentaries and documentary dramas.

I think of the central character somewhat as Voltaire thought of God. While Martin Ellis may not exist, there are good and serious reasons for inventing him. He states issues which arise demandingly out of much recent thinking, scientific and otherwise, but which no one has in fact stated... as far as I know.

That is why he is placed in as close a relation to real life as an imagined person can have. It will become clear also (to anybody who cares one way or another) why the narrator - the 'I' of the story - is more or less myself, relocated, adjusted, and projected into Martin's scene as plausibly as I can do it. Several of the main topics are topics I have been concerned and connected with in public. Several events which are recalled (so to speak) in the margin did happen. Even the Ritual of the Grail was once enacted at Tintagel. Over the years I have seen cause to believe that it was a valid magical working.

For 'SP5' I took a hint from Colin Wilson's *The Occult*. For the menu on pages 163-4 I am largely indebted to Tina Benham.

Geoffrey Ashe,
December 1972

---

*This is the Author's Note to the original 1973 Edition.

First Day

THIS ROOM IS SOUNDPROOF. So at least Annabel has just told me, and there's no obvious reason to doubt her. Not yet anyhow. The moment she showed me in, I noticed the opaque effect. Even the window seemed oddly numb when I went over to find which way it faced.

'You can open that if you want to,' the girl said, showing me how and then shutting it again with a soft thud. 'The room has a ventilator system too. But you're sealed off. You can't hear and you can't be heard.'

'Are all the guest-rooms like this?' I asked.

'Oh no. We've only two like this, and they aren't really guest-rooms. You're here because the regular ones are full. I hope you don't have a thing about feeling shut in.'

'No,' I said. 'What are these soundproof chambers for?'

'Solitude.' Some girls would have smiled. Annabel didn't. 'Well, come downstairs when you're ready, Geoffrey.'

She started through the doorway, then turned and glanced round the room again before she left. In that second or so, there was a curious flash of the off-human about her – as if she'd stepped from the cover of a vintage fantasy magazine. I believe it was the outline that did it, the spread and swirl of her complicated red dress. All the way up from the front entrance I'd been nervous of treading on her hem, or maybe her sleeves.

Now that this female patch of colour[1] has gone, blotted out by a blank door, I realize that my cell is drab. Drab, not dull. Although there's no sound, and no smell either, I'm reminded irrationally of India and that old ashram of Gandhi's outside Ahmedabad, which managed to be austere and lively at once.

The Finger and the Moon

Meanwhile it strikes me that the accident of the guest-rooms being full has made my job easier. (Query though, was it an accident? Could this room be bugged? Wait and see.) If I'm out of earshot, I won't have to put everything in notebooks. I can record my observations on tape. Some of them anyway. The record may be usable in itself. Of course the basic tapes will have to be edited and expanded.* But let's see how close we can get to an instant oral fair-copy.

And while I think of it, here's a self-reminder to keep an eye on my stock of tapes. They were meant to be used just for the interviews and actuality stuff. If I put much of the story on them as well, they'll soon run short and I'll have to send for more.

However, my stay here isn't likely to be long. As a rule my impressions come out right if I form them at high tempo. I took in enough of Israel in four days, enough of India in ten, to produce articles that got by the Features Editors, and this place doesn't cover as much ground as India... or Israel[2]. Only a few acres (to hell with metrication). Smaller than Vatican City even. But I seem to have talked myself into trying to convince the public that it could be a bigger thing, in a way, than any of them.

I'm speaking low. It's the room. Better play back a bit and check that everything on the tape is clear so far.... Yes. I happened to hit the point where I said this room was drab but not dull. A snap judgement, and correct. The room is - intense. Now why?

It's about twelve feet square, with a high ceiling. Pastelly décor, predominantly cream and pale brown. Cool atmosphere, pleasant, not stuffy; thanks to that ventilator, I suppose. But the single arched window is rather narrow. Even this fine June evening, I'll soon be needing to switch the light on. The lights are ordinary domestic fixtures, one in the ceiling, one by the bed. The electric fire isn't plugged in.

Most of the floor is covered with - what? It might be thick paper, almost white, tacked down at the edges. There's a built-in cupboard with coat-hooks, and a little chest of drawers by the window, with a plain mirror. Otherwise, no proper furniture. I'm sitting on a stool, so low I'm practically cross-legged. My bed is a mattress against the wall, with a tiny bench beside it. Cushions with geometric patterns are scattered about. On second thoughts, the effect is Japanese.

But on third thoughts it isn't that, any more than it's really Indian.

* And of course they have been.

This room rejects labels. On the opposite wall to the bed hangs a large, bold black-and-white drawing. Lots of intricate decorative motifs in the old Celtic style, surrounding a picture that grows out of them, or rather inwards from them. A rocky landscape. Near the crest of a hill there's a patch of level ground with a beehive hut made of rough stones, and a tall bearded man in a hooded cloak. He's leaning on a staff, and a fire is burning near him. A track zigzags up from the fore-ground to his ledge and beyond. He might be an early Irish saint.

The cupboard has a box in it containing a puzzle. One of those teasers with pegs and discs, where you have to rearrange the discs on the pegs, and are only allowed to move them in certain ways. Also three rolls of the same heavy paper (or whatever it is) that covers the floor, and a hand-thrown pottery jar with several felt pens of various colours standing up in it. So the inmate is invited to draw. But where? On the floor?

I'm beginning to see why this room is intense. There are so few objects in it that they all get charged with significance. Also, most of them are offbeat. They make you wonder. That's what I'm doing now, aloud. It's a room without clichés. Even the plain chest of drawers is hardly a cliché in this company.

The window should take you back into the everyday milieu, and doesn't. It looks out over a flagged pavement, a garden, a tranquil expanse of lowland Somerset. But then, as so often in Somerset, the skewed cone of Glastonbury Tor breaks the skyline. Rising there surmounted by its mind-cheating tower, it stands on the very edge of space, with nothing beyond: the holy mountain of some enclosed green world imagined by C. S. Lewis or Tolkien.

Perhaps in a sense it is, or will soon become so. If it does, however, the creative genius will be Martin Ellis. Who may just possibly be one of the most important men living.

2

That weird hill reminds me of my first meeting – and so far, my only meeting – with Ellis himself, the presiding spirit of this place, what-ever it may turn out to be. He wasn't, then. Our encounter occurred in the autumn of 1971 when he gave a talk to the Free Mind Society. He was scarcely more than a name to me, if that, and I didn't go with a preconceived wish to hear him. I'm not sure why I did go.

My recollection is that I just happened to drift past the hall that evening with time on my hands. I read the notice, and went in on impulse.

Let's recap....

The Free Mind Society is still almost the only background I can put Ellis against, and it may not help much in elucidating him. I don't think he attended its meetings often. Neither did I.

It's one of those dim high-thinking London outfits that have plodded on for a century or so, through phases of agnosticism, and theosophy, and religiosity, and humanism, and God (if they will pardon the term) knows what. Somebody once told me they used to sing a hymn beginning 'Nearer, Mankind, to thee'.[3]

To get to this lecture I walked along a bleak corridor lined with bleak busts of Herbert Spencer[4] and kindred firebrands, to a library full of chairs facing a table. Most of the books on the shelves had a redundant look. From where I sat I could make out only one title, *Errors of the Bible Exposed*. The audience of forty-odd ranged from a talkative Old Guard who, when young, probably sat at the feet of H. G. Wells and the Pankhursts, to a quiet hairy contingent who might or might not have been students, and seemed to have wandered in from a different planet.

Presently the secretary arrived with the speaker. From his introduction I gathered that Martin Ellis was an analytical psychologist, that he favoured Jung and had met the Master; and that he was going to speak on 'The Quest for Meaning'.

The secretary sat down and Ellis got up. Now that I try to picture him, I can't. In a few minutes I'll be able to check my blurred visual notion, and it may well be wrong. He was tall, I'd say, and aged forty-five to fifty, with greying hair and a nondescript suit. His voice and delivery were clear. What does come to mind is that he reversed the demagogue image. The old political spellbinders - Hitler is the textbook case - had a riveting impact while they spoke, yet afterwards, listeners declare, it was hard to remember what they'd said. The one thing I'm sure of with Ellis is that he was the opposite. His speech lingers rather than himself.

Though I don't have to rely on memory for it. The Free Mind Society issues a bulletin with reports on its speakers, and I've got hold of this one. Ellis began by talking about a psychiatric problem which had acquired vogue-status a few months before, been accorded the colour-supplement treatment, and then faded into the usual limbo. But (Ellis insisted) the problem went on and was very real. He cited Victor Frankl on this neurosis of the then-incipient 1970s, and added that he could confirm Frankl from his own practice.

'More and more of our patients complain of a sense of meaning-lessness in life. More and more often, the reason is the outlook of science. Or what has come through to them as the outlook of science. Sometimes it's called reductionism. I'd prefer to apply a phrase of Jung's and say nothing-butness.

'Thinking people tend to feel that science has cut Man down. It's explained away everything that matters in terms of smaller, meaner things that don't matter. Religion is *nothing but* wish-fulfilling fairy-tales. Love is *nothing but* body chemistry. Art is *nothing but* a surge of conditioned reflexes. The highest flights of the poet or philosopher are traced back to childhood trivia and rationalized compensations.

'Science leaves Man shut-in, futile, doomed. In Desmond Morris's words, a naked ape. Or in William Blake's, a mortal worm. It feeds on the work of its countless laboratories, to trap people in closed systems - chemical, or biological, or physical systems - where all colour has gone and all hope is lost.'

As Ellis pressed on along this line, I noticed he was being cagey. He wouldn't come right out and declare whether he agreed with his patients. He just kept hammering at the theme, 'this is how they feel'. But he did quote Professor William Thorpe, the Cambridge zoologist, on the new student generation and why it was shying away from science. Professor Thorpe, it appeared, had written an article in *The Times* blaming this on a related cause. Many students found the scientists off-putting: complacent vendors of a machine world, with moral and spiritual factors reduced to by-products, swept under the carpet almost. The whole show was pointless and irresponsible and they weren't buying it.

Thus far Ellis was making sense to me, abstractly; and reviewing it all today, several years later, I'd say a lot of it still stands up. But thus far my interest was self-centred. He was giving clinical support for some pet theories of my own. *Nothing but* that, as he might have put it. Then suddenly he roused me.

The Finger and the Moon

He mentioned a happening of the summer just past. Near Glastonbury - within sight of the Tor, within range of its formida- ble spell - a group of those people whom I knew better than to call hippies had convened a semi-mystical pop festival.[5] Or a semi-pop mystical festival. Anyhow they'd built a pyramid to occult specifica- tions, and invoked cosmic energies at the solstice, and it had all been a muddy, strident, tumultuous, beautiful scene, bubbling on for most of a week, raising protests for miles around, losing money, and carry- ing its own triumphant justification for anyone who was there. I had been there, a senior well-wisher. It transpired that Martin Ellis had also been.

This was a prelude to the second part of his argument. From then on, I recall, I could sense a creeping distress in the audience. Several faces stiffened. Several of the Free Minds, having relaxed minimally during the first part, resumed their strait-jackets.

Ellis claimed that the anti-science reaction he'd been talking about was the clue to portents like the Glastonbury Festival. The current movement of minds, he insisted, wasn't merely away from science, it was towards rival attractions - myth, astrology, magic - and an expansion of consciousness. He was right, of course, and events (some events anyway) have been bearing him out.

Among the proofs which he brandished then was a French book, *The Morning of the Magicians*, which had been selling wildly for eight years and was now inspiring more best-sellers of a similar type, occultish *mélanges* which tried to make science itself fantastic. He also drew the meeting's attention to the encyclopaedia *Man, Myth and Magic*, which had been coming out in weekly parts and defying the part-work norm by making a profit.[6] Yet another of his points was that the tools of science itself were being diverted to strange ends, like computerized horoscopes. Alien cults were taking root in the West. *Time* magazine, having lately asked whether God was dead, now asked whether he had come back to life.

'As to that,' said Ellis, 'I think it's a red herring. We aren't due for any revival of orthodox religion. It's a revival of older things. In the 1960s the big topic was Sex. In the 1970s it may well be Magic.'[7]

With the 1970s already in progress, this was not a highly original remark. Journalists had made it before Ellis. Only, he made it in a way of his own, which somehow avoided bringing the word 'trend' to mind.

He laid stress - as the journalists did - on the articulate young, their fashions in star-reading and witchcraft and neo-druidism, and the Jesus cult which was then getting to be heard of outside California. But he never gave the least hint of patronizing The Young, as such, or holding them up as exhibits. Nor did he suggest an oldster trying repellently to be 'with-it'. His conventional looks (I remember that much) disposed of any 'Swinging Curate' suspicion. So did his style, which was contemporary, but neutral. That talk never sounded like a rejected script for *Oz* or *IT*.[8] Throughout, it remained simply - a talk.

It didn't go down well, at any rate with the vocal part of his audi-ence. I have a hazy but definite recollection of hostile questioning. The hecklers' theme was that the whole magical thing was a flight from reason and therefore sinful. They expected Ellis to be defensive. He wasn't. He counter-attacked.

His reply went like this. 'You claim to speak for scientific, progres-sive humanism and you equate it with reason. I'm telling you it hasn't worked. It's supposed to instill devotion to the good of mankind. But apart from a high-calibre few, it doesn't. The more science, the deeper the apathy and sense of futility. On the one hand we live in dread of technological horrors: war, overpopulation, pollution, the entire open-ended Doomwatch[9] package. On the other hand there's a powerless-ness to do much about it. A failure of will - because of this feeling that a darkness of soul is closing in and death is the end and science has made everything hollow and pointless. Now if that's so (and I can give you evidence, clinical scientific evidence, that it is), then I wouldn't call it a flight from reason to look elsewhere for rescue: it's thoroughly rational. At least, it can be.'

The secretary thanked him, a shade uneasily, with some stock for-mula like 'giving us plenty to think about'. I wanted to ask Ellis why he went to the Glastonbury pop festival. It took me a few minutes to reach him, because he was instantly beset by members of the audience who hadn't spoken, and sounded friendlier than the hecklers. When they dispersed, we only had time for a word or two. He told me he'd read one of my books, and made a comment which confirmed that he had.

'I'd like to know more about it,' he added, 'this Glastonbury mystique you've discussed in your writings, and Avalon and King

Arthur and all the rest. It's so potent, and I still don't understand why. Could you explain?'

I said perhaps, but not in one sentence. Before we got any further the secretary whisked him off for a drink.

A few days later, however, Ellis wrote to me in care of my publisher, with a page of questions about the Holy Grail. That letter is in front of me now, with the rest of my scanty file on him. The questions are clearly worded and concise, very well-informed, very difficult to answer. He asked me what were the Five Changes of the Grail. I wish I knew.

Ellis thanked me politely for the weak replies I was able to give. Then after a year or two of silence he wrote again, from the house where I am now, 'Allhallows'. He'd opened it as... what exactly? A private clinic? A conference centre? A minicollege? His letter struck me as oddly unexplicit.

Allhallows had come to him as a legacy from a former patient. Basically it was the dower house of an estate. The previous owner had enlarged it and bought up land around. Now the property was Ellis's, with enough money to convert it for his obscure purposes. Not much more: he was running it, he said, on a shoestring. Until he took over it was still known locally as 'the Dower House', though the enlargements had made that name incongruous. The new one was his own choice. He'd opted out after his fashion and moved to Somerset.

He enclosed a brochure. This was a fairly competent job, but gave only morsels of information. His main message in it, repeated in the letter, was 'Come and see for yourself'. It contained black-and-white photos of the house (Georgian, three storeys), and a garden with a maze, and close-up portions of some intriguing statues or rather sculptures, apparently by a friend of his. He devoted a whole page, without margins, to a picture of an untidy workshop, where work was being done though its nature escaped me. Inside the back cover were further pictures, captionless, of figures described only as 'some of our visitors'. One showed what might have been the editorial board of an Underground paper; another - possibly - a teacher with a class; another, two men and a woman who were even harder to place, because, as far as I could make out, they had no clothes on.

3

I filed Ellis's letter and the brochure. His invitation to visit remained open, neither accepted nor declined. I might have gone to Allhallows sooner or later, and then again I might not. But as time passed, my attention was drawn to him in another way.

He was seldom or never in the news directly, yet his name kept cropping up, always for the same reason. A series of England's instant celebrities - evoked and paraded by the media, then consigned to chance and fate - all praised him, separately, as an influence on their lives. I couldn't see that these admirers had much in common except that they were in their twenties or thirties and outside the Establishment; even the all-engulfing post-Beatle Establishment.

They included, of course, a rising pop star. But they also included a small poultry farmer who fought a by-election as an Independent, and pushed one of the major party candidates into third place. He became a national 'plague-on-both-your-houses' figure, much listened to and much wooed. They also included a Catholic ex-docker who reclaimed drug victims and derelicts, was a self-evident saint on the ancient pattern, and told reporters that technically he was in mortal sin[10]. Both, like the pop star, referred to Martin Ellis in tones of discipleship.

Then there was the poet 'Madri', a more surprising character, with a surface *vieux-jeu*[11] effect that was deceptive. She presided over a house-commune in Islington called the Tantra Pentacle. On sunny afternoons her brightly-clad followers would emerge, and roam for miles through the streets of London, chanting and twirling. They brought out a record with Madri reading from her poems between hymns. Denounced as obscene, it climbed through the charts into the top twenty. The BBC refused to broadcast it, and it climbed into the top ten. The BBC refused again, and for a month it was at Number One. Commercial TV interviewed Madri in her commune. She dominated the interview.

One of her remarks attracted press notice. 'We don't want negative dropouts here. Sometimes they ask to join - students who've failed their exams, working people who've been fired - inveighing against the System. I listen and then tell them: "You may be right. But you have to be right for the right reasons. Prove you could succeed by the System's rules if you chose. Go back and pass your exams. Or hang on to a job for a year. After that, chuck the System by all means, and we'll be happy to hear from you again if we're still around ourselves." Critics hinted that Madri didn't measure up to her own standard, but a professor testified that she'd once been offered a Cambridge fellowship and declined it.[12]

When asked about her Pentacle's doctrines, she answered that Tantrism was a recognized Hindu philosophy, and neither flaunted its notorious sex-mystique nor played this down. She hoped to adapt it to the West more fully than had yet been done. And her guru in that work, so far as she had one, was Martin Ellis.

But it wasn't Madri who got me moving and brought me to Allhallows. It was John Rosmer, a biochemist, the culprit in a public scandal which is still reverberating. By following up reports of sick cattle in Yorkshire, he exposed an Anglo-American war project of singular nastiness, at a research station which had been the subject of official denials. When the Government saw that the game was up, a minister resigned.

For a few weeks the CND era flared back into life. At a Grosvenor Square demo, Rosmer flew over the police cordon in a balloon. Alighting on the US Embassy roof, he dropped a sack stuffed with petitions, and took off again. The police arrested him when he landed. But his trial revealed so much official confusion over the nature of his offence that the charges misfired and he was acquitted.[13]

During one of many TV exposures, Rosmer spoke of Martin Ellis's 'centre' - that was his word. His own visits to Allhallows had had decisive effects on him.

'How?' the interviewer asked. 'What exactly does Ellis do?'

'He's a magician.'

'You mean he's done wonders for you?'

'No. I mean what I said. He's a magician.'

The interviewer, for once, was ruffled. 'How do you fit that in with your beliefs as a scientist?'

Rosmer grinned. 'I don't think I can do better than pass on Martin's invitation. Come and see for yourself.'

Watching that interview, and comparing Rosmer with Madri and the others, I realized they had more in common than what I've mentioned. They shared a personal style. A certain firmness of outline, a certain unfashionable precision. They were more sharply defined than most public persons in their age-range – including the protesters and cultists among whom, on the face of it, they belonged. You never forgot that they were young, or fairly so, yet they had the distinctive-ness of veteran stage actors in third-rate films. They were vanguard people speaking with rearguard accents. Madri was sneered at by a *New Statesman* poetry critic, unjustly but significantly, for seeming not to have read anyone later than D. H. Lawrence. As for Rosmer I'd have been inclined to call him a Tory Radical, if the words hadn't carried connotations which, with him, were out of key.

Suddenly I wondered: wasn't there a story in Martin Ellis? Indeed, why hadn't the story been told already? Publicity swept its floodlights over path after path converging on that 'centre' of his, but never lit up the centre itself. Yet whatever went on in it was surely remarkable. Hadn't any journalists even approached him? Or had they tried it and found him unhelpful? Or was it simply that they hadn't spotted the recurrent Ellis news-motif because it never occurred twice in the same context?

No harm in asking... and so, for completeness, to the reason why I'm here now. I put the proposition to Trevor Herrick, the editor of the *Globe* colour-supplement, who had given me one or two jobs before. No, he replied, he hadn't considered it. If he did, could I offer anything special or exclusive? I mentioned the meeting and correspondence. I produced the brochure. Trevor glanced through it for pictorial angles. His eye paused on the maze, the sculpture details, the visitors dressed and undressed.

'It looks like a low-budget Woburn Abbey,'[14] he commented. 'What does Ellis *do*?'

'Surely that's the theme. All these different characters insist that he does something, and we never hear what it is. The idea of the article would be to find out, and publish the secret.'

'Would he talk? He might tell you that you had to enrol for a course at some ridiculous fee.'

'He didn't strike me that way. I doubt if Hoad' (Hoad was the social worker from the docks) 'could have afforded a ridiculous fee.'

'Point taken. Well, let's feel this out. Ask Ellis if you can stay there. Explain what for, of course. We can give you an advance towards expenses, and lay on a photographer if the project shapes up.'

Ellis showed himself co-operative. Today I came into the West

The Finger and the Moon

Country by rail – a two-hour journey – and connected with a wandering bus, and walked up from the village to the house. It's behind a mass of rhododendrons, out of sight of the road. A driveway curves through the bushes, and leads into a forecourt, opposite the front door. This was opened to me by the aforesaid girl, who introduced herself simply as Annabel, addressed me simply as Geoffrey despite our saddening age-difference, and took me straight up to my sound-proof room. No one else was in sight.

From outside, Allhallows looked like its picture. We went through the hall and up the staircase too fast for me to form any impressions. But I did notice an archway inside the front door, with an inscription which we passed under:

DO WHAT YOU WILL[15]
...but be very sure you will it

Enough for now. Time to go and meet the guru again after this long interval.

4

I've met him. It was neither a welcome nor a snub.

The house was quiet when I went down, unexpectedly quiet. I followed a murmur of voices to the back and found Martin Ellis in a large kitchen, talking to Annabel and an older woman, who were both seated at the table slicing brown bread. He was standing, in profile.

There couldn't be any doubt who he was. All the same, memory did mislead. For one thing he isn't really tall. Maybe figurative language plays tricks; maybe the mind fastens on a person's 'stature', and then stores him away with a false height. Anyhow, he can't be above five foot ten. Also he looks fresher, more clear-cut, better focused than I remembered, and certainly no older despite the interval. His hair is slightly longer. He has blue eyes... the point here is not that they're any special colour, but that I did register what colour they were. After Annabel I'd half expected him to be decked out in some bizarre costume. However, he was plainly dressed in an open-necked yellow shirt, brown trousers, and sandals.

As I came in he finished a sentence, then turned to me. 'Ah hallo. Glad you've finally made it. You've met Annabel, and this is Karen. Karen, you know about Geoffrey.'

The older woman, who was dressed very much as Martin was, smiled up at me.

He offered me a chair and sat down himself. 'You've come to a deserted house, as you probably noticed. Everybody else is out walking. They should be back soon.'

'I did wonder. How many are in residence?'

'How many, Karen?'

'Twelve, counting us. Geoffrey makes it up to thirteen.'

'It varies,' said Martin. 'Thirteen is near to capacity for anything more than a night or two. Of course we can take on more resident students if they camp outside. We've no campers this week.'

His voice was unusual. I'm never much good at accents. But Martin's doesn't seem to have any nuances at all which you can pin down, either social or regional. He's a hard-to-classify English-speaking person. For the moment, that's it.

Annabel said to me abruptly: 'You're Aries.'

I acknowledged it.

Martin chuckled. 'Annabel gets it right twice out of three. Eight times random expectation.'

'I suppose I must be prepared for this sort of thing at Allhallows.'

'Oh, why?'

'John Rosmer has informed several million viewers that you're a magician.'

'We've been watching John with interest,' Martin replied. 'After that interview, you know, we had the police here. Scotland Yard, no less.'

This was news indeed. 'What were they looking for?'

Karen said: 'They wanted us to help them with their inquiries.'[16]

Getting no further light on the police, I tried another approach. 'Scotland Yard must be more on the alert than Fleet Street. I can't think why no journalists have followed up these hints pointing your way. The Allhallows story seems to have been waiting in suspension for months, reserved for me.'

'That's understandable,' said Martin.

It was the first atmospheric remark he'd made, and it pulled me up sharply. Some people would have answered me with a platitude about luck or chance. Others – the kind I'd have expected in a 'magical' milieu – would have held forth on fate or astral influences, or maybe divine providence. For Martin, as for these, the strange placing of the *Globe* assignment was clearly more than an accident. Yet it was all in the day's work. He merely noted it and passed on, without discussion.

But he didn't pass very far. He'd just begun asking about my previous forays into freelancing – no doubt to size up the kind of treatment he'd be likely to get from me – when the other inmates returned. Conversation trailed off in a hubbub of boots tramping, voices calling, water running. I was crowded into a corner by preparations for supper, ignored for a long time, then invited to come and eat.

The dining room of Allhallows is big and airy, with french windows looking out on a tousled patch of grass and shrubbery. I sat facing across the room between Martin and Karen, on a bench at a refectory table running parallel with another refectory table. The meal was on a self-service basis. As the residents filed in and out with dishes, they reminded me of a team of diggers at an archaeological site. The party had the same bias towards youth but not extreme youth. It included an elderly couple. Beside them sat a handsome black man. A Chinese girl[17] sat opposite him.

No one was introduced to me, except a dark-complexioned chap of thirty or so, with short hair and a short, careful beard. His name's Paul. Like Karen and Annabel he's an Allhallows fixture, a sort of bursar.[18] It may be my fancy, but I think Annabel becomes a bit incandescent in his neighbourhood.

The talk that drifted my way was mostly about their afternoon hike. It sounded as if it had traversed half Somerset without going anywhere in particular. As for the meal itself, I'd been prepared for vegetarianism, and some of the party did have vegetables only, plus bread. Others, however, had cold meat as well. Jugs of water and cider alternated along the tables. Fruit followed.

After supper the light was failing. The residents dispersed. I could hear a transistor and a noise like ping-pong. Martin, however, asked me to join him in a small room which I assumed to be his study.

'We've got a couple of newcomers today. I like to have a few minutes' chat to start them off, and it might be helpful to you to sit in.'

The newcomers turned out to be the African and a lad from Wales. I didn't catch either name because of a yell outside the window, but gathered that the Welsh boy was a colliery worker. Martin asked them (for my benefit, he already knew) to tell what they were interested in. So far as I could follow their answers, they'd both belonged to covens and found the witches' claims unconvincing. They felt themselves to be seekers.

Martin didn't give them a discourse on witchcraft. He spoke for only a minute or two and said, in effect, only one thing.

'Our purpose here is to vindicate magic, and show the value which it can have for you. That doesn't mean we're going to train you in the techniques commonly known as magical. We don't even ask you to believe in them. You must decide that for yourselves.

'But we do ask you to take them seriously. We do ask you to try, with the rest of the group, to find a way through them to the reality behind. Allhallows exists because we're sure this reality is supremely important, and can only be attained by the magical path.

'I want you to bear in mind the words of one of the masters of Zen. *Teaching is like pointing a finger at the moon. The inquirer must look at the moon, not the finger.*[19]

'In our view, magical doctrine is the finger. It's not the moon, but it does point at the moon. Before you leave I hope you'll discover what the moon is.'

They went out, muttering 'thank you' and 'goodnight'. Martin stood silent. He was dismissing me too.

I'm back in my room getting it down. I won't worry about bugging, it seems most unlikely. What else is there to say about him at this stage? Only that he has a quality which I've struck once or twice in my life, no more. Hindu holy men are supposed to possess it, and I can vouch for that in at least one case. Martin Ellis is like Vinoba Bhave[20]: he spreads euphoria. After meeting him you feel blessed. Something memorable and reassuring has happened... even if it hasn't.

Second Day

THIS MORNING I woke late. When I got downstairs, breakfast was nearly finished. Martin was coming out of the dining room as I entered.

'Hallo,' he called. 'Did you sleep well? Good. I have some correspondence to work at, but I'm giving a talk to the whole group at two o'clock, and I suggest you attend.' He went his way and hasn't appeared since (the time is now a quarter to twelve).

After breakfasting alone, because the others had either gone or were going, I left my dishes in the kitchen. It was occupied only by a male volunteer helper, wordlessly washing up. No one took charge of me, and most of the inmates had wandered off. Once again that glint of suspicion. Were these people watching to see what I'd do when by myself? No use to speculate. No hope either of learning anything from Martin till the afternoon. I did what I'd have done anyhow: explored the house.

Allhallows is nothing very special. It's a rectangle with two short wings running backwards. The front door is at the middle of the long side, and opens on to the hall and stairway. A corridor connecting the downstairs rooms runs along the back. On the left of the house as you go in, the wing contains the kitchen and dining room. Between the dining room and the entrance hall is a big recreation room, plainly furnished, with a television set in a corner, a hi-fi record-player, and equipment for indoor games. In the corresponding position on the right of the hall is a conference room with a round table. One of the chairs at this table is older and higher-backed than the rest. In the right wing are Martin's study and a library. Somewhere underneath there must surely be a cellar, but I don't know where you go down to it – perhaps from the kitchen.

The first floor up is all bedrooms and bathrooms. My own silent chamber is at the back near the centre. The floor above that is chiefly a large dormer-windowed attic, or series of attics, Partitioned into cubicles. Without prying I can't decide whether the sexes are segregated. Certainly the cubicles aren't grouped in any obvious way.

Outside the house, round it to the right as you face the front door, is a parking area. Some of the cars stand under a ramshackle shelter. Some are unprotected. Behind the left wing is a former stable, converted into the workshop shown in Martin's brochure. My tour ended at the door of this workshop, which was locked. I was peering in through a glass panel, trying to make sense of the untidy interior, when Karen emerged from the kitchen and walked towards me.

Having spent much of the morning in her company, I can describe her better now than last night. She's a round-faced woman with longish blonde hair. As she approached she stood out colourfully against the brickwork, because of a kind of loose smock she had on, buttoned down the front, with a purple and white pattern. She also wore a green headband.

'I've been looking for you,' she said. 'What do you think of us?'

'I'm learning. And hoping to learn more.'

'Have you seen our grounds?' She pronounced the last word in quotes, it wasn't pretentious.

'Not yet.'

'Come along then.'

She laid her hand on my arm, and steered me firmly away from the house. We crossed the pavement my window overlooks. The path led on through flower-beds towards a lawn extending to the left behind a high hedge. In front were trees.

'Has Martin told you about our sculptures?'

'No, he hasn't.'

'They were done by a rather splendid American boy who evaded the army call-up a few years ago, during the Vietnam war. He belonged to an Indian sect, and he vowed to the Lord Krishna that he'd do a work of spiritual art for every year he lived safe in England. Martin put him up for a while and he's given three of his works to us.'

She talked on, giving further detail. Meanwhile we veered to the left over the lawn and passed between two pillars. The sun had come out from behind a cloud-bank and it was hotter, though also breezier, as we were well clear of the house. Karen had released my arm – she talks with her hands when she becomes animated – and now she unbuttoned her smock so that it fell apart, showing a light summery dress, and a plain cross hanging round her neck. I noticed that the dress had a pocket with a small book sticking out. I couldn't see what book.

A gust caught her hair where it escaped the headband, and blew it over part of her face like a veil. She was suddenly, if transiently, beautiful. Up to then I'd been guessing (partly because of the ageing of those well-displayed hands of hers) that she was at least forty. Probably she is. But I realized she was in that phase when a woman's apparent age can vary widely with what she's doing. Karen, holding forth on this evidently favourite theme of the sculptor, looked ten years younger. She also looked a bit slimmer, but that was because the opening out of the formless wrapper had revealed her true shape.

'There!' she exclaimed.

We stopped in the middle of the long lawn. On top of a stone pedestal stood a contorted structure of metal strips, a network in 3D. One straight rod ran through it, with wire loops on the end. Everything else was twisted and interlaced.

'That's kinetic art,' said Karen. 'You push it.'

I pushed. The strips regrouped themselves, bending and swaying. It was fascinating, but was it sculpture? And was this object a figure of any sort, or an abstract spatial fantasy? I consciously didn't try to see anything, and promptly saw: a man striding along towards the house, one foot on the pedestal, the other stepping off it. His head was thrown back. The straight rod had become a stick over his shoulder, and the loops on the end formed a bundle like Dick Whittington's.

Karen beamed. 'You can see him.'

'Yes. Yes, I can.'

'That's very interesting. You're quick. Women usually see him quickly if they see him at all. Men often don't until they've been here three or four times.'

'Hm. What are you implying?'

'Nothing you need to worry about, I'm sure.'

(Did she, or did she not, lay enough stress on 'you' to make it flirtatious?)

'Well, I'm glad I passed the test. What's that building?'

The building was a pseudo-Grecian affair, a hundred yards or so farther on, in another clump of trees.

'That's the temple. But don't let's go there now. If you see too much at once, your impressions could get confused. Let it unfold.'

'If you say so. I suppose the same applies to your maze - and by the way, where is the maze?'

'Over that way.' She waved a hand in the opposite direction. 'No indeed, you mustn't go to it yet. Come and sit with me.'

Moving towards the temple, but halting some distance short of it, we sat down on a bench facing an open vista. Karen was on my left. I saw a sundial; a sweep of rougher grass running gently downhill; a low boundary fence with three of the residents leaning on it, their backs to us; and beyond that a field, and the far-off Tor.

2

One question was overdue for an answer. 'Do you happen to know why Martin went to the Glastonbury festival - that mystical-pop show in the summer of '71?'

Karen looked at the ground. 'That was where we first met. We were so much older than most of the crowd, it brought us together. Martin was in search of clues. He'd known for years that all this land-scape is... charged. He didn't know how. But he'd nearly made up his mind, already, that this was where he'd have to work sooner or later.'

'And then he got the house left to him, precisely where he wanted. It seems an amazing piece of... should I say luck?'

Again an occultish comment might have come, again it didn't. 'Not really. The house was there all along. The last owner, Eric Blount, was a sweet old gentleman with ideas about the Holy Grail. A long time ago when Martin had his practice in London, Mr Blount used to attend as a patient. But actually, you know, just to talk. His family had gone, he was lonely, everyone here thought he was a crackpot. I gather it was mainly because of him that Martin first got interested in Somerset. When Mr Blount realized just how interested, he made a new will. Then, a few weeks after that Glastonbury show, he died and the property passed to Martin. So it's all straightforward and con-nected. No uncanny coincidences.'

I pressed on. 'Has Martin worked this Somerset lore into his ideology? Does he believe in King Arthur and Joseph of Arimathea and all the rest of it?'

'I'm sure he'd be delighted to tell you himself.' A private smile flitted across her face. Martin, it hinted without malice, can be a bore on the subject. 'But you know, Geoffrey, now you're here, I'd like to find out what you think. Martin says you're an expert.'

'That's very generous of him. I hope he understands how tentative it all is. With Glastonbury specially. As Calvin said about the Apocalypse, anybody who studies it is either mad when he starts or mad when he's finished.'[1]

'Yourself included?'

'Oh, probably! The most I'd claim is that I've been more right than wrong.'

'That sounds like plenty to go on with. Do enlarge.'

I'd no intention of letting her seduce me into giving a lecture which would not only waste time but cause her, ever afterwards, to smile in that same way when referring to me. But if Martin had fallen under an Avalonian spell, I was in contact with a vital bit of the story, and couldn't neglect the lead Karen offered. Maybe I could link it with the little I'd picked up of the Allhallows gospel, and so get back to the task in hand.

'My feeling on all that,' I began carefully, 'is in line with a remark Martin made to the new arrivals, last night – about the finger and the moon.'

'Ah, yes.'

'One has to learn to take legends seriously without taking them literally. They aren't true, or at most they're only true to a slight extent. Yet they point to the truth. Glastonbury's a supreme instance. The legends may not be facts, but the existence of the legends is a major fact in itself.'

'That's sensible.'

It was; I'd cribbed it from the great E. A. Freeman.[2]

'The trouble with most scholars,' I went on, 'is that their minds can't handle that. When they've decided a story isn't "true" in their own sense, they throw it out as worthless. I'm always surprised they keep on doing it when it's led them astray so often. Ever since they wrote off Troy as a fairy-tale and Schliemann, who took Homer seriously, went off and dug it up. Still, they go on. They put the finger under the microscope, and miss the moon.'

'But if these stories aren't true, where do they get us? What is the moon?'

I was struggling not to be trapped into the lecture - and I was lecturing.

'With the classic cycles of legend there's something that has hung on through the centuries as... well, a deep inarticulate awareness. The facts at the root of it may be lost, yet it survives. Look at this legend of Joseph of Arimathea bringing the Grail. There seems to be a fact behind it - that Christians were at Glastonbury in early times. By the Middle Ages no one knew who they were. Yet people still clung to that deep awareness. So they rationalized it. They told a tale about somebody they did know, a Bible character. They said Joseph came to Britain, and settled over there.' I gestured towards the Tor. 'The chances are, I'm afraid, that it wasn't Joseph at all. But the story points to a fact. If we care about history, we ignore it at our peril.'

'What about King Arthur?'

'Arthur's more complex. Historically he's a sixth-century British general. Mythologically he's miles deep. He's put together from masses of Celtic traditions and motifs. The clues lead you into a long, strange process, creating a hero-myth, moulding it over thousands of years, then tailoring it to fit a real person.[3]

'What intrigues me most,' I continued, 'is that none of those Arthurian story-tellers understood more than a fraction of the stuff they were handling. Yet in a blind way they got it right. They made a valid myth on a valid basis. King Arthur works, so to speak. Every so often he proves his vitality by making a comeback.'

'As in T. H. White.'

'Also as in Rosemary Sutcliff. Or John Arden[4]. It's a paradox - as if the story-tellers were guided by knowledge and insight which they couldn't have had. As if they tapped a sort of national memory-bank, a storehouse of experiences and dreams.'

Karen was sitting straight up and looking young again. I'd scored, but couldn't see why. She asked: 'How do you picture this memory, or storehouse, or whatever you call it?'

'I'm not certain. At Glastonbury it's like a living presence at a focus of power. That presence reaches out. It's around us now. All those

legends are only fragments of what it holds, filtering through distorted. Even so, they're strong magic.'

'Wait, Geoffrey. Isn't this just your own version of our friend
Jung's Collective Unconscious? The great big catch-all psychic inheritance where myths are supposed to come from?'

I perceived an opening for another move towards the business in
hand. 'Only partly. It seems to me (and I'm thinking of something else
Martin has said) that Jung helped to promote a mistake he criticized
in others - "nothing-butness". You wrap up a legend in the analyst's
formula, and stop. It's the Shadow or the Anima, or for aught I know
Oedipus, and that's it. But so often that isn't it. There's more. Like I
said, archaeologists keep proving it. Somebody digs on a site which
stories are told about, and finds a basis for them. A factual basis, not
just a psychic pattern.

'But this is the mystery: it may be something the story-tellers
couldn't have known, not by any recognized method. That's how
the excavations turned out at - Cadbury Castle, over there.' I waved
towards the hills bordering Dorset. 'When subjects of Henry VIII
asserted that Cadbury was Camelot, you'd think they can't have had
the least notion of the dark-age ramparts that were under the turf,
actually under it waiting to be dug up. But by some intuition, some
insight, they picked on the right hill-fort. The one that very likely was
Arthur's citadel.'[5]

'I know,' said Karen. 'I was digging with the Cadbury team myself
for a couple of weeks in '69.'

Then her whole manner changed. She turned and stared me in the
face. 'Yes! Oh, yes!'

Baffled, I waited. Nothing happened. She just went on staring, bril-
liant-eyed, statuesque with an excitement that was too much for her
normal mobility. Plainly I was on target, but what target? Surely some
revelation was already at hand....

It was not. Voices - or rather, a voice - drifted towards us along
the lawn. Paul, the bursar, had come through between the pillars with
the elderly couple I noticed last night at supper. They advanced at a
leaden pace while the woman droned steadily.

'...So I pointed out to her that she'd entirely misconstrued
Hoerbiger's teaching because she's too much under the influence
of Steiner that man did an untold amount of harm but anyhow I'm

certain the Somerset giants belong to the last growth-cycle I'd have thought the zodiacal evidence alone would convince anyone but you never can tell with a disciple of Steiner and as the world enters the Aquarian Age it's so vital to grasp the truth and I always beg people to go to Somerset themselves and walk over the ground with bare feet...'

Her husband put in: 'Or at any rate with thin-soled shoes.'

'Yes well when I'm within sight of the Tor I can always trust my vibrations and I pointed out to her that her rising sign is Capricorn and I've more than once seen a UFO with my own eyes following the exact course of the motorway and....'[6]

They were past us. Paul turned his head for an instant with a grimace of comic despair. Or was it comic? Was it a shade too genuine, a grimace of contempt, even hate? Ah well, a dark bearded face like his can easily look sinister. As for Karen, she'd relaxed and was smiling.

'No comment,' she said.

'No comment indeed.'

'It's nice to give them a chance to talk. Now I wonder what time it is.'

As I drew back my sleeve to look, she laid her hand over my watch. 'We must go to the sundial first and pay our respects.'

We went. The sundial's a modern piece of work, but not much easier to read than an old one. I did my best, and then saw an inscription running round it:

TIME IS THE MERCY OF ETERNITY[7]

Circumnavigating as I read, I glanced up at the sun.

'Yes,' Karen repeated, taking my right hand in her left. Again that intense mysterious deadlock. But only for a second or two. 'You can look at your watch now, if you want.'

I did.

'There are jobs waiting for me indoors,' she said. 'But let's make a detour. I never like to go back the way I came.'

The Finger and the Moon

3

Still holding my hand with a soft, unvarying pressure, she guided me through a shrubbery and past a greenhouse and a vegetable garden. As we walked, I realized I hadn't made the slightest attempt to get any data for the article: even on Karen herself, her status, her relation with Martin. Of course it mightn't have been tactful to probe. But thus far I'd hardly even conjectured. I did notice, at some point, that she wore no ring.

This place (I must put it on record as something that's got to me even in a few hours) has a curious, insidious quality. It affects thought. Queries that would come straight to mind elsewhere don't occur to me here. Not spontaneously, that is. I feel that I'm functioning with an altered bias. Consciousness is enhanced. Memory is strengthened to a point near total recall, at least in the short term. Sitting in my room I can see and hear the whole of the morning, parts of it as plainly as if they were filmed. What man can describe a woman's clothes an hour after leaving her? I'm no exception, yet I can describe Karen's. Logic, however, seems to slacken off here. Or maybe it's only different, logic-of-the-situation that's odd because the situation is odd.

As we re-entered the house through the front door, which was standing ajar, I looked again at that motto over the arch and kept quiet. This wasn't the time to get sidetracked into a fresh discussion. Karen went through to the kitchen, buttoning her smock again, and examined potatoes. While she worked I began belatedly questioning, filling gaps, as a run-up to this talk of Martin's, in which I hope his 'moon' will clear the horizon.

To summarize... Karen's title is 'house-warden', but she has a share in all major activities. About herself and Martin in a personal sense she gave nothing away. She stymied me with a cool assumption, whether real or put on, that I already knew. The other staff members are Paul and Annabel.

Allhallows runs a programme of social and cultural events - music recitals, conferences, outdoor happenings - which draw a ticket-buying public from a wide catchment area. This accounts for the photos of 'visitors' in that brochure, except the nudes, whom Karen couldn't recall. Two film companies have hired the grounds for country-house sequences.

The resident students, however, who enrol for at least a week and often much longer, are the reason for Allhallows. They alone undergo Martin's training. He doesn't accept just anybody. Each applicant is interviewed. (I'd like to know how that pair in the garden got through – but never mind.) According to Karen, the types they're most on the lookout for are 'systembreakers': people of any age, in any kind of job or profession, who have proved they can make it by the rules of the game and have then elected not to. Martin's phrase, she tells me, is 'the willed rejection of success'. Now I know who Madri was echoing in her interview at the Tantra Pentacle.

Every student joins a rota for helping around the house or outdoors. There's also an unwritten law that every student adds to Allhallows by doing a work of his[8] own choice, suited to his own talents, which he leaves behind him or brings back later. Hence for example the picture in my room, and the sundial, and a lot of the present furniture, all made by Martin's trainees. There have also been a couple of cash legacies for specific improvements.

When Karen explained this custom it sounded arty-crafty, and likely to disqualify most of the population – I thought again of the Catholic ex-docker.

'What did Hoad do?' I asked.

'Hoad?'

It struck me that they scarcely ever used surnames. 'Terry Hoad, the social worker. What was his contribution?'

Karen became grave. 'He cured Annabel.'

Before I could press for details, Paul entered the kitchen. No sign of the elderly couple. 'What did you do with them?' I said.

'They're upstairs meditating.'

'Do you have much difficulty with cases like that?'

'Not often, but sometimes. The worst are the ultra-enthusiasts. The ones who get it all wrong, bore everybody to death, stir up trouble, and LOVE Allhallows so much and would be so HURT if we tried to ease them out.'

'I know what you mean.'

'The proper treatment,' said Karen, 'is to give them a job to work at – a real job, not a made-up one – that'll keep them happy and harmless.'

'Easy to say, not so easy to do,' Paul retorted. 'Let's face it, Martin takes on some pretty weird characters. And afterwards you're apt to hear that the person – it's usually female – has been going around spreading nonsense about us, giving us a crank image, making it harder to convince the people who matter that we're sane and sound. Then, if I breathe a word of complaint anywhere, the answer comes back: "But she's so sincere! She means so well!"'

'How would you solve the problem?' I asked.

'We ought to put applicants through personality tests, as if they were applying to an industrial firm. I used to be with PCS. Personnel Consultancy Service.'

'Surely that could standardize your intake too closely. You might lose good applicants who didn't take kindly to your tests.'

Paul's voice was creeping upwards in pitch. 'Suppose we did screen out a few with disguised potential. What would the loss amount to? Five per cent?'

'It'd still be bad if your five per cent happened to include an offbeat genius.'

'Look, Geoffrey, that's hypothetical. You can never tell what "would have happened"[9]. Even if a reject did blossom out in some other context, it needn't prove he would have done the same here.'

Karen had turned her back on Paul and was making coffee, a bit pointedly, I thought. He pontificated on about selection procedures. After the coffee I asked him if I could see the library.

'Be our guest,' he said.

He took me to the other end of the house and threw open a door, then lingered. 'Are you getting the material you want?'

'I'm playing by ear so far, and waiting to listen to Martin this afternoon. One thing's puzzling me a little.'

'Only one?'

'One to go on with. Magic's alleged to be about power, directly or indirectly. According to W. B. Yeats, the magician seeks to attain control over the sources of life. Aleister Crowley[10] described magic (with or without a k) as a method of producing results. But here, you have this anti-success thing. You like people who reject power, who choose not to do what they could do. Or have I misunderstood?'

'No. You haven't misunderstood. Let's say, simply, that you will get an answer to that. You may think it satisfying or you may not. Now, if you'll excuse me...'

He left me in the library, pulling the door to as he went, but not shutting it. I appraised the books.

W. B. Yeats and Aleister Crowley, whom I'd just cited, caught my eye at once. They were ranged with Arthur Machen, Algernon Blackwood, A. E. Waite, and a history of the Order of the Golden Dawn, the magical fraternity which I remembered all five belonged to. Another shelf contained Robert Graves's *The White Goddess* alongside Margaret Murray and Gerald Gardner. John Cowper Powys filled half the shelf below. I spotted Eliphas Levi and earlier demi-mages. Among the moderns were Colin Wilson, Richard Cavendish, and a superb assortment of eccentrics. A rack on the table supported a much-handled set of *Man, Myth and Magic* in brown and gilt binders. Beside it were stacks of old magazines like *Gandalf's Garden* and *Quest*.

Not all the library was magical. It offered a broad selection of classics including the Bible, as well as some unforeseen authors like Marx, Bertrand Russell, Vance Packard. The works of Jung were predictable. Less so were those of Rabelais and the Marquis de Sade. Blake was represented by facsimile volumes as well as standard texts. Asian matter took up plenty of space. So did paperback fiction, much of it science-fiction.

A shelf-unit standing in a corner held books on Glastonbury, King Arthur, etcetera, including one by John Michell and one by myself. I guessed these had belonged to Eric Blount, the previous owner of Allhallows. It was sad to see four pamphlets written by him and printed at his own expense.

On a desk lay a large bound manuscript in Martin's handwriting. I dipped into it but couldn't decide whether it was a diary, a dream casebook, or a literary experiment. Now I come to think of it, that MS is very peculiar indeed. If it's a diary, it might imply.... No. I won't put anything on record that could get him into trouble.

4

Martin's afternoon session is over. A golden dawn, or a vaporous anti-climax? Time will tell. It had better. Before trying to sum up what was said, I take due note of a fact which is emerging: Allhallows can't be stampeded into self-revelation.

However, most of its inmates have begun to take on individuality. At the midday meal – described as dinner – I found myself recognizing habits of speech, ways of moving. Martin had turned the students loose all the morning to drift around in small groups. Paul, one felt uneasily, might call this 'relating to each other'. When we sat down to eat I was at the end of the second table. My neighbours were a red-haired, redbrick[11] character named Norman, aged about twenty-five, and a solemn girl he's brought with him.

Norman belongs to a new movement, Cryptocracy, which maintains that the right method of organizing mankind for survival is through an elite secret society on three levels. The Cryptocrats have roughed out their world-system on paper and are looking for superior types to slot into it. Norman is a 'staff officer' of the movement. He is all for Action, and has come here partly in search of recruits.

Throughout the meal his girl spoke only one sentence, and I can't recall what prompted it: 'We never did that in Women's Lib.'[12]

Martin asked me to step into his study before the meeting. When I got there he poured out wine in a tall, rather flamboyant goblet, and slid a plate of biscuits across the desk. 'Karen was telling me your views on legends. This is intensely interesting. You remind me a little of Charles Fort. That American, you know, who collected mysteries the scientists wouldn't face.'

I did know. But I didn't want a private lecture when I was waiting impatiently for the public one.

'Fort had the same idea,' Martin went on, 'that we must get free from an academic true-or-false logic....'

My eyes absorbed details of the study. A straight sword on the wall. A plastic curtain-rod on a tray. A curtain-rod?

He noticed, and broke off. 'I use that for dowsing.'

'Water, or what?'

'Water mostly. Can you?'

'I did it once or twice on an archaeological site, looking for foundations.[13] Dowsing strikes me as a typical Fort-type case.'

'Yes, well.... At present, Geoffrey, I'm more concerned with another sort of divining. I should warn you, you're very welcome here, but we can't promise you a smooth passage. Something is building up. A disturbance. Annabel read the I-Ching this morning, the Chinese lot-casting device, you know. She only does it on special occasions, but when she does she's seldom wrong.'

Mentally buffeted by his mercurial leaps, but still upright, I accompanied Martin to the conference room. (By the way, what was today's 'special occasion', and who decides when an occasion is special?) The students were sitting round the table, eight of them altogether. They now wore name-tags issued for the opening of the formal course. Martin shepherded me into a chair, and went over to the single high one himself. Before he sat down in it I made out a design on the back: a diamond, with a line across dividing it into two equilateral triangles, and a circle inscribed in the upper triangle.

Martin settled, and signalled to me to start my tape. He began very slowly, looking down at the table in front of him.

'Not this; not that.'

Very slowly he raised his head, and then went on at a slightly faster tempo, staring into space, almost motionless.

'I expect you know those words – the supreme utterance of India, at the brink where words fade into stillness, and infinite denial is infinite affirmation. Today I want to apply them in another sense, to the mental travels of the West, to what our civilization has lost and can find again.'

A pause.

'Not this; not that. History traces two paths of truth. This' (a movement of his right hand) 'is called science. That' (a movement of his left hand) 'is called religion. What is the relation between them? You must have heard at least three opinions.

'First. That they go together as the two modes of approach to life and reality, complementing each other.

'Second. That science alone is the true path. That religion is an irrational, primitive, at best transitional thing, which science fought and defeated some time during the reign of Queen Victoria. It hangs on only as wishful thinking, exploited by priests and politicians.

'And third, the retort of some religious believers. That since God was swept aside, unchecked science has given us nuclear weapons, technological slavery, pollution, and many more evils which the age of faith never dreamed of.

'Yet, you know, all these opinions beg the question. They assume it has to be this and that and nothing besides, science and religion distinct for ever. Valid – one or other or both – as the only roads there are. As the highways through a wilderness where all else is trackless fancy and superstition.

'For us here and now, however, I say: *not this, not that.*'

Having said it, Martin made a gear-shift which the tape, I realize, doesn't bring out. He unfroze, moved, became more conversational. The only change in his taped voice is a further quickening and easing. But he timed this well. One more sentence in the previous manner and he'd have begun to sound like a mystagogue, his credit trickling away. As it was, he continued:

'I reject this, because it's a false choice and a wrong restriction. It's bad history. Go back to the formative days of civilization, you won't find science and religion even distinguished, let alone opposed. You'll find a single system of knowing and doing. It varies from place to place, from age to age, from teacher to teacher. But always it's simply Man coming to grips with the cosmos.

'In the youth of classical Greece you'll find Pythagoras at the head of a mystical order, laying the foundations of mathematics and physics, yet treating even a theorem as an act of worship. Farther back in Egypt you'll find astounding technology, complex myth and ritual, an immortality-cult, all united in one of the most creative cultures that has ever existed. Farther back still perhaps, here in Britain, you'll find advanced astronomy and engineering techniques embodied in megalithic observatories which were also cult-centres.

'History doesn't show us an infantile "religious" phase followed by a mature "scientific" phase, taking over and getting progress under way. But neither does it show us human societies being formed and set rolling by priests in communion with their gods. It's neither this nor that. Man took his first strides before science and religion had distinct identities. His major advance began when both were branches of the same tree, and the life of the tree was the life of both. That tree was magic.'

Several of the students, after a blank start, were taking notes. The elderly couple were scribbling madly, both of them; I wondered about duplication of effort. Martin talked on, with no attempt to slow down for the note-takers.

'Of course the split did happen. Elements of magical craft and lore – astrology, numerology, alchemy, the arts of healing – evolved into sciences and forgot their origins. Meanwhile, elements of magical ritual and cult evolved by way of myth into the higher religions. In both cases there was growth. Man gained. But he also lost.

'Take science first. I needn't dwell on the modern nightmares which you all know. But I invite you to look at science's deeper effects on thoughts and attitudes. With all its achievements – its glorious, often priceless achievements – it has cut Man down, shut him up in his body, reduced him to elementary existence: birth, food, shelter, sex, death. It has taught him that this is all and death is the end.'

The words sounded familiar. Martin was repeating the first part of his talk to the Free Mind Society. Apparently this had been built into the course. Soon he referred, as before, to nothing-butness and Frankl and Thorpe. He also mentioned Arthur Koestler and somebody called Lalkov.[14] However, the follow-up was new.

'Perhaps then we should accept the believers' claim, that religion fills the void science has left, that it preserves the spiritual dimension science has lost.

'But wait. With religion likewise, hasn't there been a loss – a deadly loss – as well as the gain?

'Since the split, religion *has* often opposed progress, *has* obscured truth in the name of dogma. The scientists have a case there. But even on its own terms, does religion work today? Outside of a minority, does it satisfy, does it inspire? It doesn't. The believer may say justly that the scientific view of Man (or the view which passes as scientific) is shutting-in, debasing, hopeless. But his own religious view is also apt to be shutting-in, debasing, hopeless.

'Humanists (so-called) argue that religion is wish-fulfilling fantasy. The best answer to that, and a most significant answer, is what the humanists say themselves when they want to prove something else – that religion does NOT fulfil wishes. It's much more obsessive than wish-fulfilment, and much less pleasant.

'I've heard humanists compare God to Father Christmas. As if anybody ever changed his whole life for Father Christmas! Or starved or suffered or died for Father Christmas! Yes, or persecuted in Father Christmas's name!

'But look at Christianity. In the Bible Belt it's a stunting life-denying bigotry of Thou Shalt Not. In liberal circles it's shrunk to a mere morality, drying up the higher life of the spirit. Christians may still promise life after death while scientists deny it. But their heaven is a meaningless pie-in-the-sky Elsewhere. Belief in it doesn't enlarge our life as we live it, or release human beings from their bondage and hangups.'

I took a note myself, mentally, to ask Martin about his own religious background.

'Where do we go from here? Is there any escape from the tyranny of closed systems that paralyse the will to advance? I put it to you that when science and religion diverged, as the two heirs of Man's ancient wisdom, they both left something behind. There's a part of the legacy – the source of the deepest vitality in all of it – which neither of these heirs possesses. As a result, something in Man has fallen asleep, or has sunk below the threshold.

'You can guess what I mean. A cliché is best for summing it up. *Religion has lost its magic...* and so has science. What we call "magic" now, of course, isn't the great original magic. Mostly it's a feeble, distorted remnant. Yet it's never quite lost hold of what was once the central reality. It's never quite lost the power to revivify and re-awaken. It can show the way to recovery. That is the truth we shall explore while we're together.

'Before throwing the discussion open, I want to give you one further talking point.

'I suggest that mankind is haunted by an awareness of this very fact. Haunted by a feeling of lost potentialities and a fall. Think of all the myths of a golden age, far back. An age of Titans; of men who conversed familiarly with the gods, and had no fear of death; of superhuman works, profound knowledge. The glory of Atlantis. The enchantments that raised Stonehenge into place.

'Here in Britain, and especially here in Somerset, we have our own version of it – with a further belief that this enchanted age isn't really lost, and can come back. Our guest Geoffrey can tell you more about the reign of King Arthur and the acts of Merlin, and Avalon and the promise of Arthur's return. Probably also about the sleeping Giant Albion who is behind all the mysteries of Britain.'

I wondered what I was being let in for.

'And it isn't just in early traditions that we find such ideas. All the novel theories that have been aired over the past few years – all the mystical-occult revivals that have been in the news – have you noticed how often they appeal to the same conviction about a lost marvellous age? It's alive. Desperately alive. I think Geoffrey would agree if I said that this was one of the reasons for public excitement over Arthur, and the Cadbury excavations in quest of Camelot, a few years ago.

'But apart from that, look at all the modern theories on the same lines. Theories about primeval giants; lost secrets of technology; aircraft and atomic power in the ancient East; culture-bringers from outer space, thousands of years back. Theories about Mu, and Tiahuanaco, and flying saucers from Venus. Explanations of all the gods as helpful astronauts coming from remote planets around 10,000 B.C. – give or take a few millennia.[15]

'There may be truth in some of these notions, and then again there may not. What I do urge you is to reflect on the way most of them show a yearning to give shape to the same belief. There *has been* something marvellous, it's no longer with us, but perhaps we can recapture the secret and reinstate the vision.

'Often such theories bring in magical motifs, even if they're dressed up in scientific disguises. That instinct at least is sound. Magic is the golden string which can lead us back to the roots of the tree of life and the heart of the human mystery.'

That was the end. As soon as he showed that he was ready for questions, Norman, the Cryptocrat, burst out.

'I must say, this leaves me nowhere. I assumed the object of the exercise was so that we could get together to discuss action. If we're going to be given academic lectures I don't see any point in coming.'

A faint, unsympathetic murmur. Martin replied gently:

'Tell us what you would like to do.'

'I said, get together on a programme.'

'A programme for what, Norman?'

'Action. Magic's supposed to be a technique for getting results.'

'Can you give us an illustration of what you mean?'

'Er, well, I represent a movement...'

Laughter and protests. Clearly they'd already been made aware that he represented a movement.

'We'll be pleased to hear about it another time', said Martin. 'But I think, now, we should pass on. Yes, Kwame?'

The black student spoke up in a resonant voice.

'To an African this is familiar. We know that human societies have gone backwards as well as forwards. We have only to remember Zimbabwe. But we know too that many tribal societies live even today in this state you describe, governed by magical beliefs, without religious or scientific development. I do not deny some of the tribal witch-doctors have much practical wisdom, but I cannot see how you would assert this was ever a good way to live.'

Martin's answer was careful. 'Very likely not, in the cases you have in mind. Conditions may be too adverse. What I am thinking of is a potentiality, which has been realized far more fully in some societies than in others. I hope this can be spelt out in the next few days, if you'll be patient.'

The elderly husband (I couldn't read his name-tag across the table) asked abruptly: 'What about Hitler? What about all the mysticism of the Nazi movement in Germany, the superman stuff and the noble Aryan past which they had to revive? Do you approve?'

'No, I certainly do not. The Nazis threw reason overboard and "thought with the blood". The sleep of reason engenders monsters. Myself, I believe in reason. The important fact about Nazism is that it could get such a hold on a civilized, technically advanced nation. It was a mystique that offered escape – into self-transcendence, earthly adventure and fulfilment, the rebirth of mystical glories which modern Man feels he's lost. Hitler grasped truths of human nature which liberal types ignored. He exploited and perverted those truths. Our job is to grasp them as he did, but reverence them, and come to terms with them in a rational spirit.'

I noticed – surely one of the few signs of a real generation gap – the unreality of this Hitler issue to most of the students. It's practically Dad's Army.[16]

The young Welshman spoke next. 'How do you think Stonehenge was put up?'

Martin smiled. 'I don't know, and I don't believe anybody knows. Archaeologists have their explanations. I'd like to see them do it themselves.'

This fourth exchange set the students off like a box of firecrackers. They began chattering to each other instead of questioning Martin. It was what he wanted. He sat back glowing benignly.

After a long, wild, wide-ranging conversation he called the meeting to order. 'Time to adjourn. I'd like you all to come to the recreation room this evening at eight, for an experiment. And one other thing. In the next day or so, would each of you try to recollect an event in your own life which might be called "supernatural" – an event that's hard to explain by the approved methods. If you've got one, write a short account of it in a form we can collect and discuss together.'

He spoke to me as he left. 'You too, Geoffrey, if you will.'

5

In the hall there's a letter-rack, one of those green baize contraptions with crisscrossing ribbons. As I emerged from the conference room I saw a piece of paper stuck in it with my name on. This was a message to ring Trevor Herrick at the *Globe*. The Allhallows phone, by the way, is near the kitchen, with an extension (I think) in Paul's room upstairs, which he uses as an office. It gets answered promptly, I haven't yet heard any prolonged ringing. For outgoing calls they have a separate pay phone.

I got through to Trevor. He told me that a photographer, David Jacks, would be arriving tomorrow. I warned that this might be premature. So far we aren't within sight of any answers. What does make Martin's graduates tick, John Rosmer and Madri and the rest? The gap between effects and causes is still absurdly wide. But David Jacks, it seems, is in Yeovil with his equipment on another job, so they've arranged for him to take in Allhallows before he leaves this area.

I acquiesced, and asked if some more tapes could be sent to me. Meanwhile Martin had vanished. I went out through a door near his study to the back of the house, and saw Karen inspecting a myrtle bush. She checked that I'd found the message. I confessed my qualms.

'Not to worry,' she replied. 'Once Martin gets going on those "strange experiences", there's daylight ahead. A first instalment any-how. Have you got a few to tell him yourself?'

'Maybe. Mostly to do with picking up the inspiration for a new book. Like when I was at a loss for ideas once, and had a long vivid dream that made no sense, and then, the very next day, happened to run into the only person who could interpret it – and that made a lot of vague notions jell, and started me off. But it could have been telepathic.[17] My feeling is, Martin's angling for things that go beyond all the telepathy-ESP stuff. Hints at contact with higher powers perhaps. Am I getting warm?'

She shot me another of her illuminated, unilluminating looks.

'Yes. You are.'

We began pacing along the lawn in the sunshine, through the pillars, towards the kinetic sculpture. 'Most of the students do trot out experiences like your dreams,' she said. 'They're apt to be so proud of them too. But we have to coax them past it. Past so much of what they think of, when they think of magic – fortune-telling and spell-casting and so forth.'

She took me farther along the lawn than this morning, to the pseudo-Grecian structure set among trees, which is near the edge of the property.

'Come and look at our temple.'

It had a pillared front. 'Eighteenth century?' I asked.

'It's supposed to be nearly as old as the original dower house. The only modern improvement is the sculpture inside. Another of the three by our American friend.'

We entered a bare, oblong, stone-floored chamber with a few dusty chairs. Three steps led up to a carved stone table, some neo-classicist's conception of a pagan altar. Above it, attached to the end wall, was the American's sculpture. It was in very high relief, made of metal strips, like its elusive colleague outside. But there could be no doubt what this one was: a phallic human figure at least six feet tall, with the right hand raised, and a face like a glowering Japanese mask... and horns. My eyes dropped to the feet. They were ambiguous, neither clearly hooves nor clearly not hooves.

Martin's brochure hadn't conveyed this.

'The Devil in person?'

'The Horned One,' Karen replied. 'You can take him any way you please.'

'Is the temple – well – used?'

'Why, yes. We get witches here, and a few Satanists. Some of them give us demonstrations. Some... appreciate the facilities in earnest.'

'Is anything of that sort likely to happen while I'm here?'

A second's pause, then a quiet 'Yes.'

'And Martin doesn't object?'

'Hardly ever. It's therapeutic for them to work freely. Our local historian says the temple may have been put to this use in the eighteenth century. The landowner belonged to the Hell-Fire Club. Sir Francis Dashwood and Wilkes and all that set.'

I remembered what was written over the entrance to Allhallows. 'Do what you will, but be very sure you will it.' The same motto, or part of it, was over the door of Medmenham Abbey where the Hell-Fire Club held its orgies.[18] But a whiff of caution still deterred me from mentioning this. Instead I asked: 'Can my photographer take a picture of the Horned One?'

'Of course.'

Feeling slightly happier about Jacks's visit, I let Karen pilot me on a more extended tour – down that slope with Glastonbury Tor in the distance, and then to the right along the boundary fence to a point behind the house, which was partially screened from us by trees. I didn't talk on the way, because the sight of the Tor had again come as a reminder. It recalled other happenings which I was trying to sort out.

Karen sat on a bank of grass and I sat beside her. She guessed what was in my mind and said: 'Have you thought of any more experiences to tell the class?'

'I don't know about telling the class. But the cases I'd really like to canvass opinions on – that is, from people who do believe in ESP and whatnot – are the ones where explanations of that kind are no use.'

'You're still talking about these inspirations of yours?'

'Well, yes. Take my books on Glastonbury and related matters. That place interested me for ages. But I got hooked seriously by a single incident I can pin down. At Toronto Public Library I dug out a book which mentioned one tradition (no need to go into details now) that caught my imagination. It did the trick and did it at the right moment, and I started work.

'Here's the point, though. After researching for years and reading swarms of other books, I realized that the one in Toronto was very rare, and the tradition it quoted was highly dubious and not on record anywhere else. So I'd hit on the single right book to get me moving, in the right place (a damned unlikely place, far from home) at the right time... and the odds against were colossal.[19] You can't account for it by talking about the Unconscious, as a psychologist might. But what use would it be to drag in notions like ESP either? How would they help?'

'How indeed? But go on, Geoffrey. There's more, isn't there.'

'Only this. Again after years of research, it dawned on me I'd been surrounded with hints all my life. Things that sound silly in cold blood, and yet they pile up. Relatives of mine had names out of Avalonian legend, or were born on the saint's-days of Glastonbury saints. That sort of coincidence had happened over and over, in my own life too. None of those relatives knew or cared or influenced me. The realization all came later.'

'Do you draw any conclusions?'

'Take it with the book incident, and it's as if some unknown agency was working on this for decades, even before I was born. Not to give me messages which I couldn't have read, but to fix matters so that a conviction would take shape gradually as I found out more and more. A conviction that there was a plan, a meaning, behind it all, and this was a job I was meant to do.'

'Not a plan or meaning you could have been responsible for your-self.'

'No. Not even if I had occult powers. To contrive that string of coincidences I'd have had to cause events backwards in time, as far back as 1897, when the first of the relatives - my father, to be precise - was born on a Glastonbury saint's day and given a significant name.'

Karen sat for a while without comment. Then she said: 'You understand a lot. In a way Allhallows exists because of something like your "book incident". I don't see why I shouldn't tell you. It's about Martin and me. Do you want to hear?'

'If you want to tell.' Was that part of the story coming now?

'When I met him, you know, at the Festival, none of that Glastonbury mystique meant a thing to me. I was in an advertising agency, and I went to pick up ideas on trends in the pop scene. But after I'd been with Martin a day or two, it flashed. There was a moment when I saw him at one special place in the field there, a place I could show you now, with hills behind and a crowd of the kids whirl-ing around - and he was so much older, and so different, and yet he belonged and it was all wonderful - and that image wouldn't go out of my head afterwards. It said "This isn't Martin-over-there-and-me-over-here, it's us."'

Karen stopped and I tried to think of something to say, but didn't have to. She resumed.

'Martin was married, long ago. I don't know if he's told you.'

'No, he hasn't. Nothing personal at all.'

'He hardly ever speaks of his wife. (This is partly a hint to you, what to avoid mentioning.) She died of cancer. He got over it but wouldn't marry again.'

'Were there any children?'

'No. Students often assume he's a lifelong bachelor, and some of them go on and assume he's a consenting adult, implying he's never known where it's at with heterosexuals. That causes a blockage from time to time.'

'It must.' But if she was his girl-friend, and the Allhallows consensus allowed visitors to be told so on a single day's acquaintance, how did such rumours get off the ground?

'We kept on seeing each other after the festival. Whatever had hit me, it worked both ways. He was phoning me almost before I got home. Soon, the inevitable happened. We never exactly lived together. He stayed with me sometimes and we used to travel a bit. It was a funny informal sort of understanding.

'But I could see what he needed ... I thought. He was a genius who wasn't selling himself. I tried to be a female Svengali. My job helped. And you know, he could write a best-seller if he chose. Or do well on television or radio. Don't you agree?'

'Yes indeed.'

'Quite so. I introduced him to the right people, I set up lunches with publishers and producers – and yes, he co-operated. What he did do, like reports on scripts for publishers, he did splendidly. But I couldn't involve him. He made me furious. Once we'd been having dinner at a restaurant and I stormed out. Oh yes, he followed. But before he did, he picked up his glass of brandy and finished it.'

She smiled, not wryly, but warmly. 'What I'm leading up to, Geoffrey, is our Crisis. It came the next summer over the launching party for that magazine *Cosmos*. Martin got an invitation for two because he had an article in the first issue. It was a marvellous chance for him to make contacts.

'But they muddled the dates. I think they sent a notice saying the 16th and then corrected it to the 15th, and for some reason Martin got the first notice but not the second. He spent the 15th, the real date, entertaining some cousins of his, and then came to me on the 16th with the news that he'd just found out. He was apologetic because he'd had a chance to check and didn't, so I'd missed the party. It didn't upset him for his own sake. He told me he couldn't have gone the night before anyway because of his cousins. That did it. We had a flaming row over attitudes and priorities and God knows what, and then...'

'Then?' I prompted.

'Then we were past it all. Martin's public career faded out. I stopped trying, we were at peace. What he wanted from me ... he called it comradeship. We're still together after our fashion, only it's a different fashion. But that mix-up over dates! It was extraordinary.'

'As if a guardian angel had been at work.'

'That's how I felt. It came through like that from me to Martin, and it made an impression on him. More than just about us.'

'How do you mean?' I asked.

'You'll be finding out soon, probably.' The sky had clouded while we were talking. 'Let's go in.'

We took a path through the trees and she led me into the house by the kitchen door. I thought of the ghosts from her advertising past that might still be hovering upstairs. Dead correspondence, files on clients' campaigns, stylish dresses and trouser-suits in the fashion of several years ago. Or had she banished the former things entirely? One doesn't know, not in detail, what happens to these people whom association with Martin alters so much.

Annabel had made tea and was handing it out to students.

6

Midnight. I spent most of the early evening shut up in this room of mine, recording the events of the afternoon, and reconsidering tapes, and writing notes. Another fact has seeped through. Allhallows isn't standing still. At least, not securely. It could develop new features while I'm here catching up with the present lot. Quite likely it will, during the months between my drafting the article and getting it into the *Globe* magazine. Something is in the air, something not docile.

There's more to this than Martin's obscure warning in his study.

After tea, I managed to grab a few minutes alone in the library for another attack on his manuscript. A few minutes, no more. Norman's morose girl came in, the one who never did it in Women's Lib, and I preferred that she shouldn't see me with that book. But I did have time to puzzle over the last few lines.

They look as if they've been added lately, on a sheet inserted in the binder. Where many of the pages are thumbed or frayed, this one's fresh. I can't repeat its contents word for word, but here they are approximately.

> Climbed C before dawn. Path slippery, dark. Twisted ankle. Summit as ever. Constellations only slightly distorted, but 3 Archons blazing & angry above the Mendips. Presence M cloudy, ambiguous.
> Patterns suggest Spectral subversion, close. MIDSUMMER?

Like the rest of the book, this didn't chime with anything else at Allhallows. But now I've noticed a clue I missed earlier. Slightly but undeniably, Martin is limping. Yes, he's twisted his ankle. That book has almost got to be a diary of some sort. A diary of madness? But he leaves it lying around – and he's so unflappably self-possessed.

Midsummer, meanwhile, is three days off.

At supper Martin seated me by a student I don't seem to have mentioned, a waiter at a London club. His name is Steve. He enjoys his job, and tells good stories about the club members. I praised him for being so observant. That triggered him off on his special topic: numerology. He's perfecting his own system for classifying people by numbers, and he does a character-reading act at the club.

When our company met in the recreation room for Martin's 'experiment' I saw why he'd placed Steve in my path. It was to help me gather material on the star of the evening. Steve was going to show us his technique.

Dark and curly-haired, he confronted the group (which included Karen and Paul) and began. He made a gauche start. It had probably struck him at the last minute that his usual patter wouldn't do, and he wasn't quick enough with words to fake a new introduction. But he had the knack of making an audience warm towards him.

'Er well, numerology is a very ancient art – as I'm sure everybody here knows – it goes back to the Kabbalistic lore of the ancient Jews, and there are instances in the Bible, at least I've heard there are, I hope you'll correct me if not—'

His eye swung round and paused on Martin, who gave a just perceptible nod of reassurance.

'Yes, well, for my own readings I use a chart based on the Jewish system. It was used two hundred years ago by the famous magician Cagliostro.' Steve pronounced the name as you would in English, sounding the g. I would guess he's seen it in print but never heard it. He fumbled in his pocket and extracted a sheet of paper, folded like a motoring map, which he opened out and displayed. Too visibly it had gone through the same process many times. On it was written, with a black felt pen, a layout of numbers and letters:

1	2	3	4	5	6	7	8
A	B	C	D	E	U	O	F
I	K	G	M	H	V	Z	P
Q	R	L	T	N	W		
J	S				X		
Y							

'As you see,' Steve continued, 'the chart gives a number – that is, a single digit – over each letter of the alphabet. The basic operation is to take the person's name, add up the digits that correspond to the letters in it, and keep doing that till you've got a single digit. This is called the digital root and it's the personality key. Plenty of numerologists do the same, but I've fed in some ideas of my own as well. Also I've related it to the astrological signs. Now can I have...'

Almost certainly he was going to say 'a volunteer', but checked himself because he wanted to choose his victim. He wavered, then said: 'Sorry about that, I got lost for a moment. I'll try to demonstrate.' He looked at the elderly couple, whom I now know as Mr and Mrs Frobisher, and addressed the husband. 'Would you be willing?'

'By all means.'

'Your first name is?'

'Alan. With one L.'

'Right. The A comes under 1, the L under 3, the next A under 1 again...' He made ALAN FROBISHER add up to 45, then added the 4 to the 5, and declared 9 to be the digital root. Next he asked for a longish series of further details, including birth date and parents' names. He scribbled on an envelope, stared at the result for a few seconds, and began.

'There's a feeling of trouble early on. Your parents did stay together, I mean they didn't separate, but they weren't too happy.'

'Fair enough, I'm afraid.'

'But you weren't hurt by it yourself. Not badly. You had an up-and-down sort of record at school. Did a teacher ever tell you something like this: "You could do well if you paid attention, but you keep wandering off on your own"?' Steve gave the teacher a posh accent. He's a clever mimic.

'Almost word for word,' Mr Frobisher said. 'That would be my form master. He told me I was erratic.'

'Good. After school you trained for a job but found it off-putting. So you gave that up and tried a different line.'

'Right again. I spent a year as a medical student and couldn't take it.'

Steve glanced at Mrs Frobisher, then returned to Alan. 'Maybe now I'm on thin ice, but the signs are powerful. Don't answer unless you want to, and tell me if I'm wrong. But I'd say that when you were about twenty-two, you got engaged to somebody else, before you met your present wife, and it didn't work out.'

'Near enough. I was twenty-three.' Aside: 'That would be Eunice, dear. You know about Eunice.'

It went on like this for a quarter of an hour. Steve diagnosed Mr Frobisher's occupation as 'art', and Mr Frobisher confessed to being a fabric designer. He also assented to Steve's description of him as 'romantic' and to a few tactful remarks about his marriage and off-spring – 'two children, perhaps three' (it was two).

The only statement he turned down flat was that he'd been defrauded in his thirties by a confidence trickster. Steve tried several re-phrasings but got nowhere at all – at least, not directly: Mr Frobisher was so emphatic he hadn't been swindled, you suspected he had. Steve broke the deadlock with a couple of happier shots, and finished amid applause.

Martin spoilt his triumph. 'Now do it again with someone else.'

Steve demurred, muttering that it might bore the audience.

'Never mind that,' said Martin. 'Do it again. That's an order.'

He spoke pleasantly, but you could see it actually was an order.

Dashed, Steve picked out the Welsh colliery lad, and took down his full name. It was Owen Griffith, which gave 55, and 5 Plus 5 was 10, and 1 plus 0 was 1. Steve assembled his further details and began. Instantly he was in trouble.

'You got on well with your parents.'

'Never knew my dad. He walked out when I was two.'

'With your mother then.'

'She used to get drunk and belt me.'

And so unhappily on. Owen seemed perfectly good-humoured, not hostile, and not making it up to discredit numerology. Once or twice, as Steve groped for a footing, he even stretched the facts to make them fit better. But apart from a few generalities, the second attempt was a fiasco.

'It does happen like this,' said Steve glumly. 'Some people just don't. No offence, Owen. Regrets all round. I never like to go from one to another without a break.'[20]

'But if this numerology is a mathematical technique,' objected the hitherto mute Chinese girl, 'then ought it not to give its results the second time as it does the first time?'

'Maybe it ought. I only know it doesn't. Not so you can rely on it.'

Martin interposed 'I'd rather we didn't discuss this experiment till tomorrow. Each of you mull it over and form your own conclusions. Thank you very much, Steve, it went well. Better than you think, perhaps. Now let's have some music.'

I looked at the record-player, but nobody moved towards it. Instead Annabel appeared with an instrument which she explained was a Welsh harp. Having shown how it differed from a non-Welsh harp, she launched into an unsettling Celtic melody. Owen recognized this and joined her, singing softly in Welsh.

The evening's entertainment was closed by Paul with a most bizarre poetry reading. Once again I think we're meant to draw inferences, and once again the clues are frail. He stood at a small table, the only one within reach. It had a litter of newspapers on it. Having squared them up fastidiously, he announced his first series of extracts.

'I will read some passages from the Babylonian Epic of Creation, composed nearly four thousand years ago. The senior gods enthrone the young Bel-Marduk, called the divine Son, and give him their commission to destroy the Old Ones, the terrible pre-human powers led by the monster Tiamat.

> 'From this day unchangeable shall be thy pronouncement.
> To raise or bring low – these shall be in thy hand....
>
> We have granted thee kingship over the universe entire....
>
> Go and cut off the life of Tiamat.
> May the winds bear her blood to places undisclosed.'
>
> Bel-Marduk constructed a bow, marked it as his weapon,
> Attached thereto the arrow, fixed its bow-cord.
> He raised the mace, made his right hand grasp it;
> Bow and quiver he hung at his side.
> In front of him he set the lightning,
> With a blazing flame he filled his body.
> He then made a net to enfold Tiamat therein.
> The four winds he stationed that none of her might escape....
>
> Then the Lord raised up the flood-storm, his mighty weapon.
> He mounted the storm-chariot irresistible and terrifying.
> He harnessed and yoked to it a team-of-four,
> The Killer, the Relentless, the Trampler, the Swift....
>
> For a cloak he was wrapped in an armour of terror;
> With his fearsome halo his head was turbaned.
> The Lord went forth and followed his course,
> Towards the raging Tiamat he set his face....
>
> The gods, his fathers, milled about him.'

Paul was silent for a few seconds, then said: 'Now I will read some passages from the sixth book of Milton's *Paradise Lost*. God the Father enthrones his divine Son, and sends him to expel the forces of evil, led by Satan, from Heaven.

The Finger and the Moon

'Hear all ye angels, progeny of light,
Thrones, Dominations, Princedoms, Virtues, Powers,
Hear my decree, which unrevoked shall stand.
This day I have begot whom I declare
My only Son, and on this holy hill
Him have anointed, whom ye now behold
At my right hand; your head I him appoint;
And by myself have sworn to him shall bow
All knees in Heav'n, and shall confess him Lord.

Go then thou mightiest in thy Father's might,
Ascend my chariot, guide the rapid wheels
That shake Heav'n's basis, bring forth all my war,
My bow and thunder, my almighty arms
Gird on, and sword upon thy puissant thigh;
Pursue these sons of darkness, drive them out
From all Heav'n's bounds into the utter deep:
There let them learn, as likes them, to despise
God and Messiah his anointed king.

Attended with ten thousand thousand saints,
He onward came, far off his coming shone....
So spake the Son, and into terror changed
His countenance too severe to be beheld
And full of wrath bent on his enemies.
At once the Four spread out their starry wings
With dreadful shade contiguous, and the orbs
Of his fierce chariot rolled, as with the sound
Of torrent floods or of a numerous host.
He on his impious foes right onward drove,
Gloomy as night; under his burning wheels
The steadfast empyrean shook throughout,
All but the throne itself of God. Full soon
Among them he arrived; in his right hand
Grasping ten thousand thunders.'

Unexpectedly. Paul stopped reading. 'Try to fix those images in your minds, the Babylonian and the Miltonic, three and a half millennia apart.[21] That is all. Thank you for your attention.'

In this Allhallows atmosphere, where something seems always about to happen and never quite does, the passages sounded incantatory and foreboding. Yet the apt mental comment was 'So what?' I did, however, observe Paul himself. He read those two sets of extracts differently. The Babylonian text came through calm and even. The lines from Milton seemed to clutch him by the heart. He delivered them with mounting excitement and a flush spreading over his cheeks, as if the War in Heaven concerned him personally. Why?

Afterwards coffee was served, somebody did start the hi-fi, and the party dissolved into four separate conversations. Martin withdrew looking sleepy. I was cornered by the Cryptocrat Norman. He'd picked up that allusion to me at the afternoon meeting, and wanted to consult me on some grisly scheme for a society or order which would 'remobilize the Arthurian mystique' as part of British Cryptocracy. I was tired, and the music (Higher Pop) was loud, and I didn't catch half of what Norman said, and to judge from the rest of it I didn't miss much.

Third Day

I

TEN HOURS to put on record, and still plenty to come. I slept soundly for as long as I did sleep. But about 6:30 a.m., half waking, I went through what psychologists call a hypnagogic experience. It had the same flavour as one that happened to me in India – a flavour of anguished urgency. A single image appeared and faded and reappeared, over and over again for several minutes. I felt that it was charged with meaning and that if I failed to construe it my loss would be incalculable.

What I saw was a tall gaunt figure of doubtful sex, in a blue robe. He (if that's the correct pronoun) stood facing me but with eyes turned down. He was pouring water from a cup in his right hand into a cup in his left. They were of metal, contrastingly coloured. The first might have been silver, the second gold. Although the water could be seen flowing, this picture was outside time, because the flow never stopped.[1] At last I woke fully, dazed and shaken.

Struggling up from my mattress, I looked out of the window. A fresh sun shone invitingly. I decided to go and search for the maze. To judge from Karen it had to be over to the right, past the car park.

I went out behind the house, veered in that direction, and saw another vista like the one near the temple. This too fell away towards the boundary fence, with trees on the left, and a jungle of rhodo-dendrons on the right. Its gentle slope of grass wasn't empty. Thirty or forty yards down – with that inescapable Tor in the distance – Annabel was standing. Beside her stood a Great Dane. Both were very still in the morning sunshine, quarter-profile, the known girl and the astonishing dog. I advanced towards them. She turned and called 'Hallo'.

Her dark hair hung down her back. She was wearing a long yellowish dress, damp at the hemline from brushing dew off grass. Her feet were bare. Round her waist was a belt or sash, made, chiefly, of credible roses. Plastic or otherwise, they formed the semblance of a garland.

'Hallo,' I greeted her. 'I haven't met your friend. Who does he belong to?'

The Great Dane rolled a resentful gaze at me, and growled softly. Annabel murmured soothing words and patted his head. He was submissive at once.

'I don't know. He just comes and goes.'

Indeed he had no collar.

'Does he come at any special times?' I asked.

'Usually when something's about to happen. A change.'

'You use the I-Ching,[2] don't you?'

'I can read it a little.'

Deadpan. It struck me I'd never seen her face alter, not sharply. Her complexion was poor too. Yet she had an air of welcome about her. Welcome without come-hither. Those roses... I wondered if she was old enough to have taken part in Flower Power.[3] Or perhaps she was a Neo-Flowerchild of a new generation.

I tackled her again. 'How long have you lived here?'

'I live here. I don't count time. Why count?'

'And before you came?'

'Before? Nothing.'

'Nothing.' I felt blocked.

'Not to spell out. Dirty needles. Doorsteps. Horrors on the floor of the loo at Piccadilly Circus.'

I understood, and remembered Karen: Terry Hoad had 'cured' Annabel. Presumably this was what he cured her of. It wasn't a subject to pursue. Better to change course.

'Mm. Actually I got up to go and look for the maze.'

'It's over there,' she replied. 'Through those rhododendron bushes.'

'What sort of maze is it? Can you reach the centre by just turning to the right, like Harris?'

Even while saying this, I thought: they don't read *Three Men in a Boat* any more.

'No, you can't,' said Annabel. 'The centre doesn't connect with the outside.[4] It's designed as a mandala, of course. I'll take you through it if you like... later. You won't be going into it yet, but that's the path to it, if you want to look.' She pointed at a gap in the bushes.

Dismissed, I followed her path. It led through to what was once a big formal garden at the corner of the property, with a brick wall taking over from the boundary fence. Today the garden survives only as an unkempt tangle around the fringes.

Martin's maze fills most of the space, an imposing affair eighty or ninety feet across, which must have swallowed a large slice of his resources. The effect is like Hampton Court, with a high clipped surrounding hedge, too high to see over. This barrier is much more impressive now than it is in the old brochure picture, where part of it seems to be hardly more than a rail, with similar rails lining the pathways further in. If the inner ones have all become hedges too, there must be a background of elaborate transplanting and tending, followed by healthy growth. The shape of the maze - as I learned by walking round - is hexagonal, with a pillar at each angle.

Completing my circuit and arriving at the entrance, I debated whether to go in; took a step or two; glimpsed a passage a yard wide, running between hedges, and turning sharply. Then the maze said *No* to me. I don't see how else to put it. Hurriedly I retreated through the bushes. Annabel was still there, facing me as I emerged, not exactly waiting, but knowing.

'You didn't, did you.' She stated rather than asked.

It was irritating. 'I didn't want to, just at this moment.'

'No, you wouldn't, not yet.' Then her manner changed, and she smiled at last. 'Excuse me.'

Allhallows had woken up, and Paul was in sight. Annabel ran towards him with the dog bounding behind - Paul didn't move, he let the girl come to him. I had my feelings about those two in the first evening. Their relationship may be none of my business, but now I've observed both of them, it jars. It definitely jars.

2

Before breakfast Martin and Karen commandeered me with a proposal. They took me into his study to present it.

'The session this morning is likely to be a longish one,' Karen explained, 'and it's very important. I've suggested to Martin that instead of just speaking to the students himself, he should bring you in as well.'

'I'd be honoured. But how?'

'You could tell them some of the things you were talking about yesterday. They fit in beautifully.'

'I would appreciate it, Geoffrey,' said Martin. 'It sounds as if you could make various points a great deal better than anybody else will. Three of the students handed me their scripts last night – on their "experiences", you know – and if these are typical' (he lowered his voice) 'they may not take us far.'

'And as we've got you here,' said Karen, 'it's a pity to let you just sit and listen, when you could contribute so much.'

This was my first straight encounter with them in partnership. It was rather touching, the way she still tried to manage him, but now worked on activities he chose himself, instead of activities she chose for him.

'Yes, of course,' I answered when they'd both stopped. 'I'll do my best.'

At breakfast Martin announced that in view of the fine weather, the group would meet outdoors. He also collected two more scripts. Presently his morning session took shape on the grass near the sun-dial. A little mound enabled him to sit a foot or so higher than the students, with a sheaf of notes on his lap. He told me to sit on the same mound, with the same slight elevation. Karen, Paul and Annabel remained in the house.

I was a bit apprehensive about the chances of taping a session out in the open, but the air was very still, and most of it can be retrieved....

Martin began by reviewing last night's numerology. 'Steve did it well. Probably you all agree. Yet we saw what does often happen: success in one case, then failure in another. Mei-ling' (nodding towards the Chinese girl) 'asked the crucial question. If it's a technique, done by rules, why do the results vary?

'This isn't confined to numerology. It's the norm with all magical methods of character-reading and prediction and so forth – with astrology, crystal-gazing, palmistry, fortune-telling by cards, you name it. Sceptics can always make a technique look foolish. You know the line. They ask six astrologers to cast the same person's horoscope, and get six different readings, none of them convincing.

'Yet you also know that expert astrologers do succeed. Not every time – there's always that on-and-off quality – but enough. At Freiburg University they have case-histories of astrologers like Walter Böer, who cast the horoscope of a teenage delinquent he'd never met, and told exactly the same story as the psychologists who examined the boy.[5]

'Or with crystal-gazing, you'll have heard of scryers like Jeane Dixon, who's been at it for years in America. Then there's our own Annabel here at Allhallows, who uses several methods. So also with numerology. We saw Steve's first result, and I could recall famous instances from history such as Cagliostro, whom Steve mentioned.' Martin pronounced the name correctly. Perhaps he intended a tactful tip to Steve, and to anybody else who might refer to the same seer. 'By numerology Cagliostro foretold the fates of Louis XVI and Marie Antoinette.'

Mrs Frobisher, who had been gazing dreamily at the landscape, snapped back to attention and wrote.

'Our basic fact,' continued Martin, 'is neither consistent scoring by any of these techniques, nor consistent non-scoring. Nor is it a hotch-potch of half-results that might be guesswork or might not. No, it's a record of some brilliant successes by every method, often in a series by the same person, but always in a strange now-you-see- it-now-you-don't pattern, with a scrapheap of failures all around.

'Most modern interpreters of magic would agree what the likeli-est reason is. *The technique is not the secret.* The spelt-out drill, the conscious acts which a magician performs, don't account for whatever success he has. They focus his mind on the subject, yes. Or perhaps they just keep it occupied. They may do this better, for him, than any-thing else would, and he may be right to use them. But the real inner process, of character-reading or prediction or whatever, is... *other*. The same is true of minor magical workings to produce effects, like casting a spell. When a spell gets cast it isn't because of any words the magi-cian recites. If he hits his mark and then tells you how it was done, he's probably rationalizing. He may even be deceiving himself.

'This isn't a theory of my own. I could quote you several authorities, but I'll quote only one now, Aleister Crowley. Magic, he said, "eludes consciousness altogether" – these are his words – "so that when one is able to do it, one does it without conscious comprehension, very much as one makes a good stroke at cricket or billiards."

Martin looked up from his notes. 'I won't apologize for citing Crowley in this day and age. All I feel unhappy about here is his posh choice of games.'

Some of the students laughed. Some didn't. Both Frobishers were distressed. Martin went on.

'When I had the privilege of meeting Jung, he told me of his experiments with techniques such as the I-Ching. He convinced me it was wrong to dismiss them out of hand. They might be valid through mobilizing the latent powers of the Unconscious, in ways that still escape science. I'd say, now, we must go further than Jung. It isn't even worth debating whether a magical technique is "valid". Sometimes you can prove that, scientifically, it must be absurd. How can astrology make sense – that is, literal sense – when it's based on a false astronomy?' (Mr Frobisher shook his head.) 'But the technique doesn't have to be valid. Even if it's total nonsense, we can grow into deeper understanding by asking what happens when people use it.'

Martin addressed me. 'Geoffrey, I believe you take a parallel view of legends.'

He was tossing me my cue to repeat bits of that first talk with Karen, about Glastonbury and Arthur and stories which aren't facts yet point to facts. I did. Most of the students had heard of the excavations in Somerset during the 1960s, and they asked me questions that threatened to sidetrack the whole proceedings. To pull them back to where I judged Martin wanted them to be, I recalled his remarks on modern crank theories – 'Was God an astronaut?' and that kind of... well, speculation.

'I've found the same there,' I said. 'With theories about Atlantis for instance. Ignatius Donnelly and his school. They may be all wrong about Atlantis, and geology may have proved they're wrong, yet their ideas do repay following through. The crank may get a grip on realities unconsciously, like the legend-weaver, and then cook them up into a story which is nonsense, yet gives clues which you'd miss by being sensible. I've got a rule covering all this. *There is a wrongness which can lead to rightness more effectively than rightness itself.*[6] Here today you're applying this rule of mine to the study of magic. It's very interesting. Also encouraging.'

Martin seemed satisfied with my return to base.

'Now,' he said, 'let's relate these things to the Unconscious as Jung proposed. In magic the "wrongness", as you put it, Geoffrey, would have to be a signpost pointing to a "rightness" below the mental surface. With twentieth-century Man at least. Once, it was closer to the surface – and perhaps even above it.

'Freud wouldn't take us far. Jung made me see that Freud's main motive was to oust the supernatural and mystical. His psychology does just that. According to Freud, everything that gets into us gets in through our senses and physical experience. When it sinks below conscious level, the Libido and other resident demons do tricks with it. These account for dreams, inspirations, myths, religions. Anything beyond elementary existence – the cycle of birth, food, shelter, sex, death – is explained away by these juggleries below-deck. It's another of those closed systems which so many feel trapped in.

'Jung broke with Freud on "nothing-butness". Freud taught that if we can explain A in terms of B, it's nothing but B. If a religious dogma can be explained as a sublimated genital image, it hasn't any further meaning. Jung thought it had. He evoked his vast cloudy Unconscious. Some of it was collective. He said we all have the same archetypes or patterns inside us. When life has supplied images to jigsaw into the patterns, we create myths, religions, all the rest, which are a lot richer and broader-based than Freud allowed, and have a family likeness the world over because the whole human race has the same inherited kit.

'Now it's true you can explain away plenty of mysteries if you make the Unconscious clever enough. But we'd surely agree, here, that there are limits. If we appeal to the Unconscious at all, we'll have to picture it as harbouring knowledge – not merely patterns – which can't have got into it through the senses, or the normal life of the conscious self. Like a magician's knowledge of a stranger's character, or the future, which he acquires in some unknown way and then lures up into consciousness as best he can, by using his technique.

'A Catholic psychologist argued once that the Unconscious might be open on the far side, as it were, and have direct contact with God and spiritual beings. Jung wrote a preface to his book... Still, let's keep our feet on the ground. We could say that when the magician succeeds, his technique (numerology or what have you) is like a combination unlocking a door. It lets the knowledge through from his Unconscious - correct or muddled - to where his brain and tongue can handle it. We could say something like that about the creation of one of those legends, or one of those crank theories, where unexplained insights into the past seem to struggle through. The insights are there, deep down; the legend or theory is the brain's attempt, probably a pretty garbled attempt, to dredge them up.

'But how does the Unconscious get hold of the knowledge in the first place? Are we any further?'

He was genuinely inviting ideas.

'Faculty X,'[7] Owen's Glamorgan voice cut in.

'You've been reading Colin Wilson,' said Norman.

Martin assented. 'Colin Wilson does use that term. He believes we all have a latent power to "reach beyond the present", beyond the here-and-now limits of the body. He invokes his Faculty X to account for magical phenomena, and telepathy, and much more besides. But does this help or is it simply a word?'

Suddenly Mei-ling spoke, with the precise eloquence of the educated Chinese, and only the shadow of an accent. 'Pardon me. I can offer no opinion on this Faculty X. But surely we are concerned with much more than magical feats and ESP, real or alleged. I refer to the inspiration behind major scientific advances. This has the same quality. The scientific pioneer seldom attains his insight by conscious technique, through the work of the laboratory. The insight simply appears, often when his mind is not on the problem. He performs a leap of imagination which he then, if I may put it so, "rationalizes" by formula and experiment.

'History furnishes many proofs. The chemist von Kekulé hit on the ring structure of organic molecules while dozing by the fire. He dreamed, or half-dreamed, of a snake with its tail in its mouth...'[8]

Murmurs of 'Ouroboros!' - which, however, didn't deflect Mei-ling.

'Clerk Maxwell's electromagnetic equations came into his head out of nowhere and were not tested till much later. Several Nobel prizewinners would confirm what I say. Quantum mechanics, the concept of the double helix, also had their origin in pure intuition. Behind it, one often finds aesthetic rather than inductive thinking, a sense of cosmic order or beauty which transcends space and time.

The Finger and the Moon

Scientists have been forming their ideas mystically, and stating and proving them afterwards, from Kepler on. Einstein himself spoke of mystical experience as "the sower of all true art and science". Dirac has confirmed him. The key knowledge rises first from unconscious levels, and no one has explained how it gets there.'

'You've been reading Arthur Koestler,' said Norman.

'Among other authors. I am working at a doctoral thesis on the history of science.'

Norman missed it, but the solemn girl he brought with him – her name's Janice – had sprung to life and was staring at the accomplished Mei-ling with rapture. I thought of her involvement with Women's Lib. But perhaps that wasn't all.

The rest of them sat silent. Martin tried me again. 'It would be hard to improve on that. But Geoffrey, before we take a break, could you comment from your own standpoint? Say, about literary inspiration?'

I didn't want to pile it on. 'I'd only raise one point. People who've studied mystical experience tell us it often seems like an answer to a long-standing question. That may have been so with some of Mei-ling's scientists... by the way,' I addressed Norman, 'allow me to fore-stall you, I've been reading Marghanita Laski. With myself though, and such ideas as I've had for books, inspiration has tended to be different. What I get first is more like an answer without a question. A topic gives me a conviction of Something There, something that'll turn out to be a revelation if it's looked into, before I've looked into it. I became certain Glastonbury was charged with meaning, burningly so, long before I found what questions it's the key to.'

'That's like Robert Graves,' Owen interposed, 'when he read Taliesin's riddle. It led him on to the whole of *The White Goddess*, and the secret of the Old Religion.'

'You're right,' I said, 'Graves is a far more important instance.'

'Would you add anything further yourself?' Martin pressed.

'Simply that in a case like this, the "rational" explanation won't work. It's no good saying "Oh well, you were thinking about that problem subconsciously for years", when you didn't even know what the problem was.

'Once or twice I've known instantly which of several legends had substance in it. Instantly, without studying them. There are two Celtic stories of men who crossed the Atlantic before Columbus:

the Irish tale of St Brendan and the Welsh tale of Prince Madoc. I knew at a glance that research into Brendan would lead to interesting results, and research into Madoc - with respect, Owen! - wouldn't. It took two years to confirm it and discover what questions the Brendan story does shed light on.[9] My first notions were miles out and took a lot of unlearning. But right from the start I had that instinct. Deep down, I knew something I couldn't know.'

'Yes. Thank you very much,' said Martin. 'It all converges. Magic has steered our thoughts towards the Unconscious. But we must ask whether the Unconscious - with or without Colin Wilson's Faculty X - can explain all the deep-seated knowledge and insight that we have to explain.'

He consulted his watch. 'We should be summoned for coffee fairly soon. Let's relax a while.'

3

Allhallows has an effect on its inmates like (*eheu fugaces*) a ship at sea on its passengers. Tempos alter. On the one hand, conversations are long-drawn and exhaustive as they seldom are in everyday life. On the other, personal relationships - and I don't mean only the sexual kind - take shape faster. You pick up signals more keenly, you push ahead more frankly and single-mindedly, because there isn't the elbow-room for leisured appraisals when contact will end so soon. Therefore, your time-sense gets confused. More may get confused with it.

When Martin reached his halting-place, it was clear that as soon as he resumed he would lead up quickly to his punch line, or to the first of a series of them. I sensed the cliffhanger. Yet I also felt: 'This won't be it, not really.' Whatever was going on at Allhallows alongside his teaching was far away from it, out of phase. He'd used the word 'converge', but a more obscure, more serious convergence was still to come and not yet in sight.

After some general chat, Karen appeared between the pillars. Martin, who had been watching for her, announced a twenty minute coffee break. He didn't get up himself. Everybody else did, and headed for the house, leaving him on his mound shuffling the students' scripts. Janice took Mei-ling's arm and the pair moved slowly, engrossed. Norman was haranguing Steve about numerology. Owen was with

the Frobishers; one heard Mrs Frobisher saying 'Faculty X' at intervals. Kwame walked alone.

Most of them collected their coffee, in paper cups, and returned. I
drank mine with scalding haste in the kitchen, because I felt a need
to revisit the outer world. As I walked through the hall, the bell rang
and a man entered through the open door. He wore a suit with tie, as
nobody at Allhallows does, and he carried a small oblong parcel.

'Excuse me,' he began, 'can you tell me...'

He had no time to ask. Paul rushed downstairs, shot a rather sour
look at me, and hustled the stranger up, talking about - ye gods! - the
weather till they were out of sight. Above, a door closed.

I strolled down the rhododendron-shaded driveway and came out
on the road. A few yards along it, in a lay-by, stood a Volkswagen
which I assumed to be the visitor's. On its front passenger seat there
was a binder stuffed with papers. Some had slid partly out, revealing
diagrams and tables of figures. The binder was labelled WESSEX
LABORATORIES. I turned and walked back up the drive. The
visitor was already leaving. He looked different. Of course: he no
longer had that parcel.

I rejoined the party. Martin held the scripts in his hand. He read
them out and went over them respectfully, without identifying the
writers. These 'strange experiences' sounded like the ones a magazine
gets from its readers if it extends the same invitation, though they
were better described, in more detail. One of the scripts told a ghost
story, another was concerned with an answer to prayer, another with
a message from a dead friend, two with dreams. Such happenings as
are stored up everywhere in spiritual self-defence, hinting at mysteries
and hopes beyond the squalors of the rat-race. But Martin had been
right when he spoke to me in his study. This material wasn't much
use.

He asked me for my own. I repeated what Karen wanted me to
repeat, and added another case, when I'd received an inspiration
that seemed a blind alley, and only realized many years later, after I'd
written a biography, that I could now re-interpret the inspiration as
guiding me towards that topic.

'The point is,' I explained, 'that it made sense only in retrospect. So
how and why? When that inspiration first struck, it simply couldn't
have had the meaning for me which it came to have later. It combined

two nicknames of the man who was the subject of the biography, nicknames which I only discovered after I'd done a lot of research on him. If this was a divine message, as some might say, why should God give me guidance which I couldn't grasp till I'd actually undertaken the job and the guidance was superfluous?[10]

'Those nicknames did get into my Unconscious, and not by any accepted route. They did slip through into consciousness with an air of trying to tell me something. But at the time, without meaning – and necessarily without meaning.'

'What would you infer then?' said Martin. He was angling... prompting.

I recalled Karen again, and plunged. 'It's as if there was a higher being with plans for me; but not God. A being who is linked with me personally, who has knowledge and powers which I don't. He, or it, arranges events over long periods. He also drops hints. Often valuable hints. But not always. Sometimes they're grotesque, useless. And yet they snag the mind. They might have been concocted on purpose to make me ponder, ask questions, suspect that the being's there and I should take notice. A kind of' – I risked it – 'a kind of guardian angel.[11] If each of us has one, communicating through the Unconscious as best he can, poor fellow, I suppose it could solve most of the problems we've been discussing.'

Had it fallen flat? For a few seconds Martin looked remote. Then he returned. He spoke very deliberately.

'I see we've travelled a long way. What you're suggesting, Geoffrey, is still in the closest touch with magic... but now with a higher magic, with the tradition of the Kabbalah and much else... the ancient belief in a realm of spiritual entities that we can contact, converse with, even control. A realm of power and wisdom, and also danger.

'Some of you will have heard of a famous occult group, the Order of the Golden Dawn, which the poet Yeats belonged to. Its head, MacGregor Mathers, translated a French text entitled *The Sacred Magic of Abra-Melin the Mage*. This book is supposed to derive from a medieval Hebrew original. It contains the lore of angels and demons. Crowley, who served his magical apprenticeship in the Golden Dawn, made use of it. He came to believe that what magicians call the Great Work, the sovereign process which raises human beings above their mortal confinement, is no other than attaining "the knowledge and conversation of one's holy guardian angel". If his Christian language puts you off, let me remind you that he pursued his holy aims by the most unbridled sex-magic.

'I do indeed put it to you that such entities may exist, closely bound up with every one of us. That they may be knowing and powerful. That their lives may be counterpointed to the lives of our conscious selves. That their presence may account for those mysteries below the threshold which magic unveils, and also for the cryptic phenomena of insight and inspiration.

'I do indeed put it to you.'

He paused, then made one of his rapid gear-shifts. 'Enough for now. We'll be meeting again this evening.' There were a few subdued questions, but the session was over. Martin had delivered his punch line.

At least, I assume that's what it was. Now it will be interesting to see where he goes from here. I fancy this evening may bring us to his first steps in practical wizardry.

4

Meanwhile, however, the afternoon has not been devoid of incident.

When the party dispersed I went indoors and found that my photographer, David Jacks,[12] had arrived. His car stood in the forecourt, and he himself, by Karen's leave, was busy in the conference room. He had already strewn the table with cameras, black cases, yellow cartons, tins, folded tripods. Seeing him with his portable studio, swarthy and intent, I placed him. We'd met once at an exhibition of his work in a Mayfair gallery. I wondered how his flair for the hideous and sordid – for war, disease, government – would adapt to Allhallows.

After a few polite exchanges, he said: 'I've only seen the front of the house. It isn't much good. With all that foliage I couldn't stand far enough back, and anyway it'd look like *Country Life*. Or Country Death. Have you got the story?'

'It's elusive,' I parried. 'Also this is a two-way traffic. They're drawing me out as much as I'm drawing them out. Truth emerges from dialogue here. But not overnight.'

'What would be the best visual angles on this crowd? Do they wear funny clothes, or do exercises?'

'Not so far.'

'What *is* it all about?'

'The part I can follow is beginning to add up to a kind of Spiritualism. Unseen beings around us, communicating and guiding.'

'Hm. Look here now. Last week I was in Glasgow, in the home of an unemployed shipyard worker with five children. The week before, I was in an approved school, a stinking dump fifty years old, crammed with juvenile Paki-bashers and rapists. Tell me, have you heard anything here which you could pass on to them there, and do the slightest good?'

'Not in a direct way, no,' I admitted. 'What seems to happen is that Martin Ellis inspires his students, and they go off and do the good themselves.'

'Yes, I know of Terry Hoad, and Rosmer, of course. But surely the crux of this project is, how does it happen?'

'That's still far from clear.'

'My feeling, frankly,' Jacks persisted, 'is that Allhallows is just another crank-leisure outfit, making uplifting noises, but never producing a result you can gauge. Years ago, my wife used to take me with her every few months to a retreat house run by a religious order. The priests were charming, the nuns were sweet, the laity were scrubbed and blameless. But after a spell in Vietnam or Bangladesh (yes, I know it sounds phoney, but it's true), all that pleasant bourgeois goodwill was simply a nothing. Is Allhallows so different?'

No pat answer came to mind. We went in to dinner. During the meal he reminisced about his assignments. I felt he was genuinely sensitive to the big issues he'd beaten me over the head with, but in his own style. They got to him through the image, the stark visual image. To make a comment on India he described a woman he'd seen walking along a street in Calcutta, staring straight ahead, with a dead child lying across her arms. Even when Jacks got on to cheerful themes he was oddly lugubrious. Several times he led up to some brilliant scene he'd captured, some scene that was 'really exciting', his all-purpose phrase for excellence. Yet in each case he did it with the same look of fixed despair. This was encouraging. Underneath, he might not be quite as unsympathetic as his manner had suggested at first.

Throughout dinner his eyes were scanning the room taking in its twelve occupants besides us. Afterwards we returned to his array of equipment. 'This has to be a rush job,' he said. 'But we can manage something. You've got an inter-racial angle. I'd like to get the black chap, and that Chinese girl.'

'They'll be around.' Karen had mentioned that all the students would be busy on household chores.

'What have you got on Ellis himself?'

I had to confess, very little. Jacks listened to the little there was, looked a degree sadder still, and muttered names like 'Buchman' and 'Hubbard'.[13] Luckily he was in too much of a hurry to dilate. He handed me some apparatus to carry, and took a small camera himself.

We found Kwame at once, riding a motor-mower across the lawn. 'Oh, superb !' said Jacks. I introduced him, and he got Kwame to talk, and held up the little camera to his eye taking picture after picture, snap, snap, snap. Kwame, it transpired, was a trainee civil engineer. I hadn't known.

Jacks's next target was Mei-ling. We sighted her in the vegetable garden, with Janice.

'That other lass,' the photographer murmured – 'she was in Women's Lib, right?'

This time I knew. 'She was.'

'Yes, I've got some pictures of her. She led a squad of activists who set out to dramatize the unequal public lavatory facilities. They occu-pied the men's place at Green Park tube. The Mirror ran a front page headed SIT-IN.'

He went up to the girls and repeated his routine with them both, singly and together. Janice was a bonus, a protest angle to add to the racial angle. She recognized him as a figure that had slipped in among the police during the Green Park eviction. He'd presented her to the public in an undignified posture. However, she seemed to bear no grudge. Her mood was transformed. We left her to her idyll.

Jacks now focused on the kinetic sculpture. He photographed it in various phases. I got him to see the walking man, and he promptly observed what I hadn't, that if you stood by the figure and looked the way it was walking, you had one of the few 'really exciting' views of the house.

Next I took him into the temple. He exclaimed at the Horned One, and set up a larger camera for time exposures. The phallic portion raised a nice question of judgement. If he shot from in front, *Globe* readers might miss the point entirely. If he went to the wall and shot in profile, they might complain. He tried a range of intermediate aspects.

'Any chance of a ritual?' he asked.

'Yes, but they haven't told me when.'

'We must look into that.'

'Somewhere,' I said, 'they have a third sculpture. Come to think of it, I don't know where. Maybe we can find out.'

I took him round to the workshop, which had been emitting noises. It was unlocked, and Paul was inside, chatting to Norman as the latter mended a chair. Paul was the first staff member Jacks had met, apart from his short encounter with Karen. The possibilities of the meeting dispelled thoughts of art.

He asked Paul what the students' motives were.

'Generally speaking,' said Paul, 'we follow on from that phase a few years back when the vogue-terms were "permissiveness" and "hippie" and "Underground" and "alternative society".' (Already it was illuminatingly plain to me, and doubtless to Jacks too, that he was repeating – almost parroting – a set speech.) 'There was a revolt against the Establishment; a pursuit of taboo experience, drugs and free sex and whatnot; a sense of disaster closing in, and a struggle to escape from the trap; a dream of spiritual breakthrough that would change society.

'Some of it blew over, it was too shapeless. But some of it went on – and not solely at the junior level. The new-type Glastonbury pilgrimages, for instance. And the causes of disquiet didn't just go away. People went on sensing disaster – through pollution or the population explosion or nuclear war – and reacted. Only, their reactions got less anarchic and more constructive. Without going into Martin's programme in detail, you could say he's been helping them to find positive ways.'

The speech was machine-made. Paul had gone through it before and was bored with it. Still, was that the whole reason why he sounded as he did?

Jacks asked about Martin, repeating his remarks on unemployed shipyard workers, etcetera, and insinuating that Martin had led a sheltered life.

'Actually that's not so,' said Paul. 'His early career was rather colourful. War service with Intelligence, a wound that put him out of action, then a string of jobs in three or four countries. He worked as a miner and as a farm-hand. Somewhere along the line he was a Communist. He's shown me a Canadian magazine called *First Statement*, published around autumn 1944, that had a pro-Communist piece in it by him.'[14]

The photographer fired another shot. 'But this crowd who come here. Aren't most of them pretty cosy? Isn't this NeoMagic just a hobby with them? Your Mr Ellis may have turned a few into do-gooders. But have any of them had real, deep, personal problems which you people have solved?'

I thought: Paul can deal with that one at least. He may not want to name Annabel by name, but he can mention the case.

He didn't. This was his moment for loyalty to Allhallows, and it passed. 'I understand what you're driving at,' he replied, 'and you aren't the first to bring it up.'

In that instant I knew. *There is something wrong, something very wrong.*

Jacks consulted his watch. 'I'd like to scout around a bit more, by myself, if you don't object. I need to be alone for a while to get the feel of a place.'

'Go ahead,' said Paul. He went.

I began a probe of my own. 'That's fascinating about Martin's background. I'd no idea.'

'He avoids the past... in a personal sense.'

A further aspect occurred to me. 'I'd have thought that if this were brought out more - that is, what a lively history he has - it would enhance him for the students. For prospective students, too.'

'Right enough. He's never learnt to project himself. No PR talent at all.'

'He could be built up into a picturesque public figure. Even a television pundit.'

'Good lord, Geoffrey, do you think I haven't told him? I keep trying. It seems counter-productive, but I keep trying. This article of yours could help.'

So Paul was out of step with Karen as well.

The Cryptocrat put his hammer down, leaving the chair unmended, and spoke. 'This is only part of a wider issue. It's more than personal. You've got the base for a mass movement here, and you don't exploit it.'

'How do you mean?' I asked.

Norman turned to me. 'You ought to appreciate this better than anyone. What we were discussing last night.'

('We' hadn't discussed anything. However.)

'The King Arthur mystique,' Norman insisted. 'Glastonbury and the Grail. The prophecy of Arthur's return and a new age for Britain. It could be tied in with Blake too - plenty of kids are still reading him - Blake and his myth of the Giant Albion.'

'Actually,' said Paul, 'we're well aware of Blake. He comes later in the course. You may have noticed that monogram on Martin's chair in the conference room. It has all the letters of "Albion". Some are a bit contorted, but you can make them out.'

'There you are then,' said Norman. 'A ready-made emblem to put on badges and banners. You could found a new national Order of the Round Table.'

That generation gap again, almost the only real one. 'It reminds me too much of Nazism,' I objected. 'It could stir up some rather diabolical passions.'

'Why not?' retorted Paul. 'Those passions are a fact of life. They can't be suppressed. The thing is to form a system, an organizational structure, that channels them positively.'

Norman was pacing back and forth. 'Suppose we take this further. I'll invite a few of my friends in Cryptocracy to come down. Can you handle visitors any time?'

'Given a few days' notice,' said Paul. 'Monday or Tuesday would be fine.' He spoke absently; he was thinking fast himself. 'You know, I've got an idea, Geoffrey. While you're here we ought to make use of you. Isn't there a legend about Midsummer at Cadbury?'

'A famous one,' I said. 'If you keep vigil on top after sunset, inside the earthworks, the ghosts of Arthur's knights will ride past. You can hear the hoofbeats. Or something.'

'I thought so. Now, every student group here has at least one major outing. Let's make it the Cadbury vigil. It's the day, or rather the night, after tomorrow. I'm sure Martin will go along with this.'

'It could be fun. As long as they don't expect too much.'

'You can put it in the right perspective beforehand. Now here's still another thought. Often we stage a little indoor performance. A piece of ritual magic, or witchcraft ceremonial, put on by students. Have you got anything yourself? Like, a short play on some Arthurian theme?'

'I once did a mock-up of the ritual of the Holy Grail. That was one of my own ventures in television.[15] I could send for copies, and a friend of mine in Bristol still has the costumes.'

'Fine. We don't have time for much rehearsal or learning by heart, of course. But hopefully, we might put this on as a dramatic reading.'

'I'll see what can be done. In fact. I'll see right away.'

I made two phone calls with satisfactory results, and went back to the workshop to report. After a while David Jacks reappeared.

'Have you got what you want?' I asked.

'Some.'

'Did you see Martin?'

'I did. Not much joy, though. The whole thing is too static. It's visually unmeaning. I have to go now. But I could come again for a second bite if it was worth while.' He addressed Paul. 'Have you got, say, a ritual you could stage for me?'

'We were just considering that,' said Paul. 'Yes, we should be able to give you a show or two, if you can get here.'

'Good. So keep in touch.'

I helped him pack. 'Did you find the maze?'

'Yes, but I didn't go in. Couldn't risk getting lost.'

He gave me a phone number for messages and drove off. We never did sort out that third sculpture.

Query: ought one to be playing along with Paul, when he and Norman are so blatantly trying to set up a sub-programme within the programme? A sub-programme with publicity value, but not for what at present exists?

Oh well, it's no use to fight against being drawn in. I've already been drawn in, by Martin. Pure detached observation is a mirage, even in the sciences. An observer does get involved himself, he does affect what he observes, so he may as well face it honestly. Let it unfold, as Karen said. There's no risk of this becoming a rival show. They can hardly arrange a flood of Cryptocrats, or a Cadbury vigil, or a Grail ritual, without Martin's OK.

But Midsummer... and that entry in the manuscript book, the diary or whatever it is. One does wonder who is planning what.

It's supper time, nearly. This room can get oppressive. The window stays open now, except when I'm recording on tape; and the voices of Allhallows float in.

5

11 p.m., back here in my room. Martin's diary (yes, it is a diary – of sorts) lies on the bench in front of me, with a large notebook beside it, allegedly the key to what it's about. I have not yet opened either.

Martin didn't do any post-prandial wizardry after all. He simply talked again in the conference room, not for long. This may be the last lecture that I sit in on. Tonight we re-align, and soar off into skies unknown. For the present his message is all that matters of the evening. The tape-recorder acted up, and I've had trouble piecing a text together, using notes jotted from memory to eke out the inaudible parts. But here, roughly, are his words.

'Earlier today we conceived a realm alongside our conscious selves. A realm of unseen lives, bound up with ours, counterpointed with ours. I now ask you to accept this realm as a fact. We shall soon be exploring it. We shall enter the region which Yeats used to have intimations of between sleeping and waking, and called "Anima Mundi" and knew with a poet's vision to be fierily real.

'But at its gate there's a trap we must avoid. The trap of looking outwards first. Of picturing the unseen entities first as *out there*, around us.

'That false priority has led Man astray ever since the fading of his original magic. His mind – his conscious, reasoning, restless ego – has got off balance. It has ranged outwards in quest of order. It has spun its webs *out there*... but spun them, always, from its own purblind inadequacies. Religion: a system of gods ever more remote, leading up to Plato's geometrizing Creator, and St Thomas Aquinas's diagrammatic Trinity. Science: a system of abstract physical laws, leading up to the huge, cold, clockwork universe of the era since Newton.

'Modern Man reaps the harvest. To lay the primary stress on what is or may be outwards is clutching at phantoms. Now everything has slipped and drifted away. God, for most, is no longer relevant.

85

The Finger and the Moon

The universe of science is alien, dwarfing human beings and crushing them into its own vast deadness.

'Recently some have tried to draw this estranged universe closer. One of the motives of science-fiction has been to persuade us that we can spread ourselves through all worlds, and master and humanize them. Another motive has been to populate the dreadful void with life we can relate to. With men on the other side of the moon, UFO voyagers from Venus, canal-builders on Mars launching artificial satellites.

'But more recently still, science itself has been ruining these Wellsian dreams. It has given us technological horrors which overshadow its triumphs. It has destroyed fantasy after fantasy. The other side of the moon is as sterile as the side we see. Venus is too hot to support life. The Martian canals are strips of sand-dune, or "rills", or optical illusions. The Martian satellites are not artificial, they are dreary lumps of rock. Space probes are confirming the heavens' indifference. They are driving Man back upon himself after all.

'That, however, is where he should be. It's where we should be tonight. The alienation is due to our approaching reality with a false priority that denies us the equipment we need. We should not be looking first *out there*, even to the space closest at hand, for the unseen powers of our own being: not first for surrounding spirits or angels, any more than for gods or natural laws.

'Magic has always clung to a truer wisdom, however twisted. That is why it mistrusts Spiritualism, as teaching a false emphasis, rather than as teaching a falsehood: an emphasis on outside entities like our own conscious selves, and on guidance from them. Magic's higher tradition tells us to look inward to Man first as the "microcosm", the pattern of the universe in himself, and *therefore* the master of its secrets – including the secrets of whatever invisible life does surround him – if he knows himself fully and undertakes the quest rightly. The Kabbalists created the myth of Adam Kadmon, the cosmic humanity. Blake translated this into his own myth of Albion, who is primordial Britain but also eternal Man. Until the mental fall I have spoken of, Albion comprised all natures within himself, within his own spiritual being. "But now the starry heavens are fled from the mighty limbs of Albion."

'I say to you: before looking outwards, wait. Before confronting external nature, confront human nature. That is what Freud began to do, and although he never acknowledged it, the Kabbalah influenced his thought. It is what Jung did better, and still with the aid of magical studies. It is also what Aleister Crowley did, under the stimulus of the Golden Dawn. As a beginner in magic he described the Great Work as attaining "the knowledge and conversation of one's holy guardian angel". But later he described the same work as attaining "the knowledge of the nature and powers of one's own being". Had he changed his mind? No, he had not. Even he, however – even Crowley with his wild dark speculations and orgasmic rites – never went far enough, to the new model of human nature which I propose to you.

'We glimpsed what seemed an answer to riddles in the idea that a guardian angel, a spirit-watcher, a higher self as it were, does hover near each one of us. We suggested that this being is linked with the conscious mind through the Unconscious. But that suggestion defies a sound rule of logic, economy of hypothesis. It's complicating matters unduly. We can do better.

'*The Unconscious, so-called, and that other self are the same.* Or rather: what Freud and Jung found in each person's psyche, beyond the reach of waking awareness – what they therefore called "subconscious" or "unconscious" – is really an aspect of the life of another being within him, another self from which his ego has split off, but which is still there, still active, still thinking, still in its own way conscious. Viewed under a different aspect, that inner being is also the guardian angel.

'Scientists may be right when they contend that you and I (meaning what those words commonly mean) have no preternormal powers. But we each carry within us an allied being who has. That is why occult phenomena continue to happen. If you want a technical term for that being, I think we might call it "the protoself".[16]

'Let me offer you an image, a well-worn image. The pioneer psychologist Fechner compared the psyche to an iceberg. The conscious ego is the tip. That small fraction above the surface is sentient, looking out over the waves, viewing the ocean and its contents in its own way – through the senses. Until now, we have treated the much greater portion below as unconscious, because the sentience of the tip doesn't extend downwards; because the upper part of the iceberg doesn't look down into the lower part, or out through it, and is therefore not aware of it, not directly.

'But now conceive that this is all question-begging and mistaken. The part below the surface has an awareness and sentience of its own. It looks out *through* the ocean, and views its contents differently: the hulls of ships instead of the tops; the below-surface portions of other icebergs; and fishes, weeds, rocks, seabed, which the upper part never catches sight of from any angle. It has methods of knowing the ocean which the upper part lacks, and can't even imagine. It's sensitive to vibrations through water, for example, and to changes of temperature far down.

'Not to press the analogy too far – that's how a familiar image should be construed. But as to how the ego becomes divided from the protoself which is its own deepest reality; how the split takes place in everyone, and has grown sharper with the passage of history; what are the relations between the two, which psychology can disclose a little of; what the world of the protoself is; and what are the prospects of reunion, the recovery of psychic oneness and wholeness by Binary Man, the "integration" which Jung aimed at and much more... these are mysteries we shall make our way into.

'The first step is to think of your mighty invisible companion as present, inside you. And the first commandment which follows is: LISTEN, LISTEN TO THAT COMPANION.'

Afterwards, Martin steered me into the empty library. His studied manner dissolved at once. We had a circling, fumbling conversation. Something was trying to get said, and for an awkward time it didn't. He gave me chances to comment on his talk, and I let them pass. I was in the throes of mental readjustment and couldn't decide how he meant me to take all this. Also he made no reference to Paul's projects, and left me wondering whether Paul had told him, and if the answer was "no", why not, and if the answer was "yes", whether he approved. Meanwhile I tossed him pathetic semi-jokes like 'We're all schizophrenics now' and 'If you're right, there are four of us in this room'. But they rang eerily. That manuscript was lying on the desk like a murder clue.

At last we struck a spark. I spoke of his 'new model of human nature', his 'Binary Man', as a startling hypothesis.

'It isn't,' said Martin.

'Startling to me anyway.'

'I mean it isn't a hypothesis.'

'Let's not quibble over words. It's a conception you've thought out as a step beyond your predecessors...'

'Not altogether.' He hesitated, then said: 'Geoffrey, I don't know if you've looked into my magical diary there.'

'Yes, I have. Just to dip. But it's rather bewildering. Why do you leave it around for any student to read?'

'They're welcome to make whatever they please of it. Or whatever they can. You've got to have the key, and I'll be glad to lend it to you. Wait.'

He bustled off to his study, and bustled back with the aforesaid notebook. 'I'd advise you to read that first, then tackle some of the diary. Take them to your room if you like. Don't discuss them with any students, not yet, anyway.'

'Thanks very much.'

He'd been slowly boiling up to this. Now it was done, he blurted out a 'goodnight' and left me. It seems fairly predictable what this key is going to say, in its main gist. But then?

...Before making a start on it, I've been standing at my window, breathing. The air that drifts in is fragrant. Nostalgic. It recalls I don't know what. For an indescribable moment I wasn't 'now' but twenty years or so back, foreseeing myself standing at this window.[17]

An ardent moon, out of direct visual range, is floodlighting the lawn and the two pillars.

Other-Scene

HEN I OPENED Martin's notebook it confirmed my fore-
bodings. His big, prosaic writing (it doesn't quite fit him,
somehow) blew the gaff in one sentence.

Prolegomena to Diary
The purpose of these experiments, begun in May 1972, was to study
the effects of a serotonin[1] preparation briefly designated as SP5.

Just so, I thought. Another chapter in the stale saga of drug revelation. What was novel in Martin's trips? Also, what about Annabel,
whose cure is chalked up as an Allhallows success?

Sitting on the mattress with my back propped against the wall, I
attacked the technicalities in his next few paragraphs. They unravelled as I recalled certain facts from another source. Serotonin... it rang
a bell. A secretion, surely, of the pineal gland, that oddity embedded
inside the skull which used to be held in awe as the contact point
between body and soul. Doctors have credited serotonin with strange
properties, mostly having to do with intelligence and concentration. Was anything ever said – I asked myself while wrestling with
Martin's preface – about its use in a drug? Not that I knew. Yet as
far back as the date given in his notebook, he'd volunteered for a programme of tests with this Something described as SP5. Which must
somehow have led him to his notions about the protoself and Binary
Man. Well, I would have to find out how.

His tone in the first part of the notebook was anticipatory. He'd
written it in spring 1972 before trying the stuff. He didn't give the
formula, but he did record various facts, as of then. Its inventors had
told him that SP5 should be non-addictive and harmless. Taken in pill

form, it should cause whatever it was going to cause within about half an hour. The effect, they figured, would be a burst of mental enhancement. To quote Martin, an 'intenser and fuller realization of whatever the psyche is most deeply concerned with'. At least they hadn't cherished any something-for-nothing delusions. If all went well, they theorized, SP5 would simply awaken one's latent powers and focus them swiftly. It would cut out that long phase of subconscious pregnancy which scientists and poets alike have to endure. Instant, total inspiration, in fact. The fullest enlightenment the subject was capable of, coming quickly instead of gradually.

Martin's notebook passed on to sketch the frame of mind in which he'd approached this experiment himself. He had a practical reason for welcoming any fresh light. His own psyche was then 'most deeply concerned' with issues arising out of Cases 364 and 389 and... a string of three-digit numbers. After a few seconds' bafflement I took these to refer to patients of his. Their files of course would be secret. Next, however, came a personal statement that was plainly a summing-up of the issues which these cases had raised for him.

Leafing through it to find how long it went on, and what followed, I was mystified to glimpse near the end of the notebook (in a different-coloured ink suggesting a later date) an array of what looked like mini-crosswords: Ximenes[2] type, with no black squares. Abandoning the text for a moment, I stared at them. They were five squares by five, and filled with unmeaning alphabetic jumble. A footnote gave me the hint. They were key-charts for passages in the diary which Martin had chosen to put in cipher. So, not quite everything was exposed for any student to read! I had another skim through the diary. In a few places the handwriting was indeed broken by blocks of capitals that didn't spell any words.

As the crossword-charts led me to suspect at once, Martin uses the Playfair cipher. He'd have learnt Playfair during his wartime Intelligence job. (So did Lord Peter Wimsey, as narrated by Dorothy Sayers[3] in *Have His Carcase.*)

With that diversion disposed of, I turned back to Martin's statement. It showed that his main concern when he volunteered for SP5 was a topic already familiar to me, the major theme of that lecture where I first heard him, and of his opening Allhallows talk. Cases 364, 389 and the rest were those very patients whom he'd cited at the Free Mind Society: the troubled souls who felt their lives to be meaningless, because of reductionism and nothing-butness and the cutting down of Man by science. Theirs was the problem which was most occupying Martin when he first sampled his mind-enhancing drug. Things were beginning to link up.

As I read, it struck me that he'd composed the statement during his private lacerations with Karen. Whom he thus implied to have been something less than his main concern. Furthermore she must have read this notebook herself, and drawn her conclusions. But perhaps that kind of concern didn't count. Or he could have let her assume it didn't.

Here are the chief portions of his statement verbatim. They show the budding, towards May 1972, of ideas he is voicing now at a later stage.*

...These patients are not morbid, but perceptive. They have grasped a truth which Blake grasped ages ago, according to Case 402, the professor of English. They are distressed by aspects of the scientific era which have been taking shape for centuries. Even Bertrand Russell, that arch-apostle of scientific humanism, said we were being forced to regard the universe as a vast Indifference, and mankind as doomed to nullity and oblivion. Why he expected anybody to work for his own various causes, I can't conceive.

Several patients feel that knowledge itself has been withered up by a scientific blight. Once (they say) religious faith allowed Man to trust his experience. He was made in God's image, so all God's works could make sense to him, and he could know the world through kinship. Purpose and beauty in his own life, even his pleasure in sounds and colours and scents, linked him with all creation: the morning stars sang together.

This rapport has vanished. Science piles up information, but with the religious picture gone we don't know what it's information about, or whether it's about anything... except a phantasmagoria of particles which even the scientists can't see; an abstract model that gets changed every few years, and wanders farther and farther from any image we can relate to ourselves. The single certainty is that normal experience tells us nothing about the events which the scientist claims alone are 'real'. So we're cut off from Nature. Sometimes scientists justify their claims in a sense

* All the longer transcripts are taken from authorized photo-copies made afterwards.

by producing a result that hits us, a new medicine or an atomic bomb. But we, the rest of us, don't understand it. We live under the shadow of daunting mysteries as the men of the age of faith did not.

After this passage came a series of quotes from individual patients. Most of them, I felt, expressed a half-baked emotional recoil which Martin needn't have made so much of, except as a psychiatric datum. But the one patient whom he quoted at any length, Case 413, was different.

413 lectured me on Descartes and Newton. For him, science's leap forward in the seventeenth century was a kind of Fall, with Descartes as its devil. 'He was a mathematician, and he convinced people that mathematics was the sole and sufficient key to Nature. Which meant in practice that Nature had to be trimmed down to what mathematics could handle. To dead, aimless, but measurable matter. Centimetres, grams, seconds! (Descartes was before the metric system, but you know what I mean.)

'As the mind wasn't tractable, it had to be trimmed down likewise. They closed it up inside the skull. All it was still permitted to do was interpret signals trickling in through the senses, as its only sources of knowledge. Light-waves stimulating the optic nerve. Sound-waves wiggling through the ear. Even those didn't give direct contact with reality. They hadn't any worthwhile message till after mathematical processing which scientists alone understood.'

Thus, according to 413, science divorced the mind from the world and left it alienated. The morning stars stopped singing.

But, I suggested, couldn't science itself bridge the gap? 413 denied it. No Babel-tower could reach an acceptable Heaven. He turned to Newton, who, he asserted, carried Descartes' falsehood to final triumph. After Newton the 'real' universe was the blind amoral mechanism which scientists could reduce to equations. 'Nothing but.' Colour and sound and scent, beauty and purpose, no longer meant anything out there. They were huddled away into our brain-cells – minute portions of minute organisms, very meagerly informed. Reality became what the scientists said it was. Not what Man lives, but a system constructed in his brain out of 'pointer-readings', and then projected into infinity.

One product of this today (413 didn't mention it, but it supports him) is the notion that everything real can be computerized. Man will be outmoded because anything he does a computer will soon be able to do better. All those computer jokes are nervous attempts to exorcize a fear.

413 argued further that the trail-blazers of science transformed our status without knowing what they were doing. They installed a muddle at the heart of the thinking process, which has had to be swept under the carpet. On reflection I take his point.

During my own training I read Locke, who worked out a psychology for Newtonian Man. Now I can see Locke and his followers in a new light. Famous paradoxes fall into place. Like Berkeley's proof that if this view of the mind is correct, if it's an enclosed ego that just receives messages via the senses, then we can't know that physical objects exist outside us at all, or conceive any separate context as truly there. We're all dreaming, the message is the medium,[4] and the only basis for the scientists' alleged cosmic machine would be the awkward supposition that our dreams are harmonized by God! Likewise Hume... who proved that the scientists' own conception of universal cause-and-effect and cosmic order has no grounds in any kind of experience they'll admit as evidence. The senses don't give it to us. Why then accept it?

Here I took an overdue pause for breath, marshalled my recollections of Berkeley and Hume, saw more or less what Martin (or 413) was driving at, and pressed on.

The nub of these paradoxes is that they are paradoxes. Of course the objects around us exist. Of course there is order in the universe – not as something which science finds or invents, but as a precondition of science itself, of inductive thinking. Einstein said it: 'The basis of all scientific work is the conviction that the world is an ordered and comprehensive unity.' That's basic in everything, not just science. Magicians realized it, or half-realized it, in the Stone Age. We couldn't plan or devise techniques, we couldn't reason or even use language – Hume himself could never have argued his way to his own paradox – if we didn't KNOW that the world has some sort of coherence for the mind to seize and handle. A child would never learn to say 'cat' if he hadn't the innate trust that when he sees a feline patch of colour walking around, the other qualities making cat-ness can be relied on to go with it.[5]

But science has left us guessing how these primary intuitions get into us in the first place. Even Russell confessed that he could see no answer to

Hume. Even Haldane confessed that on standard scientific assumptions he couldn't see how knowledge was possible. There had to be laws of thought and science gave no account of them.

Then why go on pretending that this strait-jacketed world-view works when it doesn't? Why do people have to be oppressed by this cloud and driven, often, into utterly mindless escapism? It's the obsessiveness that amazes me. Most would-be scientific thinkers, rational humanists, and whatnot, have a stubborn compulsion to keep the mind's prison intact. To go on cowering inside their skulls, petty, divided from all the grandeur of Being; erecting closed systems out of statistics and diagrams, manipu-lating them, and thrusting them blindly into Nature.

Martin's choice of words in the last sentence halted me for a moment. Surely anyone with his training would.... Well.

Sometimes they set up as sociologists and try to force everybody else into their mean little patterns. When anything threatens to upset the sys-tem - religion, ESP, even science itself in its more inspired moods - such people's balance deserts them. Talk about objectivity! They get heated and dishonest. They sneer at anyone who ventures a word on behalf of the dangerous idea. They refuse to look at the evidence, or lie about it, or invent ploys to explain it away (as Freud did, alas).

The smarter sort rig the rules so that they can evade any issue they daren't face. Some demand 'proof' pre-defined so as to be impossible. The Watson school of psychology swept aside all the data of consciousness by saying consciousness was a myth so they didn't have to discuss it.6 Many of my own fellow-students favoured a philosophical fad called Logical Positivism. Its attraction was that whenever they were afraid to discuss an idea, they could dismiss it as 'meaningless'. Today, scientists like Monod want to re-base human life on an 'ethic of knowledge' which simply isn't knowledge, only a question-begging confidence trick with biological and statistical concepts.

I caught echoes of past arguments, probably of gibes at Martin and those he sympathized with, which he was anxious to refute. Too anx-ious perhaps. One would need to allow for bias....

The Finger and the Moon

There seems, often, to be an urge in the psyche to cut *yourself* down, shut *yourself* in. To reject any enlargement of that mini-ego which is all the scientists allow us, and the assembly-belt career of the body it's supposed to depend on - birth, food, shelter, sex, death. To orate about progress, yet make it pointless, and undermine the motives to work for it. My patients may protest that they don't think like that, but I can see they're spellbound by the prestige of humanists (humanists!) who do. I have no answers. Freud actively abetted the process, Jung isn't positive or clear-cut enough.

The juniors' revolt into mind-changing drugs has been partly a reaction against homuncular elders. For the trend isn't confined to intellectual heights. A psychic cutting-down factor, a kind of false selfhood and self-reduction, has been gaining ground for a long time. Plenty of 'naked apes' trapped in the system find it easiest now to acquiesce in that status, and buy books telling them how to live with it. Case 402 quoted Yeats on 'that slow dying of the heart which men call the progress of the world'.

I warmed to Case 402. Clearly he'd helped to restrain Martin from soaring off into metaphysical space, and shown him that his theme could be transposed on to various levels. But what did it add up to? A profound analysis of modern Man's spiritual condition? Or a verbal box of tricks rationalizing the neuroses of patients who'd let the age get on top of them - victims of a Doomwatch[7] syndrome? Either way, this was what Martin was thinking about when he took SP5, so this was what mattered. The rest of his statement was tentative. He noted how he'd cast around for another way of looking at things, a way that would 'restore meaning and value to the human experience without betraying reason'. Hereabouts his notebook musings acquired a touch of priggishness. A touch, also, of Messianic daydream. I felt that they struck a curiously young note for an educated professional man in his forties.

His reading had included studies of mysticism by William James, Richard Bucke, Marghanita Laski. All of them, he found, described ecstasies that gave people a vision of cosmic order and unity. The ecstasies didn't seem to oppose science, they seemed to transcend science, even to put it in its true setting and make better sense of it. Martin was intrigued to learn that Descartes himself, 413's villain, was set going by a mystical experience. But all this left him with a frustrated feeling of hovering on the outside. He didn't have ecstasies himself. Nor could he go to one of his patients and say 'Have an ecstasy'.

Meanwhile he was already dabbling in magic. The scientific repute of Renaissance magicians, such as Paracelsus, surprised and impressed him. They laid stress, he observed, on unknown potentialities, on power and wisdom below the threshold of everyday consciousness, on occult keys to the cosmos in Man himself. I judged that in the pre-SP5 phase, Martin had reacted to most of this as weird and way-out, yet had also felt that he was picking up hints which he never got elsewhere.

Perhaps it was this background presence of magic which had caused him to describe the diary to me as his 'magical' diary. In the notebook it was occultism that steered him back to a closing flourish on his own topic.

Modern minds often give an impression that salvation is pressing in from unexplored regions of the psyche, but is being resisted because of a dread that it would be too strange, too subversive. Even my patients resist, whatever it is they say they want.

The personality needs the invading elements. Yet the ego braces itself and thrusts them back. An atheist may well be fighting a religious belief below the threshold – I don't mean a consoling fiction, I mean a psycho-logically valid belief, that would fulfil his being if he stopped fighting and let it through. Only, he's determined he mustn't. That would ruin the pseudo-scientific pseudo-reality which he's made for himself and clings to with masochistic fervour.

If SP5 causes what its inventors predict, an 'intenser and fuller realiza-tion of whatever the psyche is most deeply concerned with', then I sus-pect it will do so by weakening this inner force that thrusts back. Then a richer comprehension, already prepared below the threshold, can burst open the gates into consciousness. I don't claim to be an exception. I may well be resisting a solution already latent in my own psyche. If so, let's hope this experiment will indeed burst open the gates. Let's also hope I shall be willing to accept whatever conclusions it may suggest.

2

So to Martin's diary. The drug, though, isn't mentioned in it, as far as I can see from a quick sampling. Browsers in the Allhallows library seem to be denied that clue. The closest he comes is when he refers to 'State E', meaning, I suppose, the 'Experimental' state.

Scanned coolly this diary has a disjointed air, which I think I can explain. After his first SP5 trip Martin wrote up a record and put it in the binder. Then he waited a month or more before trying a second dose. That must have continued to be his pattern. The gaps were long because he needed time to ponder the results of each test. Hence, the total sequence covers a period of years. Hence, it reflects changing preoccupations. There's no single story line.

Also you can see how growing familiarity with the drug's action made him cut corners more and more freely, and jettison detail. The entries soon begin tending to get shorter, and, for an outsider, more obscure. There are further complications still. Pages of afterthoughts have been interleaved. Other material has been withdrawn – as I found when I turned to the end, to check my memory of that last, cryptic 'Midsummer' item. It isn't there any more.

The way Martin composed this diary, his writing of unique long-hand entries instead of typing with carbons, and the signs of tinkering with the contents, all made me wonder as I read it about his relations with the research unit that ran the test programme. It wasn't clear how his information got into their files, if this holograph text was the sole report. That, however, could wait, as indeed most of the diary could. My present business was with the first section, telling what happened when he embarked on SP5 against that backdrop of clinical and philosophical labourings, and thus got launched towards the orbit where I now tracked him.

Some of the notebook pages between the personal statement and the Playfair appendix gave a few details on each test. The first, it appeared, had taken place at night in Martin's consulting room, in Kensington I believe. A member of the research team was in charge, identified only as T.R. He handed Martin a red pill which was duly swallowed, and they sat in the lamplight waiting. At which point the diary record starts.

A quiet lead-in. T.R. made conversation. He asked about my practice, my interests, my motives. Half an hour passed and nothing happened. Then something did. I just managed to signal with my hand as the change-over hit me.[8]

I can only compare it to simultaneously falling asleep and waking up. Zen masters have said that the prelude to satori is like that. It was happy. A few times in my life I've had a blissful awareness of dropping off to sleep in the instant of doing so. A similar bliss occurred now.

At first the room looked the same. Then for a few seconds it went colourless, as if on black-and-white television. Abruptly it flashed. Colour returned, and with it came a difference of quality. The scene had been replaced by an identical scene, having the brilliant strangeness of hyp-nagogic images that dart into the mind between sleeping and waking. Unlike most such images it persisted, and was mobile, not static. T.R. leaned forward in his chair without breaking the spell.

Time also changed, or memory did. This is hard to describe. Let me attempt another comparison. You're walking down a lane that leads into a straight stretch of main highway. You emerge on the highway, and walk along that for a few hundred yards, then look back. Your lane and its entry-junction are now out of sight, hidden by trees. Instead you see miles of the main road behind, far beyond the place where you entered. It's *as if* you'd got where you are by walking along the main road from the most distant point you can see. The lane is still in your mind, but what you now seem to have behind you is a different journey altogether.

As State E took hold I still remembered the lane, i.e. the series of events in time as we know it, leading up to this moment: going out to meet T.R. at a restaurant, returning to this flat in a taxi, and so on. But I also had what felt like the impression of a main road behind me which the lane had converged with – another past, another train of events leading up to the present, which was far more significant.

I tried to recall events in that other sequence. None came. Instead came a rending and tearing in the psyche. I plunged, out of control, into an abyss of infinite shock. No, that won't do. The plunge occurred, the shock was real and appalling, but I have no words to define what it was that plunged. Hardly the person who is now writing this. Nor do meta-phors of direction apply. The movement wasn't downwards, or upwards either. It was a zero-gravity rush into Elsewhere.

At last an 'I' reassembled. It reassembled, however, in another centre of consciousness.

'Martin' – I've got to put it thus – was still present and awake, still sitting in the chair. But 'I' wasn't Martin any more. I was a distinct being, observing that too-familiar self from within, aware of what Martin saw, heard, even thought, but by a kind of wire-tapping. (Re-evoking this, I am reminded of Morton Prince's classic case-study of a split personality. Prince's patient Miss Beauchamp carried a sub-personality inside her that sometimes took over, an impish entity known as Sally, who spied on Miss Beauchamp's thoughts. I'd become rather like Sally towards my own normal self.)

This appraisal of Martin-from-within gave me my first glimpse of the shadowy main road behind. I wasn't having a bizarre dream. I was sharing, somehow, in a long-established inner knowledge of Martin, a long-established attitude to him. The other centre was deeply rooted, with a past of its own. I had been drawn into a separate psychic life, which must have been flourishing inside me since... there was no telling when. The attitude to my late self which shot through me was far from neutral. It was a strong and troubled love-hate, at high intensity.

Focused by that emotion, the experience began to cohere and gain fresh dimensions. Martin grew more vivid as a distinct entity, through bodily signals which I caught by eavesdropping on his nervous system: a slight itching of the scalp, a slight nausea, feelings of contact with clothing and the chair. But unlike Martin, I could pass beyond those sense-impressions into the reality they all stemmed from. The human body which I too occupied now disclosed a marvellous, lucid inner logic. I knew, quite simply knew, the nature of the organism, the pattern forming and defining the whole animate mass of matter.

I don't think this vision carried any religious overtones. It gave me no sense of having a God's-eye-view, or being let into the secret of a Great Architect's design. This was a straight intuition of being. Once it had stamped itself, I could see that everything about the human organism would branch out from it, like geometry branching out from the axioms.

It was beautiful. Not that dreary middle-aged hulk itself, but what I saw in it. I hung suspended in a rapture of insight till a movement by Martin disturbed my reverie. His (or our) head swivelled towards a table, and his (or our) eyes rested on a bowl of cherries. Promptly the sight blazed up into a second illumination. It wasn't so rich in meaning, but it was the same kind of event. Because I'd had the primary insight into myself, I possessed the clue to further insights, to any number of them. I could know those cherries as I'd known my body. The inner form of the human creature initiated me into the forms of all things which that creature could experience.

Each of the cherries WAS. Blindingly. Each tiny red surface, which was all Martin perceived, gave me entry into a splendid and complex pattern. A sort of crystalline structure in non-space. The eye seemed to occasion the vision, rather than produce it: when the eye saw, the insight - in whatever state of being I now was - occurred.

The cherry pattern was utterly different from the human pattern. However, the several instances of it which the bowl displayed had a fraternal likeness. Every cherry was fierily itself, with its own character and glory, yet all were companions in a fellowship.

This was a new species of knowledge. It was knowing things in themselves instead of merely knowing about them. It was also knowing how one implied another. The vision of my own human nature had been my springboard into the world around. But that was only a start. The first step, once cleared, gave me access to many more. Object led to object, in a boundless web of correspondences.

I found this out during the next few minutes, as Martin's gaze drifted around the room. He looked at the clock, at a stone paperweight, at an ashtray. Every time his eyes came to rest, I saw, again, the inwardness of the object. But I also had increasingly potent glimpses of its relations with other objects, Only glimpses, I wasn't ready for more. But I did grasp a vital truth. Each inner landscape was a territory and a map at once. From what-the-cherries-were, I could infer a little of what-the-clock-was. From what-the-clock-was, I could infer a little of what-the-paperweight-was. By taking them together, I could infer much more of what-the-ashtray-was. It was like proving theorems from previous theorems. Things without life were less dazzling than the cherries, but they all glowed, so to speak, with a charge of being.

Case 402 once quoted Blake about seeing a world in a grain of sand. If State E were prolonged, I suspect it really might show you how to infer everything else, in some degree, from that single grain. With rising joy and relief, I realized it dissolved the philosophers' paradoxes like acid.

Berkeley and Hume could go their way. Physical objects, things-in-themselves, were *there* - intensely, patently there. No sophistries could reduce them to phantasms. I could go out to a thing. I could get inside it. I could almost become it. And because I saw, not only the inner patterns of things but also how these were linked together, I stood face to face with the universal order which Hume obscured. That too was there. I would know henceforth that the mind does have firm foundations to build on, if it can discover them. Also that the sudden unexplained inspirations, by which science makes its own best progress in spite of itself, are indirect insights into a cosmic scheme - a scheme which I, in State E, could perceive directly. Perceive and rejoice at.

I must take care, though, not to intellectualize too much. To judge from this first trial, State E isn't a mode of thinking. It's a mode of being, with a special flavour and tone. An ecstasy seizes you which is this-worldly rather than other-worldly. You still perceive through the bodily organs. At least, I don't recall seeing or hearing anything but what Martin was seeing or hearing. But sensation transcends itself. It's no longer confined, no longer confining. In the words of Blake yet again: 'If the doors of perception were cleansed every thing would appear to man as it is, infinite. For man has closed himself up, till he sees all things thro' narrow chinks of his cavern.' In State E as in the mescaline state, you feel that the doors are cleansed and you're perceiving as everybody ought to perceive.

There, however, the likeness halts. You aren't merely drifting in a diffused beatitude as with mescaline and other drugs. You're alert and positive, understanding the why and wherefore. The cosmic harmony isn't merely beautiful, it makes sense. Practical sense. I don't mean that you see the answers to problems. I mean that you see they were never problems at all. The ego has spun them out of its own inadequacies. With the enlarged vision you see the truth and simply comment 'Of course', as you'd assent to the statement that two and two make four.

I spoke of a love-hate emotion towards my everyday self. It had a tincture of wry amusement. I viewed Martin and his non-problems as a bird might look down at a man lost in a maze.

LSD used to go with anarchic behaviour for much the same reason. It made society's labyrinthine routines look stupid. Those who took it were apt, for example, to be proof against army discipline, not so much from moral motives as because the entire flim-flam of drill and regulation became so absurd for them that they couldn't conform. State E didn't carry me as far out as that. But it did put the ego and its myopic techniques in their place. During it, Martin spoke to T.R. two or three times.

(Martin was still functioning in a dull way.) The plod, plod of his verbal signals was weirdly clumsy. In State E, I would say, language plays only a minor role.

I've mentioned knowing what Martin thought, as well as what he saw and heard. I did, but until the end his thoughts made no impact. They reached me muted and sluggish, and faded away as dreams fade on waking. But at last his brain was jolted into asserting itself.

Somebody in the flat above switched on a record-player. The music was strident. It didn't touch off the same fireworks for me as visual images. It was enriched, yes, but chiefly by an odd heightened sensitivity to its physical groundwork - the needle of the record-player, the groove on the disc, the hi-fi equipment. While I was digesting this, Martin reacted to the music in his own fashion. It surprised him, because he hadn't heard anyone go upstairs, and it annoyed him, because it was too loud.

...Whereupon the doors of perception grew murky. State E broke up. The music was music and nothing more, and then for a while it wasn't even music, only a rumble. The room became trivial and slipped out of focus. There was a void instant, a closing and opening of eyes, and all was over. Martin was himself again. Being himself, he was also me.

'That's it,' I said.

T.R. glanced at his watch. 'About sixteen minutes.'

'I seem to remember telling you I felt sick, and then suggesting it might be something we ate.'

'Correct. I wrote your remarks down.'

No, it hadn't been a hallucination.

3

This then was the background to Martin's new map of the human psyche. I noticed he never used his term 'protoself' in it. That must have emerged from his morning-after reflections, when he sought to define the other mind-centre which had taken him over.

I was sleepy. But I couldn't leave it there. I had to know what happened when he explored the same country a second time. His notebook showed that he did it several weeks later. He'd gone to Somerset to take stock of Allhallows, then still in a lawyers' limbo, willed to him by Eric Blount, privately assigned its new name, but not yet surrendered. As the day, though cloudy, was mild, he decided to sample SP5 on top of Glastonbury Tor. Hardly prudent. However, the hope of psychic adventures on that haunted summit must have been too alluring.

The watching brief was held by a companion called 'K.' whom I suspected of being Karen.

Two friends travelled with them, labelled Robert and Caroline. Under his original note Martin had squeezed in several further lines describing this pair. I inferred that their role must have turned out to be bigger than foreseen. Both were in their twenties. Robert was a sociology lecturer influenced by B. F. Skinner.[9] As a disciple of that relentless professor, he had published papers on social planning in exactly the spirit that depressed Martin's patients. Caroline was a primary schoolteacher, unmarried. Her main interest in life was a faith-healing cult. This, I assumed, was going to be a factor in the SP5 record.

Martin swallowed his red pill in the lane below the Tor, so that the climb could be performed, and pulse-rate and breathing could return to normal, before his drug trip started. Robert and Caroline wandered off. Martin and K. trudged up to the small summit plateau where a sub-king in Arthur's time built a stronghold. They sat down on a bench near the ruined tower of St Michael's chapel.[10] People came and went but didn't disturb....

There was less wind on the Tor than usual. We could keep warm. I took care to arrange myself facing towards the Mendips, several miles off, so as to find out whether State E vision was affected by distance.

The overture was much as before, but the main transition, when it hit me, was easier. After only a moment of chaos I was safely installed in the other centre, looking out on the world through a distinct Martin. His eyes were aimed at the green hilltops near Priddy. An insight into those remote masses did occur, and was no less intense than it had been with close objects like the cherries. It was confused, however. The hills jangled. They were beyond my power to sort out. Space itself was not the reason, as I understood when a raven[11] flew slowly across my field of vision. To the eye it was a black speck, but inwardly it sang its way through me, a comet of polyhedral splendour.

A new influence was encroaching, though. This time I was far more keenly conscious of Martin's thoughts. Instead of merely twitching, they buzzed and flickered. I even caught hints of a two-way traffic. He, also,

responded to the raven - not as I did, but with more than a casual interest, as if he'd been oiled with a drop from the centre where I now was. It
struck me that this second foray couldn't simply repeat the first, *because
Martin knew about the first.* After all, he'd written it up! He was aware
of the other centre. Though his selfhood barred him from direct access to
it, he was deeply curious. A faltering rapport had begun to take shape.

Some impulse made me wonder what the grass would be like. A faint
echo bounced from Martin's brain, and his eyes turned down obligingly
to the grass near his feet. He didn't know why. Nevertheless, it happened,
Then I wasn't purely a passenger. After a few enchanting seconds with
the shrill chorus of grass-blades, I tried to produce other body movements, and to put ideas in Martin's head. The results were uncertain.
Again things happened, several times, but never with a firm conviction
that I was causing them. It felt more like a series of irritating coincidences
- as if Martin and I kept hitting on the same notion at the same instant.
Two clocks chiming together with no mechanical connection.

But whatever the reason it worked more often than not. I was closer
to a sense of control, less liable to be whirled about. I began a subtler kind
of probing. Up to now I'd feared that any involvement with Martin's
thoughts would be incompatible with State E and liable to disrupt it.
Before, that single flurry over the music upstairs had been enough to jerk
me back. It seemed not to be so any longer. Perhaps we could co-think.
With the utmost caution I shifted my attention to Martin's brain.

Events in his brain-cells had a catalytic effect, just as events in his
optic nerve had done when his eye focused on objects in the consulting
room. They touched off revelations. Very different, though, and hard to
come to terms with. What Martin dimly imagined or recollected, I saw.
The Somerset landscape was still there, but like the half of a split screen.
The other half hung noiseless in an indescribable hyperspace, alive with
pictures.

Looking out over Glastonbury, Martin recalled a previous visit four
years ago. For him it was a blurred muddle of imagery. For me it was
present and precise. I saw the Abbey ruins in mellow sunshine, and the
late Eric Blount talking genially as he guided me round. He carried a
walking-stick with a gold band, and the light glinted on it. A few seconds
later the scene dissolved and Allhallows appeared; Eric was a reminder
of his house. While the building itself was as solid as the ruins had been,
faceless wraiths were flitting through it. They were prospective students

whom Martin's sanguine fancy was peopling it with.

The next phase was a step beyond that. Martin's brain began to evoke symbols rather than sights. One might compare them to the inner realities of objects, the cherries for instance; but these were realities of the psyche.

The fuse was lit by an external event. Robert and Caroline, who had been away on their own devices, re-appeared down the slope below us. They were sauntering along what is said to be the worn track of a druidic ritual path, spiralling round the Tor.[12] Hitherto State E hadn't given me a straight look at another person. That lack was now remedied.

As they drew into eye-focus, the inner perspective of human nature assailed and excited me again. It was far less detailed than when I experienced myself. But with each of those others it had a starry freshness, a likeness-in-unlikeness, which was exquisite joy. Robert and Caroline, strolling by, were successive waves of being. The female was distinct from the male with more than a biological difference. Sex was only an aspect of a quality that went deeper. Might one in linguistic despair say 'gender'?

Martin's gaze followed them. They paused, and the waves soared up without breaking. Now there was more, even more. They stood a few feet apart and both were haloed. Around the head of each, and the upper part of the body, was a transparent glory of light: an iridescent globe.

I understood. I was seeing – or rather, I was being shown through a visual image – the hidden and greater selves of each, their counterparts of that Other in which my own consciousness was planted. Watching through Martin's eerily reinforced vision, I saw that the light was mobile. On both Robert and Caroline it rose and fell and changed shape. One moment it lengthened into a flame wrapping the whole figure. The next it dwindled into an aureole above the shoulders, or a glow off to the side and barely in contact.

As they stood talking, both their light-forms began to warp as if gusts of wind were blowing them. Robert's light was affected strongly. For most of the time it streamed behind him, moored only by a thin strand of shimmering silver. At every gust driving it that way I sensed a blankness in him, as if he were sleep-walking. Caroline's light withstood the psychical wind better. It clung to her head and shoulders without getting swept completely back.

Why the difference? A clue offered itself readily. Perhaps too readily.

Robert's temper of mind, his would-be scientific rigour, was excluding the source of his own best wisdom. Preferring the cerebral fetish of the laboratory, he had denied inspiration and treated his profounder self as a tempter to be exorcized: 'get thee behind me, Satan'. The State E picture of him agreed with my own ideas, and the Bible text for it came pat – hence, it was suspect. I had enough critical alertness to grasp that at the time. But I also grasped that the picture of Caroline was more interesting, because I resisted it. I couldn't accept that her soft-centred pseudo-religion was any wiser. I resented the image, yet it refused to alter.

She remained stubbornly present, vexing me with her clinging prismatic mist.

Then in a rush the partly-achieved sense of control slipped away from me. The sequel was a chaos which I never recovered from till State E passed off entirely. I can recall its main features and see the logic of it after a fashion, but the rest of this record will be less coherent.

First, some obscure reflex impelled Martin to turn sideways on the bench and look at the tower. That famous landmark is the remnant of a chapel built in the Middle Ages, replacing another which was one of the few English buildings ever destroyed by earthquake. I saw the tower standing as usual, grey and upright. I also saw a tower which was its twin, or nearly so – a shade higher, maybe. Then a blaze of light, like the light round Caroline's head but huge and terrific, exploded at the top. The tower (that is, the State E tower) collapsed in the quake that was seven centuries gone. I believe this mindpicture even had an accompaniment of sound, a muffled rumble.

But before the last stone had come to rest, Martin's imagination pitched me into another scene, grotesquely remote from my surroundings. I saw Case 407 in his studio. Here too I witnessed events that couldn't be taking place now; and, as soon transpired, they could never have taken place literally at all.

That sentence in the diary was at the foot of a page. The next page began:

This whole sequence of events in the studio, so plainly not 'real', had a different quality from the straight memory-pictures of Eric and Allhallows which Martin's brain had projected earlier.

The Finger and the Moon

I stopped reading, went back, stopped again. What sequence of events? My earlier disappointment over the Midsummer entry supplied an answer. A page had been removed from the binder. Something about this patient, Case 407, needed to be kept secret.

It was tantalizing. Still, perhaps Martin would fill me in when we discussed all this. Meanwhile his second trip was nearing its end....

It is almost as if I entered the world of dream, the world of significant symbols which Freud and Jung groped for. They did it by dipping into what they regarded as subconscious. There must be far more to this than they supposed. Anyway, however construed, State E seems to reveal an inwardness of the psyche as well as an inwardness of matter.

I must revert, before I forget, to the tower's fall. Though it ripped through me very fast, I remember one aspect of the event which wasn't in State E previously. As the masonry and beams shuddered and split I had an inner sense of them that fused with the visual image, and this now included specialized knowledge.

Let me make the novelty clear. When I looked at the cherries and the raven, my insight hadn't supplied any facts about them - facts in the cut-and-dried objective sense - which I didn't have at least some glimmering of already. Even though the cherries and raven were physically there, not just visions, State E hadn't turned me into an instant fruit expert or ornithologist. It would have helped me to become either afterwards, if only because it made them, the fruit and the bird, so much more precious and worth one's love. At the time it enlightened on a different level. Whereas with the visionary tower, odds and ends of outright technical expertise were darting about in the mental uproar. I felt the tower crumbling, with a precision that presupposed architect's knowledge, mason's knowledge, carpenter's knowledge. None of which I possess.

Martin was staring at the tower - the real tower that's there now - throughout the downfall of the predecessor it conjured up, and throughout 407's crisis in the studio. When both had faded, it still rose in front of me. I realized that the looker at the tower was myself, and State E was gone.

K. scribbled a few notes.

'How did I behave?' I asked.

'Absent-mindedly.'

The record ended.

Fourth Day

I'VE SPENT THE MORNING with Martin, following up (what else?)
on SP5. My night was disturbed again, though not as before.
Curiosity had carried me to the finale of his Tor scene. As soon
as I got there, sleep overwhelmed me. I just managed to lay the diary
aside, switch the light off, and slither down, still more or less dressed.
At some point in the small hours when the night was cool, I half-woke
and pulled a blanket over. Between then and my full waking came
a long meandering dream. It was prompted, of course, by Martin's
diary. But not by his descriptions of other-consciousness. Instead it
fastened on K., that unspecified watcher who had sat beside him, a
loose end in his story.

I was wandering in a network of narrow paths on a steep hillside.
They wound upwards and downwards through the grass, like goat-
tracks. I was trying to reach the top of the hill or perhaps the bottom.
Sometimes it was one, sometimes the other. Any progress either way
had an air of frustration as if the other way was intended. There was
no room in these paths for a second person to walk alongside. Yet
someone did. K.

My guess that the initial meant Karen came through in the dream,
but fitfully. Certainly my companion was female. I'm not sure whether she was meant to be guiding me. My frustration did attach to her,
as if she'd been to blame for our taking wrong turnings. Whatever
role she was really playing, her identity wavered. Several times we
faced each other for tangled dialogues which I don't recall. She wore a
long low-cut flounced dress[1], most unwieldy for climbing. As for her
face, I can only say she was Karen and then Annabel and then both,
an Allhallows composite. Visually that's absurd because they aren't
alike, but she contrived it somehow.

The Finger and the Moon

We never reached the top... or the bottom. The sole change in the situation was that Karen-Annabel glided off along a track of her own, causing a pang that woke me up. A disquieting dream to have, not wholly to be accounted for by Martin's loose ends, or by that damned maze in the grounds either.

Breakfast lightened the mood. My neighbours at table were Kwame, Alan Frobisher, and Janice. Kwame was as handsome and dignified as ever. Mr Frobisher (I think of him by the formal style) had come down alone, leaving his wife upstairs because of an omen. Janice too was unpartnered. Her male escort Norman had gone to the other table to expound Cryptocracy. This she mightn't have minded, but away in a corner Mei-ling sat talking to Annabel, their heads close together. Janice looked morose again and her voice had an edge.

The conversation got rather interesting, and drifted into an aftermath with second and third cups of coffee. Mr Frobisher had been pondering Martin's last lecture. His own special pursuit is astrology, which has led him to the esoteric writings of Yeats. It's piquant to meet somebody who knows Yeats well as an occultist, scarcely at all as a poet. At breakfast, however, Mr Frobisher did at least quote him in relation to literature.

'Yeats wrote: "We make poetry out of the quarrel with ourselves." He believed that every poet has a concealed anti-self who is unlike him, even his opposite. This is the source of his inspiration, though he may resist.'

'It would fit in with Martin's ideas,' I ventured.

'If the poet accepts his calling,' Mr Frobisher went on, 'his anti-self masters the surface personality. I've memorized some of Yeats's sayings on this.* "We meet always in the deep of the mind, whatever our work, wherever our reverie carries us, that other Will." And again – the power comes "not as like to like but seeking its own opposite." It's a mystical anguished sort of process, he says, the advent of a "dazzling unforeseen wing-footed wanderer". Again: "We could not find him if he were not in some sense of our being and yet of our being but as water with fire, as noise with silence."'

'And with a masculine pronoun,' snapped Janice. 'Why "he" all the time?'

---

* Mr Frobisher culled his Yeatsiana from *Per Amica Silentia Lunae*. I don't know whether he quoted them accurately. He told me the source later and I have transcribed them from there.

'Yeats is discussing male poets,' I countered. 'But the Muse who aids the process is female. So I've always understood, anyhow.'

Kwame interposed. 'The high priest of my coven recommended to me the book *Cosmic Consciousness* by Doctor Bucke. Do you know this gentleman?'

'I've read *Cosmic Consciousness*, yes.'

'He is another who writes of literary genius. He puts much stress on an American poet – I have forgotten the name—'

'Walt Whitman.'

'Thank you, yes. He affirms that Whitman wrote nothing good or original till the age of about thirty-five, and then altered suddenly, as though a new spirit had taken charge of him from within.'

'That is right,' I agreed. 'In one of his poems Whitman describes how, as a boy, he heard a sea-bird calling its lost mate and suddenly realized that he too was destined to be a singer – only it was many years before it actually began happening. Of course it makes a difference whether you think Whitman was a great poet, even after that. Bucke did, so do I. Many don't.'

'I must read his poetry. But it seems that this transformation must be like what the poet Yeats means by the "anti-self" taking control.'

'Careful,' Janice put in. 'We've got to call it the "protoself" here.'

'Surely though—' I began, then recalled that the students hadn't been let into the SP5 secret. I'd have to keep this vague. 'Surely Martin intends the "protoself" as a larger concept. It would include Yeats's, but a lot more besides.'

'It might need to be,' said Kwame. 'Possibly, Geoffrey, you can explain to me a part of Doctor Bucke's work which was not clear. He was of the opinion that the works of Shakespeare were written by Lord Francis Bacon. He admitted that they wrote in very unlike styles, but argued that when Bacon was in the state of cosmic consciousness, he changed and became Shakespeare. Would this not support the idea of a protoself which is more than Yeats implies? That when this high inspiration takes control of a man, he may be possessed by a whole superior personality rising up from inside?'

'I think we must distinguish,' I said. 'That Bacon thing – it's only a crank theory. But it's one of those cases where the crank has a point even if he gets it wrong. Shakespeare really is puzzling. He really has a sort of duality. The works don't fit the biography. He might well have been an extreme case. A dull businessman of the theatre who was turned into a genius whenever a deeper self took over.'

I spoke absently, trying to remember whether Martin had said any-thing about the protoself making takeover bids. Kwame looked lost. His knowledge of English authors was plainly limited. Janice asked me, with an air of personal affront:

'Why shouldn't Bacon have written Shakespeare?'

'Well, take their styles, to look no further. I doubt if you could find one scholar or critic of any standing who favours the Bacon theory.'

'The good solid Establishment spokesman,' Janice retorted, picking up a fork and stabbing at the table with it, but fixing me with her eye all the time. 'Scholars and critics indeed. With jobs to lose. Bacon won't do because he was gay and ran up debts. Shakespeare, oh, yes! a straight heterosexual male who got Anne Hathaway pregnant, tied her up in marriage, and then ran off to his dark lady and wouldn't even pay his wife's bills. Oh, yes, Shakespeare's all right!'

I wondered whether to try Mr W.H.[2] on her, but feared it would get too complicated. 'I don't say I like him as a person. Or dislike Bacon. It's a question, surely, of one's judgement of literature.'

'You mean *English* literature. Which is the only standard, of course! Everybody in the world is expected to know it and have the proper responses to it! Kwame could tell you a few things about that – the missionaries who went out to Africa and sneered at its culture, and forced African children to struggle with *Hamlet* for the greater glory of the Empire.'

Kwame's tact was admirable. 'I must not speak rashly of what I do not know well. It is true the colonists and missionaries ignored much that could be of value, even to themselves. Certainly I would say that this inspiration which we were talking of... that some light could be shed on it from other societies at other levels. From shamans and witch-doctors. From voodoo spirit-control among African-descended people in the West Indies. Who perhaps are taken over and swept into ecstasy by a deeper and different self. I must tell you in justice to my coven, we did study these matters, and also Robert Graves's work on poetic inspiration, which we saw was related.'

'That's a point,' I said. 'You can't object to Graves, Janice, even if he is Eng. Lit. He claims we all lost our souls thousands of years ago when we gave up goddesses for gods.'

'Not goddesses,' she contradicted. 'The single female principle which they all expressed. The world-wide Mother and Muse. The White Goddess.'

She'd fallen into the trap I'd barely avoided myself. Kwame grinned with unshaken good humour. 'White, Janice? Do I detect colour chauvinism?'

She emitted a sort of gasp but didn't reply. Kwame spoke on. 'Graves calls the Goddess white because white is her principal colour. A moon-colour. According to witches of the revival, this is all very important in the Craft.'

Mr Frobisher got a word in. 'It would link her Muse-aspect with "lunar" knowledge. Yeats has thoughts about that too.'

'So does Colin Wilson,' I corroborated. 'Though perhaps her title really is rather a pity.'

'Some Black Power leaders,' Kwame remarked, 'demanded that everybody should say "pale-skinned" instead. The Pale-Skinned Goddess. But do you happen to know, Geoffrey: is there any Muse among non-white nations? And if so, what colour is she?'

I fumbled in the memory ragbag. 'The Hindus have a Muse. Sarasvati. Now you mention it, she's white, and so are her clothes. She floated in a lotus on the primordial waters, strumming a veena, till Brahma lured her out and fathered most of the gods on her. She invented the alphabet in her spare time and she's the patroness of literature.'

'Does anybody explain why she's that colour?' asked Mr Frobisher.

'Hindus revere pale skins in general... and of course some of the higher-caste people actually have them. An aristocratic Indian may be, well, whiter than white.'

'Even so,' he persisted, 'the lunar knowledge idea would help to account for her. The mysterious wisdom of the seer and bard, taking shape below the threshold of normal consciousness. In the anti-self, to use Yeats's word, or in the protoself, to use Martin's. The Goddess, as Muse, would stand for an upsurge in the soul which is ruled by the moon.'

At that moment Mei-ling finished her conference with Annabel. The Chinese girl got up and made for the door. Janice, who had been watching her, got up too leaving a half-finished cup of coffee, and, without a word to us, darted off in the same direction. Before either of them was out of the dining room, Martin banged on the table. They halted. Everybody stopped talking.

'This morning,' he announced, 'Karen will be in the chair. As it's fine again, she suggests you gather on the lawn in the same place as yesterday. Half an hour from now.'

While the students dispersed, he said to me in an undertone. 'Geoffrey, I'd like to have your reactions to that diary stuff.'

'Yes. I've got questions, of course.'

'I'll be in my study. Just give me time to attend to a few letters – twenty minutes or so – and then come along.' He walked off down the corridor.

That settled my programme. The choice lay between Martin and Karen, and it had to be him, but there was a tremor of loss all the same.

Up in my bedroom I checked over the tape-recorder, in view of its misconduct last night, and loaded it. Coming back downstairs I heard male voices in the recreation room. Steve, Owen and Norman stood round a table talking loudly. It seemed to be a fresh instalment of some earlier discussion. Owen and Norman both had plastic puzzles on the table in front of them, disc-and-peg sets like the one I found in my cupboard on arrival and haven't touched since. Steve was explaining the method of solution to Norman, with a slight air of impatience, I thought. Owen seemed to have grasped it already. Every few seconds he stuck in an oral footnote.

'Look,' the numerologist was repeating, 'you've only got to follow the rule. It's perfectly simple. When you're moving an odd number of discs, you move first to the peg you want to get them on to—'

'Like if you're moving just one,' said Owen.

'When you're moving an even number, you move first to the peg you don't want to get them on to—'

'Like with two.'

'Here,' said Steve, 'have another go. I'll time it. At 9:10 precisely, we'll see how far you've both got.'

They drew chairs to the table and sat down. Owen picked up a disc and shifted it confidently to an empty peg. Norman picked up a disc in his own set and hovered with it. Finally, but not quickly, he settled on the peg corresponding to the one Owen had moved to. After a minute or two, Owen was clicking away methodically and a pile of discs was mounting on a new peg. Norman was bogged down.

I remarked to Steve: 'I've heard there's a temple in India where the priests are doing a puzzle like this with sixty-four golden discs. The story is that when they've shifted the whole stack on to another peg, the end of the world will come.'

Steve smiled. 'They should put Norman on the job. Not much danger of the world coming to an end then.'

'I favour the Steady State anyway,' Norman retorted. He'd stopped altogether. 'No end of the world. No beginning either.'

Owen, without even slowing down, said: 'Me, I'm all for the Big Bang.'[3]

Steve and Norman both laughed at the phrase, as they mightn't have done a few years and a few million American paperbacks ago. The unforeseen pitfalls of science. I left them and wandered out on the lawn.

Fine weather, but with a hint of break-up in the hard clarity of the hills (or does that apply in Somerset?). A cuckoo, far off. In June he changes his tune. I reached the rendezvous for the morning session, but no-one had arrived yet. Then a muffled thump drew my attention to the temple. Several boxes and packages were stacked on a trolley just in front of it. As I approached to examine them, the door opened and Paul came out.

'Ah, hallo,' he said. 'I'm getting a few things ready in there.'

'Ready for what?'

'For when the Cryptocrats come. Norman's been on the phone and a party of them should be here the day after tomorrow. We're going to hold a ritual and invite your photographer, remember?'

'I gather this isn't my Grail Ritual, the TV thing. Is that off now?'

'Not at all. We can do both.'

The trolley-load was oddly assorted. There were some oblong boxes which might have contained laundry. There were three awkward-shaped parcels wrapped in brown paper; one had torn slightly and a metal leg stuck out. There was also a plastic bag which Paul picked up to carry into the temple. Its contents, whatever they were, slid down inside with a clinking noise. In the temple he laid this bag alongside two further items already beside the altar – a second, larger bag, stuffed out into a cylindrical form, and a plain carton like a monster package of cornflakes, suitable, I thought, to hold a scale model of the UN building in New York.

'Offerings for the Horned One?' I asked. The sculpture towered above us.

'Not exactly. But part of his scene, yes.'

'I didn't grasp that Cryptocracy had any connection with - well - with this sort of activity.'

'Norman's been telling me a lot more. It's fascinating. He's explained what amounts to an entirely original plan for remoulding society. His friends can stay for a while, so we'll have plenty of chance to talk.'

We were outside again. Paul was trying, without success, to pick up all his brown paper parcels together.

'It may sound naïve,' he went on, 'but I honestly believe this could be the start of a revolution. A revolution through disciplined groups and properly mobilized mystiques. Who knows, Geoffrey? You might have a big part in this.'

'Do you mean as an adviser for that Neo-Arthurian business Norman was on about?'

'Not quite in the way he suggested, no. That was kids' stuff. But he did get me thinking.'

Settling for two parcels instead of three, he shouldered the temple door open - I'd pulled it to, out of habit - and passed inside again. I glimpsed the Horned One and, suddenly, didn't feel like following. It wasn't a repetition of the mysterious 'No' of the maze. That had hit me with an impact as from something extremely positive, if unknown; this was merely a vague unease in myself. However, it did deter. I called out an excuse to Paul and retraced my steps. There was still nobody else on the lawn. Twenty-five minutes after Martin had spoken to me I entered his study.

2

Martin was at his desk. He waved me to an armchair. I took in more details of the room, but it hasn't all that many to take in. It's surprisingly bare and office-like. Two grey filing cabinets. A single bookcase full of psychological works, which I assume to be relics of Martin's practice. A single picture, on the wall that faces the hanging sword: swallows in flight.

One point, or rather two, needed to be cleared up promptly before

Paul's burgeoning sub-programme put me in a false position.

'While I think of it, did Paul explain that idea we had for a reading of my Grail Ritual?'

'Yes, he did. I'll be most interested to hear it.'

'And see it too, I hope. To some extent anyhow. I'm trying to get the costumes sent as well as the scripts.'

'Good. Tell me when they arrive. I'd like to phone Madri - the Tantra Pentacle, you know - and see if she can come for it, with a few of her community.'

This was a bonus. After all, the Allhallows graduate Madri was (and is) among my chief reasons for being here. Now Martin was tossing me the chance of an interview. But had he an undisclosed motive? Was he countering the influx of Cryptocrats? Or did he even know about that? I decided not to mention it. But one further thing I had to mention. 'Paul had another idea. A night excursion to Cadbury Castle, to keep vigil.'

'At Midsummer.'

'Precisely.'

'I'm sure we can arrange that too. We'll go before it gets dark and you can give us a conducted tour. Camelot and so forth.'

The proposed date, of course, raised issues.

'When I looked at your diary two days ago, in the library, "Midsummer" was the last word in it. That page is missing now.'

'Yes.'

I pushed ahead. 'Wasn't there another page missing, in your second SP5 test? The Tor episode?'

'Yes.'

'Did you take those pages out of the binder?'

'Yes.'

Momentarily I assumed he wanted to shut me up on the subject, but this time he continued. 'Bits of the diary are kept back in a private file. I had second thoughts on that Midsummer entry soon after putting it in, so I took it out. You just happened to catch it. But the Tor incident - that had to be withdrawn when I first put the diary in the library. It involves a patient, unmentionably at that. But yes, for completeness, I ought to tell you what's on the missing page. It doesn't matter now... except I'd rather you left it out of your article. He's dead, poor chap. A motorway pile-up. He wasn't thirty.'

Martin unlocked the cabinet, opened the middle drawer, and pulled out a folder. Sitting down again, he spread some of its contents on the desk and talked. The notes were handwritten and illegible from where I sat. He leafed through them back and forth, extemporizing rather than reading.

'Case 407 was a sculptor. Not the American who worked here, though the American came to Allhallows because of him. They met at a gallery, I believe. Anyhow.

'407 was among the cases in that notebook. A romantic who saw the world as full of beauty. Wasn't ashamed to admit it either, as long as he trusted his own convictions. But he was over-suggestible. After an upbringing in a sheltered C of E setting - Cathedral Close set - he went to art school, and met some cynical types who killed his faith. He got it into his head that Science (with a capital S) proved his sense of beauty to be a subjective delusion. Artistic conscience and rational conscience tore him apart. The universe just had to be beautiful and meaningful, but Science (with a capital S) wouldn't let him enjoy it.

'You may be thinking, "What an old-fashioned story". This great problem I've been concerned with does often afflict people in old-fashioned ways. But 407 really was old-fashioned. He had an air of the Yellow Nineties. He even drank absinthe.

'I doubt if he'd have come to me because of these hangups alone. But his art began to suffer. He fancied he could kick Science if he could create beauty which was "self-evidently valid" - his words, not mine - so he studied aesthetic theory, and lost his touch.

'Even that mightn't have made him a psychiatric case. But he got seized with ungovernable desire for a girl who wouldn't have him. After months of torment he brought his troubles to me. It was some time, though, before he told me what he'd been doing. He'd made a nude life-size statue of the girl, half recumbent, from memory and photos. Modelling the statue gave him a certain release, he said.'

'Eric Gill had an experience like that.'

'Eric Gill...?'

'The chap who carved the "Stations of the Cross" panels in Westminster Cathedral.'

'Did he indeed? I must take a note of it.' He actually did. 'Well, 407's statue was rather good, unlike most of his work in that phase. He kept it under wraps and seldom showed it to visitors, but he did draw me a sketch.' Martin picked it out of the file and held it up. 'He left the face blank in the sketch, for anonymity, but the rest of her is pretty graphic.'

'One doesn't feel that aesthetic theory was uppermost in his mind. Did he tell you how he knew what the rest of her looked like?'

'He'd photographed all but a few square inches on the beach at St Tropez.'

'Fair enough. But how did he get into your SP5 visions?'

'Be patient. Under analysis he confessed to having a private sexual ritual. After dark he'd turn out the lights in his studio and uncover the statue. Then he'd take off his clothes, contemplate the pale female form, and masturbate. It was self-defeating, of course. He dared not go too near the statue or touch it. Also he had guilt feelings from child-hood: this was scarcely Cathedral Close behaviour. Consequently he seldom achieved even what he tried to achieve. He'd drive himself frantic for a few minutes and then collapse without orgasm.'

'He sounds a sad case.'

'Very sad. Now as to my SP5 sequence. That image of the tower brought him to mind – for obvious reasons. The braincells projected a picture of him in his studio. Let me repeat, this wasn't a memory image. I'd never been there. Yet I did see 407 having one of his ses-sions.' Martin smiled wryly. 'The analyst is supposed to be unshock-able. Verbally he is, if he's any good. But it still takes some adjusting when you actually watch what your patient's told you about.

'We're on the missing page now. My point of vision in the studio seemed to drift. The sequence began in semi-darkness. 407 had already taken the wraps off his statue, stripped, and, ah, proceeded. Then I got an SP5 effect within the effect. I saw the same human light I'd seen round Robert and Caroline. With 407 it was poignant. There he was, writhing in his prison of sense and ego-obsession – while behind him, entirely behind, almost detached from him, a luminous cloud swirled in the air like a mobile rainbow. I say a rainbow, it was more silvery than anything, but it did change.

'It didn't reflect back from objects around or make the studio brighter. I was glad; I couldn't shake off a sense of intrusion. That man's psyche was exposed as well as his body. I knew, if only he could let his aura sweep round and engulf him... but he couldn't. There was something in him that fought. On two fronts. It was pushing back the healing light and it was also holding him in physical deadlock.

'The crucial part of this was the way it ended. He jumped up and moved closer to the statue. My own focus shifted round to it. Then... this is hard to describe... the cloud of light smashed the barrier and surged forward. It encased both the figures, as if they were inside a great shining sphere.

'And the statue came to life. Or rather it wasn't the statue any more. Or the real girl, either. It - she - was more humanly coloured than the statue. Her hair showed (yes, all of it, she was dark) and so did her nipples. Conversely though, she had a poise which the real one mightn't have had. She was simply *there*, in a curiously lovely way.

'That was it. Neither of them spoke. He had a couch in the studio and they lay down. Presently he relaxed.'

'After which, it faded out?'

'Yes. You've read the last bit of the record.'

'What do you make of it?'

Martin stared into vacancy for a few seconds. 'The point is, you see, it didn't happen. I wasn't tapping some dream or hallucination which 407 really had. Nor was I getting some distorted view of the girl yielding after all. She never did. In fact she'd already gone to New Zealand. No, I was witnessing events in a realm of the psyche. Symbolic ones. Because, in what passes as real life, 407 did find his release. It sounds comic, yet it saved him. He joined a group called the Astrosophical Buddhists. All through the last year or two he lived, he was at peace with the cosmos, and doing his finest work.'

'Did he join that group before or after your SP5 vision of him?'

Martin consulted his notes. 'He was involved in it but hadn't yet joined.'

'I'm not sure what this means. Was Astrosophical Buddhism his substitute for sex?'

'Or was sex his substitute for a fulfilment he needed, but didn't find till he joined the Astrosophical Buddhists? Surely the answer must go deeper than both.'

3

We talked for hours. I ran my tape and scrawled notes. Before getting down to what Martin's experiences were supposed to have proved,

I asked him about the test programme itself. Why those handwritten records? Without carbon copies, how had his information ever reached the research unit? Privately I wondered if the programme and the unit were largely imaginary. However, he replied without hesitating. He preferred to write in his own hand because it was more personal. When he re-read the script after a lapse of time it brought back the experience, which was so foreign that it could soon become unreal to him otherwise. While the programme was going on (it's finished now) he used to meet the research director after each trip. They'd go over the record together, with a stenographer taking it all down. It was a better, more sensitive procedure than putting typescripts in the post.

The main report is still being compiled, it seems, and may take years. Meanwhile they allow Martin to continue on his own account so long as there's no publicity. His students aren't normally told about SP5. Not ever. Martin – or Karen when she stands in for him, as she did this morning – presents them with ideas that are in fact based on his SP5 adventures. Also they're free to dip into his diary in the library. But only a select few who go further, his PhD's so to speak, get to read the notebook which is the key to it all.

When I understood the setup I didn't care for it much, but rather than comment, I switched to a query about the other test subjects. How many people besides Martin had taken SP5?

'They tried it on six others. We were kept apart while the programme lasted. At the end they let us meet and compare our results.'

'Did all six get the same results as you?'

'More or less. The scope was narrower. They hadn't, you see, been concerned quite so appositely. I happened to be a psychologist. So this inner unfolding, or whatever you choose to call it, gave me a psychological message. A very sweeping message which I was already attuned for. But yes, it unleashed hidden faculties in the others as well. One was a vet. Under SP5 he practically became Doctor Dolittle. He picked up signals from animals as if they were speaking to him.'

'But you see, Martin, this raises the whole drug issue. We've heard it before. What effect, what solid effect, does SP5 have? Could this vet handle animals any better when it wore off?'

'I'm told he could. If you ask about performance in general, there aren't enough facts. People in the SP5 state can learn to put the body through actions that aren't too complex. One subject folded paper hats. Another played "Twinkle, twinkle, little star" on the piano. After they've come out... like the vet, they all seem to have a better grasp of jobs that interest them. But the major advance is in a different area. Resolving problems. Fulfilling oneself in depth.'

I wanted to keep our feet on the ground as long as I could, pressing him on aspects we could be factual about. 'Take the basic functions. What happens with eating under SP5?'

'Physically it's normal. Mentally it's surprising. Tastes and smells are evocative. You peel a banana, a nerve tingles in your nose, and while you're eating this banana you see a vivid replay of a scene where you ate another. Or some staple item can touch off a documentary. A loaf can project sequences of Christ at the Last Supper, and bread and circuses in Rome, and Paris rioters in the Revolution – all based on associations stored in the brain, and ready to be activated in ways the brain can't manage unaided. Afterwards, eating reverts to what it was before. No loss of appetite, no indigestion or constipation.'

'And sex? Or is there time for it?'

'There can be time, easily. With a strengthened dose the SP5 state can last an hour. As a body-function alone, sex weakens. The male with a casual partner may be impotent. The female is passive without orgasm. However, there's more to it than that. When the psyche is deeply involved' (I'm not sure whether Martin used the word 'love' hereabouts) 'the other centre – the protoself – is roused. It surges in with a drive of its own, which makes up for the shortcomings of the nervous system. Then, intercourse is ecstatic. If both partners are under dosage it's so ecstatic as to be super-fulfilling. Back in normal life they don't want to come together again for ages. Sex gets cycled. It's marvellous when it happens but it doesn't happen often, because they're satisfied for months without it. They may seem downright apathetic towards each other, without even enough feeling to make them possessive or jealous.'

'So a couple could have perfect sex and fewer children as well. It sounds like an answer to the population explosion.'[4]

Martin laughed. 'That's quite an idea. I never thought.'

He still hadn't given away anything I could be certain was personal. I sat back while he continued interpreting. Plainly, however he might deploy his case for students, he believed in the protoself because of the drug. SP5 had transferred his consciousness to another centre. Therefore, he knew the other centre existed. He'd been there!

I did demur. Mightn't his experience be simply a drug state? It was too happy, the way he described it in his diary, too much like wishful thinking. A touch of real sordid pain or misery would take the gloss off these visions. Anyhow, couldn't it all have been inspired by his patients' neuroses? He'd been brooding over their yearning for enlargement of spirit, significance, etcetera. SP5 obligingly cooked up a solution for him, crediting Man with this second self tucked away inside, full of power and insight. Maybe too obligingly. I even hinted that it wasn't his own solution, that he'd borrowed it from Gurdjieff,[5] who also taught that Man has more than one centre of consciousness.

Martin stood his ground unruffled. 'As to its being too full of sweetness and light – no. Suspend judgement till you find what SP5 showed me in cases you didn't get to in your reading. As to validity, my point is that it always opens the gate to the protoself – that's how it helps to resolve problems – only with me this was so complete, so mind-blowing, because the problem I was concerned with myself could only be resolved by my protoself grabbing me directly. Saying in effect, "Here I am, here's what all human beings have in them if they only knew it."'

But, I urged, did this alleged protoself actually settle anything? Could Martin offer an account of it which would hold together and give an authentic new look to the human condition? Why should his drug-scenes, with their crystallized fruit and allegoric voyeurism, be any truer than the LSD or mescaline types?

He talked. Bit by bit, as the morning progressed, I drew out his opinions. Or some of them. I don't think it would be much use trying to reconstitute that immense, rambling dialogue. I'll leave my stuff on it aside and have a shot, later, at distilling Martin's theory into a few paragraphs.

(Done, later. The result inserted herewith. – Editorial note.)

4

PROTOSELF PSYCHOLOGY[6]
Abstract of the Ideas of Martin Ellis

The 'other centre' or protoself which SP5-takers find annexing them is as individual and personal as the ego. It is the Being of each one of us. It is not merely an aspect of some universal Collective Unconscious or, in Hindu terms, Atman. Martin's use of the iceberg metaphor when introducing it to his students is precise and carefully stated. Each human entity is a separate berg, not a peak jutting up from a single concealed mass.

In relation to everything else, the protoself's power may be summed up as its access to *the Inwardness of Things*. (This phrase reminded me of Teilhard de Chardin[7], but Martin called him 'seductive and dangerous' and wouldn't admit any influence.)

The light-auras Martin saw round people whom he looked at under SP5 were valid images of their protoselves. The protoself is there all the time, active, probably never sleeping. But in adults, it only pierces through into the ego's everyday life erratically and indirectly: by way of dreams, sudden inspirations, and what people are apt to call 'feelings'. It is thrust down by a divisive agency in the psyche, a sort of perverse will, a watchdog. Hence Binary Man, with an inner conflict and mixup of signals, often leading to neuroses and delusions.

(This of course is standard psychoanalytic doctrine pushed further. Freud and Jung got through, clinically, to a great many glimpses of the protoself's workings; but they regarded it as 'subconscious' and without individuality. It is far more than they thought. When SP5 takes effect, which it does mainly by quelling the watchdog, the protoself asserts its domain from within, with resources which the analysts never caught any inkling of.)

We are not born binary. We become so. The protoself is there at the start, embracing the entire psyche. Its innate sense of reality and order supply the groundwork for learning, especially learning to speak and employ language, which cannot be explained without going beyond the reach of experimental science. (Somewhere about this point, Martin said 'Chomsky'[8].) As a child grows older his ego-consciousness distils out. His brain verbalizes the body's experi-ence to build up a limited 'I' largely cut off from its psychic origins, entrenched in spurious selfhood. The protoself is still there inside him observing the ego, but the reverse is not true.

The split has become more marked with the advance of civilization. In ancient society, magic flourished as the expression of the protoself's role in the human unity. Adults, however mature, were less cut-down and shut-in. But priestly religion and science gradually branched off. These were products of the cerebral, system-weaving ego. It grew away from its roots and neglected magic. To say so is not to belittle its achievements. The brilliance of the intellect is, in occult terms, solar. But the sun's glare blinds us to other lights.

A vague awareness of psychic loss is part of the reason for the wide-spread nostalgia of mankind – the feeling voiced in numerous myths, that a golden age when Man was in harmony existed long ago and has perished. A life-pattern of disorientation and dwindling has set in, with death as the end because the ego has no way of seeing beyond it. The mystery cults of the Greek and Roman world were filled with a sense of spiritual fall which their initiates were supposed to retrieve. In the mysteries of the Great Goddess, the initiate's supreme ecstasy, as reported by Apuleius, was to 'see the sun shining at midnight': to be illuminated by all the lights of the psyche together.

The maturing individual is apt to develop a sense of loss which is the same as mankind's. Nostalgia for one's submerged protoself, one's own golden Atlantis, explains that stubborn illusion about the idyllic days of childhood. Childhood is seldom idyllic in that sense, any more than the golden age was naïvely golden. Yet the instinct of looking back and seeing it thus is well founded. Children still have a potential which is usually lost later. Their happy acceptance of a realm of crea-tive imagination – of legends, fairy-tales, magic itself – is a glow of the protoself and the glory not yet departed.

Genius has been described as an inspired childlike state, or an ability to be young again. What Man does in his higher flights is in fact attained through the freshness and energy of imagination that is commonest in children. It re-opens doors that were closed in growing up, so that the protoself can sweep in again carrying consciousness upward, outward.

(On this 'childhood' business Martin reeled off a series of texts which I suspect he got from his patient 402. Wordsworth's Immortality Ode of course – 'Heaven lies about us in our infancy', etc. – and Blake's Organized Innocence as the highest spiritual state. He was more excited, however, about a passage from the mystic Thomas Traherne[9] which he told me came nearer to catching the SP5 atmosphere than anything else, and was written as an evocation of childhood:

> The corn was orient and immortal wheat, which never should be reaped, nor was ever sown. I thought it had stood from everlasting to everlasting.... Boys and girls tumbling in the street, and playing, were moving jewels.

Martin quoted this with emotion and then added: 'Crowley, you know, even black Crowley, prophesied that the coming age of enlightenment would be the Age of the Child. That wasn't sentimental Peter Pan rubbish, it was far more profound.')

Childhood and the lost golden age shed light on each other. The era of the old higher magic was one of immense potential and of immense achievement too, in Minoan Crete and early Egypt, for instance. Likewise a child under three, who, for instance, learns a language *from nothing* and not from another language known already, is functioning on a level which adults can no longer conceive. To talk of reinstating the lost vision, in the individual or in society, doesn't mean regressing to infantilism. The Beginning is the original richness, the prerequisite of all growth. Crete and Egypt may even hint that progress could have gone forward without the psychic splitting-up and the consequent loss.

To revert once more to language. This is a vital key to the inner relationships of Binary Man. The protoself seems to have an inbuilt proto-language, a scheme of patterns that corresponds to the structure of reality. Some of it gets through to the brain – far more in childhood than later – and the brain builds up verbal language on it. Everyday speech, followed by mathematics and so on. But these are not the same. They are like computerizations, often crude ones. The brain is shut up inside the skull and narrowly dependent on the senses and nervous system. The protoself ranges wider. Its messages about the world struggle through, and the brain verbalizes, rationalizes; ably perhaps; but the word-formula which the brain cooks up is never the real message in its fullness. So the cerebral ego constructs its little cosmos in a mould of half-truths and mangled insights. That is one reason why 'intellectuals' and 'experts', who fancy the little cosmos to be the whole show, have such a boundless capacity for being wrong... witness, for example, economists.

(When we reached this part of the discussion I began to see dimly how my own pet notion on legends fitted in. 'Wrongness can lead to rightness.' A fantastic yarn which the brain spins may be utterly garbled. But on Martin's showing this can be the garbling of a valid message conveying a deep appraisal of the facts of the case, which the protoself is trying to slip through the barrier, past the watchdog. The story may be quite beyond credence like the legends of Merlin. Yet if you toss it out for that reason, as the scholar is apt to do, you lose the message. Whereas if you take it seriously, ask what it's about, trace it back, it may lead you... closer anyhow, much closer.)

Variations on the theme.

Unexplained actions, Freudian slips. Often these are responses to wise and far-sighted promptings from the protoself. Indirectly it may guide us more than we know. The brain translates its signals into rational 'motives' which satisfy the ego but aren't the genuine causes of what we do.

Unexplained inspirations, such as those of really great scientists, like the ones Mei-ling recalled in that session on the lawn. At bottom they are flashes of the protoself's insight into the logic of the cosmos, glimpsed by Martin when he first took SP5. It discharges its lightning-bolt into the scientist's brain when the watchdog is off guard. Then – ploddingly, half-blindly – he translates it into equations and experiments.

Poetry. The supreme evocative shorthand. It too, in another way, reflects proto-insight into the inner reality of objects and human beings. The poet's language succeeds briefly in being more than computerization. One reason is that the incantatory spell of rhythm is too much for the watchdog.

Philosophy. Because language isn't the Real Thing, only the brain's makeshift, our verbalizing creates problems that aren't there. We all grow up with the protoself's basic wisdom still in us, knowing the world around us is real, knowing it makes sense. But as we've forgotten where this came from, philosophers try to wrap it in verbal proofs. The attempt is futile. As Somerset Maugham put it, 'Metaphysics is the finding of bad reasons for what you believe by instinct.' Hence the paradoxes of Berkeley and Hume. Under SP5, reunited to the protoself, you don't solve them, you simply see through them.

(Martin went on to relate Plato's Ideas to his experience with the cherries, but I lost him.)

5

During our marathon dialogue Annabel came in with coffee. She was gone within seconds, yet she jerked me out of the theoretical mood. I asked myself whether Annabel thought like that, and found it mattered that she probably didn't.

I was still meant to be digging, after all, for the answers to a practical question: how Allhallows produces Rosmers and Madris. Something deterred me from asking Martin point-blank. The answer couldn't be extracted, not in a form that would be any use; it had to emerge. Instead I asked him how he fitted magic into all this. His own magic, rather than his alleged Wisdom of the Ancients. Why, to begin with, did he call his SP5 manuscript a 'magical' diary?

'Remember the finger and the moon,' he replied. 'The mere patter, the mere technique, that's largely another lot of verbalizing. We already made the point. But this particular finger points at a very special moon – the protoself in its own nature. I'd say, the essence of magic is the discovery of the protoself and its powers, and the liberation of Man through inner reunion. That's what the Renaissance magus-scientists were after – Agrippa, Paracelsus, Bruno. They approached it on intellectual lines, through the vision of Man as key to the universe himself if he can only realize himself. Modern Tantrists and sex-mystics have tried other ways, ways of internal unleashing, so to speak. SP5 is another way again, and a better one. I count SP5 as authentic magic.'

'You just mentioned the protoself's powers. That raises a big issue, you know. Yesterday you claimed that the protoself is the source of magical workings. When a clairvoyant or numerologist pulls it off, that's what actually does it. But if so, what special channels of information does the protoself have? What can the bottom of your iceberg do which the top of it can't? ESP perhaps?'

'I've gone into that pretty critically. I haven't found that proto-knowledge short-circuits ordinary methods of knowing. Not habitu-ally. Under SP5 I've seldom learnt any facts that couldn't have got into me by everyday routes. The facts are different in quality, yes – they aren't static or self-contained, they're alive, infinite. But they come by way of plain honest seeing-and-hearing, more often than not.

'One thing, though, which the protoself does seem to have is total recall. Which explains a great deal. (Those Renaissance magi had the same idea.) Freud and Jung proved that we remember far more than we think we do, only it's sunk below the threshold where access is lost. To put it in my own terms, the protoself remembers. SP5 con-firms that. Again and again it's unpacked my own brain-cells for me. It's produced memory-sequences like Eric Blount in the Abbey. Or I've found I could pour out all sorts of things afterwards which I couldn't have called to mind normally. That might have sounded like preternatural knowledge to anyone who was listening, but it wasn't. It was perfect remembering. Often of details about a person or place which I must have heard as a kid and (on the face of it) forgotten.'

Here he did surprise me. Had he come down on the sceptics' side after all? 'This certainly tallies with a lot of alleged mysteries that aren't. Like Bridey Murphy. That case of the woman under hypnosis who recalled a previous existence when she was Bridey Murphy, and it turned out to be a mix-up of "forgotten" scraps about herself and a neighbour with that name.'

'Precisely so. When it comes to the crunch, SP5 evidence often favours the orthodox scientist rather than the occultist.'

'It reminds me of the way they account for the *déjà-vu* experi-ence.'

'Quite. And mystical feelings of direct contact with the past. I'd say SP5 confirms that it's often – not always, but often – just submerged memory of a similar scene, or a history book you've read.'

'There was a popular theologian, C. S. Lewis probably, who sug-gested that unfallen Man would have had complete access to his subconscious.'

'Then SP5 is a partial restoration of Eden. I could believe it.'
Wistfully.

Anxious to divert him from his enamoured mood, I tackled him
about his exceptions. 'Sometimes, though, SP5 does show you things
by abnormal methods. Is it like ESP?'

Martin reflected. 'You didn't read the whole of the diary, did you?'

'No, only the first two episodes.'

'Then suspend judgement till you've finished it. Briefly, I've had
proof of telepathy in a sense. Also of precognition in a sense. The
protoself can detect all sorts of curious patterns, in time as well as
space, so that it can see ahead – even into what you'd swear were
random events. But ESP as Professor Rhine claims... knowing physical things without the senses in some clairvoyant way... I'm not convinced that it happens, even on the proto-level. I suspect the data have
been misinterpreted.'*

Martin's reminder that I'd read only a fraction of his diary was now
clearly going to be used to end our discussion. He repeated it when I
took him up on his falling chapel-tower during the second trip.

'You had flashes of special knowledge – architectural, wasn't it?
– and couldn't understand where they came from. Wouldn't that be
a kind of ESP?'

'I hit on an explanation I like better. But wait and see if the rest of
the diary sheds light on that. It should.'

Silence. A suspicion was taking shape in my mind that Martin's
whole theory had a flaw running through it. If we're cut off from our
protoselves, and our brains mangle the deeper truths by putting them
into words, then what about the words of Freud, Jung, Martin Ellis
himself? How can their accounts of the psyche be better than garbled
hints at a reality which is likely to be quite different?

---

* At the time I didn't feel able to absorb any more. In a later talk Martin told me what he
meant. He thinks that Rhine's alleged proofs can accounted for by precognition. In the
experiments, cards with symbols on them were dealt out, and a subject who couldn't see
them tried to 'sense' each symbol as it came. With some subjects, when the cards were
checked afterwards, an improbably high percentage of the guesses would turn out to have
been correct. Therefore.... But Martin's view is that the subject in such a case doesn't sense
the cards as they're dealt; his protoself has a preview of the checking process a few minutes
later and enough of this trickles through into consciousness to give him a high score. There
are ramifications of this involving telepathy as well, but not extra-sensory *perception*,
which Martin is distrustful of.

I tried this idea on Martin before leaving him. 'Haven't you fallen into the mystic's trap – speaking of the Indescribable and then pretending to describe it?'

He gave me a sad smile. 'I've seen that danger. Mind you, it's not as bad as anti-mystics make out. Words that can't describe can still point the way, can start people thinking on lines that get them there. But yes, of course, I'm dealing in verbal shadows. Mine are more like reality than some, that's all. Reality itself – what one sees *there*, under SP5 – oh no, that's another story. The temptation isn't to spin more webs of words. The temptation is to stop talking altogether and stay there.'

'Then SP5 is addictive.'

'Not in the medical sense. Only as a place or a woman will sometimes be. Short of a downright sick compulsion, the honest truth, usually, is that you can keep away if you must – and if you must, it's nowhere near a cold turkey treatment.' He gazed out of the window. 'But you often feel that you'd love to be where you aren't.'

After all this time, all this elusiveness, he was speaking personally at last. Perhaps I could gain just an inch or two more ground....

'Tell me, has anyone taken SP5 besides yourself and the other test subjects?'

The question pulled him back. 'A few. But the research unit still does all the dispensing, mostly on my recommendation. It's very hush-hush.'

'How about Karen, for instance? And Paul and Annabel?'

'Karen, yes. Paul... has tried it. Annabel, no.'

'Because of her drug trouble before?'

'She told you?'

'Enough.'

'That's interesting. Yes, she was a hard-drug case. But that isn't the main reason. You see, Geoffrey, Annabel doesn't need SP5.'

He paused, I waited. He went on in a voice pitched a shade lower. 'She's a natural genius. Karen and Paul and I are not what's described as "psychic". Annabel is. She's an extreme instance of something I first heard of in this part of the country, around the time I took over Allhallows. Just about then, some of those new Glastonbury communities were forming – youngsters, you know, whom the locals insisted on calling hippies. Radical neo-mystics and Jesus freaks. Lots of them had been on drugs. But when they settled over there, the place turned them on so spectacularly it made acid seem old-hat. I expect you know more about it than I do.'[10]

'A fair amount anyway.'

'This Avalonian place-magic... it didn't exactly cure the habit, it took them past it. They moved forward. Dreaming dreams and seeing visions. Annabel came there as a worse case than most. She'd been under treatment, in a straight medical sense. But she lived three months in a little commune south of the Tor, and afterwards she joined us here, changed utterly. I'd be scared to let her take SP5. Also, she's never asked for it.'

'Are you telling me she goes around in a trance?'

'Not at all. She's still herself, still functioning on the usual levels, often as foolish and tiresome as the next girl. But Karen and I have learnt to... recognize, and be silent.'

I wondered how Karen's version of the same cure - that the ex-docker Terry Hoad did it - fitted in with Martin's. But I veered away once again from perilous ground. 'Do any of your students take SP5?'

'Not so far. The brighter sort read my diary and make guesses. Few of them persevere in asking. Surprisingly few. Our best graduates, like Madri and John Rosmer, know but don't discuss in public. At present I won't approve a supply for them. They're safe themselves, but there could be leaks.'

(So SP5, as such, isn't the secret which the *Globe* is paying me to unearth.)

I stood up to close our session at last, with the obvious polite murmurs. Something - Martin might say my protoself - forbade me to go till a final question had been put.

'Could *I* try SP5?'

I'd have been prepared for him to shut off, and start dropping hints about going home. His face, however, had no expression at all.

'I wouldn't rule it out.' There was a pause. He looked down, drumming his fingers on the desk, then up at me. 'I'll have to think it over. Stay around, we can reach a decision soon.'

6

Evening – my fourth at Allhallows. Clouds blew in over the Poldens during the afternoon, and a drizzling rain started. Time, as I remarked before, has an altered rhythm in these surroundings. Talk is apt to meander on and on, pressureless, without urgency. But events shape up faster and with a sharper impact. This damp evening is unlike the three before it. A bridge has been crossed. Possibly more than one.

When I left Martin's study after that long conversation, I found the post had arrived. On a table under the letter-rack, which it was too big for, lay a package addressed to me. Inside were the scripts of my Grail Ritual, safely and promptly transmitted by the TV producer who had been keeping them. I told Martin at dinner. He said he'd phone Madri and fix a date for the performance, when she could bring some of her co-Tantrists to watch.

'Would three days from now be all right if she can make it?'

'Quite all right. I can stay, if you can put up with me.'

Three days. Norman's Cryptocrats were apparently going to descend sooner, and they might still be at Allhallows when Madri came. There'd be no shortage of copy. Though it was a nice question how far it would be legitimate copy, when one had injected so many new factors into the system one was supposed to be observing.

Meanwhile I gathered that Karen had spent the morning expounding protoself theory to the students. Precluded, of course, from mentioning SP5, she'd carried on where Martin left off last night, still relating it all to magic. Students told me how ancient teachings were adroitly shown to have foreshadowed his concepts. In dinner-time retrospect the Kabbalah loomed large. I heard how Jewish mystics had worked out a doctrine making the nature of Man the key to the nature of all other beings, and the relations among them, so that the universe became an intelligible pattern of patterns'. I also heard how these mystics had divided the psyche into the *Ruach* or ego and the *Neschamah*, which, they declared, is more profound but only articulate in so far as the *Ruach* gives it a voice....

Never mind these esoteric particulars. What Martin has plainly done is to state his theories in the jargon of an established Higher Magic, one that was much in favour with his friends the Renaissance magi. I admire his resource. He, or Karen when he isn't around, can present the package as a modern version of the Kabbalah without disclosing that this is four-fifths afterthought, and he reached his conclusions by a totally different route. Still, if Jewish mystics offer a terminology that carries his message, that surely means they were on the right track and deserve credit. I've given up the ethics and simply let it flow over me.

I joined the students - the whole complement of Allhallows in fact - for an afternoon session in the conference room. It hardly promised to be exciting. Exciting or not, however, it has given a crucial twist to my destiny here. I'm still wondering how, precisely.

The theme was alchemy. The round table wouldn't hold all thirteen of us. Martin and Karen stood back while the students disposed themselves, and then sat on spare chairs outside the circle. So did Paul, separately. Annabel? She was on the right of the speaker's chair, the one with a high back. That chair itself was occupied by Mei-ling, whose grave dark head didn't reach the top. Janice had tried without success to slip in on her left, and was slumped moodily two seats round, beside her original escort Norman.

It seemed to be Ladies' Day. After Karen's morning it was Mei-ling's afternoon, and Annabel introduced her. I assumed this was what they'd conferred about at breakfast. Annabel began speaking in her deceptive near-monotone. She was as self-possessed as a Roedeaner,[11] but without the cutting edge. Very hard to place.

'You know we like to spend some of our time studying classic types of magic. Usually we find there are several members in a group who've specialized already, and can explain to the rest of us. The evening before last, we had Steve's demonstration of numerology. Now we're having Mei-ling in this chair because she knows about alchemy. That's partly on account of her research in the history of science. Alchemy was the old form of chemistry. She also tells me there's plenty about it in the Chinese Taoist tradition.'

Martin, like some other teachers I've known, has mastered the art of getting students to take the load off his hands.

'Alchemy,' Annabel went on, 'has to do with the Philosopher's Stone, which turned base metals into gold, and also with the Elixir of Life, which made you immortal. After what we discussed before dinner, it's interesting to find that the Wandering Jew appears in this setting. But alchemy brings us closer to home than that. John

Dee, the Elizabethan magician, thought he'd discovered the Stone at Glastonbury, complete with instructions for its use. Or at least he thought his assistant Kelley had – who's said, by the way, to have become Aleister Crowley in a later incarnation.' Annabel got as far as a faint smile. 'I understand Mei-ling may be telling you a story about John Dee and a warming-pan. But now, over to her.'

Mei-ling began to talk, or rather to half-read from copious notes in what looked like a medley of Chinese and western characters. I'm afraid she lost my attention almost at once and recaptured it in snatches only. It wasn't her fault. She spoke English with the same English-plus elegance as before, and held her fellow-students. But as for me, I was mentally fatigued and SP5 had started too many hares... and a fresh question was overshadowing all others. Would Martin let me sample the stuff? If he was right, it would unleash an apocalypse of my own deepest concerns. Which made me wonder what these were, and what would happen when the unleashing occurred. My protoself that harboured them was, if real, a total stranger.

The next quarter of an hour was the time Allhallows began to bite into me. It was a funny way to be caught. I wasn't meditating cross-legged in my soundproof room, alone in flight to the Alone.[12] I was crowded with nine adults at a table, leaning on my elbows, while that Asian voice glided past. Yet I was grappling with basics in a state of feverish detachment. Mei-ling's phrases wove in and out of the reverie.

'...In part, alchemy was a pre-science. Besides leading to chemistry, it foreshadowed modern physics with the concept of transmutation. But our object here must be to treat it as a species of magic, and decide what are the truths which it symbolizes. Historically it...'

My concerns. What are they? For tax purposes I count as a 'writer'. That's why I'm here. To cover Allhallows for a newspaper's readers. The editor wants it done because, for some reason that still escapes me, Allhallows is having an impact on the contemporary scene. But was that what actually got me moving? Did I sincerely want to inform the public? Or was it merely a journalistic angle, a gimmick to get me an assignment?

Why should I want the assignment anyhow? And why did Martin hint, on the first evening, that there was some special reason for me to have it? What did he see?

'...Alchemic manuals are obscure because of the cryptic language. Alchemists believed that their art was very mysterious. It was also very laborious. It demanded a lifetime of devotion. An alchemist had to be prepared for many mistakes and disappointments, and for countless repeats of even a correct process before he could hope for the great transition. The work was so secret, and so much a world of its own apart from everyday life, that aspects of it were given code names instead of descriptive ones. Such as the dragon, the grey wolf, the black crow, the king and his son, the royal marriage, the serf, the Ethiopian . . .'

Most likely it was the location that pulled me. When Martin spoke at the Free Mind Society, he didn't get at me till he mentioned that Glastonbury festival, and then he did. After which he settled here in the nimbus of Avalonian mystique. My own long-standing theme. The spell seemed to be working at Allhallows to some purpose. Therefore I wanted to find out how, to get to the bottom of it. If a paper would pay me to do that, so much the better.

'...The Philosopher's Stone itself is as hard to describe as the art which brings it into action. Alchemists write of it in contradictions. It is precious beyond price, yet also it is found everywhere and despised because unrecognized. It is divine and not divine. It is made out of fire and water, it is made out of flesh and blood. It is a stone in the usual sense of the word, or alternatively, it's not a stone at all. The Rosicrucian Michael Maier says: "From a man and a woman make a circle, then a square, then a triangle, finally a circle, and you will obtain the Philosopher's Stone." Others again...'

Go back further, though. What was it that started me on Glastonbury and Arthur and the rest? Why did I write books on them, long before Martin entered my life? To cash in on a popular chunk of British mythology? Or because I really cared about digging down to the roots of the legends? Or was it to express something inside myself, some need or conviction, which the mythos offered me a ready-made daydream for? Or perhaps (remember that chat with Karen) because Another hammered me into the shape I am, for obscure purposes of his (its) own?

'...Stress was laid on the alchemic vessel where transmutation was set in motion. Often this was a glass globe. It was called "the philosophers' egg", not only on account of its being round, but because of a cosmic symbolism. Ancient myths affirmed that the world was hatched from an egg. So also the Stone, which was a new birth of matter, would appear in the vessel. But in a more esoteric sense, the vessel stood for human nature – in fact for the alchemist himself, who would undergo rebirth and fulfilment through the work. Gold-making for profit was not, or should not be, the chief end . . .'

Then there's this business of Paul, who is facing me now over Kwame's shoulder. I'm not sure what he intends, but he's trying to involve me, and I play along. Even though he's so obviously stirring things up.

'...Another symbol of the work is the Ouroboros, the snake bent into a circle, eating its own tail. Several of you pointed out yesterday that this was the image which gave von Kekulé his chemical inspiration. The snake is one and all, an endless cycle of life and death and birth and renewal. The transmutation of base matter is the regenerative impulse that keeps the wheel turning . . .'

Why did I give Paul the go-ahead? Because – honestly now – I can use this Neo-Arthurian interest to build myself up at Allhallows as an authority, a VIP? Or because it truly matters to me that the interest should flourish, for the sake of... well, except in nebulous terms, I hardly know what? Either way, does it imply that I care more for promoting my own concerns than for doing the job I've been commissioned to do?

'...With Dr John Dee[13], who was royal astrologer to Elizabeth I, alchemy was only one pursuit among several. But his helper Kelley did give him a crimson powdery substance which he claimed to have found in the ruins of Glastonbury Abbey with instructions in cipher, and Dr Dee did test it on a warming-pan and turned part of the pan to gold. So he said. This case is typical of the mixture of occult theory, mundane practice, and probable fraud and self-deception which extends through all alchemy...'

Ye gods, why DOES an author write, and do the things which writing leads to? What are the real motives, the real compulsions in the Unconscious – or, if Martin prefers, the protoself?

From the last auto-interrogation I couldn't see anywhere else to go. My thoughts trailed aimlessly, till a change in Mei-ling's voice drew me back. She'd got to the Elixir of Life. On that topic she was sprightlier and less academic, because she knew jokes about

Taoist sages in China who had sought the recipe with unwished-for results. In Europe, she continued, the Elixir and the Stone were held to be the same thing. One legend declared that the Wandering Jew had the secret. A more favoured figure as its possessor was the Comte de St-Germain, who frequented high society in the mid-eighteenth century, and was reputed to be two thousand years old.

'As with Dr Dee,' said Mei-ling, 'we find a strange blend of facts which are really interesting with facts which point to a commonplace charlatanism. The "deathless" Comte de St-Germain was an impostor in his major claims...'

'But my dear, he wasn't.'

Mrs Frobisher had surfaced after days of near-silence. Recollecting the only long speech of hers I'd heard – on the lawn during my first time with Karen – I wondered apprehensively what was in store.

Mei-ling flashed her a polite smile. 'He wasn't?'

'Oh no, certainly not. I've met him'

Norman laughed ungraciously. Mei-ling, losing her aplomb at last, looked to Martin for guidance. He rescued her. 'This is news indeed, Mrs Frobisher. Would you like to tell us?'

Glassy-eyed, she outpoured. 'I thought it was common knowledge that St-Germain was a great Adept and Master nobody is sure when he was born but it was many centuries ago and when he revealed himself publicly in the eighteenth century he was a superhuman genius a linguist a musician a scientist – and Madame de Pompadour knew he had the Elixir and was immortal and he was received at the court of France and sent on diplomatic missions and he made jewellery and painted pictures with techniques no one has been able to reproduce and, well, in the end his enemies conspired against him and he had to withdraw so he arranged a mock funeral but came out of hiding a few years later to warn Paris against the Revolution since when he's been living mostly in eastern Europe and known to Theosophists as the Hungarian Master,' she paused for breath.

Nobody stirred. The spate resumed. 'Now I want to make this very clear, I don't want there to be any confusion about it, in 1960 or was it 1961 I was at the Haushofer Memorial Conference in Stockholm and Baron von Blumberg read a paper on the theory that the Earth is hollow and the inside is inhabited and afterwards this distinguished-looking stranger stood up and none of the delegates had any idea who he was only they believed he was a Hungarian and he told us the theory was true and when Bulwer Lytton wrote his novel *The Coming Race* about the advanced humans who live underground and use the vril-power it was meant as a serious warning - and I talked to him later and while of course he revealed no secrets he gave me a copy of Bulwer Lytton's novel which he, the Master I mean, inscribed to me in his own hand and I've brought it because I foresaw the Elixir would raise the subject.'

Mrs Frobisher rummaged in a huge handbag and extricated the book, a cheap reprint. She laid it down in front of her, open at the fly-leaf. Even across a wide arc of table-top one could read the flamboyant signature: Janos Korda.

We sat there trying to cope with this monstrous non-sequitur. As a senior member I felt it devolved on me to comment. 'But Mrs Frobisher, that doesn't say "St-Germain". It says "Janos Korda".'

'Naturally he travels incognito.'

The silence thickened. Then she began once more, and her voice held a sly foretaste of the knock-down climactic proof which was about to explode on us.

'When I got home I did some research on Bulwer Lytton and discovered that he was known to have met the Comte de St-Germain as he was then still called and put him in another novel *The Last Days of Pompeii* or was it *The Haunter and the Hauntings?* anyway you see there couldn't be any doubt of it.'

Five seconds must have crawled by before we grasped that this *was* the knock-down climactic proof. Martin came to the rescue again. 'Thank you very much, Mrs Frobisher. I'm glad you've kept our attention on the Elixir. Alchemy is such a vast field, it's easy to skimp one aspect of it. I hope Mei-ling hasn't.' He turned to her and spoke. 'You do have more on this?'

She had, but not much. When she'd finished, Martin thanked her and then, without preamble, addressed me. 'Any comments, Geoffrey?'

The invitation was loaded. Since my request for SP5 I was on trial and it mattered very much what I said. Having listened so sketchily, I could only make a wild clutch at me of the bits of Mei-ling's talk which remained with me.

'The question, surely, is what it's for. Perhaps even who it's for.'

'Could you enlarge on that?'

'Alchemy seems to me to be a species of magic which you can take two ways. I think that's brought out by what is said about the alchemic vessel. Its function may be crudely literal, or it may be spiritual and symbolic. Either the alchemist is transmuting lead into gold, or he's being, somehow, transmuted himself. One way he's exploiting the technique egocentrically, for profit and power. The other way he's taking part in a process that's higher and subtler. In a sense, divine.'

I noticed that Paul had a resentful expression. Martin looked more cheerful.

'Right,' he said. 'We must view crude gold-making as a temptation, or an incidental at best, never as the true aim of the work. Alchemy underlines a rule we should bear in mind: that *exploitation is no part of the higher magic*. To use secret lore purely for your own ends is to be shut up in the prison of your ego, your false selfhood. Then you very likely become what's known as a "black" magician.

'In the light of our thoughts here at Allhallows, we can define what it is that alchemy points to. Under some aspects at least, the Stone can be construed as a symbol of the protoself, which is our deepest being, the source of all we have the power to become. Spiritual rebirth means enabling it to work its way up towards rejoining the ego which has so nearly lost touch with it. In doing so, in coming into its own, it transmutes the psyche. As alchemy implies, this will be a long, hard, hit-and-miss process. Remember the resistance that holds the protoself down, the weight of base metal, so to speak, in human nature...'

Martin continued for several minutes. It was all very Jungian. He seemed to be arguing that alchemy supplied guidelines for a revamped psychotherapy. At the end, Kwame spoke up. 'You have been talking of the Philosopher's Stone, and the reality which you say it points to, a rebirth of human nature. I think though that you have given us no interpretation of the Elixir. To what reality does that point?'

'To just what you'd expect, Kwame. Eternal life. But eternal life linked with transformation.'

7

As we filed out of the conference room, Karen stood waiting in the hall. She took my arm and it was like a reunion after long parting.

'The rain looks as if it might ease off. I was thinking of going for a drive. Would you like to come?'

She led the way to the car-shelter and unlocked an elderly green Triumph. The rain hadn't stopped, but it was thinner, and the sky had patches of wan blue in it. We climbed into the front seats. Karen kicked off her sandals and rested bare feet against the pedals. On both of them the second toe was perceptibly longer than the first.

'Where are we going?'

She had plans for me. 'I think you ought to visit your sign. Aries the Ram.'

I understood. One of my occupational hazards has been expo-sure to notions about the Glastonbury Zodiac. The first morning at Allhallows we'd heard Mrs Frobisher briefly on those two-and-three-mile-long signs which are alleged to cover the Central Somerset landscape. There had been many such folk in my life before her - trac-ers-out of gigantic figures on Ordnance Survey maps, using roads and hills and streams, with rival opinions as to who made the figures and when.

'You believe the Zodiac's really there?'

'I'm determined to take you to your sign, whether it's there or not.'

She drove coolly, skilfully, as fast as the wet surface allowed. We left the main highway and plunged into a network of lanes. Twisting Somerset lanes with a guileless Chestertonian logic.

Before the Roman came to Rye or out to Severn strode,
The rolling English drunkard made the rolling English road:
A reeling road, a rolling road, that rambles round the shire,
And after him the parson ran, the sexton and the squire.

We were tranquil. Very little was said, and there was no pressure to make conversation. With Karen silence was already no longer awk-ward. It occurred to me that she too used SP5 and I ought to learn more of this, but when I put out a feeler she gently blocked it. To my relief if anything.

Aries, according the astral topographers, is a sheep-shape of land stretching west and southwards from Street. The Triumph nosed into the grey shoe-dominated town and swung through angles. 'Now we're on the Ram's head,' said Karen. 'Now' (as we passed a school and the road began to climb between fields) 'we're running along his chest.' A wooded ridge rose ahead. I'd traversed this area before, but there was plenty I'd never noticed. A final sharpening gradient brought us to the crest of the ridge, and the trees.

Our road ran on down the far side. But before it dropped away another road crossed it, winding along the ridge. Also a lane led off obliquely. Karen swerved across into this lane and parked the car by a patch of grass adjoining it. 'Marshall's Elm,' she announced.

'What happens at Marshall's Elm?'

'I show you a mystery.'

I'd had a besetting fancy that my dream of last night was to be fulfilled – but no. Nothing like my dream-hill was in view. Karen wasn't dressed for the part, either. She was wearing a plain skirt, about the shortest feasible for her build and general aspect.

Here, for the moment, no rain was falling. We even had a glint of sunshine. She unclasped her safety belt and dismounted.

Without putting her sandals back on, she took a step or two into the long grass on our left. I joined her.

'This is where you and I intersect,' she said.

'How do you mean?'

'I was born on May the eighth.'

'So?'

'Taurus. Over there' (she pointed along the ridge, to the left of the road that had conveyed us up from Street) 'is the Bull's head. Behind us is the Ram. You and I come together at this crossroads. Your planet's Mars, I expect you know that. Mine's Venus.'

We scrambled down a low bank on to the roadway. She padded across it on her bare feet, and led me over a second patch of grass to a stile. A few seconds later we were in a spacious field, climbing up along the ridge between copses.

'Now we're on my territory, the Bull's head. By the way, have you ever worked out what your rising sign is?'

'The ascendant? Scorpio.'

'Mine's Scorpio too. Dark, secretive, sexy.'

Her mask of youth was firmly and credibly in place. I wondered how much further this was likely to go and what was expected of me. The trees gave no cover and the grass looked discouragingly damp. 'You should be warned,' I said. 'Aries and Scorpio make a dangerous combination.'

'That's been evident for days.'

Her hair was straying with its accustomed charm, and she showed to great advantage going uphill, stepping lightly and breathing easily, avoiding the thistles in the grass without seeming to be aware of them. At the open top of the ridge a warm breeze was blowing. We looked downwards into a valley on the south side, over it to Dundon beacon, and further along the ridge to the pillar of the Hood monument thrusting up above tree-tops.

Then an image popped out of one of my memory-holes – a blown-up map of this part of the Zodiac, expounded by a tweedy gentleman at a lecture....

'Your Bull is only a fractional beast. No farmer would want him.'

'Why not?'

'Follow him through on the map. They've only traced his head and foreleg. The body is somewhere else.'

We looked each other full in the face and after a second or two the laughter came.

'Yes, Geoffrey, you're right. It is.'

'Mind you, I wouldn't despair of finding it.'

'Neither would I. But the map's the map, isn't it. I expect those Druids who laid it out had their reasons.'

We circled back amicably to the stile and the car. Our wordplay had pleased her out of all proportion to its content. She drove into Glastonbury singing Post-Folk and we ate an ample tea, during which she reminisced about her spell on the dig at Cadbury, and made plans for tomorrow's Midsummer vigil. The rain had resumed, heavier than before. But Karen was confident it would be all right on the night.

During our return journey we both sat silent again. Except once. She said: 'You must have had time to go into the SP5 thing fairly thoroughly.'

'Yes. Up to a point at least.'

'Is Martin letting you take it yourself?'

'He hasn't told me yet.'

'I'll try to get a ruling for you this evening.'

'What would your verdict be? Should I or shouldn't I?'

'If you don't know whether I want you in the family' (the road ran straight ahead and she squeezed my hand) 'you're stupider than I think you are.'

8

Midnight again. Whatever she urged on my behalf, it worked. After supper Martin came up to me. 'You can have those SP5 pills if you want.'

'Thank you. Yes.'

'Let's go and attend to it then. I have just three left in the place. They're here in my pocket. You can take those – I've reordered – but they have to be released to you formally. Paul handles the paperwork with Wessex Laboratories.'

We went upstairs to Paul's room. He was there and opened the door into a tidy bedsitter, with none of the eccentricities of my own quarters. Besides the basic furnishings, he had a desk with the extension phone and a typewriter on it and nothing else. The Well-Organized Workplace. By it was a dispenser for stationery. A wall chart showed the dates and durations of various Allhallows programmes, with red, green and blue tapes stretched across an overgrown calendar.

A TV set, with video-cassette fittings, dominated one corner. It was balanced by a combined cabinet-bookcase, more of the space in this being taken up with magazines than with books. A photo of a group of uniformed teenagers stood on top of it, maybe a school cadet corps. On other walls hung abstract paintings. In the middle of a shelf was an electric clock... an intruder: Allhallows (as I suddenly realized when I saw it) doesn't have any clocks on public view. Time is kept privately by watches, with radio checks.[14]

The SP5 ritual was undramatic. Politely, with few words, Martin and Paul went through a routine that reminded me of getting a prescription filled. Paul took a thin pad of forms from the dispenser, with carbon paper between the first two sheets. He wrote on the top sheet and handed the pad to Martin. Martin signed. Paul took it back. Martin drew a stoppered tube from his pocket and gave it to me. I unplugged it and saw three ovoid red pills inside. Paul handed me the pad and I signed in a space where it said 'Received'.

'What about the clauses in fine type?'

Martin took that more seriously than I intended. 'There aren't any. We don't tie you up with conditions or disclaimers. If I've decided I can trust someone to act sensibly, that's it. But mind you do, eh?'

'I'll do my best.'

'I must warn you of one hazard. Since those early tests, they've improved the formula. It's the same stuff, but it takes effect very much faster now. You don't have the half-hour wait.'

'Glad you told me.'

'You and Paul may like to have a chat. I'll be on my way.'

With Martin out of the room Paul's manner altered, though I didn't feel he relaxed. He opened the cabinet, revealing some bottles, and poured me a gin and lime. He drank Scotch himself.

'So you've got on to Martin's select list. Congratulations. When are you going to take the plunge?'

'I'm not sure yet.'

'Do it at Cadbury tomorrow night. On the site of Camelot. For you, it should be spectacular.'

'That might be a good idea.'

He talked on about the Cadbury visit, and the promised Cryptocratic advent, and the Grail performance after that, and the *Globe* article which I'll doubtless produce eventually. I wasn't, of course, taping this or taking notes. But reviewing it now a couple of hours later, I'd say Paul's tone has become frankly proprietorial. Cryptocracy may be Norman's show, the rest may be mine, it doesn't signify. They are Paul's now, and he's making the most of everything that his status here has channelled towards him.

He insisted I must persuade the photographer to return. 'David Jacks, isn't it?'

'Yes.'

'Tell him he's got to come. The feature will have more for him than he thinks before we're through. And media-wise, it may well be only the beginning.'

'I'm a bit... uncertain... about the thing you're staging in the temple.' (What were those packages?)

Paul topped up his glass. 'Ah, so you detect a whiff of sulphur. That doesn't worry me. I have a theory on this topic of Satanism and so-called black magic. It gets a bad press because it goes with efficiency, which the sweetness-and-light brigade can't stomach.'

'Would you go over that more slowly?'

'An action replay. Fair enough. Well now, you're a student of history. Think of Rome and Carthage. If we're to believe Rome, the Carthaginians were the biggest devil-worshippers of the ancient world. Roasting babies alive for Moloch and all that. But does it strike you that they were also the greatest merchant venturers, the most practical businessmen of their time?'

'So?'

'Just this. Whatever spirits the Carthaginians tapped, divine or infernal, those must have been the Spirits That Get Things Done with no nonsense about it. They'd never have bothered with any others.[15] Or take some of the Satanists of the Christian era. Gilles de Rais – a successful general. Madame de Montespan – a royal mistress who did very well for herself. Shady magic interests me as being practical magic. The good boys smear it because they're impractical themselves.'

'You believe in it? Literally?'

'Why all the propaganda against it if it isn't effective? Do you know what – I'd love to try a bit of necromancy. Questioning the dead. You start by stealing the grave-clothes off a corpse and wearing them for nine days. You recite the burial service over yourself so as to get as near death as possible. Then you open a grave soon after midnight and touch the corpse with a wand, and lay it out with its head to the east, and adjure it to answer you. They say it'll stand upright and do your will.'

'You're welcome to find out. Personally I'd rather not.'

Paul wasn't listening. 'Procedure. Ritual. Such a field to explore... and so many inhibitions. That stuff of Martin's today about the inner meaning of alchemy, transformation of the magician and so forth. What he doesn't tell them is that there's far more to it than vague uplift. The grades in a magician's progress are all defined. There's a hierarchy. (And I do understand hierarchies. I told you I was an organ-ization consultant, and before that I was assistant personnel manager at Hadley Transistors.) Only... the magicians who've explained all this are the sort Allhallows doesn't dwell on. Like Crowley.'

'That's hardly fair. Martin's mentioned him several times.'

'A kid-glove approach. He likes some of his ideas in the abstract, but he soft-pedals the techniques and the motives. Crowley's rituals are meant to raise you to higher and higher levels of power.'

'Self-promotion up the magical pyramid, in fact.'

'The lowest rank of magician is Neophyte. Second is Zelator, the trainee in self-discipline. Third is Practicus, the trainee in intellectual matters. Fourth is Philosophus, who learns the ethics of the art. Fifth is Adeptus Minor, who applies sex-magic to unchain his true self. Sixth is Adeptus Major, who enjoys the fruits - wealth, knowledge, women, power over others. Seventh is Adeptus Exemptus, who perfects the previous training. Eighth is Magister Templi, who attains understanding of the universe. Ninth is Magus, who uses that understanding with total mastery. Tenth and highest is Ipsissimus, who is beyond all this and beyond the comprehension of those in lower degrees.'

I'd heard it before, and knew where to look for it in print. Paul's researches have been less than profound. However, he did spring a surprise on me now. 'I want to show you a film. One of a series that the Therian Constellation has just put out.'

He loaded a video-cassette into the TV and a figure appeared on the screen - a bearded man rather like Paul himself, but older, wearing a white coronet and a clinging white robe. He was standing inside a circle drawn on the studio floor, three paces across. There was writing around the rim of the circle, but the camera angle made it unreadable. There was also a shallow metal bowl on a little table, with a low flame burning in it. Beside the bowl was a jar. The man sprinkled the flame with the contents of the jar. Greenish smoke swirled upwards. An offstage drum began to beat a slow rhythm. Walking round the circle, he chanted.

> Thee do I invoke, the Endless.
> Thee, that didst create the Earth and the Heavens.
> Thee, that didst create Night and Day.
> Thee, that didst create darkness and light.
> Thou art Asar-Un-Nefer: whom no man hath seen at any time.
> Thou art Ia-Besz.
> Thou art Ia-Apophrasz.
> Thou hast distinguished between the Just and the Unjust.
> Thou didst make the Female and the Male.
> Thou didst produce the seeds and the fruit.
> Thou didst form men to love one another and to hate one another....

The magician paced more and more swiftly, chanting without a break. His words grew more outlandish, the drum-beat grew faster.

Presently he halted, stared at a point in front of him, and appeared to go into a trance. When he resumed, his voice was still his but subtly changed, as if another being had taken partial control of him.

> *I am He! the Endless!*
> *I am He! the Truth!*
> *I am He! that lighteneth and thundereth!*
> *I am He, from whom is the shower of life on earth!*
> *I am He, whose mouth ever flameth!*
> *I am He, the Grace of the Worlds!*
> 'The Heart girt with a Serpent' is my name.[16]

The camera zoomed in on the speaker's face, which was certainly re-shaped in a disturbing way. Then the screen darkened. Paul switched off and thrust a booklet into my hands. 'Read that, it goes with it, you'll find all the words and a commentary.'

Undoubtedly the film had affected him. He'd been drinking right through since Martin left, yet he wasn't exactly drunk. It was alcohol plus ritual, ritual plus alcohol. He now seemed high, peculiar. He ran his hand over his beard and fidgeted, prowling backwards and forwards, opening drawers and disarranging their neatly sorted contents. After several remarks jerked off into vacancy he tossed me a question.

'Where did she take you?'

The anti-climax was so grotesque that it took me a moment to adjust. 'Do you mean Karen?'

'Yes of course I do, I mean her, I saw you go off.'

'That was clever of you. Where were you?'

'Around. Around.' He didn't keep still, he went on with his gyrating and rummaging. 'Well?'

'We drove out to Street and then Glastonbury.'

'To Street and then Glastonbury. In the car all the time? No stops?'

'We walked up a hill to see the view, when the sun was out.'

'Listen, friend. Nobody makes passes at our lady housewarden. Nobody.'

'I didn't.'

'Just a word to the wise.'

'Mind you,' I said, 'she doesn't strike me as past it exactly.'

He spun round and confronted me. He had a pistol in his hand. It was too startling to frighten, and anyhow he was wiping it nervously with a cloth.

'What are you going to do with that, shoot me?'

'No, no. I wouldn't. Martin wouldn't either.'

'Martin?'

'You know how it is with those two. You must.'

'They haven't told me. Why should they?'

'SP5. You know about it. They go on SP-trips together every three months and aren't seen for days. In between, nothing. Separate rooms. Couldn't care less. *He* doesn't care... but she doesn't either. I tell you, nobody. NOBODY.'

An ugly rise of pitch betrayed him. This wasn't a wholly disinterested assessment But after all, I reflected, he's younger than Karen. Maybe ten years. Meanwhile he was still polishing that absurd gun, and his train of thought was still changing course like a snooker ball bouncing off the cushions.

'We don't have eternal triangles here. Not even the magic sort. Magic squares though. You take my meaning.'

I did, not to my relish. I didn't speak.

'The young one now, the reformed junkie. You'll have run your expert eye over her too. Anything to report?'

'How could there be? I've seen very little of her.'

Paul wasn't so far gone as to crack the senile joke about 'seeing more of her', but he shot off again as if it had cracked inside his head. 'That hippie gear she wears. California Late Sixties, all covered up and no shape. You mightn't guess it, but oh yes, there's something underneath. Very definitely something. I could unfold a tale. In moderate doses, you understand . . .'

I got up and edged towards the exit. 'Yes, you don't have to enlarge. I noticed Annabel yesterday morning. Now I'd better say good-night—'

He didn't detain me, but he edged with me. 'You noticed. Talk about spying, eh?' (No one had, but still.) 'You're quite a noticer. I see why your editor sent you here. Another thing you noticed. That Wessex Labs chap yesterday bringing the stuff, right?'

'Why yes, now you mention it.'

The Finger and the Moon

He was about to say more, then didn't. The door closed behind me. Those last words are nagging now like a piece of grit in a shoe. I can't lay my finger on the reason. Too tired.

Fifth Day

RAIN FELL RUTHLESSLY through the night and was still pelt-
ing down at breakfast. However, the forecast was hopeful.
Everybody agreed that our Cadbury vigil should still be on.
Now - five hours later - the weatherman has yet to be vindicated.
The rain is lighter but hasn't ceased.

After breakfast the students dispersed to do household jobs.
Nobody has hinted that I ought to pitch in myself. I keep my room
tidy, and wash the odd dish or sweep the odd patch of floor to show
willing, but I've not been put on the rota. Theoretically at least I can
sit and read or ruminate without guilt. But I keep a reporter's notebook handy and am seen to be writing in it at intervals.

About 9:15 I went to the empty recreation room and settled into
a chair near the window. That tube with the three pills was in my
pocket. When and how? What were the likeliest effects, what would
be the most favourable milieu?

I had Martin's diary with me, and explored it beyond the first two
sections in search of guidance. It was strangely unhelpful. On my
initial survey I'd noticed that it got harder to understand as it went
along, but assumed that once I grasped the main drift, the tangled
parts would unravel. To my distress I found that most of them didn't.
Martin's insouciance in exposing the diary to his students doesn't
seem as rash as it did. Only a genius could fight his way through it to
any purpose.

Several of the entries describe (or fail to describe) Martin's further
ventures in body-control and brain-control while in the protoself.
Others try to spell out his insights into material objects. He devotes
three pages to an egg. Such passages make only fitful sense to me.
They're full of short cuts, cross-references, even non-language, squar-

ing visionary circles with *ad hoc* formulae that look like chemistry but surely are not. Also there are the paragraphs in cipher....

My judgement after a longish perusal was that the entries likeliest to repay effort – apart from the first two – were those that involved people rather than things. As Martin had hinted, several of them were sombre. Networks of brain-cells charged with his suppressed memories had been stung into disgorging hideous loads of pain and squalor. I felt more respect for him as I traced him through these uncharted nightmares. But another feature intrigued me more. He often reverted to that experience of looking at somebody and seeing the light-cloud or aura which he supposed to be the protoself. The entries where he did, though scattered throughout the diary, had an air of composing a linked series. He used plainer language in them. He drew comparisons. Also, nearly all had cipher texts after them, as if carrying some special message.

I'd left the diary's notebook-companion in my room and couldn't tackle the cipher at once. For the same reason I couldn't look up the circumstances of these visions. Mrs Frobisher was vacuuming the stair-carpet, and caution counselled me to put off fetching the note-book rather than risk getting caught in a verbal deluge. Even without background details, I could still guess.

The following, for instance, appeared to have happened on a big public occasion where Martin had seen the crowd from above, prob-ably from a high building.

Each individual's light was vivid. Where people stood close-packed the shimmering globes and flames often touched, but I don't think they mingled. The sun set and the park grew dim: even in State E the aura is never visible light. The crowd was good-humoured.

Suddenly it all fell away from me as if the space had grown huge. Myriads of human light-dots blended into one mass. Stars forming a Milky Way. The mass was not equally bright over its whole area, The dots were like those in a newspaper half-tone photo, and like those, they made a picture. I couldn't see it well, you might say the screen was too coarse, but I got an impression of a wide bright valley leading into the distance, and an ineffable sense of peace and homecoming.

The cryptographic pendant ran thus:

FIDFA DBVCZ NAOGN DMJCE APSFE WGXFC
GEZWF BFVPF EGUPK UWVEM DAZOK SANLT.
BFNOA DDYFN ZWOZW AVQUE UEEWZ OLTON
SFEGZ JKZRF

No key, no message. You can't break a Playfair by a simple frequency count. Mrs Frobisher was still noisily within earshot. While waiting for her to finish I read another test-record of the same type, which told how Martin had swallowed his pill in a hospital and then sat beside a patient watching him die – by permission, I inferred, of a 'Dr J.' who figured twice in the record. Martin's aim in this macabre exercise was obvious, and he was rewarded with... something.

Dr J. recognized the moment of death and signalled. The patient's aura had been glowing throughout, despite coma, and hanging over the body without any movement. Death made no difference. The aura persisted, and had not gone when I returned to normal.

Evidence for 'survival'? Yes and no. In State E there was no excite-ment, no sense of an age-old riddle solved. The fact wasn't responded to as evidence, because I had no awareness of a case to be proved or disproved. The fact was simply the fact. It is only in retrospect that I feel it as more.

The cloud of light over the bed was iridescent as usual, with gleams of red, blue and other colours, though the prevailing effect as usual was sil-very. After death a faint golden-yellow was seeping into it. The strange-ness of the tinge made me think that this was exceptional, that this part of the spectrum hadn't shown for me before, in the auras of living persons. (Must watch for it.)

Again the cipher:

CNHLW DMEAR FABHB YFCNJ WFWZL FEPVW
YBAZA JDBWD IOAHA OMFSO PZ

2

Karen came in. 'I think we've got the chores safely under way, so I'm putting my feet up for a while. Are you busy?'

I explained. She did put her feet up, on a settee within quiet talking range.

'Yes,' she commented, 'I remember those bits of Martin's diary. They tie in with my own first sampling. Would that interest you?'

'Immensely.'

'I wasn't part of the test programme, but he persuaded them to dole me out a few pills. By the way, has he given you yours?'

'Yes.'

'Good, and when will you start?'

'I'm still wondering.'

'Don't wonder too long. If you have an impulse that says "now", that's it.'

'Did you?'

'Very much so. It was a few days after our Glastonbury Tor session.'

'I guessed that K. was you.'

'Yes, well, Martin doesn't give you the whole story there. He was more restless during that SP-trip than I let on to him afterwards. Robert and Caroline stopped walking, if you remember. The real reason was that I called out to them to stop, in case help was needed. That conversation of theirs... they told me later they were arguing about the experiment. Robert thought Martin was making a fool of himself, Caroline was open-minded. And all the time they were looking out of the corners of their eyes for fear he'd come tumbling down the hill.',

'He didn't, though.'

'No. But he took a while recovering. We sent Robert and Caroline home and wandered on into Cornwall. I drove - Martin couldn't have kept his mind on it. He was interpreting his visions and writing madly. I wasn't in an idyllic mood myself, we were near our crisis then, the one I told you about.

'He was pressuring me to take my first SP5 pill. I think he felt lonely till I did. But it seemed like getting hooked somehow, even if the stuff didn't do that. Also I was trying to groom him for a conference I'd wangled him an invitation to - oh dear, it's all so tragi-comic and long ago. Sorry.'

'No need to be.'

'We stayed at a pub near Tintagel and walked down to the cove very early in the morning. It was cool and the tide was coming in. No one else was about yet. We went into that cave under the headland. You must know it, the one that pierces right through, and when the tide rises the sea floods into it with a lot of roaring and spray.'

'Merlin's Cave.'

She nodded. 'I'm glad you confirm it's actually called that. When Martin told me, I wondered.... Anyway. The sea was pushing in at the far end and getting towards the narrow part of the tunnel. We clambered around for a few minutes, then walked back and out to the cove. I stood on the beach and looked at the cave-mouth we'd just come out of, and it hit me. NOW.'

'SP5, you mean.'

'It wasn't very logical. The tide was encroaching on us, and after seeing how Martin reacted on the Tor, I'd more reason to be scared than he knew. But this just had to be it, this was where SP5 would speak for me.'

'And did it?'

'I put the pill in my mouth. (They dissolve, in case Martin hasn't told you, you can take them without water.) I wandered about the beach and then sat on a rock, and presently the thing worked. At first it was a let-down. Yes, I could see what he meant about the world being more significant from that vantage-point. It was as if everything I looked at was The Product in a perfectly fabulous TV commercial. You remember, I was in advertising. But it ended there. I didn't catch a glimmer of those beautiful patterns of his. I've seen them since, in a way, but not then. Only one thing happened, really, and yet you could say he's built up half his ideas on it since.

'Two people walked out of the cave and stood on a patch of sand. I was surprised – no, that's wrong – I felt I ought to be and wasn't. There hadn't been anybody around when we went in ourselves, or since. There they were all the same, a tall man with longish hair and a beard, and a young dark woman. They had funny clothes on, but no funnier than I'd often seen on pop fans and hitch-hikers. The man had a fawn-coloured cloak fastened on his shoulder, a long heavy shirt, baggy trousers, and sandals. His cloak had an emblem on it. The way he moved made me think he was middle-aged, but exciting middle-aged. He could have made girls fall for him, like Picasso. The woman was bare-footed and wore a cape over an ankle-length dress with long sleeves and a decorated belt, rather off-Carnaby[1]. That dates me.'

'Not so you have to worry.'

'Let's hope not. Well, I did see the auras of these two, like Martin had seen on Robert and Caroline, only more so. They were part of him and part of her, and the auras were what they *meant*, what they were *about*. The person belonged to the light, not the other way round. They were great big splendid lights – rainbowy flames whirl-ing and touching each other, responding back and forth in the air.'

Karen turned to me. 'If I said they were responding sexually would you believe it?'

'I'd try. You saw them, I didn't.'

'I saw them and they were. They – the couple I mean – were simply talking, not touching. I don't recall catching any words. But it was all so different at that level. The woman made it plain. She wasn't like me, but I felt close, I seemed to be thinking with her mind... and I hated it. The flames were inter-twining and dancing, caressing each other – that couple were made to be lovers and their flames knew – but the wretched little mortal selves were all at cross purposes. The lovely thing that was meant to be couldn't get through to them. Something hideous was building up in that woman – something calculating. They were doomed because she wanted to use the man more than love him, and it would kill whatever she felt for him now.... This must sound muddled.'

'No, I follow you all too closely.'

'That's it, then.'

'But what came next?'

'Nothing. My dose wore off, and when I opened my eyes the couple had gone. Only—'

I interrupted her. 'May I guess what's coming?'

'Do.'

'They'd never been there at all.'

'Full marks, Geoffrey. Martin said the beach had been empty all the time. I ran down to check for footprints before the sea washed over the patch of sand. Not a trace.'

It sounded disturbingly like a ghost-story or Versailles Adventure[2]. 'You know, Karen... if I were going to criticize... my comment would be that it's too good to be true. Those characters in that setting! Right in front of his own cave! It doesn't fit the theory either. Surely

Martin's imagination-pictures weren't in the real landscape. They were apart from it, weren't they? Like on a screen.'

'Exactly what he complained of himself. He went over and over my story trying to shake me. That's why it's still so vivid, he grilled me so long.'

'Well then?'

'Well then. The part he approved straight off was the coupling of the flames. He built a lot on that. He decided in the end (I quote) that *protoselves are in direct contact with each other.* Or can be. Quite apart from what the people are doing. You and I may not be communicating at all, you may be downstairs and I may be upstairs, but our protoselves may be communicating like mad, and bits of it may seep through to us. Thoughts, promptings, who knows?'

'This must be what Martin meant when he dropped hints about telepathy.'

'I expect so. But you see what he got out of it. He could have it both ways, be scientific and mystical at once. He could go along with his friends who told him we don't have preternormal powers, and keep the door open just the same for telepathy, occult influences, even spell-casting. They all work, but through the other part of his Binary Man, the part scientists can't get at. Magicians' routines make sense too – as gimmicks for persuading the protoself to cough up.'

'Wait,' I said. 'Let's make certain I've got this right. A fortune-teller deals out her cards and tells me about myself and my prospects. The suggestion is that her protoself locks on to mine and they converse, and the card-reading that's going on all the while is...'

'An incantation. A ritual. It helps her protoself to come through with what it picks up from yours. Remember Steve's numerology. You get brilliant successes and total flops. Sometimes the protoselves make contact and sometimes they don't. The technique can only work when they do.'

'Which accounts for... quite a range of phenomena. Clairvoyance, to go no further. Like that American Edgar Cayce, who diagnosed illnesses in a trance and prescribed for them and seemed able to tap all the medical expertise in the world without any training.'

'Yes,' said Karen, 'I've heard of him. But he only did it in the trance. His waking self couldn't. It was the Other that roamed around getting inside patients and picking doctors' brains. You do see?'

'I think so. Then in ordinary life – those curious impulses, and acting as if you knew what you don't know—'

'What you told me about yourself. Yes. It has to be everybody, not just clairvoyants and fortune-tellers.'

Karen swung round into a sitting posture and faced me. 'It's true, you know. When it's pointed out to you, you see it. I realized long ago, this... communion or whatever you call it... is the secret of love. X and Y may quarrel and claw each other and behave like idiots, while their other selves are in blissful harmony the whole time, knowing better. In fact X and Y may not be much more than a silly underplot in the real action.'

Cool it for now, I thought. 'Tell me about the rest of your Tintagel scene, how you figured it out.'

'Martin spotted the same thing you did, it was so obvious. I didn't though, I had a blockage. You could say it was the "inwardness" of my own psyche. Too close for comfort.'

'I'm not with you.'

'You will be. Martin cross-questioned me and finally came down hard on one detail, that emblem on the man's cloak. He asked me to draw it. I could only remember it was in two parts, red and white. But he insisted I should take a pencil and try, and then an outline came back to me. Two winged animals, one red and one white, posed as if they were fighting. Martin told me a legend of how a red and white dragon fought each other, and Merlin became famous by making prophecies on the subject.'

'That's correct. It's in Geoffrey of Monmouth.'

'So then, the man simply had to be Merlin and the woman had to be Merlin's girlfriend, the one who got her teeth into him and exploited him, and then trapped him in a cave with his own spell. Nimuë, wasn't it?'

'The name varies. Nimuë, Vivien.'

'I had to admit later, after our crisis, that it was a bit like the situation we'd been getting into ourselves. Which I hope I needn't go over again? I was tuned to pick that episode up. What bothered Martin, though, was that it wasn't memory and yet he couldn't explain it as fantasy. I'd actually seen Merlin and Nimuë fourteen centuries ago – is it fourteen?'

'Probably nearer fifteen.'

'A long time anyway. We solved this in the end, but it meant taking an awful leap. Martin said: "If protoselves can contact each other, pass ideas back and forth, and so on, we've got the answer to this too. There was a middle-man. That scene was transmitted by the protoself of somebody else, who saw it at the time and re-projected it for you." I said: "All right, but this witness of yours must have been dead more than a thousand years. You're suggesting his protoself is still hovering in the cove, reminiscing for my benefit?"

'Martin jumped at it, just like that. After he'd done a few more trips of his own he concluded we'd found the real immortality. Protoselves go on. The *being* of you and me - it goes on. When we die we're re-absorbed into presences that don't. You into yours, I into mine.'

'So those survive and communicate with the living and... now you're accounting for Spiritualism too.'

'If you like.' She glanced at her watch. 'Excuse me, Geoffrey, I have to go and keep an eye on the kitchen. We've got something special cooking - literally. I tell you what, though. You've got the diary there. Do you know how to read the cipher bits?'

'I think so, but I haven't tried yet.'

'See if you can. You'll find they tie in with the things you said to me the first morning you were here.'

3

(Memo for further consideration. Can you ever complete an inquiry into a man's ideas, if every step forward places a fresh question-mark over what those ideas are really based on and why he holds them? What becomes of a guru when his woman is bright enough to blow the gaff?)

Mrs Frobisher had long since finished her vacuuming. I climbed an empty staircase and fetched the notebook from my room. After one false start I ascertained that the Playfair diagram for both the texts I'd singled out was keyed by the word WONDERFUL.* The appendix to Martin's story of the dying patient unravelled as:

* For an explanation of the method see any cryptographic handbook, or Dorothy Sayers, *Have His Carcase*, Chapter 26.

GOLDEN SOLAR LIGHT OF EGO
RETURNS TO THE SEA WHENCE LIFE COMES

A shade flowery, but I re-read the preceding text and saw how it fitted. The longer cipher, following the crowd scene, was in two parts:

A COLLECTIVE UNCONSCIOUS
MADE UP OF INTERCOMMUNING PROTOSELVES
QUERY.
CROWLEY QUOTE
EVERY MAN AND EVERY WOMAN IS A STAR

I recognized the 'quote' from the ubiquitous Crowley - it's in his
alleged revelation the *Liber Legis*. However, the preceding Jungian
notion was the nub of the message. It looked here as if Martin was
striding out far beyond his master.

With Karen's advice in mind, I tackled the other cipher texts.

Hindsighted familiarity had doubtless made them easier for her
than for me. Still, by leafing back and forth and sifting the actual drug-
records carefully, I was able to put together a new section of Martin's
mosaic.

I'll have to check with him later, but as far as I can see he has a
theory of the Collective Unconscious which purports to unveil what
Jung left wrapped in mystery. According to Jung, every psyche
shares in a vast vague racial inheritance, which has in it the archetypes of our dreams, our myths, our religions; and we all draw on it
in our various degrees. Martin has personalized this limbo. I think
- in fact I'm sure - that he has taken a hint from Yeats, who wrote of
the same unseen realm (before Jung himself expounded it) as 'Anima
Mundi', and conceived it as a 'sea of commingling spirits'.

In this case, protoselves. At that level, the hidden-part-of-the-iceberg level, each of us has a zone of occult contact with the whole company of protoselves: those of the living and those of the fellow-humans
whom we dismiss as dead. With the 'being', in fact, of everybody who
has ever existed. The proto-realm is inside us and all about us.

We have only glimmerings of its nature. It has another time than
ours, multidimensional. The Australian aborigines' Dream Time,
where the events of myth take place, reflects a twilight awareness

of it which has slipped away from civilized peoples. It is not a realm of mirage but of deepest truth, 'inwardness', a source therefore of living patterns and symbols. When Jung argued that conscious life obeys the unconscious archetypes, he was putting abstract words to a process which is anything but abstract. 'As above, so below,' in the language of a major magical document, the Emerald Table of Hermes Trismegistus. One world of life is geared in with another world of life.

When the protoselves are out on their own, detached from the mortal binary, Martin is apt to call them 'presences'. He doesn't picture them as embalmed in changeless eternity. They experience; they interact; and through the living, they affect our world and our minds and our behaviour. Things *happen* in the proto-realm as they do in our visible surroundings. There, much of what the superstitious regard with awe and terror is generated – apparitions, spell-castings, strange influences, irrational events. Sometimes in part through conscious human co-operation. Witchcraft in the vulgar sense is not total self-deception, it can tap energies, even when the witch is a silly old woman who has no idea what she's doing.

In the proto-realm, creative imagination finds its models. This is the abode of gods and dragons and giants, and malignant devilish powers too... or of entities that come through to mythweaving Man under those images. In our normal waking lives we can't encounter the other-world directly. But myths capture fragments of it. Sleepers dream of it. Poets and prophets have shadowy glimpses of it. Magicians who invoke spirits conjure up visitations from it. The success of the makers of myth and ritual, from the Sumerians to Tolkien, has depended on their skill at translating the proto-realm into images that strike chords in those for whom the making is done.

Very rarely we are given a near-proof. Hence Paul's reading, on my second night here, from the Babylonian Creation-Epic and *Paradise Lost*. Both passages describe or rather interpret the same events. Yet Milton could not have read the Creation-Epic, which wasn't rediscovered till two centuries later. He and the Babylonian author both 'saw' proto-events through their other selves.[3]

Martin's map of the unseen world certainly has advantages over Jung's. Because he builds it up out of individuals, he can include memories in it, memories of the protoselves' earthly lives. It isn't a

Collective Impersonal God-Knows-What outside history. Real experiences, scenes actually gone through on our mundane sphere, have streamed and are streaming into the flux. Which means that the legend-maker, the seer, the medium, may recover bits of the past through his own protoself and then give them his own colouring without entirely effacing them.

Karen was right. I do see how this would resolve the mystery she beguiled me into lecturing on, the other day - the mystery of legends, their bizarre retention of madly distorted facts, their rightness by way of wrongness. Take this faërie Avalonian landscape. Conceive a few master-protoselves or 'presences' lingering in it over the centuries: That-which-appeared-as-Arthur brooding like a mist on Cadbury-Camelot; That-which-appeared-as-Dunstan, the great abbot, shining among the ruins of Glastonbury. Then all this local mythology unfolds as a fabric woven by the living, half-blindly, out of wisps of their august revelations. Mainly garbled and fanciful, but still passing on enough facts to... to vindicate those who've taken the legends seriously, and gone excavating in that faith, and punctured a lot of 'exact scholarship' in the process.

This, I infer, is how Martin construes his vision of the falling tower. The light blazing above it would be one of the Glastonbury presences. A medieval builder saw the tower fall, saw with an expert eye, and his immortal nature flashed the memory into Martin when SP5 opened the gate. That was Martin's first inkling of the proto-realm as alive. The diary shows that as his use of the drug progressed, further contacts gave him some of those hints of telepathy and precognition which he'd told me to watch out for.

To sum up what I think I now understand. The proto-realm combines the Jungian Collective Unconscious and the Yeatsian Anima Mundi. Or rather it makes them out to be the same. It's also the Astral Plane or 'Akasha' which Madame Blavatsky and Rudolf Steiner discoursed upon - the storehouse of cosmic memory, where countless past happenings are on record and recoverable. An all-embracing conception indeed.

How far back in time can it take us? Martin has a diary entry that refers to a barrier. I gather he thinks that beyond a certain point, archaic humanity is too alien for us to reach. But myths of a lost golden age, however misplaced as to date and setting, still have traces of factual memory in them: memory of the days of the high original magic before Binary Man, before the split-off ego began to trap itself in its own systems. The presences have not forgotten that era. They have haunted later generations with tales of the primordial union of Earth and Heaven, when men walked with gods and spirits in harmony, and death held no terrors because immortality was simply a fact of experience. Tales of an age when the doors of the proto-realm were still partly open....

4

I went in to dinner a little late. All the students were standing around chatting, with glasses in their hands. In spite of the greyness and wet outside, the atmosphere was almost festive. Karen was popping in and out of the kitchen helping to carry culinary supplies for a chap I hadn't seen before. He was long-haired, clean-shaven, not young but seeming so, one of those over-thirty male evergreens who began to be noticed in the 1960s and are now common. His chief garment was a caftan, worn with some panache over loose-fitting trousers.

'Who's this?' I asked Mr Frobisher.

'I gather his name is Hugh McTaggart and he's the leader of a commune near Butleigh.'

That rang a bell. 'The one Annabel was at?'

'Was she? I wouldn't know. They have theories on food and drink. This' (he raised his glass) 'is a hot infusion of leaves. In a moment we're going to be given some recipes, and then eat them.'

'May I have your attention please?' shouted Hugh. 'I'd like to tell you about the meal we're putting on.

'First, the stuff in your glasses. It's a herbal brew. Herbs are valuable foci of cosmic forces. They trap the subtler rays and transmute them into a form we can absorb. This particular drink is made from the Holy Black Mint.' He waved a specimen. 'I crushed a handful of leaves gently, dropped them in a teapot, filled it with boiling water and let it stand for three minutes, repeating the process in further teapots till we had enough to go round.

'We're following up with Spring Herb Soup. For this, you put a finely chopped onion in a pan with some vegetable oil. You cook till it's transparent, add five tablespoons of millet flakes, and stir with a wooden spoon. Add two pints of water and a dash of sea-salt and bring to the boil – still stirring. Let it simmer for ten minutes and put in four sprigs of parsley and one each of mint, sage, marjoram and thyme, all finely chopped. Stir some more.' He showed specimens of all the items he mentioned, with an approximate dumb show of the actions. 'We had to treble everything here, because we've got such a big party.'

Most of us sat down. Steve, reverting with a flourish to his profession, waited at table. 'I'll expect tips,' he said as he dispensed dishes of creamy green liquid.

Martin played up to the prevailing mood. 'This gives me an idea. Magical menus. We could start with witchcraft. Any suggestions from the covens, Owen? Or Kwame?' They shook their heads. 'How about the brew in *Macbeth*? Poisoned entrails, venomous toad...'

Other members of the party began to quote ingredients of the cauldron.

'Fillet of snake.'

'Eye of newt.'

'Wool of bat and tongue of dog.'

'Root of hemlock.'

'Nose of Turk and Tartar's lips.'

'Jew's liver.'

'There you are then,' Martin summed up when nobody could remember any more. 'A gruel thick and slab. Wicca Special. You could suggest it to the chef at the club, Steve.'

'Don't put them off,' said Hugh. 'We have more to come.'

Actually the main course was orthodox. But when that had been cleared away, Hugh introduced his version of muesli. 'A lot of people have no use for muesli because they think it's boring. Also they grumble that it causes wind in the bowels. The secret is to start with a sweet apple of the right kind. Ideally, the kind we grow in our Avalonian orchard near Butleigh. Grate it into a bowl and add an equal amount of oats and some raisins. Squeeze in the juice of half a lemon, and add milk. You can sweeten it with a tablespoon of Barbados sugar. In our commune we don't, but I've made a concession to your weakness. That'll give enough for two, so here we've used seven apples, and everything else in proportion. To liven it up some more I've given you a few strawberries.'

The muesli passed round. It was nicer than I thought it would be.

Hugh wasn't staying long, but I had a chance to talk with him. It turned out that he'd been at a lecture I gave in the meeting-room of another community not far from his. He approved. 'We have a good relation with that group. It's all different aspects of the same New Age⁴ thing, the same polyhedral life-style. Our own line is macrobiotics, but we like to aim at a broad non-technical appeal – as with these recipes today.'

'You're in a great tradition with your diet ideas. Pythagoras onward.'

'Pythagoras is a special study of mine. You have to see him as a whole, with the geometry as part of a spiritual wisdom. Of course he's the same person who is known in the East as Buddha. The name "Pythagoras" is a Greek corruption of "Buddhaguru", Buddha the Master.'

I groped helplessly for an adequate response. Hugh rattled on. 'Buddha attained enlightenment under a fig-tree. 'The figs were of a rare species and he'd been living on them for weeks. *Ficus religiosus*. It has ingredients that strengthen the inner vision. That's why, when he travelled westward and taught the Greeks, he laid so much stress on diet.'

'Tell me,' I said, 'is your commune the one Annabel lived in for a while?'

'Yes, that's us. We all love Annabel. But I'd met Martin before, of course. We helped him to get Allhallows ready. I designed the maze. Have you been into it yet?'

'Not yet.'

'Annabel can tell you about it when the right moment comes.'

Somebody else wanted to put a question on herbs, and time was short, so I took my leave of him. He did look extraordinarily healthy.

5

Up here though in my room, that agreeable interlude is past and I am thinking aloud at my tape-recorder, the immediate issue unresolved. Am I any nearer to a decision about my own SP5 plunge, which is probably my sole chance of getting behind this Allhallows word-magic?

Deep concerns. True purposes. I recall what I told these people two days, three days ago. Details in my life do seem as if contrived by some unseen agency, to steer me on certain lines and confirm that I was being steered. I'm not fancying myself to be the Elect of God. Only noticing what I think happens to many people, but they usually overlook or forget it. On Martin's reading I must presume that my protoself – whatever and where-ever it is – has always known best, and has been consulting its colleagues and pulling wires in the other-realm, to make events in this one come out as intended for me.

I see a flaw, though. What about those significant coincidences before I was born, like names and birthdays of senior relatives? How could my protoself have contrived those? Apparently Martin asks me to believe that it will go on after my death. Was it also around before my birth? Does he bring in re-incarnation on top of the rest?

Come to think of it, that could be what he's driving at in a most peculiar diary passage. He scribbled a reference to Jung in the margin, and I got the book from the library but haven't looked it up yet....

The paragraph he means is in *The Integration of the Personality*. Jung says that what he calls the Unconscious doesn't seem to have a distinct personality. Instead it has traces of many personalities, which come to the fore in dreams. Yes, I can see why this would have pulled Martin up. If accepted it knocks the protoself, the other pole of his own Binary Man, squarely on the head. Not to mention exploding its immortality. If it isn't a single entity, what survives, and what is the proto-realm composed of?

The SP5 trip which has this note in the margin, now.... It's very short. Its background is a visit to an unnamed woman novelist who claimed to 'remember' the reign of Henry II. I know who Martin means, she was interviewed when her book was published. He writes that he found this woman attractive, that he took SP5 in her company and... the record ends almost before it's started, with a diagram that doesn't make sense to me

Wait. This is like Case 407, the sex-troubled sculptor. At least one sheet has been pulled out of the binder. Have we a scandal here? I believe Martin's in his study. Let's see if he's willing to divulge.

*   *   *   *   *

He divulged. Not as expected.

I showed him the open diary with its obvious gap, and was shocked at the effect on him. He looked sad and old, and stumbled over several answers before he got a grip on himself.

'Yes, Geoffrey, I was wondering if you'd ask. I decided I wouldn't draw your attention to it, but you could read those pages if you did ask.' He took a folder from the same cabinet as before, and handed me two sheets from it. They filled the gap and completed the record.

I can't even begin to reproduce what I read, and I'm not seeking his permission to make a copy. It was incoherent and utterly harrowing. A few seconds after the drug took hold, some inner probe touched the most deeply buried nerve of all, his memory of his dead wife – Frances was her name – and her cancer. The ensuing vision was a kaleido-scope of anguish. Even the handwriting was shaky. I gathered that in the final phase of her disease, Frances had been almost unrecogniz-able. He saw her again like that, only worse, because of a twist of SP5 insight making the cancer repulsively alive and its victim a wraith. He also saw her as she'd been in her best days. But his glimpses of Frances were jumbled in a geometrical nightmare (whence the diagram) with glimpses of other women. He searched desperately among the figures presented to him, trying to identify the real Frances. One moment she was none of them and the next she was all of them, and then she was various permutations of them. The nightmare lasted as long as the drug did.

Comment was hopeless as I handed the sheets back. I could only mumble: 'I appreciate the honour – the courtesy – of your letting me read this.'

'You had to read it.'

'Does anything follow from it?'

'Nothing did at first. Gradually though, I've been forced to face what her death has meant in my life. When it happened – or rather, when I'd recovered enough to think – it set up a conflict. I wanted to... I'm not sure it was exactly to believe in immortality, or meeting Frances again... but to know, to find out. I couldn't forgive the prud-ery of scientists. Millions can be spent on orthodox projects, not a penny on exploring what's called The Unseen, because the scientists won't allow it as a proper field for research.'

'Sir Oliver Lodge[5] did.'

The Finger and the Moon

That's a long time ago. And mind you, Geoffrey, I was never in danger of succumbing to wishful thinking like Lodge. This was the other side of the coin. It was so plain that... the organism that died... was only doubtfully Frances at all. If she "survived", what did that mean? What is a human being? What does a human being amount to? The immortality problem and the identity problem fought to a standstill, and at last it all froze over.'

'But it surfaced again when you got interested in patients who were also fretting over the nature of Man, in their own way.'

He had brightened somewhat as we left the horror behind. 'I think I'd admit that. Perhaps I'm like Tennyson. He lost Arthur Hallam and tortured himself for years over immortality, to a point where it actually made him do his major work on another Arthur - your friend the King - who was supposed to be undying and due to return. By the way, would you agree Tennyson's underrated? He sees the issue better than most. He knows immortality couldn't be just this wretched transitory individual spun out forever.'

> A shadow flits before me,
> Not thou, but like to thee:
> Ah, Christ, that it were possible
> For one short hour to see
> The souls we loved, that they might tell us
> What and where they be.

'Even when he's convinced himself Hallam is alive, it isn't crudely as Hallam.

> What art thou then? I cannot guess;
> But though I seem in star and flower
> To feel thee some diffusive power,
> I do not therefore love thee less.'

'To use your own word,' I said, 'Hallam has become a presence.'

'Quite. I can believe that, where I can't believe in a neat capsule-soul winging off to Heaven. Or transmigrating either.'

'Still, there do seem to be cases (not Bridey Murphy, but others) of people recalling past lives under hypnosis or in dreams. Like with

Arnall Bloxham, and that Cathar affair.'

Martin acknowledged. 'Before the SP-trip you've just read about, I'd been studying immortality ideas in mystics eastern and western, and spiritualists, and the less absurd of the humanists. What struck me was that every party has spokesmen who can make a good case, and yet they all contradict each other. Christians are sure we have just a single earthly life, and then pass on to an endless destiny which depends on how we've led it. Hindus are equally sure we have a whole series of earthly lives, and gain or lose ground in keeping with the total effect up to now. In England the dead return to tell mediums they don't transmigrate, in India they return to assure us they do. Most of the humanists deny we go on at all. Some of them turn religion upside down like Camus[6], and argue that any after-life would devalue this one.

'That vision now' (he pointed to the two sheets on his desk) - 'I think it's a hint that everybody may turn out to be right, if we can get the role of the protoself into the open. We have to drop normal logic. Frances is all those women and none of them. She's still alive and she isn't. Her "being" doesn't correspond, purely and simply, to the person I married at a specified time and place.'

'Sorry, I've lost you.'

'Maybe I've lost myself. I can only put this very confusedly. But I've drawn up what seems to me a defensible credo. It's given out to some of the students. Here.' He passed me another, longer sheet of paper with photocopied typescript on it.

Many of the protoselves - perhaps all - came into being before the human bodies they now inhabit. How we should relate them to our own space-time, whether they are earth-bound or from other worlds, are questions beyond the scope of this note.

They can subsist in their proto-realm as 'presences' without human form. But they project themselves into matter. Whenever one of them does this, it appears as a human organism with the results we know. The ego develops into a distinct self in the everyday sense, which lives in the body and dissolves with it. After death, this self may keep up a kind of separate existence for a limited time. But in due course it is fully reabsorbed into the protoself from which it emerged: into a higher entity which has been there all along and does not die with the body.

The extent to which 'I', the ego, will go on at all in that state depends on what 'I' have been and done. If 'I' have kept the doors open to my protoself during life so far as this can be; have fulfilled my nature; have recovered integrity – then 'I' have defined myself in harmony with the proto-life I re-enter, and will go on as a factor in it. A great personality makes a great difference to the immortal presence which it rejoins. But a small mean one doesn't. It has cut itself off in its own hard-shelled egoism. After death it will wither.

The discarnate protoself may enter matter again, and form another person. Hence the same protoself can appear through the course of time as persons A, B, C,... with or without enrichments from each of these lives. In a sense A, B, C,... are the same. In a sense they aren't. The immortal being from whom they all stem transcends personalities as we know them.

Therefore:

The Christian is right to say that A, as such, lives only once and then passes into another state with no earthly recurrence.

The Hindu is right to say that A reappears as B, C,...; in a sense he does, because he is part of a protoself that does.

The materialist is right to say that A ceases to exist at death. Simply as A, he does cease to exist.[7]

I read through it twice. Was it a blinding light or a verbal fiddle?

'You're saying something like this. Take a case where one gets a strong feeling of re-incarnation. Voltaire and Bertrand Russell, for instance. Russell isn't a repeat performance of Voltaire. But somewhere in your unseen world, there's a "presence" with a certain temper of mind. That "presence" appeared on earth as Voltaire, absorbed Voltaire after death with his pretty impressive contribution, and then reappeared after a few decades' breathing-space as Russell.'

'I'd say the truth is something like that,' Martin replied.

'In which case, yes, you've accounted for people who remember past lives. If a protoself becomes A, absorbs him at death, and later becomes B – then psychic fragments of A, including his memories, could seep through into B.'

'So that under hypnosis, B might well recall incidents from A's life. That still doesn't make him crudely A-over-again.'

'Doesn't this apply more widely? Those standard characters who keep turning up in dreams and fantasy...?'

'Precisely,' said Martin. 'The Anima and the Shadow and so on. Jung claimed they were aspects of the dreamer's own psyche. I'd suggest he was more right than he realized. Often they preserve bits of the protoself's previous lives, recreating scenes as advice or warning.'

Still another thought. 'All those figures you saw with your wife were women. Would any given protoself always come through as a person of the same sex? In fact do your protoselves *have* sex?'

'Too speculative. I haven't a notion. To judge from Freud, though, the protoself must throw itself fairly heartily into the sex life bubbling below the surface. Also, with SP5 one's apt to see a profound difference between male and female. Much more than *la différence*.'

'Equal or unequal?'

'Is a diamond equal to an emerald? There's no inequality in anything I can see to measure.'

'It does occur to me,' I mused, 'that if you admit a male protoself might get into a female body just for kicks – or vice versa – you have a neat explanation of homosexuals. With no offence to anyone.'

* * * * *

Back in my room again, the way ahead is a little clearer perhaps. I can see no end to the ingenuities of Martin's ideas. I can also see no end to the winkling-out of the motives behind them. Analysis and criticism won't get to the bottom of Allhallows. The only road is to *think* Allhallows. That could give me the key to my situation.

Very well then. I adopt the opinion of the house. I'm linked with a protoself which is more than just an aspect of me. He's been around, how long? – quietly preparing my life, building hints into my background, twenty or thirty years before my birth. Oh, not for my sake alone. 'I' am merely the current manifestation of a being who's manifested himself before, very likely, as a whole string of people whom I may or may not have heard of, and who are now sketchily infused into me. Maybe I embody whatever is left of my namesake Geoffrey of Monmouth (that would be nice), or François Villon, or the Thames bargee whom Dr Johnson had a slanging match with. Or Jack the Ripper... though I doubt that. He, this multi-being who sojourns inside me and observes me and prompts me, surely has a maturer appreciation of issues than I have, and has been acquiring purposes through his series of lives which it's up to me to fulfil.

How would Martin suggest putting a name to him? I don't know. But that need not prevent me from addressing him and asking advice. Purely as an experiment. Summoning my guardian angel, since that's one of his disguises. Or in Whitman's phrase, Inviting My Soul. Why not?

In a magical milieu the first step towards contacting unseen beings is to draw a circle on the floor. As, for example, on this curious near-white floor which I took note of when I arrived. As, for example, with one of those felt pens which I also took note of. All present and correct. There - a circle. So speak to me, True Self whatever your name is, I'm listening.

Listening and hearing nothing. But seeing something. The rain's stopped trickling down my window. In fact it's stopped altogether. The sky is clearing. So our Cadbury-Camelot excursion is on. Which means we watch for the shades of Arthur's knights. Then if SP5 is an entry-pass to the world they inhabit - yes - and especially after Karen's Tintagel yarn. I'll try it on top of Cadbury. Paul was right about that if nothing else. Settled then. Now I must go on inviting....

After sitting in my circle for five more minutes without getting an answer, it's just dawned on me that I had my answer five minutes ago.

6

I've lagged at least twenty hours behind events. Since that last taped monologue in mid-afternoon, there hasn't been a moment for more than scattered jottings. However, I'm now in a lull and may be able to catch up.

The next hour or so after my stint in the circle was devoted to a plenary session. Its venue was the conference room and the speaker was Mr Frobisher, in his role of astrological mage. I don't think it was important, except for the way it ended.

Martin supplied the run-up. 'So many people today are familiar with astrology, we don't usually go into it in detail. I just like to put it in perspective. If we're right in our view of the protoself, one of its major powers is its insight into the order of the universe. Man, at that level of his being, relates to the whole system and can know it through his affinities with it. Astrology is a majestic attempt to spell out certain parts of the cosmic order, by correlating the heavens and times and seasons with human life. The astrologer attunes to a vast web of influences, and if he is successful they pierce through into consciousness.

'I've asked Alan Frobisher to talk to you about horoscopes, partly because he'll remind us of the main motifs as interestingly as anyone can, and partly because he has an invention which he'd like to show us.'[8]

Mr Frobisher seemed in no hurry to begin. He had brought a big flat case, and was peering into it when Norman suddenly assailed him. 'It strikes me astrology raises difficulties, to say the least. After all, astronomers tell us the stars are all different distances away, and aren't where we see them anyhow, because the light has taken thousands of years reaching us, so your entire Zodiac is an optical illusion.'

'You mean,' said Mr Frobisher, 'there's reason to feel distrustful of astronomers. Yes, certainly there is. Charles Fort made an excel-lent case for believing that the stars are quite near. According to the Bender theory the earth is hollow and we're on the inside, not the outside, and the stars are nodules of light in a globe of bluish gas at the centre.'

'Bender died in a concentration camp,' Mrs Frobisher put in. 'He was a martyr.'

The Cryptocrat had tried vainly to retort and now did. 'No, of course that isn't it. I'm saying... well, quite apart from astronomers... if you just look at the sky intelligently without a telescope even, or read up on space probes, it simply doesn't work, it doesn't agree with what astrology makes out is going on up there.'

'You mean,' said Mr Frobisher with good-humoured patience, 'we can't do astrology just with the naked eye. No indeed. It's the whole substance of our claim that this is an art which requires study and calculation and special aids.'

Norman subsided muttering. Mr Frobisher lifted his invention out of the case and set it on the table, where it stood unsteadily upright: a wooden frame two feet square with a rotating disc like a dart-board in half a dozen segments, and smaller discs pinned to the big one and turning on their own axes, and graduated rods pivoted on the frame which could be swung at various angles across the disc. Every inch of surface was covered with figures and letters and zodiacal symbols and dates. Mr Frobisher had painted the structure in several colours, with violet predominant, for some reason which escaped me. He explained that he had drawn on the astronomy of the Druids and had therefore built his machine out of oak wood.

Once fairly launched, he grew curiously impressive. His voice expanded, his grey hair gave him dignity. He talked of planets and sun-signs and ephemerides and birth-charts and houses and ascendants, with a polite nod or two towards the great Zodiac of Glastonbury. Yet it was promise without performance. He was always on the brink of showing us how he used his machine, but never actually did. The lecture petered out. Martin, however, brought matters down to earth before dismissing the class.

'There's one simple thing I'd like you to do. Give me a snap judgement on Allhallows. The four of us who run it are all here - Karen, Annabel, Paul and myself. We can tell you our birthdays. See what you can make of them.'

'Hm. I warn you, this judgement is going to be far too snap for my liking. Still, I don't mind having a go. When's your own birthday?'

'August the tenth.'

'Leo. And Karen?'

'May the eighth.'

'Taurus. And Annabel?'

'February the second.'

'Aquarius. And Paul?'

'October the twenty-ninth.'

'Scorpio. That's amazing. Leo, Taurus, Aquarius, Scorpio. The four fixed signs.'

'Why do you call them fixed?' the Welsh voice of Owen interjected.

'Fixed, by contrast with those signs where the sun makes its transitions from one season to another. Having all four of them combined must be a potent clue.' Mr Frobisher looked as if he were genuinely concentrating. 'To take these signs together is to think of you four as a team rather than individuals. A team in relation to what it's a team for - the running of Allhallows.

'Leo, Taurus, Aquarius, Scorpio, the fixed signs in the circling year as it obeys the laws of Nature. Together, if I may say so, you form a pattern of productive constancy in the midst of change. The things that happen here will tend to make sense - not always at once - but through a logical progress. Bud to flower, and seed-time to harvest. Muddled ideas should get sorted out. Suppressed problems should be brought into the open. Vague projects should become plans that can be discussed usefully. People who come to you may learn a lot and be affected a lot through being here, it'll always tend to follow a path, step by step. As a group you "stand", so to speak, and you can help others to work out where they stand themselves.'

7

Just as the astro-session was ending, a car arrived. A young fellow emerged from it and appeared in the entrance hall. I didn't know him, but he turned out to be the son of my theatrical friend who stored the costumes and props for the Grail Ritual. These had been disinterred as requested and were in the car. A stack of unwieldy parcels, dusty from a Bristol attic, but undamaged. I helped him to shift them into the hall and thanked him. He declined nervously to stay longer.

I was bracing myself to lug them up to my room. Karen had other ideas. 'No, let's take them to mine. I'd love to see them, and the clothes may need checking for repairs.'

We went up. For several minutes we were busy unpacking. Her room, however, was registering on me throughout. Mainly green décor. A divan bed, wide, but single as opposed to double. A hand-basin with H & C. Furniture a shade awkward - bought, I would judge, for a trendy flat long since abandoned. Two low bookcases. Designs for advertisements on the walls, defused souvenirs of her professional rat-race: one with a rose filling the foreground and a woman behind it, another inspired by Leda and the Swan. Also an oil painting of a blue-point Siamese cat. The room was not as neat as Paul's. The atmosphere struck me as easy and informal, but with no marked letting-one's-hair-down tone.

Karen exclaimed over the costumes and props. Light armour and a cloak for the questing knight, robes and gowns for the inmates of the Grail sanctuary, a golden crown, and the four sacred objects, the Grail itself, the lance, the sword, and the dish.

'You've got some of the makings of good television here. What programme did you say this was for?'

I told her. She examined the items one by one, wanting to know about the designer and actors, and the percentage of budget allocated to the Grail sequence. Finally she had the whole lot arranged on chairs and coat-hangers.

'When are you staging this?'

'The day after tomorrow, I believe. It might depend on when Madri can come.'

'Ah yes, the Tantra Pentacle. You'll like them. Sit down and let's have tea.' There was a grill in the corner, also an electric kettle. She filled and started the kettle, and began boiling eggs and laying a small table. 'Do you have theories about sea-salt, like Hugh?'

'Nothing dogmatic.'

'I use it,' said Karen, 'in memory of Gandhi.'

She set down a tiny bowl. My eyes focused on the crystals and I was again where I once walked, on a beach in India beside the slow breakers of the Arabian Sea, while an ageing school inspector talked to me of a far-off morning when that beach was covered with a weaponless army, and a small defiant man scooped up a few grains of unlicensed salt, and the British Empire began to die.[9] But no! This wouldn't do. This was an SP5 experience and I haven't taken it yet. I was getting suggestible.

Karen's hand passed in front of my face. She was laughing. 'Come back.'

'Sorry.'

'Tell me,' she said, 'are you a dog-person or a cat-person?'

'Definitely cat.'

'I could have guessed.'

I asked her about the last bit of the astrological business. 'You must have done that before, you must know already what your signs are.'

'Of course we do. We ask all our astrology speakers to go through that routine. It gives them a chance to vent opinions. Some of them tell us that with four fixed signs this whole outfit must be stick-in-the-mud. Others turn it round into a compliment, we're steadfast or reliable or something like that.'

'I see. What about Mr Frobisher's assessment?'

'Unusual. In fact, unique.'

'Odd that Paul's sign should be Scorpio, and you and I both have Scorpio rising.'

'The sun-sign and the ascendant are quite separate. They can be opposed.'

Cautiously I led up to a mental pinprick which I'd at last realized the reason for. 'I keep feeling that this is an abnormal time for you somehow. Maybe disturbing. Martin's dropped hints to me, and he said Annabel read the I-Ching the other day and only does that on special occasions, and it was ominous. Then, didn't you drop a hint yourself when you showed me the Horned One? That you expected the temple to be used... or words to that effect?'

She hesitated. 'Yes, I - I suppose it ought to be said, now. The main reason is you.'

'Me? Why on earth?'

'Don't get me wrong, Geoffrey, you aren't to blame for anything. But you see, Martin's never been anxious for press coverage. When the *Globe* proposition came from you, of all people, we saw this would be more than journalism. It would open up issues... the forces at work in this piece of country... which could be alarming. Also, whoever did it, it would mean putting Allhallows into words. A fixed printed statement. When in a sense, part of our message is that that's the very thing which can mislead.'

'When you say that, it doesn't sound like you.'

'It isn't, it's Martin. He thought you were the person who could do this right if anyone could. Because you do understand the mystique that brought him here. But then again, if the media once got in, it could start all kinds of deviations.'

I felt cast down. 'Perhaps you'd rather I cleared out.'

'No. We're stuck with you now, dear. And I'm very glad.'

'So am I. But there's one thing I wish you'd tell me. What was Paul's attitude?'

'Paul was your strongest supporter. But I'm not sure it was the kind of support you'd welcome. He was all for "putting on a show" and "projecting an image".'

'To judge from a talk we had last night, he still is. He made a remark then that puzzled me.' Now it was coming. 'He mentioned a consignment of SP5 being delivered two days ago - and it was, I saw him receiving it. Yet last night Martin said there were no pills in the place apart from these three of mine. He said the stuff was on order, he didn't seem to know it had got here.'

She put down her cup. 'Oh no.'

'It needn't be more than a mistake.'

'It probably is, though. Geoffrey – you're in the family now, I'm trusting you to be careful – I'm afraid Paul may have kept the stuff for himself.'

'Would he have to do it like that?'

'He isn't meant to take SP5. Martin authorized it once and then said "Never again".'

'What happened?'

'Martin wouldn't tell me. It came under medical ethics because he'd had to treat Paul as a patient.'

Karen was running her eye over my TV props. She picked up the sacred dish and gazed at it from several angles. 'Has Paul told you his life story?'

'He mentioned working in that consultant firm, and being assistant personnel manager in a factory.'

She chuckled. 'He wasn't assistant personnel manager, he was assistant to the personnel manager. There's a world of difference. It's a non-executive job. Never mind, we all window-dress a bit, and Paul really was a bright lad. I met him during his consultancy phase. He came into the ad agency I worked for, to give it a going-over. He impressed me. He still can. I invited him here after he had a break-down and he's never left.'

'What was the matter?'

'Destructive impulses, they called it. When he was a consultant he was madly efficient and ambitious, but just occasionally – just enough so it wouldn't do – he flew into rages and insulted the clients. He got fired and then... I'm not certain of all the details. Do you remember Hell's Angels, those boys with Nazi outfits and motor-bikes?'

'Vividly.'

'Paul was too old to join, but they had a weird fascination for him. Martin helped him over his breakdown. I believe the upset with SP5 was some kind of a relapse. All the same, he's pulled his weight. He handles our accounts and so on most expertly.'

'Last night he was talking about... well, the setup... and he said some curious things.'

Karen flushed. She looked down at the dish and rotated it slowly in her hands. 'I suppose we've got to go through this. Once when Martin wasn't around, I went to Paul in his room about some perfectly routine item - probably a grocery bill - and had, shall we say, difficulty escaping. He told me how much more interesting I was than girls his own age. The situation got very sticky. His idea of chatting-up - it doesn't work. Of course a younger man with designs on an older woman is liable to think he's doing her a favour. One makes allowances. But Paul came right out with it, almost. I have a dreadful impression that he even said "I thought you'd appreciate it".'

I made such responses as one could, then probed from a fresh quarter. 'Annabel... figured in our conversation.'

Karen had laid the dish aside and donned the prop-crown, eyeing her image in the mirror. 'In a way I'm responsible for her too. She worked for me once as an office temp. Very young, very naïve. Those staff-agency ads make desk jobs sound too glamorous. When she got depressed I took her under my wing for a while. She was one of those spontaneous types who go around saying "Why can't you take life as it is instead of discussing it?" and "You shouldn't plan, things should just happen".'

'Those easy-riding children of nature,' I commented, 'are often just the ones who get into the most God-awful complications.'

'She did. But there was more to it. These psychic gifts of hers, they were driving her round the bend and we neither of us knew what the matter was. On the surface she was simply a victim of - the vogue-word was still "permissiveness" - not genuine freedom, but plastic-permissiveness, the big media con game.

'Annabel smoked pot and I didn't mind, but she drifted into an acid set, and when I tried slowing her down she snapped back at me with some old-hat cliché about lesbian jealousy, which she thought was the last word in sophisticated insight. Do I look it?'

'No.'

'The tragedy was, she got hooked on hard drugs through her own spiritual hunger. We can skip the horrors, but she turned up at last in Hugh's macrobiotic commune.'

'Martin mentioned that. He said it cured her.'

'It put her in the way of a cure, yes. That was where she found her Grail, so to speak.' (Karen had transferred her attention to the prop-Grail and was testing various methods of holding it.) 'But there was more to that too. I heard where she was when Hugh came over. Terry Hoad[10] – you asked about Terry – was here at the same time, reporting back on his social work, and he went to see Annabel. He convinced her that her mission in life was to make full use of her powers. Or whatever you call them. When she found she had more in her own resources than drugs could give, that clinched it.

'The only trouble was, it got Terry himself into a tangle. As a good Irish Catholic he was giving her advice which his priests couldn't approve of. That's why he tells interviewers he's in mortal sin.'

'Why did Annabel come to Allhallows?'

'Terry persuaded her.'

'That's all there was between them?'

'That's all, I'm certain. Whatever conclusions one's dirty little mind may jump to, Terry's sin is not carnal.'

Perhaps now I could extract the rest. 'I don't know whether... the way Paul spoke of Annabel... is anything I have a right to inquire into.'

Karen put the Grail down and turned deadpan. 'I wouldn't think you'd need to inquire. Not that Annabel seems to care who hears what. You could say she tried to do what permissive birds are supposed to do. In London she got as far as a feeble affair that broke the ice without much enlightenment. Then, after she came here... oh hell. Did you see that film *Cumulus*?'

I had, and caught the allusion. A few remarks filled it out. Annabel (so Karen gathered) had decided that she fancied Paul and undertaken a textbook seduction in what she imagined to be the style of the 1970s. She walked into his room one night wearing an old shirt and nothing else, and then took that off. Unfortunately he was almost asleep, it was dark, and she shed the garment before he was properly aware of her. She impinged on his drowsy eyes merely as a pallid form standing near his bedside. Startled, he did what no film or novel had prepared her for -switched the light on. *Savoir-faire* deserted her and she made a grab to recover the shirt. A few minutes later her object was attained, but with an initial disadvantage she could never make up.

Only, in practice, it wasn't funny.

'She's involved now,' said Karen.

'I had that impression.'

'No one ever taught her how it's apt to be with the poor female. She really did not suspect that once the ultimate had occurred, it could build up on itself. Even at her age.'

'In every couple,' I quoted, 'there is one who loves and one who consents to be loved.'[11]

'No prizes, either, for guessing which is which. One thing though, this doesn't seem to have harmed Annabel's psychic talents. In fact they're blossoming.'

Silence. At the back of my mind a nasty speculation was taking shape. Karen, however, looked at her watch and halted the process. 'Early supper. You're taking us to Cadbury-Camelot.'

'If you put it that way. This has been an enlightening session.'

'For me too, in my fashion.' She set the Grail aside.

'Do you think you are Nimuë? According to Martin's notions of re-incarnation, that is.'

'Do you want him to be Merlin?'

'I'm open-minded. You did draw the parallel. Could this have been the same story coming round for a replay, only working out differently?'

'He wouldn't allow that. He believes he's contacted Merlin, or rather a "Presence M" who took shape as Merlin, and there's nobody alive at this moment corresponding to him. That wouldn't prevent me from being Nimuë, though.'

'The Lady of the Lake, according to some.'

'I'd like that.' She brandished the prop-sword. 'Excalibur. You have to take it out of my hand.'

'Only when you're under water.'

'Perhaps that can be arranged.'

'Karen ...' I'd forgotten till now. 'I want to try SP5 tonight, at Cadbury.'

'Yes?'

'If I can make some excuse and slip away from the party. Could you sit with me while I'm doing it?'

'Yes, of course.'

She was so matter-of-fact I didn't feel the conversation was over. But it was. Moving towards the door, I glanced again at the five props: the crown, the Grail, the lance, the sword, and the dish.

The Finger and the Moon

'You approve?'

'They're well made, they'd be effective on the small screen.'

'You've given them all a pretty good scrutiny. Except the lance.'

'You could hardly expect me,' she said, 'to handle anything so pointed.'

Other-Scene

WE DROVE TO CADBURY in three cars. Karen's green Triumph led, carrying herself, Martin, Owen, and me. Behind was Paul with Annabel, Kwame, Steve and Norman, in a small van. Last came the Frobishers' Cortina, Mei-ling and Janice in the back.

Owen had latched on to me with a sudden contentious interest in the Arthurian Legend. He argued most of the way, bombarding me with obscure folklore gleaned in his local branch of Plaid Cymru. His pronunciation of Welsh names is doubtless correct, but as I know them in print rather than orally (if at all), I had the utmost trouble grasping who or what he was talking about, while being uneasily aware that the least show of ignorance would destroy any credit I might have. With a certain amount of bluff I just managed to stay abreast of him till our convoy reached the foot of the hill.

Karen pulled over into the parking space. So did Paul. The Frobishers shot past. It was a little while before everyone was assembled and the climb could begin.

Light was still abundant. The steep path through the woods and crumbling earthworks was muddy and slippery. The party straggled out. A few yards behind me, Martin and Annabel were together. She was close beside him and talking, too low to hear. His voice answered: 'The path would have had four days to dry, but of course this down-pour has washed it all out again.'

Conversations were dwindling as breath grew short, and he said no more. But, four days. Since what? Several memories fitted together. The vanishing last page of the diary. 'Presence M', repeated to me by Karen. A natural suspicion as to the meaning of 'C', now confirmed. His twisted ankle. He must have gone to this very place, the night I arrived, to consult whatever oracles he supposed it to harbour.

We trudged out of the wood on to the humped expanse of the hilltop enclosure. After a rest pause I led them farther up to the summit plateau, the site of the hall that stood in Arthur's time, and the houses and workshops and Druid temples of generations before him. In every direction the ground fell away from us to the three-quarter mile perimeter of the top rampart, its grass hiding the superimposed stone walls of Iron Age Celts, Arthurian warriors and Anglo-Saxon burgh-builders, which made this place a 'castle' in an older sense than the mediaeval. On one side we looked across to Durotrigian hills on the fringe of Dorset; on the other side, to Glastonbury Tor with its tower far off, visible to the right of the sinking sun.

'You never get away from that thing,' said Steve.

'You can see Glastonbury from Cadbury,' I said, 'but not Cadbury from Glastonbury. At least, not so that you can pick it out easily from the other hills. This one's elusive. Too big to take in, too big to photograph satisfactorily.'

'But is it Camelot?' Mr Frobisher asked.

'In the sense that anything could be – yes, I believe so. Not as a medieval dream-city with Vanessa Redgrave strolling along the battlements. But as the reality which legends could have grown round, the HQ of the British commander-in-chief Artorius about 500 A.D., who beat the Saxons and saved the country from devastation.[1] Yes. The right sort of man did turn this hillfort into a citadel at the right time. If you slice through those earthworks you'll find the remains of a colossal fortification system that can be dated to Arthur's period. Nothing like it has been found anywhere else in Britain.'

Most of them asked questions and clustered near, except Mrs Frobisher, who was staring back abstractedly the way we'd come. Owen mentioned the cave where Arthur is reputed to lie asleep till the day of his returning, and challenged me to point out where it was. 'You have to come at the right moment to find it open,' I told him. Norman was unexpectedly pressing. He wanted precise details on the acreage, the length of different sections of rampart, the sub-surface locations of ancient buildings. These details weren't always easy to provide, but I was glad to keep the talk on that level and soft-pedal hopes of the supernatural.

Dusk fell. Rugs and torches and bags of food were distributed. I had no trouble getting away from the rest. The party divided into groups without urging, and dispersed to sheltered places under the banks.

'Where?' said Karen.

'Down here perhaps.'

Scrambling down a slope, we crossed to the gap in the rampart over Sutton Montis.

'This is the old gateway. Of course, you'll remember – you were on the dig. The shades of Arthur's knights ride through it.'

We worked round and pushed uncertainly out into the trees. Cadbury's woods are rough going. The taller and denser parts are disturbing Tolkien-forest, not Malory-forest.

'Watch for nettles,' I warned her. 'They grow everywhere, and for some reason there's very little dock growing with them. Better pull back.'

'I don't think this is the place for you,' said Karen. 'You should be at the top where you can survey the whole show – the part where they lived, and the walls and gate, and the Tor over yonder.'

'It may get chilly up there.'

'So?'

We clambered back to the hill-crest, the heart of a city of Celtic ghosts. A calm night, hushed and starry, was gathering round us. Lights were beginning to dot the Vale of Avalon. The other Allhallows groups were tiny patches of movement at immense distances, or nothing at all.

Presently there was a place to sit, a place to spread a rug on the moist grass, clear of thistles, crushing no buttercups.

'Should I wait?'

'Wait till it's a little darker. You know this is the new faster-acting kind?'

'Martin told me.'

She sat soft-voiced a couple of feet away, not being discreet, just sitting, and reminisced further about her own spell of digging there in '69, and the time she'd unearthed an Arthurian knife that wasn't, and the questions visitors asked her. Through the blue-black above, a meteor drew a brief trail of fire.

'Now,' said Karen.

I put the pill in my mouth. It was unyielding. I bit. It released a faint sweetish flavour and then broke up.

2

'Faster-acting' turned out to be an understatement. I was still writhing my tongue round in pursuit of a last particle when the Midsummer Night's Apocalypse hit me.

After a few seconds of confusion and vertigo, the proto-vision (if that's what it is) began roughly as Martin had described. With me too its opening phase was a sharp inward sense of the human organism that bears my name: both in its own nature, and as a kind of prism through which the outer world looked different. The clumps of grass at my feet, the rising and plunging earthworks, the black tree-silhouettes, all had a crystal lucidity and an air of speech without sound. Some of those voices were very young, some very old. They hinted friendliness and a strange courtesy, even though they were utterly alien.

But somewhere in my scrambled identity a muffled voice could still play the devil's advocate. Was this, it asked, any more than my own fancy's version of what Martin had led me to expect?

The question brought a rapid response, as if whatever-it-was-that-had-annexed-me were proving itself real. Without any effect of motion, the image of myself grew external. I was in the air, looking down from outside at me sitting on the rug. Mountain-climbers who fall hundreds of feet into snowdrifts, and tell the tale afterwards, sometimes report that they saw their own bodies falling. The analo-gy's there for what it's worth. Under SP5 though, I looked through myself as well as at. This is hard to interpret, because it was not done via an optic nerve and can't have been physically seeing. Let's say I had images which came through as visual - or perhaps, even, which I now recall as visual - in the absence of any other mode of presentation.

My focus narrowed down to a cluster of brain-cells inside my seated figure. I knew these were resisting an unseen force that was beating on them. I also knew the defence was futile, like trying not to think of something. Soon the blob of grey tissue began to change colour. It gleamed deep orange - a coppery light reminding me of the glow with which the moon fights back during lunar eclipse.

Even now the experience was not too remote from Martin's diary. What tore me apart an instant later was an event neither he nor Karen had prepared me for, shatteringly foreign to nearly all they had told me. SOUND. A strident terrible horn-blast. Another, another, and a monstrous convulsion of space and spirit. The glowing brain-segment turned inside out and expanded to infinity, devouring the universe; and then the whole scene, including the phantom which I now was, reassembled inside it.

The brain-engulfed landscape appeared to be unchanged, except that the coppery light covered it like a ground-mist. The ramparts, the Vale of Avalon, the distant Tor, all showed phosphorescent. I had an impression that there was no tower on the Tor, but it was hard to be certain. Overhead was still implacable night. The seated figure of myself was still there. Karen? No sign of her. Yet her absence caused no feeling of loss or loneliness. If she was part of this, she would be part of it in some other way. It would have been as irrelevant, as unaffecting, to observe that there was no sign of Helen of Troy.

The horn-blasts had not ceased. They went on and on. Where were they coming from? The hill was shuddering, the stars reeling. Fact, not metaphor. The Great Bear wavered in the sky and its shape altered. Polaris lurched sideways. New lights glared over the Mendips like supernovae. And still, intolerably, the horn blew. I at last connected its pulsation with a sort of white shadow that hovered far off in the direction of the Tor. How far off exactly I couldn't judge, but it slowly enlarged as if it were moving nearer. Different noises were mingling now, a medley of unhuman bayings, and the white form was convoyed by smaller ones that had firefly-sparks of red dancing above them. While the apparition drew closer, the clamour seemed not to. If anything it dwindled. I had to wrestle with a *bouleversement* of space-perception.

Not – fortunately for me – with fear. Detached from body-reflexes, from sweat and trembling and flight, I was unafraid. I could still feel awe and bewilderment, and, as I was soon to learn, several further emotions. One of them assaulted me now.

The horn rang out stereophonically behind me. Amazement spun me round, or shifted my vantage-point, I don't know how to put it. Anyhow I was looking back over the hilltop plateau of Camelot, and it was occupied.

About fifty horsemen were drawn up in a loose formation facing me, at the far end of the plateau. Almost at once they moved forward at a walk, wheeling towards the old gateway so that I saw them from several angles, though never close. The horses were big, with ragged chain-mail (it glinted in the light) draped untidily over their bodies. Several of the horses, but I think not a majority, were black. The men rode without stirrups. They wore metal-studded leather jerkins and breeches, and cloaks pinned to their right shoulders. Spears, long swords, and white cross-marked shields were slung round them. Most of them were stocky and bare-headed, but a helmeted group at the front included one who was tall. His helmet had a device on its crest.

Something was wrong with the whole troop. At a distance, in that doubtful light, I was unsure of details. But they appeared ramshackle and unnaturally ugly. Also they were heading for an abrupt down-ward slope where the descent towards the gate would be hazardous. The tall leader, in fact, halted at the verge and the rest closed up round him. 'I', whatever 'I' was, drifted nearer. I saw that the white Tor-wraiths had reached the hill and were floating above the old gateway. The largest had condensed into a nebulously human figure, also on horseback. The remainder milled about like a pack round a huntsman. Across a dip of ground, riders and spectres faced each other. The horn had stopped blowing.

I could make out the riders' faces. They were hideous. These were dressed-up corpses rather than men. Skulls with decaying flesh and thin strands of beard sat on bodies upheld by stiff leather as much as by their own firmness. One raised a mercifully gloved hand to push his hair out of his eyes, or eye-sockets, and some of it fell off. I looked at the leader, but his helmet hid his face altogether. The device on top of it was a scarlet dragon.

He and his troop advanced again. They didn't have to attempt the slope, they rode through the air towards the spectres, with a muted jingling of harness but no speech that I could hear. The tall leader joined the White One, drawing so close alongside that they almost merged. Meanwhile the rest were crossing. The horn-blast boomed yet again – I think the leader had a tangible horn which he raised and blew, though no normal instrument could have made such a din – and the combined company streamed off airborne towards the Tor. Hooves brushed the treetops and made them tingle with fire.

Surging along at a hand-gallop, the procession ought to have been past in a matter of seconds, but it was not. A comet-tail of newcomers kept forming behind it. More and more ex-humans gathered and were launched into space. Few of these were mounted. Most went on foot, those that still had feet. Many moved as if they were being dragged. Men, women, children, and lumps of flesh which I believe were stillbirths and abortions, swarmed in zero-gravity over the hilltop and soared off in the wake of the first company, drawn by a suction that did not disturb the air. Half of them perhaps had tatters of clothing. The styles of the garments on those collapsing frames seemed to span many centuries. Roman-type armour, Elizabethan ruffs, even Victorian top-hats and boys' sailor suits, made parts of the mob into nauseous masquerades. They swept in to rendezvous on the hill from vast perspectiveless spaces, generation upon generation of vanished sons and daughters of Albion; they converged along pathways of pale fire – laser-beams traversing the map – and fell in behind those who were already departing. All with an incessant murmur that swelled to a hubbub without ever becoming speech.

Away over the lower Somerset levels, I could see the procession's leaders still airborne, half-way to the Tor in a haze of white. The rest followed them, an unbroken column. The horn was still summoning from the front, quieter with distance, but not proportionately. I found myself swept out with the cavalcade and hurtling along much faster, so that I overhauled the leaders. The coppery glow had weakened and the land underneath was in near-darkness, with none of the twinkling and creeping lights of my own time. I guessed that I was looking down on the Summer Land of antiquity, and the guess was confirmed as I made out sheets of water – the old lagoons that covered what is now drained marsh round the Isle of Avalon, deepening here and there into paths for ships.

The Tor loomed ahead and then underneath. The light was a little stronger again and showed its greenness. There was no chapel-tower on top, but there was a squat circular building like a Highland broch, with a crudely domed roof. The lagoon hundreds of feet below was flat calm, a mirror. I took in a helicopter's-eye-view of the attendant hills, the bulge of Chalice nearby and the ridge of Wearyall stretching away seaward, and streams coursing down.

The White One had halted by the summit broch, with the chief horseman beside him. The column wrapped itself round the Tor in a descending spiral, with a rustling and twittering that resembled no sound caused by living crowds. Its tail-end – it did at last have a tail-end – trailed off along the base of the hills.

I must pause to record that this SP5 vision of mine, unlike any of Martin's so far as I know, had a different time-scale from normal life. The drug's action lasted less than half an hour. The vision, up to the Tor assembly alone, must have been three or four times as long. I infer this from the logistics of the flight and its aftermath. The tempo was fast, but never so fast as to seem irrelevant to the leg-rhythm of the pacemaking horses. Even in the air they looked as if they were propelling themselves at an easy gallop. Whirled along at a hundred miles an hour they would not have done.

As for the rest of the vision, I have no way of timing it.

3

I was close to the summit. Two of the horsemen dismounted with puppet actions, and their leader almost fell from his saddle into their arms. They laid him on the ground and jerked off his helmet, which I saw had been holding a rough pad in position. Alone in the company he appeared fully alive, and I would know his face again, but half his head was soaked in blood.

The White One stood beside them. He was still indistinct, not above human height. He faced northward with his arms raised and I understood that he was calling. His call was answered. Out of the north, at terrific speed, something approached. One had an awareness of motion rather than a sight of anything moving. But a moment later another figure stood among the group by the broch, a stalwart old man with a long beard and a tunic. He carried a hunting-spear and a net full of fish. In that setting he was grotesquely real, a person such as you might meet in a pub... until the White One bowed to him, and he stretched a hand out in a gesture of blessing, and the hand was silver instead of flesh.[2]

Words passed between them but I still couldn't catch any. The old man had been sent for as a healer. He bent over the warrior on the ground, drew a silver finger across the gruesome scalp, shook his head gloomily. The blow which had fallen at some dis-helmeted moment was too much for his art.

I am not sure what happened next. Without warning my vantage-point shot away through the air. The sky was dark; so, now, was the land. Only the Glastonbury area gleamed dully. From a sudden distance of miles – though not from any great height – I saw the Tor in profile, with the broch dotting its apex, but the host of figures had blended into it and could no longer be distinguished. The lesser hill undulated down to its left, and left again I saw the entire ridge of Wearyall pointing seaward. A lake spread alongside, very faintly reflecting the contours.

I found myself drawing comparisons with the twentieth century. No houses. More trees, but no heavy forest blurring the outlines. Paler now, not green at all. That was surely an effect of the weird light. Presently though, I began wondering whether the light could also cause optical illusions. The proportions were strange. Was I seeing from an angle quite new to me? The Tor was smoother and more symmetrical, Chalice Hill less bulbous. Most certainly, too, the ridge of Wearyall had gone wrong. Its outlying crest had sunk, it was now highest at a point nearer the Tor.

Implanted habits of mind remained tyrannous. I shut out what was going on till it had gone much further. Wearyall was in motion. A stirring at its sea-pointing end threshed the water, a new promontory heaved up. Several hundred yards back, where the ridge was rising highest, an improbably wide cave yawned underneath and I saw through to another stretch of lake beyond. Size still restrained me from accepting what must, by now, have been obvious. The ridge had become a colossal human leg, the leg of a recumbent Titan who was drawing it up. A huge foot was breaking the surface at its end. A huge knee was lifting in the middle.

When I did finally acknowledge that mind-cheating limb, it carried my attention to the rest of the figure. A second disturbance was upheaving torrents of spray at the inland extremity of the hill-cluster, to the right of the Tor. Waves were spreading over the lake. A shoulder humped up above tumultuous water and gave me a belated clue to the torso, which I had been staring at without seeing. The Titan, to be accurate, was a Titaness. The Tor was her left breast, complete with a nipple formed by the building on the summit, which no longer had the look of a building. As she rolled herself over and hoisted herself up, the convex surface that had been Chalice Hill spread downwards between enormous hips. The destined acreage of the Abbey contained her womb; the destined site of its Old Church – St Joseph's shrine of the Virgin, and the focus (they say) of spiritual forces far more ancient - was an alarmingly placed shadow.[3]

Her right arm and leg, which had been bunched and largely submerged on the far side, unfolded and appeared. Her head, flung backwards in the region of Stone Down, came level with what had been the Tor. She propped herself on two terrible arms, she knelt, she stood, ten thousand feet tall. Miles of water rose with her, swirling and streaming like a translucent robe. My vantage-point rose too, holding her in profile. She turned west. Her face was none I could remember. Her hair was encircled by a garland like apple-blossom.

She took a step and another, the robe clinging round her and trailing out behind. Her feet trod on the sites of Sharpham, Ashcott, Shapwick. She splashed with unhurried grace through lagoons and over hills, as if she were walking through seapuddles on a sandy beach. The light travelled with her. I was drawn along behind in her track, through the lonely air, miles behind, out over Lundy and then the ocean. There was no fear in this, only awe. She was striding into the west on the wavetops, weightless now, making for the drowned Altantean ranges.

It was growing less dark around me. Even at her leisurely pace, the goddess moved faster than the eastward rotation of the earth. We were overhauling the sunset. The sky shone red and then gold in front of us, and turned bluer above. I could see a sky-scape with drifting cloud-strata. As I crossed a gulf of clear space, the wisps that hung low in it cast shadows on the luminosity of the sea. I was not quite alone, a raven was winging along beside me. Now the goddess broke silence. She sang, a sad yearning Gaelic-sounding melody that filled the heavens.

Within minutes the west displayed the foreseen yet outrageous thing, an overtaken sunset reversing into sunrise, far swifter in fact than the sunrise of the earthbound. Gold and azure and pink brightened into dawn. The ocean spread away to indefinite horizons. It was not empty now. An island basked in the speed-created morning ahead.

Knowledge came to me that the vision was near its ending. With that knowledge came a change of scale and perspective. Space contracted into itself. The goddess was no longer gigantic. I saw a woman step ashore on the island, a human-sized woman with a white gauzy robe and a garland, her bare feet ankle-deep in foam. I have a confused

memory of seeing her walk along an avenue between standing mega-
liths, four on each side. The raven perched on one of them. At the
end was a low hill with a cavern, or perhaps a burial mound with a
passage-grave.

She passed through into the heart of the hill. I saw a central chamber, dimly lit through clefts in the roof where birds fluttered in and
out. Around the mural-painted walls were statues and mysterious
furnishings, but I recall nothing of that. The goddess made straight
for a slab of gold-coloured rock. A man lay on it asleep, and he had
the same face as the wounded leader of the horsemen. She bent over
him and placed her hand on his forehead. He woke and began to stir,
very much as the goddess herself had stirred when she rose from her
waters.[4]

But I am not sure whether I saw him upright. The rest was simply
a brief ecstatic chaos. My last impression was that I was back at the
cave-mouth. All those dead of Albion who had coiled round the
Tor and faded into the goddess's body were still present. They were
exploding into new life and youth, and skimming homewards over
the sea – myriads re-limbed, re-born, delivered.

4

I was cold and stiff. Karen was still beside me. 'Yes,' she said.

'It was different. Not like Martin's, or yours either.'

'I thought it might be.'

'More like something from an Old Testament prophet, only without the Lord's comments. Or Blake.'

'You'd better tell me while it's still fresh.' Composedly she produced a notebook and switched her torch on. 'I can do shorthand.
Secretarial college.'

I started and then broke off, noticing a third person in the starlight,
sitting cross-legged only a few yards from us. Annabel.

'How long has she been there?'

'Most of the time. Don't let her distract you. Go on.'

Sixth Day

I

NORMAN'S CRYPTOCRAT GUESTS have disrupted and dominated the morning. They arrived during the last clinkings of a breakfast which was late and staggered. The Cadbury vigil had been kept till long after midnight. Breakfast was a catena of small postmortems, two or three yawning residents at a time, pursuing arguments begun on the road back as to what (if anything) had happened. Kwame talked of a special atmosphere beside the north rampart. Mrs Frobisher recited five spirit messages, including one from Sir Galahad. Owen was the sole actual ghost-seer. With a plain-spoken, all-in-the-day's-work air, he reported watchers in the trees whom he couldn't identify, and then appeared to lose interest in them.

Myself, I'd faced questioning as we left the hill, and when it was renewed I told the same story. SP5 of course remained a taboo topic with the students. I disguised my experience as a nap with a dream, and made it brief and imprecise. Even so, Owen started expounding it; or rather confirming, out of Cymric lore, certain recognitions I'd reached unaided.

He put a name to the White One, adding picturesque details. 'His own servants wear red and blue liveries. His hounds have red ears and you never can judge how near they are to you, because when they give tongue, they sound louder from far away than they do close by.'

Had or hadn't I told him the portion of the vision which that folk-belief fitted? Memory was dimming and I was glad, as I'm now gladder, that Karen was on the spot with her shorthand. He was still discoursing when the Cryptocrats' car drew up. Norman rushed out to greet his guests. Paul, whom I hadn't seen at breakfast, appeared and followed. I joined them.

The car had a sticker in the rear window:

GOD IS BACK
and boy, is he mad![1]

I took this to relate to the theology of the driver. He clambered out,
a massively built young man with flowing hair and a beard like Karl
Marx's. 'Peace and love!' he thundered, making the sign of the cross.
'All six of us bless you.' His four passengers, count 'em, were out of the
car. Norman faltered an instant, then seemed to recollect a response,
which he gave in an embarrassed undertone.

'Er ... May we behold him soon.... This is Herod,' he said hastily to
me.

'Herod.' It didn't sound appropriate.

'I'm atoning in this life for the other,' the driver explained. 'For
killing the babies and cutting off John the Baptist's head. Jesus my
navigator be praised.'

'I've told you before,' said Norman, 'it wasn't the same Herod.'

'Two Herods,' a rasping female voice put in, 'are better than one.'
The pasty brunette looked as if she were costumed for a circus, and so
did her male companion. She was a simplified Annie Oakley – Wild
West hat, heavy decorative shirt, gun-belt, three-quarter-length skirt,
boots – and her partner was the ringmaster, except that he was hatless
and... I was about to add whipless, but I have a suspicion, now, that
the thing sticking out of his right boot-top is a whip, though a puny
one.

The more conspicuous of the other two men introduced this couple. 'Joe and Freda Bamberger.' The speaker himself was older, forty-
ish. His protruding thyroid eyes put me off. 'You know Arnold Gore
of course,' said Norman. I didn't, but realized that I should. Who on
earth?

Arnold Gore and the rest were swapping remarks about the journey while the fifth Cryptocrat hovered unacknowledged, a short
dark gentleman, bespectacled, grey-suited, plain-tied. His sober rig
made him grotesque in this company, but only when you took notice
of him, and at that point nobody did. The name which I got for him
subsequently, not then, was Simon Calthrop.

After an involved discussion with Karen, and a false start, they
sorted out their arrangements. Paul bustled attentively. They were to
camp behind the parking area on the stretch of grass set aside for that

purpose, with a water tap and a brick surface for barbecue gear. The Bambergers had an igloo tent which they assembled. Herod dragged an oversize plastic bag very slowly to the far corner of the camping space, shouting remarks at intervals, and halting every time he did. At length, however, his tent emerged from the bag. Arnold shared a third tent with Simon Calthrop. While debating some technicality Arnold happened to say 'No problem,' giving the cliché an unusual sound, with a prolonged o in the first word. I suddenly recalled who he was. For some reason I'd had a mental stoppage and his name hadn't registered.

This Arnold Gore is the man who runs the Noel Community projects in the wilderness of north-east London, and gets publicity every so often with shock statements on housing and similar issues. He has a high reputation which seems deserved, and yet...

A few years ago someone took me to a conference of the Union for Non-Violent Change. At their morning session Arnold was the star speaker, and he held forth eloquently on love, co-operation, and kindred subjects. At the afternoon session, a review of the Union's programme, he leaped up and launched into a diatribe referring back to some previous row I hadn't been in on. Apparently he'd been urging the setting up of an 'action committee' and now claimed that the Union's officers had been frustrating him. He became so abusive, and the meeting was getting so turbulent, that the chairman and secretary hustled him into the next room for a private chat. They returned announcing that they'd agreed to put his proposal to the members. About a dozen supported Arnold, and joined him afterwards to arrange their first get-together.

In spite of his manner I was attracted by some of his ideas, so I signed on for his new committee. Over the next few weeks I attended five of its meetings. At the inaugural one he didn't show up and sent an excuse. At the second he arrived late, said almost nothing, and left early. After that he neither appeared nor communicated. The committee was futile and I drifted away. However, my name was now on his mailing list, and I became the recipient from time to time of many-paged statements about the Noel Community, full of self-justifying bulletins on his incomprehensible quarrels with colleagues.

Seeing him at Allhallows I wondered what he had in mind. He showed no sign of recognition, and as he was busy with his camping equipment I strolled over to Joe and Freda.

'Have we met you before?' said Joe.

'I've been to some of the same meetings as Arnold.'

'For instance?'

'The Union for Non-Violent Change.'

Joe made a scornful gesture. 'A load of crap. He only goes to build up contacts. Me, I don't have his patience with them.'

'I know about his Community's work, of course. That's admirable.'

'Admirable?' snarled Freda. 'Who wants admiration?'

'Well, I don't know how else to put it, at a distance. The Community does seem to be a serious attempt to live differently...'

'They're not living differently. They're just living. People.'

'You work for the Community yourselves, do you?'

'Some of the time,' said Joe. 'We keep the business end straightened out. Simon Calthrop is our accountant.'

'Ah, I see.'

'We work on neighbourhood affairs too,' said Freda. 'Arnold can't be everywhere. In the last few months, one damn fool after another has been trying to horn in and start a new area committee, race-relations or women or kids' lib or some codswallop. All they ever do is obstruct. So Joe and I go to their meetings, and interrupt and raise points of order till they get tired.'

'Does this fit in with Cryptocracy?'

'Fit in with it? What does, what doesn't?'

'I'm hoping to learn more about it.'

She laughed. '*You'll* be lucky.'

Without warning they both dived into the tent and rolled on the floor in a close embrace, making noises. Four boots threshed in the entrance. It was one way of breaking off a conversation. I walked over to Herod, who was still wrestling with his own tent.

'Trouble is,' he roared, 'I can't seem to locate half the pegs.'

I made a show of helping him search. 'Do you know this part of the country?'

'Look, this is where I came to life. Over there at Glastonbury with the Jesus freaks. I saw John the Baptist in that field behind Chalice Well. Exactly like he was in the desert.'

'How did you know it was John the Baptist?'

'Man, it just had to be. He told me who I was myself - Herod. I'm atoning till he comes again. Jesus, that is. Right over there on top of the Tor.'

'That's where you expect the Second Coming.'

'That's where it's got to be. Here, don't I know your name somehow?'

'You might have seen it on a book they sell at the Abbey.'

'Of course. You explain about those secret chambers inside the Tor.'

Actually I don't. He was mixing up my book with another, which is also sold at the Abbey, and which I discourage people from buying. However, it was all goodwill. 'Have you any theories on those chambers yourself?'

He shook his head. 'I'd just like to find the entry passage. Somebody once told me Jesus's blessed mother is lying asleep in one of them. I suppose you wouldn't happen to know which.'

'Not offhand, no.'

He had got the tent nearly up, but not quite, and had lost the mallet. 'They say another of those chambers belongs to Lucifer.'

'Lucifer. Do you mean the Devil?'

This was evidently a crucial point with him. 'The so-called Devil. John the Baptist appeared to me again and told me the truth. Lucifer is Jesus's younger brother. Satanism is another form of true worship.'

'But I assume Jesus comes first.'

'Of course he does. First, last and always. Alpher and O'Megger.'

'Then where does Cryptocracy fit in?'

'Man, Cryptocracy is the key to the new order of God's whole earth. It's the same as the catacombs in Roman times. The early Church was a secret society like us for two hundred years, and then it came out and ran the world. So will we.'

The tent collapsed.

'If it takes two hundred years,' I ventured, 'you won't be around to see it.'

'I have eternal life like all Jesus's children. If it did take two hundred years it still wouldn't matter to me. But it won't.'

Freda Bamberger's upper portion, her hat gone and her shirt nearly off, emerged from the igloo like a tortoise's head and shot back in again. Herod looked across at her with benign approval. 'They're a wonderful pair, those two. Stacks of money and it hasn't spoilt them at all.

They keep that Community going, just about.'

'Freda strikes me as... as being hard to put down.'

'You should have been at the Inter-Church meeting in West Ham the other day. A line-up of clergy facing the audience. C of E bishop, RC priest, three assorted ministers. All supposed to be discussing high-rise housing. This padre, he was getting wound up on suicides in his parish, when Joe and Freda walked in. Right into the middle of the floor in front of him. God, you should have seen it. They just stood there and he couldn't go on. And get this, they were transvestites. Straight off-the-hook gear, but switched. Joe like a bird, Freda like a feller. She called out loud and clear: "If anybody approaches us we shall take our clothes off".'

'And did anybody?'

'Didn't dare. After a minute or so they turned to each other, bowed, and went out.'

'What was it meant to prove?'

'It was an image of alienation.'

'And the meeting got that.'

'Of course not. What could you expect from a bunch of Christians?'

I held part of his tent for him and he got it set up at last, if a trifle skewed. Paul and Norman came towards us. Annabel was with them. The three had been conferring nearer the house. The girl's face was unhappy, but the others were cheerful.

'If you're all ready,' said Paul, 'let's take a walk round.'

The Cryptocrats gathered, Freda buttoning herself, and we set off along the lawn. For me it was an odd repeat of my tours with Karen at the beginning. Passing between the two pillars, we came to the first of the American's sculptures, the one that looks abstract till you push it, and then turns into a man walking with a pack over his shoulder. Nobody pushed it.

'Is this really anything more,' rasped Freda, 'than imitation Canello?'

Her husband demurred. 'I think the system of non-representative intersection-dispersal does have a touch of novelty. Here, and here.'

'What's it meant to be?' said Herod.

Freda snorted. 'How naïve can you get? It isn't "meant to be" anything. It IS something. You don't look beyond to any irrelevant image.'

'Wait,' said Norman. He pushed it and the figure appeared.

Freda stood as before. 'I'm waiting.'

Herod , who was placed at the best visual angle, clapped his hands. 'Fantastic!' he shouted.

'What is?'

In the end three of them accepted that the figure was there. The Bambergers didn't. Joe smiled non-committally, Freda told the others they were over-suggestible.

We drifted slowly towards the temple. Annabel dropped behind with me. I realized how seldom she and I had spoken together.

'They couldn't see him,' she said.

'Or wouldn't.'

'No, it's worse than that, Geoffrey. She really couldn't, and he couldn't either because she couldn't.'

'If so, it's only a sort of mental blindness.'

'*Only.*' It was the first time I'd ever heard a word spoken by her in passion. I glanced sideways. She was dead pale and shivering.

'What do you feel is wrong?'

'You did see him yourself, when Karen showed you the other day?'

'Yes, almost at once.'

'Hang on to that. You could see. That woman couldn't.'

Annabel looked as if she might burst into tears on my shoulder, which would have been a bad thing on several counts. I was avuncular. 'Look, my dear. Is there anything that you want to talk about?'

'I have talked. Didn't you hear me?'

'Yes. I did hear you, and I'll try to understand. Now let's keep calm and go along with this for the moment.'

We caught up with our companions at the door of the temple. Getting a party of nine through it took surprisingly long. The interior was as before, except that the chairs had been dusted, and the packages Paul took in two days ago were stacked near the altar. The horned phallic sculpture towering above brought Simon to life. With a cry, the small accountant flung up his hands. 'Magnificent! Oh, that's even better than the one in Fulham.'

'Fulham?' I queried.

'The Thames Satanist Lodge. Actually, now I look at this fellow more closely, he's more like the image in the Highgate Inferno. But much more vivid. A masterpiece. Could we, oh, could we USE the temple?'

Paul smiled. 'I've been making preparations with that in view.'

Herod too relished the Horned One. He gave the figure a kind of salute. 'Greetings, brother Lucifer. All ten of us bless you.'

'May we behold him soon,' responded Norman on the statue's behalf. He was getting into the spirit of the thing.

As we came out, Simon trotted beside me. 'Have you any acquaint-ance with the Cult?'

'Only at second hand.'

'It's a pity the press won't leave us alone. The stories are so bogus. Reporters hardly ever get to the real centres. They only find silly suburban devil-worshippers carving up chickens.' His tone was aggrieved. 'It gives Satanism a bad name.'

'I've always assumed that the real centres were difficult to trace.'

'The deeper ones, yes indeed. The Cult has a great tradition of keep-ing its secrets. That's been a factor in its alliance with Cryptocracy.'

'Do you mean an actual organizational link?'

'I'm sorry, it's a secret. Nothing personal, you understand. Still it would be foolish to deny the connection. Even Scotland Yard knows it. The Pigs watch us.' Using the outworn term, this mincing respect-able little man had an air of speaking a foreign language.

Freda addressed Paul. 'Didn't somebody say your American friend did three sculptures?'

She'd hit it. In all this time I've never looked for the third. It slipped out of mind, surely for a profounder reason than mere forgetfulness.

Paul said: 'Yes, there is another. It'll take you a while to get to it.'

'Is your estate so vast?'

'No. You'll see why.'

He led the party past the rear prospect of Allhallows, and headed for the path through the bushes which Annabel showed me that early morning. At some point I think I did conjecture that the third sculpture must be inside the maze, and I now suspected that my blind spot towards it was due to my feeling that the maze shut me out. As we filed along the path, Annabel halted and I caught up with her. She clung to a rhododendron bush, swaying. I was going to say 'Are you all right?' and it came out as 'Should I stop them?'

Her voice was faint. 'You can't. They have to do it themselves. Go on, go on.'

They debouched into the ex-garden and stared at the hexagonal hedge. 'It's inside there,' said Paul. 'At the centre of our maze.'

'Your maze?' Freda shrieked. 'What is this place, a fun-fair? How long does it take to get into it?'

'Depends on how fast you walk – and whether you know the route.'

'I'd rather pass this up for the moment,' said Joe.

Freda was more insistent. 'What the hell is it FOR? And why put the sculpture in it, of all the crackpot ideas?'

'Ask Martin. Or the sculptor.'

'Is the statue obscene maybe?'

'Aha!'

'I'm going in. You show me the way.'

Arnold Gore restrained her. 'Wait. This is interesting. Tell me, Paul, is this the kind of maze you can solve easily by the turning-to-the-right method?'[2]

'No, it isn't.'

'Good. Now I happen to know a psychologist who says maze-solving can be a personality indicator. It goes back to Watson and the Behaviourists. White rats and so on, but much more. It's already struck me we might use this technique for screening people who come to us for help in the Community. Anyhow, I suggest that I try to phone him and check the main lines of his argument, and then each of you should have a go at solving the maze without being told the route.'

'Fine,' said Joe.

'There's no hurry,' Arnold added. 'This afternoon, or tomorrow perhaps.'

'All right, Arnold,' said Freda. 'I'll go along with that, but on one condition. You have to try it yourself.'

'Agreed.'

I wondered if he was risking his prestige. What did the psychologist say it meant if you failed completely? Probably something fairly flattering – that you were intolerant of restriction, for instance.

They turned back. I kept in the rear. I expected Paul to sweep Annabel along with him, but he passed her, and the rest passed her, and she was still there. This time she did fall on my shoulder, sobbing with obscure relief.

2

It's late afternoon – a breathing space. For several hours, with a minimal break for dinner, I've been reconstructing the events of the past twenty-four. After the Cryptocrats adjourned to their camp-site I succeeded in phoning David Jacks, who agreed to return tomorrow to photograph the rituals. Martin's students, I found, had broken up into three chattering groups, one in the recreation room, one in the conference room, one (a couple only, Kwame and Owen) in the library. Martin explained that these were 'project groups' working on ideas of their own. Then he asked about my experience with SP5.

'I want to go over it with Karen as well as you,' I said. 'She took it down.'

'Let's do that now.'

She was in her room. Between us we retold the vision. Its mythical content was so palpable and local that Martin didn't need many footnotes. He recognized the Wild Hunt; and Gwyn-ap-Nudd the White One, lord of the Annwn-underworld beneath Glastonbury Tor; and the Arthur figure, human but also more than human.

It was very unlike his diary, though. He grappled bravely with that difficulty. 'I believe you did see into the proto-realm, but from a new angle. "Inwardness" for you took the form of myths and folklore motifs which you were already steeped in. Or at least it was based on them.'

'Geoffrey,' Karen interposed, 'when you came back you told me what it was like. The visions of biblical prophets, or Blake, you said.'

'That was as near as I could get.'

Martin's years of psychology helped him to extend his pattern till it had room for me. 'You must be closer than I am to the sources of dreams. That could be important. I've already thought that protoself theory spotlights a weakness of European philosophy by underlining that it's a philosophy of the conscious, waking ego. That's as true of Plato and Bergson as it is of Hume and Ayer. Indians don't make that mistake. Vedanta takes account of the sleeping mind as well as the waking.'

'Didn't Gurdjieff[3] maintain that most of us are asleep all the time and ought to wake up?'

'Gurdjieff puts his own meaning to it. His "waking" would be full integration of the psyche, the protoself flooding in. The magician's moment of insight and power, the scientist's flash of inspiration, going on all the time.'

'I wonder what would happen,' said Karen, 'if you took SP5 and dropped off to sleep. Nobody's ever done that.'

I didn't want them to get sidetracked into a duet of doubletalk about sleep. 'What I saw last night, though. Was it simply my own imagination stepped up, or did I see anything real?'

'Real in a sense. You made contact with mysteries locked up in this landscape. Contact through beings - presences - which are *there*. Though they aren't literally what you saw. They mediated whatever they had to tell you (I'm not sure what it is) through established symbols you could grasp.'

My mind was running back over the vision. 'That can't be the whole of it. The character who flew out of the north, now, and landed on the Tor. He wasn't just a convenient symbol, he was a person. I know who he was.'

'I think I know too, but you'd know better.'

'Nodens. Gwyn-ap-Nudd is his son. That's how Gwyn came to summon him. Nodens was the British god who had that temple at Lydney in the Forest of Dean.'

'Hold it there,' said Karen. 'Doesn't he turn up in the fantasy scene somehow?' She pulled a book off the shelf and leafed through it. 'Here we are. Arthur Machen. He was in the Golden Dawn outfit with Crowley and Yeats, wasn't he? *The Great God Pan*. Decadent horror yarn, 1895. He quotes a Roman inscription to Nodens and calls him the god of the Great Deep or Abyss.'

'Curiously enough, I can cap that,' said Martin. 'H.P. Lovecraft borrowed from Machen, as he did from other occultists and myth-fanciers. Nodens is in *The Dream-Quest of Unknown Kadath*. Lovecraft calls him a "potent and archaic god of unhinted deeps" who can overrule the sinister powers.'

The literary excursus could be as distracting as the sleep excursus. I stepped in again. 'All I know about Nodens is what I've read in Celtic scholars. He was a major British god with a personality - that is, he couldn't be defined as the god of anything in particular. He had a silver hand, and he was a huntsman and fisherman, and connected with the sea. Also he was a healer and he found lost possessions for you, like St Anthony. Pilgrims used to sleep in his temple and he instructed them in dreams.'

Martin pounced on that. 'Dreams again. The inhabitants of the proto-realm and the ways we encounter them. When you said Nodens couldn't be pinned down as the god of anything in particular, I believe you went to the heart of the religious imbroglio. Two of the SP5 test subjects did report meeting gods. I couldn't interpret that at first, but I got ideas later, and you're helping.

'The notion that gods began as abstractions, personifications, symbols of such-and-such – that's rubbish. Claptrap from the Age of Reason. (The only man who dared think the Age of Reason through to its end was the Marquis de Sade.) No, the more you study the birth of religions, the clearer it is that the gods start out as persons. Maybe in human form, maybe not, but the worshipper doesn't invent them, he encounters them. We don't know how, not in the West anyway, because it belongs to the lost golden-age state when Heaven and Earth were one and the gods dwelt among men.

'Look at Apollo and all the things he was concerned with. Poetry and music and oracles and the sun and moderation. Or Quetzalcoatl in Mexico – wind and fertility and civilization and the planet Venus and robbery. It's only later, when priests try to rationalize the proto-self's divine contacts, that the gods are whittled down into gods of anything. It takes a long time and it isn't satisfying.'

'That,' I suggested, 'might help to explain why there are myths about a sort of decline in Heaven. The present gods are felt to be meaner. With the Greeks you find a nostalgia for gods-before-the-gods who were actually pictured as a different lot, and superior: the Titans before the Olympians.'

Martin was pleased. 'Quite so. That isn't the end, either. The gods' final fate is to be rationalized into allegories. Mars begins as a fairly versatile chap, and winds up as a dreary personification of War. You may even get a further stage with division of labour. Read St Augustine on the pagan decadence, when the gods were split into functions, and a bridal couple went to bed with a whole committee of them, one mini-god to open the door and one to shut it and one to make the man erect and one to push the woman under him and one to keep her there... I can't remember all the details, but it's the ultimate idiocy of the theologizing mind.

'It is the end, though. Not the beginning. Gods didn't start like that. Man made contact with them as beings akin to himself, male and female, but with at least two superhuman qualities. They were immortal. Also they were numinous. You knew them as gods, you responded to them with awe. Religion is simply an after-attempt to spell out the experience, which usually botches it.'

I found an opening at last. 'Are you saying the gods are real?'

'Some anyhow. Potent living presences in the proto-realm that aren't born as human beings – or aren't often. Mystics and magicians encounter them through the protoself.'

'Would you explain the higher religions like that? Christianity for instance?' I'd wanted to find out Martin's religious background and he obliged without prodding.

'I'd say this view of the matter may not give the whole truth, but it certainly helps. I had a Catholic upbringing, my parents were con-verts in the Belloc-Chesterton ferment[4]. With me it didn't take, but I can see the force of some of the arguments.

'Read the Bible honestly. There's no religion at the beginning, or at the end either, if it comes to that. None in Eden, none in the New Jerusalem. Religion goes with a fallen condition, which the God of the Jews is supposed to be gradually putting right. Now take a good look at this God. He's no abstraction, he's a personal being, very much so. From Adam onwards the people who stay close to him encounter him; they don't infer him or reason about him. Furthermore, he's con-nected with a territory – Palestine. He plants his Chosen there and he inspires the prophets there. He's a presence in other words, a very dominant presence who won't let any others count, and he has an abiding-place of his own in Zion.

'You yourself compared your SP5 vision to the biblical prophets' experiences. Fair enough. The God of the Jews, whoever he may be, made them see sights with inner meanings. Some Celtic god or gods did the same for you.'*

---

* To judge from the notes which are used and expanded here, Martin sidestepped the issue of Christianity. In a later discussion of the Holy Grail legends, I understood him to suggest that Jesus was a rare or unique case, a divine presence that did appear as a human being. His disciples sensed the numinousness, the divinity shining through. As they were Jews and admitted only one God, Jesus had to be that God in human form – with whatever Trinitarian acrobatics were needed to explain how.

It was glib and it didn't satisfy – but not for the obvious reason. A sceptic would have objected that this was 'over-belief', that Martin's casual 'yes' to any and every deity went ludicrously beyond what was required to cover the data. The truth, though, was that it didn't go far enough, or rather that it didn't go in the right direction.

I struggled to express this. 'I'm willing to admit that there may have been a revelation of sorts. That some outside agency gathered together a lot of highly charged imagery and regrouped it into a story for me. Only I feel that this doesn't cover it. I have a sense of a deeper factor, a trigger that set it off, not "out there" among those presences of yours but closer to home.'

'Why not?' said Martin. 'Your protoself is largely unknown territory.'

I shook my head. 'It isn't like that. I can't pin it down... yes I can. Under SP5 you're more or less in the protoself, taken over by it. So you accept strange things as a matter of course, right? No violent surprises. That's in your diary. Karen mentioned it too.'

'So?'

'So, I was surprised, several times. Shocked, bewildered. Whatever switched me on after the first little bit wasn't entirely in me, it was beyond somehow. I don't feel that gods come into it. Even if they did go to work on me, there was a separate influence forcing me into being receptive to them, with a pretty powerful jolt.'

I was surprised again. Martin jumped out of his chair. He was radiant, so far as he ever is. 'That's... superb.'

'How do you mean?'

'You're nearly there, Geoffrey. Don't let's kill it with premature explanations. You're nearly there. In a way, more effectively than I am.' Before I could react he was gone, leaving me with Karen.

'What was all that about?'

She parried. 'I'm sorry if Martin's approach is a mite confusing. It does work, in time. I could give you a hint.'

'I could do with it.'

'This trigger of yours, this outside thing. Picture the scene again, at the moment when you swallowed your pill.'

I made an effort. 'You and me sitting on the rug. Grass. Trees—'

'That'll do for now. And when you came back?'

'You and me sitting on the rug. Grass. And... oh, I see what you mean. You told me she'd been there most of the time.'

'She wandered over soon after you took off, and settled where you saw her. She never spoke or looked at us, she just sat.'

'So you think... no, I don't know what you think.'

'Things like this do happen when she's around. Sometimes, naturally, I might be happier if they didn't. But I've learnt not to blink the facts when they do.'

3

A most eventful evening. On Martin's invitation, the Cryptocrats came in to an early supper – or rather high tea – with the students, some of whom were still tired from the vigil and wanted to go to bed soon. The dining room was crowded. A certain fraternization occurred, but curiously little sustained talk. The Bambergers made no attempt to mix, and didn't speak even to their confrère and sponsor Norman. He tried once, in his own way, to draw them in. When Freda picked up a cake he said 'Calories, calories!' The jocosity brought him a sour look and he retreated. Conversation didn't get fairly off the ground anywhere, except for a dialogue, or rather two interlocking monologues, between Herod and Mrs Frobisher. Mrs Frobisher maintained that the true Messiah was born in 70 A.D. ('on the day the Temple fell') and is now living in Tibet awaiting his hour. Herod – I am really not sure what Herod maintained.

Arnold's maze experiment had been dropped. I asked him if he'd got through to his psychologist, and he replied curtly that he had, but didn't now think the test could be applied here.

Paul told me that he and Norman and the five guests were holding a meeting. They wanted me to be present. 'Incidentally,' he asked as we arranged chairs in the conference room, 'did you take SP5 at Cadbury as I advised?'

'Yes.'

'I'll bet you saw King Arthur.'

'Sort of.' I gave him a much-edited summary, expanding what I'd told the students at breakfast.

The end excited him. 'Arthur – or the Arthur-figure or whatever you call him – was roused from sleep by a woman.'

'Yes.'

Paul's agile mind was clearly bounding ahead of me, but I couldn't decide in what direction. 'Is anyone else invited to this meeting?'

'It's open. But I don't think many of our Allhallows crowd will show up. There's been a certain, you might say, official discourage-ment.'

Norman appeared and urged the meeting's importance. I had an impression that he glanced at Paul and Paul nodded to him, very slightly.

'Come upstairs,' said Norman to me. 'I've got some Cryptocracy stuff I'd like to brief you on. While we're up there I'll see if Janice wants to be at the meeting.'

I'd seen the two of them together so rarely – the former Women's Libber, in fact, had so nearly drifted out of my ken – that I'd almost forgotten she had come with Norman in the first place. We climbed to the top floor among the silent cubicles. Were they or were they not together? The empty cubicle which he took me into didn't give a firm answer. It was 'his' rather than 'hers', and yet a few female appurte-nances lay around as if she'd at least sat in.

Norman up-ended a big knapsack over the table and a heap of objects tumbled out. 'Our visual aid kit.' He unrolled a chart and assembled a three-dimensional tubular model, vaguely suggesting a molecular structure. Around this he disposed coloured cubes of varying size.

'Our basic theme,' he said, is 'Stevick's Power-Knowledge-Decision formula. PKD. Are you familiar with it?'

'I'm afraid not.'

'Stevick proved that in western society, the present distribution of Knowledge is adverse to the effectiveness of Power, and this sets up a vicious circle reacting back on Knowledge itself. When Knowledge flows freely through all these channels' (he tapped several of the tubes in his model) 'it has to change its character to maintain flow. It has to get simplified, tidied up, impoverished. That's why the Establishment rejects magical modes of thinking, and why we decided that Allhallows was worth looking into. Conversely, experience shows – especially in industry, we've made a special study of indus-trial engineering, Paul's told me a lot that bears this out – experience shows... wait a second, I've lost it.' He closed his eyes and opened them. 'The areas of maximum efficiency are those where there is a strict hierarchy of secrecy, and the minimum downward and outward information-flow. Paul says this was proved in experiments described by Niall Brennan and William H. Whyte[5] which there's been a conspiracy of silence about.'

He talked on for several minutes, leading up crabwise to Cryptocracy itself, which sounded like a network of initiates and under-cover agents. 'Knowledge-Centres, properly linked and activated, will become Power-Centres. We're already confident that our system can master the problems of society.'

'Tell me, if you're allowed: who leads Cryptocracy?'

'We have an Open Leadership and a Closed Leadership. The Open Leadership is, er, open.' He reeled off a few names which I dimly remembered having seen in the papers, but not linked with the word 'Cryptocracy'. I associated two with fierce, opaque letters to the quality press during financial crises.

'How about the Closed Leadership?'

'That's the real one and it's secret. The number of leaders that any given member's allowed to know depends on his rating – his rank, seniority, attendance record.'

'Where do you stand yourself?'

'I don't think there's any reason not to tell you... I'm a staff officer in a Grade 3 Knowledge-Centre. I could name four of the Closed Leadership. But not to a non-member, of course.'

The chart and gadgets were genuinely intriguing, but baffling. I wondered if they were camouflage themselves, and the real Cryptocracy was something else again.

'At present,' Norman said, 'we're short on Mystique. The meeting here is to work on that.' He glanced at his watch. 'I'll ask Janice if she wants to come.'

We left the cubicle. As we did so I had the first independent intimation that we weren't alone on the top floor. I could hear muffled breathing and giggling. Norman rapped on the woodwork outside another cubicle, stepped into it with hardly a pause, and then backed out again.

'Go away, we're resting!' a female voice shrilled derisively, while a second female voice went on giggling. Norman was flushed. He led the way hurriedly downstairs. 'I'd no idea Janice was like that.'

'Have you known her long?'

'Long enough, I'd have thought. She isn't a Cryptocrat, you understand.'

'I suppose she had Mei-ling with her.'

'That Chinese is a shock too. She's so intellectual, so academic.'

'You're quite sure they weren't just resting?'

'That was the only time I've seen Janice undressed.'

I accompanied Norman back to the conference room, feeling what I hadn't before, ever: a glimmer of sympathy towards him.

Attendance at the meeting was very much as Paul had foreshadowed: himself, Norman and Annabel, the five guest Cryptocrats, and me. The sole dropper-in was Steve. Lately he's been where I've been myself as little as Janice. When he turned up in the conference room I'd no idea how his interests might be shaping, but suspected he merely wanted to observe a new bunch of people, for the sake of his numerology act at the club.

Norman took the chair and pattered through some preliminary business. It was plain from the short discussion which followed that he worked habitually with the others. They weren't just fellow-members whom he'd happened to invite to Allhallows. Apart from a predictable item about a membership drive, the agenda sounded trivial. Norman then made a remark on the theme of 'taking our revolution a step further'. He intended this, I think, to lead into a longer speech. But Arnold Gore interrupted.

'As you know, I have views on this. To change society you must work on the poorest and most oppressed. For instance—' He dilated on programmes he was operating among the dwellers in mean terraces, crumbling overcrowded houses, soul-shrivelling bedsitters. It sounded splendid and then with a sudden chill it sounded disquieting. Once or twice he turned my way and I stared into his eyes, into emptiness. When he finished, Norman was at a loss how to proceed. Knowing they wanted to involve me in something, I tried to probe.

'Arnold, I've a query that often occurs to me when anyone talks of changing society, and I'd be interested to hear how you answer it. Somebody pointed out long ago that with all the Utopias that have been written, it's hard to think of a single one that any ordinary person would want to live in. It reminds me of a comment Chesterton made on Yeats: "The trouble with the Land of Heart's Desire is that the heart does not desire it." In your own work, how do you take account of what the people of the area want?'

'What they want? What does that mean? One thing you can depend on, you won't learn anything useful by listening to them.'

Joe Bamberger supported him. 'It isn't "what they want". You'll never get anywhere with moth-eaten clichés like that. At the closest you might say it's what they "really" want. But all you'll get by asking them is a load of media pulp thrown back at you. If you go by that, you'll be back to Square One every time.'

'But,' I said, 'do you ask? Do these plans of yours even make sense to ordinary people? This doesn't apply to me in the same way – and yet when I'm planning a book, I always think of the grocer across the street. I've been doing the odd bit of shopping there for years. Suppose he were to ask me: "What's your new book going to be about?" and I couldn't give him at least some notion of it in a few words, I'd be sure the idea was wrong. Too remote, too complicated, too would-be clever, I don't know, but wrong somehow. I'd think again.'

Freda half-laughed, half-screamed. 'What the hell is that meant to prove? Of all the antediluvian Poujadist[6] hogwash!'

'I'm arguing really, I suppose, that there's a case for treating ordinary people with respect.'

'Respect!' Arnold almost shouted. 'I don't doubt that plenty of feudal lords treated their tenants with the utmost respect...'

Norman, in the chair, had opened and shut his mouth ineffectually. Now Paul rapped on the table. 'Please. We're getting sidetracked. However you may regard Geoffrey's attitude to his grocer, I can assure you his books have been selling for many years, so we must view his technique with... dare I say respect?' He switched on a take-the-heat-out-of-it smile and I realized he was very anxious indeed to make me a good guy in the Cryptocrats' sight. Annabel, beside him, was fumbling nervously with a portion of her dress that trailed down from the shoulder. Herod and Simon sat inert. Steve had fished an envelope from his pocket and was scribbling.

Ignoring Norman (who might or might not have made his speech, but never did), Paul launched the major proposition. It began as a recap of what he and Norman said in the workshop during the photographer's visit. That the Arthurian-Avalonian mythos is still, for some reason, weirdly potent. That Allhallows is at the heart of its country. That Arthur's immortality and promised return seem to strike a deep chord in human nature.

'I can confirm that,' Arnold put in. 'Even where there's no King Arthur, people cook up a substitute for him. You may not all be aware of this, but millions of Americans are convinced that John Kennedy never died. After the shooting in '63 he was kept alive, though the brain damage reduced him to a vegetable state. Research is said to be going on with a view to curing him.'

'Is this likely to be true?' asked Simon.

'I understand that for several years an entire floor of a hospital in Dallas was sealed off. Then, when Kennedy's so-called widow married Onassis, the patient was transferred to a Greek island. In some of Jackie's wedding pictures you can make out an unidentified figure in a wheelchair. That's him.'

'It's true then?'

'According to a private informant of mine,' said Arnold, 'a man who works in the Pentagon, the US military-technological complex is holding Kennedy as an ace up its sleeve in case of need. If he can be cured just enough to talk, he'll be trundled out at the right moment to remind Americans of the Cuban missile crisis and assure them they can triumph again.'7

It was curious to hear a story in Mrs Frobisher's manner coming from such a different source. Paul picked it up adroitly. 'That shows what a strong archetype this is, the dream of the hero's return from death, and the restoration of his lost glory. Well now, Norman has convinced me that the myth of King Arthur gives us the makings of a large-scale mystique which we at Allhallows are well placed to develop.'

'What,' said Freda, 'a lot of romantic Round Table crap? For Christ's sake, it simply isn't on.'

'No, Freda,' Paul replied. 'I mean we can harness the entrenched spell of the myth, we can bring it to life in the contemporary setting, we can MAKE Arthur return.

'Allhallows has never hit the mass-media before. But now we're going to. The *Globe* colour-supplement is running this feature on us. David Jacks is doing the photo work. And by an amazing stroke of luck - if luck's the proper word - it was Geoffrey who sold them the idea, and is here now to gather material So if this comes off, we reach the mass public and we reach it by way of an Arthurian expert.'

Arnold looked interested, but sceptical. 'Where do we go from there?'

'We (that is, Cryptocracy with support from Allhallows) begin to plug the motif of a New Patriotism. When we're ready, we announce a national competition with a serious aim. Through a newspaper if one of them will take it up. I've drafted a memo on this.'

Oddly reminiscent of Martin doing likewise, he produced a sheet of paper. But unlike Martin he read it aloud.

The dream of Arthur's return remains haunting today, partly because it reflects a feeling which many people have, if not articulately: that things will never come right through soldiering on with so-called progress, that we need a clean break, a fresh start.

There is surely great readiness to believe that Somebody might appear with a new, liberating vision, springing up from the deepest strata of the national genius, and that a fresh start could come through this fresh leadership. The Somebody could be a young obscure person who hasn't risen through normal channels - like Arthur in the legend, who arrives from nowhere, sixteen years old, and is the only person who can draw the sword from the stone.

Much of the welcome over the past decade or two for heroes of an unofficial, unprecedented sort (the Beatles were the first) has reflected this instinct. I submit that it is sound. Somewhere there IS a person with a new vision or idea which could inspire new energies. Why not actively search for him - or her?

The phrase 'National Quest' occurs to me. Suppose all mute prophets and possible leaders were invited to step forward and speak up. I maintain that a single front-runner would emerge: the new 'Arthur' who can draw out the sword and break the deadlock in British society. The Quest would attract a swarm of cranks. It would require a long, ruthless process of screening and short-listing. Yet it would be infinitely worth-while if the potential leader were found.

Paul stopped reading. 'I've made a few copies,' he said, handing them out.

Arnold was almost sold. 'I'm getting it. You devise a selection procedure to pick out this Saviour from the umpteen applicants you'd have. Preferably a bright virile young chap with sex appeal, but enough substance so he can mature. As an ideas man he won't be a Führer type as well. Our own leadership can keep him under control.'

Norman got in at last. 'Then you see, a movement grows round him. We have a torchlight enthronement on top of Cadbury. We give him a title, say "Emperor of Albion" as the ancient magical name of Britain. There's an emblem ready-made for badges and banners.' He stood up and showed them the monogram on the back of the chair, with the letters of 'Albion' in it.

'If we picked him right,' Arnold mused, 'he'd be someone with an idea that could be built up and applied through the Noel Community. Some new social gospel that could be angled to catch the public's fancy. It wouldn't have to be really ideological. Even a good slogan might be enough, a good fighting phrase, like "Black Power" was.'

'Then if Geoffrey helps us to sponsor him,' Paul continued, 'that'll give him an adviser who already has status in the field. A Merlin to his Arthur.'

'Or John the Baptist to Jesus,' said Herod. 'Geoffrey looks rather like John the Baptist.'

Paul's package was more carefully thought out than I'd expected. But I couldn't let him rush on unopposed. 'Surely this is all rather contrived. A gimmick.'

He countered unhesitantly with a trump held in reserve. 'Does it have to be? Think of it in terms of Martin's belief on reincarnation. He's discussed it with you, I know. A being - a "presence" - took human shape long ago as Arthur, who passed away leaving unfinished business. Isn't it quite in keeping that this same being should reappear now, should carry on through another leader, who in effect is Arthur over again?'

'And should set up the plan we're considering,' urged Norman, 'to put this leader in a context where his role will be understood and he'll have influence. The twentieth century's instant Sword in the Stone.'

'Sorry,' Simon interjected, 'but you're miles away from me. This may be something you people teach at Allhallows, I don't follow it.'

Paul gave them a sketch of part of Martin's theory. He did it most skilfully, never misrepresenting, but steering clear of the subtler intricacies of Binary Man. I was impressed (as I'd been all through the meeting) by the charm, shrewdness and persuasiveness which a management-trained person can deploy when he wants to. Even with Annabel beside him, a silent reminder of this and that, Paul could tempt.

After all, hadn't he shown an acumen which Martin lacked? He'd proposed the Cadbury visit. He'd advised me to start on SP5 there, with dazzling results. In spite of his own catastrophe with the drug – according to Karen. Perhaps she was right and he was getting it from Wessex Labs surreptitiously. But then again, perhaps by doing so he'd mastered it and was profiting from it.

As he talked on, filling the Cryptocrats in, a heady notion seized me that he might be giving me the answer. That all those promptings and nudgings which seemed to affect my life had been a prelude to this assignment, this Neo-Merlin role. More, quite probably more than just projecting and briefing some whizkid Arthur II whom Paul's National Quest would unearth. Beginning from my *Globe* feature I could popularize Allhallows over a broader front. I could simplify and encapsulate (always in touch with Martin of course). I could strengthen this mass movement with a mass doctrine, a new religion even, growing out of the world's spiritual traditions but taking them further. A Blake-style emanation from Albion. A fulfilment of the mighty awakening which my SP-vision had hinted at. The time being surely ripe. The basis, also, being ready to hand, there at the table with me. Whatever one felt about the Cryptocrats on a glancing appraisal, Arnold Gore's organization and prestige were real. The Bambergers' cash was real, or so one presumed... I took the closest look I dared at some rings Freda had on... Real.[8]

A strange sharp image darted into my mind, an image of that hilltop crossroad, the meeting-place of Ram and Bull, and Karen in the erratic sunlight.

Paul had ceased speaking, Herod had started. 'You're raising high-powered spiritual issues. I recommend we seek guidance. We have a case here for what I call Prayer Plus. Not only praying, but providing a channel for the answer.'

Joe grinned. 'Like a reply-paid telegram.'

'Say, that's a neat way of putting it,' said Herod unruffled. 'Pray first, and then, prayerfully, seek omens. Or scry in a crystal ball. Or hold a séance.'

Paul looked sidelong at Annabel. 'We can do any of those things. Annabel is our natural genius here. I asked her to attend, partly because I felt, myself, we should try some kind of divination. But your séance is a better idea. Annabel's a medium too, though she doesn't often perform.'

'No problem then,' said Arnold. 'Let's hold a séance.'

'We might be able to raise Arthur in person,' said Joe.

Annabel whispered to Paul and shook her head. He laid a hand on her arm. 'You can do this for us and nobody else can. You're needed, love, you really are needed.' His voice was edgeless and caressing, yet it wasn't quite right. You felt the caress was calculated. Also the word 'love' sounded off-key, not the everyday colloquial nothing, yet not a frank endearment either. But she didn't whisper again.

Paul stood up, drawing her with him. 'We'll use the cellar.'

4

I guessed the house must possess a cellar on my first exploration, but never spotted the way down to it. It's behind a partition in the work-shop, in a remodelled corner which must once have been kitchen ter-ritory. We descended the groaning stairs to a vaulted chamber. Weak light struggled into it through a grating. It was smelly and cobwebby, with rusty chains dangling from the walls, and mountains of pack-ing-cases, but still plenty of room for the party. In the centre was a long table. Packing-cases were quickly arranged round this, old papers were spread over dusty lids. We sat, Annabel at the table's head.

Herod prayed to his Jesus - a surprisingly dignified prayer for guidance. Then Paul launched into an incantation. A known word here and there gave me the clue to his source. I found the book later in the library and have it in front of me. He was certainly throwing everything in.

SOTOU

AR

ATHOREBALO

MRIODOM

AROGOGORUABRAO

PHOTETH

MA

GAIA

ABRAXAS

At this point Simon Calthrop joined in with an unpleasant sneering intonation.

IAO, ADONAI, SABAOTH
ANAKTAM PASTAM PASPASIM DIONSIM
YOD, HE, VAU, HE[9]

Paul made us link hands and chorus YOD, HE, VAU, HE at least twenty times. After which, silence. Annabel at the head of the table appeared to slip away into a genuine trance. Presently her face altered. She looked older and of doubtful sex. A voice issued from her mouth, deeper than her own, speaking disjointed words with a Welsh accent.

'Apple-trees, apple-trees. Dragons. Celidon. Forest.' The voice burst out into peals of ugly laughter.

'Who are you?' said Paul.

More laughter.

'Is there anyone you wish to speak to?'

'The one who knows me.'

I had an inspiration. 'Were you at Arderydd?'

A cry, almost a howl, of anguish.

I pressed. 'They say it would have been better if you'd never gone there.'

'Better. Better. The merciful Son of God forgive.'

'Myrddin ab Morfryn.'

'Myrddin ab Morfryn.'

'I do know you then.'

'As I know you.'

'Merlin.'

'Merlin.'[10]

'You're telling me that I myself...'

'Yes. You are.'

I considered. 'Do you speak to Martin Ellis?'

'I have spoken to him.'

'Where?'

'At Dinas Cadwy.'

I recognized the Celtic name from which, according to some, the English derived 'Cadbury'. So far, so good. It tallied. 'What else do you want to tell me?'

'To go my way again, but not all the way.'

'Could you enlarge on that?'

'With the man. Not with the woman.'

'You mean, with Arthur but not with Nimuë?'

'I mean mean mean...' The voice trailed and mumbled, then recovered. 'Go where I went. To the Giants' Ring.'

'Stonehenge.'

'The great stones out of Erin which I raised into place.'

I took a deep breath and spoke out very distinctly. 'Listen. I don't know who or what you are. I do know you're not what you pretend. You're not Merlin. You've only been reading up on legends about him.'

The voice, nonplussed, began shrilly. 'I cannot hear you. Your words are like the wind far away. Go to S-S-Stonehenge the great stones out of Erin which I r-r-raised into pl...'

I interrupted. 'Exactly. That's bad archaeology. You've got your dates wrong.'

The effect was violent, and now, thinking it over after a couple of hours, I'm not sure whether I did right. Though perhaps Annabel was beyond being damaged; I hope so. What we saw was another change in her, a more shocking change. Her usual facial calm - not lost even in the grip of the pseudo-Merlin creature - broke completely. A variety of frantic expressions began convulsing her features. She looked like a rapid series of women, and men too, in assorted states of savage and mounting excitement. Voices in conflict, high, low, and middling sprang out of her mouth uttering gibberish. She bounced on the packing case tossing her body from side to side, the victim of a psychic gang-bang.

Nobody stirred. Interference would have been too plainly dangerous to her. The fit raged for several minutes. Then she slumped forward on the table and was exhaustedly herself again.

Paul leaned towards her. 'Thank you so much, dear. I'm sorry if it was upsetting... was it?' She stared at him and shook her head wordlessly. 'Good. You'd better go and rest.' To us: 'I'm sure you'll agree we must congratulate Geoffrey on his presence of mind. We could trust him not to give way to wishful thinking, or let anything slipshod get past him. As to what we've seen and heard, well, it was mysterious.

But it shows we're in touch with real forces. Terrific ones.' He guided Annabel to the staircase. She leaned on his arm.

'You've convinced me,' said Arnold. 'Enough to go on discussing this proposition anyhow. Whether you raised Merlin or not, you raised something. If it exists it can be raised again. Frankly I don't care much whether this is spirits or the subconscious or whatever. A performance like that is going to impress people you can't budge any other way.'

They clumped and creaked upstairs and were gone, all but Steve. He was still sitting at the table, chuckling. 'Did you ever see anything like it?'

'Now you ask me, never.'

'We could almost put it on at the club – second show – only it wouldn't work with two straight-men. That poor kid, though. It'd be strictly fun if she were doing it as an act, but it's for real, isn't it?'

'Afraid so.'

I studied him. Here he was, a waiter, the closest thing at Allhallows (numerology notwithstanding) to the Common Man... and this was his reaction.

'Thank you,' I said. 'You may have helped me a lot.'

'Don't know how. But glad to oblige anyway. Er – that Arnold Gore bloke, he's not a friend of yours, is he?'

'No.'

'Take a tip, don't get caught in anything he tries to run. I wouldn't touch it with a bargepole, whatever it was.'

'How did you come to decide that?'

'Simple. I added up his name.'

Seventh Day

I WOKE EARLY with a negative hangover. No physical upset, simply a flatness, a let-down. I felt that a door had closed, or nearly closed. It was unconsoling to tell myself, with my mind's sober portion, that it probably hadn't been open.

The morning was bright-cloudy. As on that other day I got up and went out. Over the pavement behind the house, on to the lawn. A second, more nostalgic echo of my time of acquaintance-making. Karen's absence from the lawn was a felt absence. Down that perspective between the pillars, the sculpture stood poised on its grey plinth and the temple skulked among its trees.

Flat, all flat. A set for a film they never shot.

I reflected on my *Globe* piece. After nearly a week it hadn't jelled. I still could give no answer to the question I'd hung it on. Perhaps when Madri came, one of the actual exhibits... but the prospect failed to inspirit. The involvements that were bringing this place to life for me all seemed to have merged greyly into the hangover. Two of my SP5 pills remained. Would it be safe to take another unsupervised? Safe or not, this wasn't the time.

Near the pillars I waited, as if Karen might step forth in her outdoor setting. She didn't. Somebody else did.

'Hallo,' a female voice called behind me. Its cheerfulness threw me off my stroke. I swung round and was confused to see Annabel again, smiling. She had a deep-blue dress on. For the first time she appealed to me (that is, appearance-wise) as a straightforwardly interesting girl. Her junkie skin didn't obtrude. Maybe, though, it was just a *moyen-sensuel* response to several days of mild stimulus without action....

She said: 'I've been looking for you.'

'That's very nice, why?'

'To take you into the maze.'

'Right then, let's go.'

We started walking. After an appreciable patch of silence she spoke.

'You didn't ask the reason.'

'No.'

'If you had, I'd have changed my mind.'

'Ripeness is all.'

'You say that as if it were a quotation.'

'It is.'

'From somebody I ought to have read?'

'Shakespeare, actually.'

'Not the one with the fairies in it? I played Mustard-seed in a school performance.'

'No, not that. *King Lear.*'

'Oh yes. The one where the old king has three daughters and they won't speak to each other – I mean, the first and second never speak to the youngest. Except once when they have to.'

(I've checked, and she's right. I can't recall a single Shakespearian scholar who makes this point.)

At the entrance of the maze Annabel paused. 'Ready?'

'Lead on, Ariadne.'

We plunged into the great green hexagon. I went slowly, deliberately, gazing around. She matched my pace. The hedges were clipped and trained over wire fences that held them upright. I estimated their average height as about seven feet, and the breadth of the flagstoned paths between them as three.

Gradually it became clear to me that the main paths ran parallel with the outside, so that anyone looking on the maze from above would get a snap impression of concentric hexagons. Which, however, would be too simple. The paths doubled back most bafflingly. Several times we came to gaps in the hedges, opening inwards or outwards on to a path running parallel. Several times also we got on to transit paths intersecting the main ones at right angles. These cross-paths had steps in them which disclosed that the maze sank gently towards the centre. Each diminishing hexagon as you went inwards was about six inches lower than the one outside it. The total descent from outer hedge to central enclosure was a yard or so. A modest drop with a disproportionate impact. I was in a vortex. The maze was sucking me down into secret depths.

Annabel moved unerringly. She branched off to the right, to the left. She slipped through gaps and ignored other gaps. Twice she led me all the way down to the last hedge surrounding the centre, and then back again before I could see anything through its dense leaves.

I asked her only one question. 'How do you remember the route?'

'We have a little poem. I'll tell you later.'

After several minutes of plodding, with halts to look about and take stock, our journey was abruptly over. We rounded a corner towards the centre, and confronted a narrow arch cut in the last hedge. Only one person could enter it at a time. Annabel turned sideways to let me pass her. I stepped down a final step into a space in the thickness of the hedge. Here I could stand but not progress, because of a door facing me. Screwed into it at eye-level was a flat snake curled back on itself: not quite the alchemic Ouroboros, its tail wasn't in its mouth, but it was reaching for the tip with jaws gaping.

To the right of the snake, and hence peculiarly high up, was a massive latch that held the door closed. This was held itself by a locking device – a more sophisticated version of the wedge you sometimes see tied to a latch, which you push in above it if you want to prevent it from being raised. Here, the wedge was on a separate pivot. To disengage it and free the latch, you had to twist a tight handle, geared in with it, through a complete circle. Turning the handle (which couldn't be done in a single wrist motion), and then raising the released latch, took several seconds.

The socket which the latch fitted into projected from the door-frame. When the door was at last unfastened it opened away from me. I gave it a push. For the first few inches it moved heavily, then it gathered momentum and swung slowly inwards by itself, carried by spiral hinges through a wide arc. The entrance yawned empty. Annabel murmured over my shoulder: 'Look straight ahead and keep still.'

I looked straight ahead into, and across, the final hexagon at the maze centre. Four or five yards in front of me I saw an upside-down face. After a dizzying moment I recognized the face as my own, reflected in a concave mirror which, at that range, inverted it. The mirror was part of the third sculpture.[1]

Here indeed it was. I stared at the evasive object trying to take it in. It was of metal like the others, but larger and sturdier, maybe ten feet high. If the maze had all been on ground level the top would have been visible from outside, rising above the hedges. Apparently the centre was lowered to keep it hidden, and just enough to do so. I couldn't see anything to warrant Paul's hint of obscenity; that must have been a joke to tease Freda. The main structure, rooted in an oblong of grass, suggested a tree simplified to a capital T surmounting a trunk. The concave mirror was a little higher than half-way up it. Around and above, the stem carried an arrangement of strips, interlacing and crossing. One of them ran up to the horizontal stroke of the T. This, I realized, was a variation on the artistic theme of the first sculpture, out on the lawn. With a spectator's inverted face added, the design became a human figure head downward.

'You see?' said Annabel.

'I think so.'

'Now walk towards it very slowly. Keep your eyes on the mirror if you can.'

Before moving I glanced round the enclosure. Its floor was almost covered by two pools full of water-plants, one on my right, one on my left. Between them, a miniature stone causeway led straight over to the sculpture. Very slowly I walked four paces along it, facing the mirror all the time. I could hardly have diverged without toppling into a pool. As I advanced, the mirror image obeyed the laws of optics. It blurred, then reassembled. I reached the artificial tree and saw my face right way up, slightly enlarged. Nothing below it hinted at a human form, and above it there was no inverted man any more, only a lopsided tangle of metal. My approach had banished personality from the structure.

Going round to the back, I examined the fixing of the mirror.

It was mounted on a pair of vertical rails so that it could slide up and down the trunk. There even seemed to be a mechanism for sliding it. Some of the thinner metal strips above were bolted to the sides of the mirror, and looked as if they would flex up and down with it as it shifted.

Annabel had joined me. 'That's for adapting it to a person's height. It's wired to the door. When you start turning the handle an electric eye measures you, and the mirror slides up or down to your level before you can get the door open.'

'So however tall or short you are... within reason... you see yourself as the upside-down figure.'

'That's it.'

'I can't comment,' I said after an interval. 'You must give me time to digest.'

'Of course.'

We turned back. Annabel shut the door behind us, and secured the latch with a double twist of the handle. She led me out of the maze, not fast, but as unfalteringly as she had led me in. We emerged and passed through the rhododendron bushes.

She stopped. 'That poem you asked about—'

'Poem? Ah, yes, your mnemonic for the route.'

I fancy that the word mnemonic confused her, but she continued. 'At every point in that maze where you have a choice, you've got to do one of three things: stick to the path you're already on, or turn right, or turn left.'

'Understood.'

'On the way in, there are sixteen places where you do have to choose, if you follow the proper route. So the poem has sixteen words. A word starting with a vowel means "stick to the path you're on". If the word starts with a consonant in the first half of the alphabet - the A to M part - it means "turn left". A consonant in the second half - N to Z - means "turn right".'

'What's the poem then?'

> "'Through many bitter afternoons
> Great Odin agonized alone,
> Surveying overhead the runes,
> Their meaning mockingly unknown.'"

'Let's see now. The first word is—'

' "Through". That starts with T. Consonant, second half of alphabet. Turn right.'

'You do that, and walk on for a while, and when you have to make your next choice the word is—'

'"Many". Consonant, first half of alphabet. Turn left. Same for the next, "bitter". But then you get "afternoons", starting with a vowel.

At the next place where you have a choice, you stay with the path you're on, and take no notice of the path branching off from it.'

'I see. I'll take the rest on trust. How do you get out – by working through the poem backwards?'

'That's it, you unwind, but you have to change the rule. Vowels as before. Consonants-first-half, right. Consonants-second-half, left. You need a bit of practice.'

It struck me that when Arnold proposed using this maze for his personality-test game, he'd had no idea what he could be letting his friends in for. 'Surely it would be an appalling job to find your way through without knowing. Unless you left a trail or drew diagrams. Has anybody done it?'

'Yes, but very few. The people who get most excited about it usually aren't ready, so when they try, it's too much for them.'

Another discussion-defying Annabel remark. I didn't answer it. We had wandered out of the bushes and past the camping area, where Cryptocrats could be heard stirring. That reminded me, we were expecting more visitors, Madri and the Pentacle party.

I said: 'I gather the Grail Ritual is to be put on this evening.'

'Yes, Karen told me.'

'In view of your stage experience, would you be willing to read a part?'

'My stage experience? Oh, you mean Mustard-seed. Sure, if you want me to.'

'You could be a Grail Maiden. I'll give you a script. It really would help if you could find time to go over the movements and be ready to explain to the cast. Karen has the props and costumes.'

'All right, I'd like that.'

When she'd gone back into the house I looked at the world around me and it was different.

2

I gave her the script at breakfast and she wasted no time. Having skimmed through it while eating a boiled egg, she went straight over to Mr Frobisher, who was near me, and asked him to read the role of the Celebrant.

'The what, my dear?'

'The Celebrant. Nobody else would do.'

'But who is he?'

'He conducts the initiation,' I said. 'Annabel's right. You do look the part.'

'Very well then, I'm honoured.'

She flitted between the tables, telling Karen to fetch the equipment, warning Martin that the astrologer wouldn't be attending his morning session. Within minutes I found myself in the recreation room with the nucleus of my company: Mr Frobisher, Celebrant; Annabel, First Grail Maiden; Karen, Wardrobe Mistress. Martin was outside with the other students (it was getting sunnier) and the Cryptocrats had driven off to some *avant-garde* art show in Bristol.

I handed out more scripts.

'They tell me you wrote this for television,' said Mr Frobisher.[2]

'As part of a programme on mythology. But it was more than an act. The people who staged it were members of a society I belonged to myself. We hoped to learn something about the Grail idea by reconstruction, if you see what I mean.'

'And did you?'

'I felt we did. The script's my own, of course, but I based it on genuine clues in early literature.'

'Forgive my ignorance. Wasn't the Grail the chalice of Christ at the Last Supper? I thought it was hidden somewhere in Britain and Arthur's knights rode in quest of it.'

'Eventually yes, that's the story. But we get traces of an earlier pagan version where the Grail was a magic vessel, probably a cauldron of inspiration. The most interesting legends hint at a kind of cult blending pagan and Christian motifs in a secret initiation ceremony. Later, the romancers make the Grail a straight Christian symbol. They clean it up.'

I was lecturing again - resurrecting my own TV lines, to be precise. Karen, doubtless mindful of previous lectures, began to read from the notes prefacing the script. 'I see you've helped the producer by describing your characters. That's good. "The Initiate. A questing knight, i.e. a warrior: bare-headed, about 25-30." That's his costume over there, isn't it? It doesn't look very warlike.'

'I thought just a hint of armour would be enough. Nothing fancy.'

'The studio team were probably grateful. We'll have to think about casting in a moment. Then here's "The Celebrant" - that's you, Alan. "Much older than the Initiate but very stalwart and clear-cut..." and so on. Are you stalwart and clear-cut? Yes, that's the costume. Try it on.'

Mr Frobisher picked up a long, plain, white cloak and draped it round him.

'That's your basic outfit,' I said. 'Part of the time you wear this over it.' I unfurled a black cape with a face-concealing hood, and diagrams sewn on hinting at perilous enchantments.

'Very sinister.' His shoes stuck out incongruously under the hem of his cloak. 'Are those sandals mine? just as well.'

Karen read on. '"The Grail-Keeper. Dark. Wears a small crown and a costume conveying royalty, but no long or heavy robe." Hm, it looks a bit like a tabard, but never mind. Then finally the two Grail Maidens. One dark, one fair. Annabel, you're the dark one. "Garments like the informal gowns worn by Roman ladies."'

Annabel tried hers on over her dress, which, in fact, it resembled - she scarcely needed a special costume. 'Turn round, dear,' said Karen, studying the effect.

'What about the rest of the cast?' Annabel wondered.

'We'll wait till Madri gets here,' said Karen, 'and then decide. Those Tantra people do a lot of acting and miming. If the ones she brings can fill the other three parts, they're likely to do it better than us.'

Mr Frobisher said: 'Geoffrey, I understand David Jacks will be photographing this for your article.'

'That's partly what set it off in the first place. The idea was to put on a show that would fit into the Allhallows scene and give him more visual material. But now that it's drawing Madri in, it's become more than that. She's a person I'm most anxious to meet. I feel this could turn out - by a funny kind of accident - to be crucial for the whole article.'

A sense of discord and superficiality in what I was saying gave me a measure of the distance I'd travelled. Annabel transposed me into Allhallows language.

'It'll be all you expect and more,' she commented quietly, 'if you go along with it as what it actually has become.'

'Meaning what?'

'Meaning, personal magic of your own.'

'I wasn't thinking of it as that.'

'No, and you mustn't start now. Think of your article. But let the energies unfold while you're doing it. Oh, I forgot – here's something in return for the script.' She gave me a piece of paper with the maze key-poem and instructions, handwritten.

'Why... thank you. Tell me though, if you're allowed to write it down, why be so devious? Couldn't I simply have a paper saying "right, left, left" and so forth? Or even a plan?'

'You may not have the paper with you. Even if you have, you may not he able to read it.'

Mr Frobisher's bewilderment pulled me back. We were behaving impolitely.

3

Towards dinner time, after our preliminary Grail session had broken up and I'd gone to my room, Madri arrived. I left the tapes and notes I was working on and dashed downstairs.

She was in the hall with two junior Tantrists from her commune, being greeted by Karen. The personal appearance of poets is apt to surprise. What struck me instantly about this one was a fact which her TV interview gave no hint of: she's very small. Also, in unfamiliar profile, you notice her long cranium and puckered, protruding lips. To connect somebody with a mystique of sex and then find them to be like that... it makes you wonder. She wore a sari in what I dimly recalled as the Gujarati style. An incongruous shoulder-bag dangled beside her.

I reached her neighbourhood. She looked at me – up at me – and I sustained the first impact. A piercing, stripping gaze. After polite exchanges she said: 'Have you found it yourself yet?'

'Found what?'

'The Grail.'

'You may be able to judge when we've gone over the script.'

She nodded as if I'd answered, and introduced her driver, a handsome clean-shaven young man named Bernard.

'I've already decided,' Karen put in, 'that Bernard must be our Grail-Keeper. Can't you just see him in that crown, Geoffrey?'

'He that plays the king shall be welcome.'

The second junior Tantrist was Helen, almost a blonde likeness of Annabel, but with more surface sparkle. Loosening up after the car ride she twirled unselfconsciously round the hall, waving her arms and jumping.

Madri glanced back at the door. 'Where's John got to?'

'He was getting the bags out,' said Bernard. 'Here he is now.'

Madri's third companion came in. I recognized him at once, black-haired, solid, and not greatly falsified by television and press photos – the maverick biochemist John Rosmer, whose subversive exploits were the reason for all of this.

'Hallo,' he said, with a firm but not excessive handshake. 'Madri told me about your article, and I thought the least I could do was come along.'

'That's marvellous. Now I've got both of you together.'[3]

Karen cut us politely short. Dinner was nearly ready and they had to discuss arrangements for residence. As old and valued friends on a brief stay they could put up tents in an unfrequented part of the grounds. However, they made no move to do so immediately. The meal which we sat down to was vexatious. The cause which had brought them to Allhallows defeated any attempt to draw them out. Madri would talk of nothing but the Grail Ritual, its previous performance, its casting and stage requirements now.

'This dining room,' she announced presently, 'is the place to act it in. We can use the French windows and the kitchen door to get people on and off.'

She insisted, however, on herding the entire cast into the conference room for a reading prior to rehearsal. Bernard was to be the Grail-Keeper as Karen wished, Helen was the Second Grail Maiden, John Rosmer the Initiate. Helped along by Mr Frobisher and Annabel, who had had time to consider, they all threw themselves into it remarkably. Students appeared in the doorway and disappeared. Mrs Frobisher lingered; her husband, after all, was part of the show. Martin looked in and lingered also. When Madri led the cast to the dining room to rehearse, he held me back for a few minutes asking questions about the Grail legend. He reminded me of our long-ago correspondence in the wake of the Free Mind meeting – could I add to my remarks then? Not much, I confessed.

Madri piloted our company through several rehearsals, which I watched with some apprehension but few words. The author should always bear in mind that he is one of the least important people in the theatre.⁴ At a well-chosen moment Madri called a halt for tea to be served. Recovering her shoulder-bag, she put three cups on a tray and turned to me. 'Come outside. You too, John.'

She'd known what I wanted all the time. So here I was at last with the two star graduates and nobody else... and my taperecorder, carefully held in readiness. Madri sat cross-legged on the grass, produced a kit labelled TRIADS from her shoulder-bag, and began assembling sticks in a 3D geometrical web.

I stated the issue point-blank. What made them tick?

Madri replied: 'I can't even try to answer that till I know more about the person who's asking. Nor can John. Tell us what's been happening to you here.'

While she worked at her sticks I stumbled through a sketchy account of the last few days, prompted along by cool relentless questions from both of them. When I got to SP5, they confirmed that they were well briefed on it but hadn't been given it themselves. They didn't seem to resent the fact that I had, or feel any lack.

John put their query. 'What's the main effect Allhallows has had on you?'

'It's too soon to make up my mind. Martin has some interesting theories...'

'Granted. But I asked you something else.'

Madri's corkscrew eyes were impaling me.

'The main effect.... Heart-searchings. The *Globe* assignment keeps getting pushed into the background. Instead I find myself wondering what I'm doing here and what I ought to be doing. And what that SP5 vision meant – if anything. And then there's this National Quest notion of Paul's, it sounds so absurd, and yet in a funny way it does seem cut out for me and I have to take it seriously in spite of the séance business, and...'

John interrupted. 'Enough, you've said it all. When Allhallows "takes", it does that to people.'

'Look, Geoffrey,' said Madri. 'You've been commissioned to get a secret from us, right? But there is no secret beyond what you're learning for yourself. You don't need us. Unless maybe as pegs to hang the article on. That's between you and your editor.'

The Finger and the Moon

Where had my journalist's dream gone wrong? I'd set out to interview these prize catches and they'd interviewed me, and were now speaking as if it was all over. I clutched at the straw she'd left me.

'Are you willing to be pegs then?'

'How?'

'If you could just fill me in on your equivalents of the same story – and explain what led you to do the things that the public's heard about.'

Madri added a stick to her structure. 'All right. As for me, I'm a librarian – I mean, that's the only bread-and-butter job there's been in my life. Around the time my first poems were published I got taken on at the Pike Institute, where they have that big Indian collection. A professor who was researching Tantrism invited me to a group where they practised it. I got hooked, rather. My library work suffered and so did my poetry writing.'

(Again it made you wonder, hearing it from this unbeautiful small intense woman, but nobody would have felt inclined to laugh.)

'They were a one-sided lot, I realize now. For them Tantrism meant psychological sex-magic, the Left-Hand Path. Which is true as far as it goes. You probably know all this. The male and female principles, god and goddess, Shiva and Shakti, with Shakti equal and sometimes superior. The stirring of the depths, the awakening of your inner serpent, your *kundalini* – and the unfolding of alchemic power from within – very terrific, very dangerous. You're warned against trying any of this without a guru to supervise. People who dabble in it think you can use it. You can't. Since those days I've talked with a Hindu who saw Shiva in a forest. "You westerners," he said, "you are obsessed with the one thing, you see only the lingam, the sex. But Shiva is Lord of the Dance. He is the Destroyer and the Ecstasy, trampling all creatures into dissolution with drum and fire, and creating afresh.'

'If I may interject,' said John, 'Shakti can be formidable too.'

Madri assented. 'So men have told me.'

'With the female principle, in India,' I said, 'I suppose Kali herself is never far off.'

'Kali *is* Shakti – the Great Goddess in her terrible aspect. I've been spared the worst. But you see, Geoffrey, all that stirring-of-the-depths and illumination – I read how Crowley adapted Tantra for his western brand of magic, and then I heard of Allhallows and got interested and came on a course. I was one of the students Martin picked out to talk to the class – does he still do that, by the way?'

'Very much so.'

'Good. Well, I gave my ignorant little lecture and somebody asked for more information. A few weeks later Martin phoned me. This person had gone half-way round the bend doing unsupervised experiments. Martin was giving treatment and he wanted advice.'

(I was almost certain – I still am – that she meant Paul, and I was being given the lowdown on his misadventure with SP5. Quite apart from her discretion, however, it was clear that the victim's identity didn't signify.)

'Martin never said a word of reproach, but he made me feel responsible, so I came back here for a weekend – I probably wouldn't have, otherwise. When we'd finished discussing his patient, we discussed Tantric matters generally and he said something that came as a revelation.

'He told me that when the Greeks conquered part of India, they recognized Shiva as an old friend, the god they knew as Dionysus. That's on record in books by Greek travellers. Dionysus was the god of dance and group-ecstasy and divine madness over in Greece, just as he was in his Indian shape as Shiva. But in Greece he inspired literary art-forms as well, poetic drama, tragedy and comedy growing out of his festivals. In Greece (I'm still quoting Martin) his Goddess played the role of the Muse as she didn't farther east. The Muse herself can be terrible of course – poets are liable to be torn to pieces like Orpheus – but they do produce poetry, and their proper god is Dionysus or Shiva or whatever you call him. (Even though Apollo succeeded in horning in.)

'That did it, anyhow. Poetry was my thing and I'd been neglecting it. But if I put Tantra in western terms and saw Shiva as Dionysus too, and his Goddess as the Muse... then I could make progress.'

'Meaning what, in practical terms?'

'Oh... activities. Following the Indian line still – we don't soft-pedal it – but combined with poetry and drama and singing.'

'Tell Geoffrey about your children's group,' said John.

'That's our latest experiment. It carries on from Christopher Searle's work a few years back. Rousing children's poetic gifts by encouraging them to think rhythmically, to catch the beat of pop music and then write little essays in lines instead of straight prose. And doing it together, as fun. School verse-writing tends to be a chore because teachers demand rhyme and metre from the beginning. I believe you can approach it by a better route. It's certainly seemed to work with my daughter, she's produced some real poems already.'

Her daughter? Another loose end. But she swung the spotlight deftly away. 'Right, John. That finishes me. Now it's your turn.'

As soon as he began speaking he was very much the public John Rosmer of the media. Unlike Madri he was telling a tale he'd told most of before, in contexts tending to standardize it.

'I'm not exceptional. By now there must be any number of scientists who've had the same sort of experience up to a point. I've worked for private industry and the Government, with a spell in the States. My last job was in weapons research. I had no more inside knowledge than thousands of others, but enough to see through the entire show, not just the war preparation but the whole setup it's supposed to protect, in England or Russia or any so-called advanced country. The fetish of Growth and the Standard of Living and Success and so on, all measured by utterly phoney yardsticks... such obvious nonsense now, burying itself in foulness and frustration. Millions know it too, only there doesn't seem to be any jumping-off point.

'My last senior officer knew it as well as I did. But he used to say: "We live by it, don't we? Scrap the nuclear subs by all means, if you're really prepared to be overrun by Chinese. Stop growth by all means, if you're really prepared to have three million unemployed and starvation. But do face the facts of life." I could never think of any answer. So I carried on being conscientious and miserable.

'The Allhallows part, on the face of it, was pure chance. All that happened was that a friend brought me here on a one-day visit, and we heard some chap talk on "white" and "black" magicians and relate them to popular sci-fi images of the scientist – either "benevolent" or "sinister". I can't even say that the talk impressed me much. Half of it struck me as superstition – pacts with the Devil and all that. It just nagged me afterwards with a feeling that my own conflict was only the modern aspect of a far older one, and I wasn't being fundamental enough.

'Then... do you remember that Cumberland disaster last summer?'

'The power-plant accident?'

'That's it.'

'Vaguely. I need reminding.'

'A private generating unit was being built for a warhead research station. The metal fences got live and four kids were electrocuted. It leaked out that the plant had been ordered because in the last power workers' strike, this project had got behind schedule. The Government was spending millions on a strike-proof supply – not for the public but for the war establishment – and killing neighbourhood children in the process.

'When the report was published, my chief started again on his "facts of life", defence and whatnot. For me it was the crunch. I said: "That may be as watertight as a pact with the Devil. But if these atrocities are the facts of life, then I reject the life they're the facts of. It's about time I used whatever knowledge I may possess to show it up."

'Suddenly I realized I was the master and not the victim any more. I was on top of the situation. The forces in my own life were pulling together instead of pulling apart.'

'But was that your only contact with Allhallows? That one visit?'

'Oh no. I came back for a full-scale course. I learned a lot, but nothing that's changed the original effect.'

Madri was dismantling her stick-pattern. 'You ought to play the flute, John,' she said obscurely.

'As a matter of fact, I do. It's my only instrument.'[5]

I failed to push the interview any further. I thanked them and we returned indoors. Paul was in the dining room with Arnold Gore and the Bambergers, who, it appeared, had just got back from their Bristol art show. Freda was enthusing over the film programme – 'a preview of Blifil Grimes's version of Sade's *Juliette*' – with support from Joe. I still think the object sticking out of his boot is a whip.

Arnold turned and recognized John, whom he'd met at a conference. They shook hands.

'Do you know why Arnold's here?' said Paul.

'Geoffrey's been telling us about your National Quest scheme.'

'You could do a tremendous amount for it yourself.'

'I'll hope to hear more of it in due course.'

Only one person was needed to complete the enlarged Allhallows party, and he arrived a few minutes later – David Jacks. He was staying at a pub, but had brought his cameras to the house. Finding that he'd got two public figures in his sights, he brightened.

'This is really exciting,' he said, looking almost cheerful. 'Could we do a few pictures right away?'

John expressed willingness and they started out through the French window, with Madri following. Paul detained her. 'How about the Grail Ritual? Is everything under control?'

'It'll do.'

'Can I help at all?'

'No, I don't think so.'

She was gone. Paul wasn't. I think he feels that the Grail part of our affair is slipping away from him, and indeed it is.

What had I got? Bits and pieces. The sight of the photographer reminded me of his challenge the first time he was here. What had Allhallows done which anybody sensitive to the real human plight could treat with respect or interest? I could now reply that it had caused a few able individuals to sort out their hangups, acquire purpose, focus their talents... after which, yes, they made their mark. Doubtless Terry Hoad, the most incontestable doer of good among them, would have described a process of the same sort if he'd been present. Madri asserted that it was happening to me and was the key to the whole thing. Perhaps. But this was an anti-climax, a platitude. Nor could I understand how it linked up in any coherent way with Martin's protoselves.

4

The final Grail rehearsals disrupted supper so much that they aroused general curiosity. We had a full house for the performance. The night was fine, clear, warm, a seductive invitation to go outdoors, yet everyone turned up in the dining room. Both main tables had been dismantled and stacked. Two of the benches were arranged side by side, with chairs and stools around them, facing across the room's ample width towards the French windows.

All the students took their seats punctually, except of course Mr Frobisher, whose wife could be heard describing a pageant they'd once co-starred in at a Neo-Essene festival. Words like 'ephod' and 'menorah' drifted across to me. Her story was drowned out by the advent of the five Cryptocrats, who had shown less interest than any-one but now entered in a body with Paul, conversing noisily. Martin and Karen came in behind them, with Madri. Martin, for some reason, had brought the ornate goblet from his study, the one he gave me wine in when I was first there. He placed this on a stool opposite our acting space. David Jacks was already in, observant, separated. Throughout the scene that followed he was soft-footing it about the room, popping flashbulbs at intervals.

Martin asked me to introduce the Ritual. I ran briefly over my earlier words about the Grail legends reflecting a Christianization of pre-Christian motifs, 'an initiation' (I felt much too donnish with Madri's eye on me) 'into the secrets of divine action in Nature, with Christ set up in the role of a pagan deity, fulfilling and transcending. Some of the imagery has a sexual origin of course. The Grail is a magic vessel of plenty and inspiration, and it's also the vessel of a sacrament. When the Initiate finds its hiding-place and passes the test, a Waste Land revives – that's both literal and symbolic. He looks into the Grail and has a mystical experience, a kind of "scrying" perhaps.'

I added that at the time of composing this TV mock-up I'd taken hints from Jessie Weston and Charles Williams, and built the script imagery round the Major Trumps of the Tarot pack, which is con-nected somehow with the Grail mysteries...[6]

'You could have taken hints from Crowley's *Book of Thoth* too,' Madri put in. 'Is there any reason why you didn't?'

'Ignorance, madam, pure ignorance. At the time, that is.'

'So you thought along his lines without knowing it. That tells me more about you.'

'I did always feel there was a touch of authentic magic here. Things happened after that television performance. Though not immediately after.'

'Delayed-action magic,' she said. 'I'm glad you understand how it can be so.'

'I ought to add that the allusions to the Tarot Trumps in the script have nothing to do with occultists' interpretations of them. My idea was that certain themes had to be evoked in a certain sequence.'

Madri was still with me and so were some of the others. But the non-Europeans, Kwame and Mei-ling, were looking unhappy, and the Bambergers were making faces. I cut my prologue short and began setting the stage, aided by Steve and Owen. We put the big chair from the conference room on the left facing the audience, with a small table and stool beside it. On the right was a trestle as altar, and on top of this, a specially made prop which had come out of storage with the rest, a kind of upright frame with hooks and a shelf. Of the four sacred objects, the dish was on the table with a few crumbs of food on it and a cloth beside it; the sword hung in the frame looking like a cross; the other two, the lance and the Grail itself, were out of sight. For lighting we had a single standard lamp. The ceiling lights were switched off.

'This is supposed to be a cave near the sea,' I explained. 'The Initiate will arrive by boat. You'll have to imagine the boat. When he enters he finds the Grail-Keeper sitting in the chair, crowned, immobile, unseeing - under a spell in fact.' I gave a signal. Bernard came in through the adjoining French window and sat in the chair. 'Also, the Celebrant is waiting.' Mr Frobisher came in, strangely impressive in his white cloak and (this time) sandals. He stood between the table and altar.

'Right,' I said. 'Cameras. Action.'

John Rosmer, wearing his 'Initiate' warrior-rig, entered from the far right through the kitchen door and approached the set.

They all had to read from the scripts, of course - even Bernard, whose eyes were meant to be closed - and their rehearsing had been skimpy enough. Yet they'd hardly started when I knew it would be all right. They already had some of their speeches off by heart, and you scarcely noticed they were reading. Mr Frobisher was transfigured, a born actor. In spite of all the obscure matters which I'd drawn in from legends and never prepared this audience for, the show was alive, obscurity didn't spoil it...7

CELEBRANT. Why do you come?
INITIATE.   I seek the Grail.
             I have ridden through doubt and danger to find it.
CELEBRANT. The Grail is not in the world.
INITIATE .   Then what is this place?
CELEBRANT. You have dwelt in the Waste Land, the region under
             judgement.
             Until you are changed yourself, you stand in Hell.
INITIATE.   (indicating Grail-Keeper).

How shall I salute its prince?

GRAIL-KEEPER. (*in a trance voice*).

I am he who voyaged into the sunset kingdom,
Where the stream of Ocean circles the lands of men
And the stars revolve disposing the lives of men.
Whoever you are who tread this western beach,
May the wheel of fortune bear you round to your good.

CELEBRANT. Let this be a sign. (*indicating dish.*) You have travelled
empty and famished.
Here is bread, here is fish. Take and taste.

INITIATE. I may not eat while the prince fasts.

GRAIL-KEEPER. (*as before*).

No food passes my lips. You behold me maimed,
Unbegetting, actionless, beyond life and death.

INITIATE. How long so?

CELEBRANT. Since the lightning struck the tower.

INITIATE. Until when?

CELEBRANT. Until you free him.

(*Thus far the dialogue had run smoothly. Now came the first bit
of stage business. The Initiate sat down and ate. The Celebrant
took the sword off the frame and brought it over to him. He - the
Celebrant, that is - held it first with the handle up and then with
the point up, and then laid it on the table.*)

The plate is empty.

(*The Initiate made a quick token gesture of wiping it.*)

Those things which you have tasted, the Grail gave,
But without eating you had no eyes to see it.
Now you shall see, in part. I summon before you
What may be truth or falsehood, waking or dream.
No man but you can judge. When you discern,
Then grasp the sword and sever the web of doubt.

(*The Celebrant moved to the far right and gestured towards
the left. A French window opened - this was the best we could do
- and from the left, behind the Grail-Keeper's chair, the two Grail
Maidens crossed into the space between table and altar. The dark
one, Annabel, carried the Grail with a cloth wrapped round it,
but not over the top. The fair one, Helen, carried the lance, held
diagonally so that the point was above the Grail. It was a tricky*)

*manoeuvre which could easily have got a laugh, but they skimmed
through it like ballet-dancers. They finished up at the frame above
the altar and placed the objects on it - the Grail on the shelf, the
lance suspended on hooks and pointing down into it with a small
visible gap between. Then they faced the audience, fortuitously but
dramatically alike, Dark Girl and Fair Girl. For a dreadful moment
I thought they'd left their scripts behind because they needed both
hands to hold the objects, but they read from bits of paper pinned to
their sleeves, on which, apparently, they'd copied out their own lines
and cues and nothing else.)*

DARK GIRL. Alas for the word unsaid, the pang without birth!

FAIR GIRL.   For the place deserted, the life that came and passed!

DARK GIRL. For the mazed will, the hand upon sterile silver,

FAIR GIRL.   The turned back and the footstep into the night.

GRAIL-KEEPER.   I sit in his chair with heart reversed from his;

But the word to rise and walk, another must speak.

*(The girls glided slowly to the left, and exited. The Celebrant
advanced again from the right. He had put on the black necromantic
cape [pre-arranged on a chair near the kitchen door] with the hood
concealing his face. Coming to the table, he picked up the empty dish
and held it so that it was seen as a disc. He swung it gently from side
to side and spoke in a disguised, insinuating voice.)*

CELEBRANT. I come to give you the signal of decision.

The secret is - that there is no secret,

The Grail is barren, the Waste Land waste for ever,

*(He went to the altar and slid the dish horizontally over the top of
the Grail, an inch below the tip of the hanging lance.)*

The world stops here. Cast it off in its ignorance.

Cross the threshold and know a higher truth.

*(He beckoned. The Initiate rose and seemed about to step for-
ward, then recovered and picked up the sword from the table.)*

INITIATE .   This is a lie. Your way is into a void.

You speak with the voice of him who would not serve.

My vows are otherwise. I must return.

CELEBRANT. If with nothing?

INITIATE .   Then with nothing.

*(The Celebrant threw back his hood so that his face was revealed,
and reverted to his previous voice and manner.)*

CELEBRANT. It is well. You have opened the first gate.

The house of shadow becomes the house of trial.

(This was the Grail-Keeper's cue to open his eyes. There was another anxious moment, but just as I was about to prompt him he did open them. He looked at the floor to his right and left, then raised his head.)

GRAIL-KEEPER. These eyes are awake. The rock is under my chair.

It stretches to sea and land, to the shoals of men.

CELEBRANT. *(to Initiate, taking the sword from him).*

Because you came to the sunset beaches fasting,

The flesh cannot bind you. The life you lived ends here,

In a cavern-tomb at the world's rim.

(He made a symbolic gesture of 'killing' the Initiate.)

But hope still; for rim and centre are one.

(Going to the altar, he laid down his script, removed the dish from the Grail with his left hand, hung up the sword again, picked up his script and backed to the right. It was a further ticklish piece of business and he did it unerringly. The two girls reappeared at the left and passed to the space between the table and altar.)

DARK GIRL. The chariot of life comes round, ever round.

FAIR GIRL. Four are the seasons of the undying year.

DARK GIRL. Four are the spirits in the unwearied wheels.

FAIR GIRL. Four are the bringers of good news to the world.

DARK GIRL. Four are the Hallows in the house of the Grail.

FAIR GIRL. The chariot of life comes round, ever round.

(The fair one went to the altar and removed the cloth from the Grail so that it was fully seen. The Celebrant returned from the right, dressed as at the beginning, without his black cape. He still carried the dish.)

DARK GIRL. Let the work be performed, let the joy of the Grail unfold.

CELEBRANT *(to Initiate).*

What I shall utter now you may not hear,

The mystery of the Three and the Twenty-and-two.

Fasten your eyes to the Grail and your mind to readiness.

(The Initiate stared at the Grail, the Celebrant appeared to be muttering. The Grail-Keeper - a little slow with his cue again

*- drew his legs up on to the chair and sat sideways in a foetal pos-
ture. The Celebrant finished his unheard speech and slid back the
dish over the Grail, so that for the first time, all four ritual objects
were on the frame simultaneously.)*

> The Hallows are together, the year fulfilled.
> And now, I command you, ask what you must;
> Through your unwisdom may you arise remade.

INITIATE .   Whom does the Grail serve?

*(This question - which I didn't invent, it's in the legend - was the
key formula by which a seeker passed the test. Without studio lighting effects or emphatic close-up I'd wondered how John could give it
enough weight. He did very well, saying the line slowly, powerfully,
with a rising inflection. The rest of the charade took on a quality
which made me feel that I was watching the work of a better writer
than myself.)*

CELEBRANT. He breathed the word, the word that was one with
> him;
> And the spiritual vessel flamed, and he was born.
> You have opened the second gate. It is well.
> With the eyes of the spirit look through the eyes of the
> body
> And see the house of gold in the Lord's garden,
> And beside these two (gesturing at the girls) a third, his
> handmaid,
> The sky her mantle, the moon under her feet.

*(The Grail-Keeper stood up with arms outstretched in the pos-
ture of crucifixion. The others crossed themselves. He lowered his
arms.)*

GRAIL-KEEPER.   The sun rises and the colours return.
> *(To the Initiate.)*
> Friend whom the Grail has called, whom the Grail has
> kindled,
> Receive the royalty of the holy companionship.

*(He took the crown off his head and put it on the Initiate's, who
knelt for the purpose.)*

DARK GIRL. May the strength of the tower of David fortify you!

FAIR GIRL.   May the mirror of justice shine unclouded for you!

CELEBRANT. May the voice that whispers in solitude instruct you!

GRAIL-KEEPER. May the star-crowned empress, herself the morning
      star,
      Guide you ever back to the world's centre.
CELEBRANT. *(again removing the dish from the Grail and laying it
      down).*
      Rise, accomplish the mystery at the third gate,
      Which is the gate of Heaven, but of Earth also.

*(The Initiate stood up and faced him as he brought over the
Grail and set it on the table. At this point the television audience
had seen the Initiate's face in close-up, looking down into the Grail,
bathed in light to represent his mystical scrying. John tried to suggest
illumination by shading his eyes.)*

INITIATE .   I see the knot unravelled, the path made plain.
CELEBRANT.   Remember my words : the Grail is not in the
      world.
INITIATE .   Their truth is before me. The world is in the Grail.
CELEBRANT.   Go back in peace, and make the land blossom.

*(The Initiate bowed to him and exited the way he had entered.
The others withdrew, not too anti-climactically, through the French
windows. I nodded to Steve. He turned up the house lights.)*

Karen, who had been at rehearsals, recognized the end as soon as
it came and led a round of applause during the exits. I called the play-
ers back in and praised them suitably. Martin led the party off to the
recreation room for drinks. Before I followed, Annabel spoke to me.
'It oughtn't to have been applauded. They were nice to us, I know,
but it oughtn't.'

'Why not? Are you thinking of *Parsifal?*'

Blankness. I left her collecting up the props, and joined the others.

There was, unavoidably, discussion. Owen pressed me with questions about the witch cult and the cauldron of Cerridwen. Kwame,
Owen's former brother in Wicca, gave me an account of a West
African rite which he insisted earnestly - and erroneously - was a
parallel case. Janice muttered about sex-symbolism as if it were an
acute observation of her own. I don't recall much being said that
added to the prologue already offered.

David Jacks, his flashbulb-kit slung round him, looked as glum as
usual and was. Freda attempted a joke based on the 'tower of David'
(the only point in the Ritual she condescended to mention at all), but

failed to enliven him. He drew me aside. 'Sorry, but I don't think I got much there, picture-wise.'

'You seemed to.'

'There might be one we could use if it's kept small. But - with respect - all that a *Globe* reader is going to see in this is amateur theatricals.'

'Well, I'm sorry too, if so.'

I noticed him a few minutes later in a huddle with Paul and Norman. A few minutes later again, the huddle annexed Herod and Simon Calthrop. Two fans of Lucifer. Presently the whole Cryptocrat contingent went out with the photographer. Meanwhile the party was dwindling fast from other defections. Madri and her pair of co-Tantrists had gone too. So had Annabel. John left soon after the Cryptocrats. The warm starry night that girdled the house was deep and enticing. I made my excuses and plunged into it alone.

Other Scene

I PASSED THROUGH THE DINING ROOM and French window. The Ritual props had gone. Also, Martin's goblet was no longer on the stool where he'd enthroned it. I noticed and speculated. But I passed through.

Outside over rough grass I faced the shrubbery, a wall of gloom, greenish-black. I'd seen it at every meal, approached it during the Grail preparations, but never gone in. By daylight the shrubbery had remained a non-place for me, part of a vague barrier dividing the familiar lawn from the less familiar, but known, vegetable garden. By night it loomed up in front with a hint of jungle. A narrow path led into it. On impulse I took this path expecting it to swing either right or left, debouching near the sculpture or greenhouse accordingly. After an unnervingly prolonged struggle through foliage that closed in till I had doubts of the path, it began to seem that neither would happen.

What was in this area? I paused in the opaque darkness and tried to recall. Karen, surely, had once taken me through transversely from lawn to garden, and we emerged then not far from the house. So there should be a cross-path. There wasn't. Either my memory was out or I'd already passed the intersection without being aware of it. Where on earth had I got to? Trees were now mingling with the bushes, their tops rising featureless against the little I could see of the sky. When I turned right or left, thorny impenetrable masses repelled me. Ahead - blindly, painfully - remained my sole option.

I took a step forward into the gap still open for me in front, then halted again. The wood was not silent. A faint murmur of singing and drumming filtered eerily through. Subtle, monotonous, quarter-toned, the music declared itself to be Indian. Its makers could only be the Tantra group holding an outdoor session. That knowledge should have cut the experience down to size. But I was unable to feel that this plangent night-sound fell into place as part of the Allhallows landscape. Instead it turned a domestic English wood into an alien forest, a haunt of gods and demons.

As I pushed forward, the music grew louder. I was zigzagging towards it through the dark. There was nothing else to do, but my nervousness increased. Sooner or later I would find them. No veneer of daytime acquaintance could cover up the foreboding in the thought. Legend-weavers have always known that to stumble on something in a wood which isn't part of the wood, and doesn't belong in it, is an archetype of psychic unquiet. So it was with the Grail mystery itself: 'Down in yon forest there stands a hall' as the uncanniest of carols begins.

Common Sense assured me: 'Don't be silly, you know these people, they're friends.'

Primeval Misgiving didn't bother to reply. It simply rephrased its message in a form that enlisted Common Sense itself on its own side. Yes, it reminded me, I did know these people. They were adepts of the Left-Hand Path and sex-magic. What were they up to in this incantatory privacy? How awkward might the meeting be when I did stumble on them?

Meanwhile the wood was thinning. Stars glittered overhead and I could see patchily for some distance, though not through to open space. I guessed I must be in an extension of the clump of trees flanking the temple - a more extensive extension than I'd suspected of being there. The music was close now. Shapes gleamed through the bushes that still blocked my view directly ahead.

A gap appeared giving access to a clearing. This, like the maze area at the other end of the grounds, had once been tamed and formalized. Without going forward out of cover I could discern a pool and remnants of marble statuary. A few yards farther on, the trees stopped altogether at the boundary fence. Starlight streamed in. Above, one especially brilliant star, or planet, stood out among the rest.

By now acclimatized to the night, I saw who occupied the clearing. The three Tantrists were seated in lotus postures. None of them showed any sign of having noticed me. Madri, in her sari, was singing. Bernard was tapping a small drum and joining his voice to hers in snatches. He no longer had his Grail-Keeper's costume. Instead he wore an oddly elaborate headdress, a short tunic, and anklets. Helen was still a Grail Maiden. She too sang in snatches, and beat out the rhythm with a staccato object that could have been a coconut.

I am filling in these details as if they had impinged in the first moments. Actually they didn't, because of a fourth figure standing beside the pool, its back to me. This person was long-haired and femininely built, and had no visible clothing at all. An abrupt turn established the figure's sex, nakedness, and identity. I recognized (as I'd half expected) Annabel. Having always shown herself in gear that disguised her shape, she was, without it, a stranger from behind and a near-stranger from in front.

In that Actaeonish situation my Dark Girl roused no immediate lust but – I confess – warm interest. She was agreeably formed, as Paul had hinted. From the neck down at any rate she could have modelled acceptably for that kind of ad. Resting most of her weight on one leg, she held herself upright and immobile with no sign of embarrassment, and when she did move she moved gracefully. Her hands, however, were not free. The right hand carried my prop-Grail, and the left, Martin's goblet.

As long as she stood beside the pool, her pose had a statuesque dignity which the drum and singing enhanced. But soon she dropped on one knee and scooped up water in the vessels. She walked over to each Tantrist in turn. They stretched out their hands and she sprinkled them from the Grail, performing what I guessed to be a Hindu lustration. Then she knelt again and began scooping up more water and pouring it, meditatively, back into the pool or over the ground. All these actions subverted the previous effect of poised and grave nudity. If the whole quartet had been in the same state, like some coven or pseudocoven playing ring-a-roses for the cameras, Annabel's impact would have been milder. Alone like that, moving flexibly about, with objects in her hands but no clothes, she became disturbing. I had no idea what rite they were celebrating or what influence she was under. But some curious ecstasy had engulfed her, and the Tantrists as well. What if she looked in my direction? Would she see, even then?

Finally she did look. At least, I think she did. Having set down both her vessels, the Grail and the goblet, she straightened up lightly and faced my way. The confrontation – if it was – lasted for what felt like a long time, with the Indian sound throbbing and wailing on around us. She didn't speak. Nor (being at a loss) did I. Her body retained its female reticence, but I thought a tremor of discomposure flitted over her. As for myself, the sight was causing me more than discomposure. But with the futile excitement came inspiration. I knew, or someone inside me knew, what had to be done.

I took out my SP5 tube and just managed to unstopper it with shaking fingers. As the pill went down I kept my eyes fixed on Annabel, standing unveiled with the starlight on her breasts. The drug invaded an organism quickened by response to that image.

2

When the first upheaval passed she was still there, exactly as before. So were the wood and the pool, and the seated trio. Their singing and rhythm-beating went on without interruption. But this time I saw what Martin and Karen had both described and I had not previously seen myself, the human aura. Cool silver englobed each of the figures on the ground and rippled with pulsations of rainbow. As for Annabel, I thought for one bemused instant that she had no aura, and then realized that hers was out of scale and I had looked for its edge too close to her. It was an awesome swaying diaphanous flame that soared up from the earth to an apex a yard above her head.

I coped with the alien optics which Martin had prepared me for. This proto-light had no visual effect. I still saw by the stars alone. The stars alone showed me Annabel's next movement. Whatever trance she was in, it relaxed. She glanced to her left; nodded; and gave a strange little grim smile. Her situation had stirred a memory.

How did I know? I did know. My second SP-experience is even harder to describe than the first. Throughout much of it I was not certain (and I'm not certain now) where literal fact left off and the drug took over. For some reason there was a closer fusion of psychic levels. As at Cadbury I had a sense of the outer world being re-created in my own blown-up brain. But this time it was far more elusive and equivocal. No ghosts; no gods. The same Allhallows scene persisted and the same people appeared to be in it. Appeared. The question I have to ask, and can't answer, is 'as what?'

She who appeared to be Annabel turned in the direction she had glanced and walked off through the trees, unhurriedly but not, I felt, aimlessly. Unless I'd missed my bearings she was liable to emerge near the temple, perhaps on the lawn in front of it. I circled round and kept up with her. Going where I wanted to presented no problem. As with Martin only more so, mental scrutiny of my first trip had drawn my brain into a sort of loose rapport, so that this second one didn't divide me so sharply from my own mechanisms of action. I could control my body like the pilot of a well-instrumented aircraft The normal 'me' of the cerebral and neural structure was co-operative.

I paced along beside Annabel, not too close. Bernard had got up and was following on bare feet, noiseless except when he snapped a twig. Madri and Helen remained seated in the clearing. Thus far, apart from the auras, I was seeing nothing at all but what could be physically there, however unusual. Nor feeling anything out of the way either. My reaction to this wood-nymph strolling naked through starlight was wholly as might have been predicted. With a touch of anxiety over the near prospect of her stepping out of her wood into the open.

When she did - when we both did - it was on a stretch of lawn much farther from the temple than I'd expected. Near the sundial, in fact, where Martin had lectured and the vista sloped down with a distant prospect - in daytime - of Glastonbury Tor. I was dismayed to see spectators. Paul and David Jacks were advancing from the temple side. I paused in the shadows, but the female figure I was tailing walked on. The space between myself and that unconcerned back increased rapidly.

A flashbulb exploded. I looked at the photographer. He was fumbling with his kit, trying for another shot, I supposed. If a transition can be pinned down anywhere, that's when it happened. Separation, distraction, the change of my charming dryad into hackneyed camera-fodder, combined to break her original spell. I lurched forward over the lawn as she passed the sundial. Behind, Jacks was taking pictures again, of Bernard now, his first target being cut off from him by a hedge. I came alongside her twenty yards or so down the slope. It wasn't her.

Instead I saw the double woman whom I dreamed of after my first midnight readings on SP5, Annabel-Karen. Facially she was both of them, and the rest, unconcealed by her long dream-garment, was fuller and more mature than what I'd admired in the wood. The palpable paradox of hair being dark and fair at the same time was resolved by a monochrome pallor that made the whole figure, hair and all, unearthly. Though this woman was still naked, I had an impression, from a cautiously-maintained distance, of a necklace of heavy whitish beads. Her tremendous aura shone round her.

She halted. She turned and faced up the slope. Or to be accurate, she faced up the slope and that's it. Every attempt to recollect her in motion during this phase leaves me with a sense of wrongness.

A man had rounded the corner of the hedge and was striding down the slope towards her. His face and beard and physique were Paul's, but he was not the Paul of a moment earlier. He was dressed in an out-of-key business suit with a tie and white shirt, as Paul would have arrayed himself for boardrooms during his consultancy days. I could make out his aura... only it wasn't. It was a compact pearl-grey globe, like an overcast sky crammed into a goldfish bowl, and it trailed in the air behind with only a thin taut cord of light connecting it to him.

Annabel-Karen had taken up her stance on a patch of grass where the gradient was almost nil. When this Paul drew close to her, they were face to face on virtually the same level. At the top of the slope near the sundial a third figure had made its entry: Bernard, or someone who could have passed for Bernard, dancing about in a ring of light formed by his own aura. He had brought his little Indian drum, and beat time on it. But Paul didn't look back. He spoke to the pale-fiery woman and she answered. As at Cadbury I could hear no words.

Then with a repulsive puppet-jerk he launched himself at her. The attempted rape was grotesquely sordid and ineffectual. I am not sure whether he bore her to the ground or not. A second later, anyhow, she was not on the ground. She was upright again facing him, and he too was upright, dishevelled. Still she made no move. But the iridescent glory around her moved. It swirled between them, hardened into a blade of furious brightness, and cut off his head. In the last moment he flung up a hand and gave a demented shriek that went on while the head was falling.

It would have been ghastly enough as an allegorical vision with nameless actors. These, though, were projected or constructed out of familiar people whom I had feelings about. I simply can't conceive an event in everyday life that would cause the same emotions. I knew this wasn't literal fact. Nevertheless it was a nauseating, a paralysing shock. And yet again there was more than that to it. Blood fountained out of the headless man's neck; he tottered and fell, his raised hand sticking into the air; and his destroyer's face broke into a dreadful smile; and while I recoiled and could certainly not have smiled myself, the surest thing in that whole choreography was that SHE was right to.

Bernard was still skipping and prancing beside the sundial with grisly gaiety, and tapping his drum. Annabel-Karen ran, bounded, flew towards him. Their meeting was a sexless conspiratorial ardour. They danced off round the hedge. I lumbered up in time to glimpse them vanishing into the wood we'd come from. The photographer had gone. The night was deeper and colder.

My SP5 dose was wearing off. For evident reasons it hadn't occurred to me to look at my watch when I took the pill. But I suspected, now, that this second trip inverted the time-warp of the first, and drug-duration was shorter than clock-duration. As I wearily crossed the lawn, the brain in my skull was re-asserting its claims. In an unforeseen manner. It was buzzing like a hive with a swarm of poetry scraps. If I attended too closely to a single line, the result would be a deluge of imagery that drove me off course. I pushed on into the trees like a sleep-walker, and faded back into normal consciousness.

The stars were still shining but the wood was quiet. After a pause for recovery I made my way to the clearing. The Tantrists were seated as before, meditating – Madri, Helen, and yes, Bernard. Annabel sat with them, her back against a tree-trunk, her knees partly drawn up, her hands clasped around her shins. She was in her Grail Maiden's costume. The Grail and the goblet lay on the ground near her. She saw me, smiled, and lifted a finger to her lips.

Eighth Day

MARTIN LECTURED after breakfast this morning in the conference room. He asked me to come, and so far as lecturing can ever sew this job up, I suppose he's done it.

All the students attended, some bleary-eyed. So did Madri and John Rosmer. So, unexpectedly, did Paul. The bizarre emotions set up by last night's vision had a morning-after counterpart. If that meeting had been a dream, it wouldn't have trespassed on my waking reactions. But being more than a dream it pressed in on me, urging that although this intact person was admittedly Paul, the beheaded goblin had been Paul too, and I should reckon with both and fit them together. Which was a tricky mental feat. A good thing Annabel wasn't there.

Martin, ever the alert teacher, led in via the Grail performance. 'You saw the Initiate achieving contact with mysteries that transcend the everyday world, yet have a bearing on it. Are keys to it in fact. Mysteries of divine action, if I quote Geoffrey correctly. The Initiate's insight reveals the sources of life. He receives a call from beyond that gives him power to revive the Waste Land. Would you go along with that, Geoffrey?'

'Yes, that would do as a summing-up. Only—'

'Hold it now,' Owen interrupted. 'I've read Malory. When Galahad looks into the Grail he drops dead. Where's this "power" of yours then?'

I'd heard that question before. 'By the time we get to the versions with Galahad in them, we're also getting a deeper overlay of official Christianity. Galahad is called - to God. He dies by his own choice. But in the most important version he says: "I behold the motive of courage and the inspiration of prowess." The Grail mysteries do apply to this life, even though his own case is special.'

'That's crucial,' said Martin, forestalling a literary diversion. 'I know the idea got involved with Christian doctrine – God becoming Man through Mary for the spiritual rebirth of mankind – but surely the basic motif is older. Your Initiate accepts the human lot as Christ does. He doesn't reject the world. That's put to him as a temptation and he turns it down. The Grail vision shows him that the world is holy and hasn't lost the divine blessing. His vocation is in it, working for it.

'Which brings me to our theme for today.' (Of course.) 'I'd like to examine this whole idea of vocation. In a sense, all our studies have been leading up to it: to a great practical concept which I invite people who come here to take away with them. A concept for all, however far they diverge in their pursuits.'

He made one of his pauses, staring down at the table, then looked up.

'Don't be afraid that I'm going to preach a moral sermon, On the contrary. I'm going to urge that if you get one thing right – one thing which you can best get right by studying the topics we've studied – then you can put morals in their place. They'll take care of themselves. In making that claim I'm not echoing magicians alone. I'm also echoing (if it interests you) the finest mind in the history of the Christian Church.

'At the front door of this house, you'll have noticed a motto over the arch. "Do what you will, but be very sure you will it."

He let that sink in.

'The first four words have been repeated as a slogan of freedom down the centuries, by a strange medley of moralists... or anti-moralists. A slogan so simple, you feel there has to be a catch. And of course there is, if you take it up unqualified. It wouldn't be conducive to freedom, or anything else desirable, if everybody went around murdering, stealing and raping as whim dictated. However, I'm going to suggest that we can build up this slogan into an all-sufficient rule of life. So have others before me. Let's see what they've made of it.

'St Augustine said it first, nearly sixteen hundred years ago, with a significant word added. "Love, and do what you will." In modern jargon, align the psyche correctly and then everything else comes out right. True as far as it goes. But love what, love how? In spite of the greatness of many saints, Christian generalizations aren't a clear enough guide for most of us.

'Rabelais repeated the same words in the Renaissance, without Augustine's "love". He portrayed a Utopian community, the Abbey of Thélème, where the only rule was "do what you will". His notion was that if the inmates were carefully selected, their wills would harmonize. Maybe. But we can't all live in Thélème.

'Next is Dr John Dee, the famous Elizabethan magician we've heard a little about from Mei-ling. One of the spirits who spoke to him – so he believed, anyway – gave him this message: "Behold you are become free: do that which most pleaseth you.... Do even as you list." I'm not sure whether Dee ever decided what the spirit intended. There's a story of a wife-swapping session that didn't get very far. After him, certainly, we run into a phase when "do what you will" got trotted out again by people who simply wanted to do as they pleased. It was the motto over the door at Medmenham, on the Thames, where the so-called Hell-Fire Club held orgies in the 1750s – a club of rich men who met for sex and black magic and political plotting. Then the mere "do as you please" idea was carried further by the Marquis de Sade, to justify unrestrained egotism and cruelty: "Nature's single precept is to enjoy oneself, at the expense of no matter whom."[1]

'I hope you'll agree, there is nothing for us in Sade.'

I hoped so too.

'But the slogan was rescued in the magical revival of modem times. Aleister Crowley re-affirmed it as a revelation from his angel: "Do what thou wilt shall be the whole of the law." Adding: "Love is the law, love under will." Which sounds like Augustine over again, but not quite. "Love *under will*." "Do what you will" – not "do as you please". The heart of the matter is to find, first, your true Will. Which may be something you've not thought of at this moment, something, even, that you're running away from.

'It's what you are FOR. What will fulfil you. Your *dharma*, in Hindu terms; your "thing" which you should be doing. In fact – your vocation. Find it and live by it as the one task worth succeeding at. Then the "love" comes in. Pour out love, unlimited, piercing, creative love into whatever you *are* for... and that's it. That's absolute, final. Conventional examples would be the saint, the artist, the old-style craftsman. Nowadays we may have to adjust our ideas. But the principle's the same, always.

'How do you find out what you're for? First, of course, by wanting to! But we with our conception of Binary Man can give a proper answer in line with the higher magic. *Your ego may not know, but your protoself does.* It's your true guardian angel, your being. It was there before you were born, it set you up as you essentially are, it may have unfinished business which you're meant to finish. It knows best, because it's in contact with the inexhaustible proto-realm, with the inwardness of the human condition past and present, with the keys to the future, with the Presences and centres of occult power, with whatever gods may be, with the logic of the cosmos, with truth.

'Your vocation isn't remote from you. It's there already, the true Will in the proto-depth of your nature, for you to release. Always by enlarging your life, not enclosing. To find the way and keep it, you must go forward, not back. Into problems and through them. You'll find that's taught by magicians and hardly anyone else. The unleash-ing of your own powers - the powers that will make you what you should be - comes by pressing on, saying "yes", never retreating, expe-riencing everything till your path is clear. Including suffering, if you can embrace it and make sense of it. Enable your true Will to emerge, and then work at it - I stress "work" - without fretting over details. Do this fully enough, with enough devotion, and it'll be your best guide in everything, "the whole of the law". The quest is endless any-how. Play by ear, prove in practice, not by abstract arguments. Avoid getting tangled in rules, and avoid laying down rules for others. Be as open as you can about what you do yourself and what happens, but beware of generalizing from it. Everybody else has a protoself and a Will as you have.'

I felt that Martin was tumbling out a heap of precooked aphorisms with less than his usual orderliness. Also, that in spite of his own dis-claimer he was preaching. Possibly he felt the same and pulled himself up. His manner altered.

'We've spoken about the breaking down of the barriers between protoself and ego, the surging in of untapped wisdom and power, the reality of the Great Work of the magicians. Your protoself can come through briefly in dreams and myths, in impulses and inspirations and mystical experiences. This takes different people different ways. But I offer you one principle. The more you live by your true Will - your vocation - the more fully your protoself can come through, and the more transfiguring the results will be.

'Including results of the kind that would be counted as magical or semi-magical, beyond textbook science. A born healer who develops his gift can cure by laying on hands. A born gardener has green fingers. A born researcher has serendipity: he's always making discoveries without trying. They become wonder-workers through doing their thing, doing what they're meant to do.

'Examples like that may strike you as trivial. But we're only at the beginning. When human beings grasp their own nature, they'll go on to therapies and fulfilments and wonder-workings beyond present imagination; and they'll shake off the burden of mortality and futility, the deadly sense of things closing in on them, because they'll transcend death through reunion with the proto-realm.

'You may ask, what's holding us back? What blinds us to our true Will?

'Our own inner resistance. The false selfhood of the hard-shelled ego, turning Binary Man the wrong way up. What William Blake calls the Spectre. The compulsion – and it is a compulsion – to cut oneself down, shut oneself in, limit one's interests, nurse ghastly little hates, scheme for ghastly little pseudo-successes and pseudo-pleasures, probably based on exploiting others, or on perverting one's own sacred gifts for profit. (Remember the double aspect of alchemy.) Self-imprisonment in death.

'Civilized society fosters all that. It cuts human beings down itself, to fit systems – educational, industrial, political, military – and it holds out rewards for those who'll play along with their own computerization, probably in jobs where they aren't doing what they're meant to do in the least. That's sometimes described proudly as Meritocracy. Society dictates laws and ethical rules to serve its own ends; it prostitutes language to trap its victims in verbal formulae (which it can do because language is cut off from its roots in proto-being); and it strengthens itself by war and violence. It's the Waste Land, as a poet warned more than fifty years ago; it's Babel; and its logical end at best is the nightmare happiness of Huxley's Brave New World, with the planned stultification of Orwell's Newspeak.[2]

'If you can opt out, can reject the cutting-down with the prizes it offers, can find your true Will through free action and receptive stillness, and live by it at whatever cost – then you can make a fresh start from fundamentals.

'Yes, I know the standard criticism of all such advice. That this is a message which only a favoured few can take in. That most ordinary workers on their day-to-day treadmill, most ordinary victims of race-discrimination and sex-discrimination, most of the ordinary homeless and ordinary unemployed' (he stressed 'ordinary' more each time till it rang with bitterness) 'are in no position to do more than soldier on. At present, that's true. Moreover I don't believe society can be altered, not radically at any rate, by those who are caught in it. There is nothing revolutionary in trendiness.

'But if more and more do opt out and defy Babel; if more and more *live differently*[3] (which of course can include, say, trade-unionists with a fresh approach – in fact it already does); and if they press ahead in the spirit I'm speaking of – they'll tap the only energies that are deep and potent enough to sustain an alternative society. Excuse a worn phrase, but it's the apt one. Their influence will spread and transform. The Waste Land will return to fertility.

'Let me repeat this. Except for a few born contemplative types, the mode of life I'm describing does mean taking an active part in the world that we're in. Not withdrawing into the proto-realm on a permanent mystical trip. You'll recall I picked this out in the Grail Ritual. The Initiate is tested by being invited to quit the world for some select paradise, and he refuses. God loves his creation and cares for it. However you put this theologically, I agree that contempt for the world is a false road. The immortal presences are concerned with this life of ours. They elect to be born into it themselves. They have business for us to work on. The Initiate who achieves the secret does "go back and make the land blossom".'

Martin's uncommon passion left the students a little disoriented. It was Mr Frobisher who broke silence. 'I'm sorry to drag in Hitler again, but he does occur to me. Surely that was a clear case of a man with a mission and a fanatical devotion to it, and the results were appalling.'

Martin replied slowly and carefully but not hesitantly. 'I'd say Hitler may well have had a vocation to lead and inspire, and perhaps to rule. He did seem to have a kind of intuition... up to a point. But the plain fact is that he failed; and he failed because of a series of lunatic aggressions, beginning with his assault on the Jews, which turned so many of his potential friends into enemies that he doomed himself. To put it another way, the crimes Hitler committed united most of the world against him, destroyed his leadership, ended his life, and so were fatal to his vocation. If he'd grasped it properly and pursued it with real devotion, real wisdom, he'd have had the sense not to commit them. But his warped psychology perverted the Will that might have put him on a beneficent course.'

Madri put in: 'My understanding has always been, Martin, that you think we're ethically OK as long as we're really doing our true Will, because the protoself sees far enough to know crime doesn't pay. At least, not so as to be any genuine use.'

'Right. A bit over-simplified, but right.'

Norman had been getting restless and half raising his hand. 'You talk as if you foresaw a revolution. I can't make out when it's supposed to happen, or how, or why. You don't mention any organization like a party or movement.'

Martin was bland. 'I prefer to leave organizations to those who enjoy organizing. But may I draw your attention to a fact of history? Revolutions never actually happen till the top people who run the show, the Establishment, get demoralized and disorganized themselves. No party's going to do that alone. But I can picture a panic setting in at the top, when the Anti-Establishment of people who live differently is seen to be healthier, better-defined, more productive... and also, when it's seen to have convinced a lot of candidates for the Meritocracy that the system is a lie and a cheat. My feeling in fact is that it's more fruitful discussing how a change can come than trying to be precise about the sort of bodies that might take over, or the methods they'd use.'[4]

Owen asked: 'But what kind of new society does this lead to then? Would it be Socialist?'

'Frankly,' Martin answered, 'I've only the vaguest notions. I don't deal in Utopias either. The future begins today, with us. It can only be what people *now* are planting the seeds of.'

Another silence. Then Mr Frobisher spoke again. 'You talk about vocation and purpose and so forth. But suppose somebody, say an interviewer, were to ask you: "What's the meaning of life?" Could you give a short answer?'

Martin sounded remote yet near. 'The meaning of life is the overcoming of death.'

On that note the formal session ended. I gathered this lecture was the last in the course. The rest of the students' time at Allhallows would be devoted to group projects already undertaken. I stayed for their interim reports on these. The first project was on ESP, the second on palmistry, the third on ritual. During a leisurely coffee break I chatted with Martin about the projects and then about the lecture.

He wanted my reaction. 'Did it give you what you need for your article?'

'It gave me... well, I can make something of it, yes. I do see how this is a common factor. How John and Madri and your other big names have all found a vocation and it's made them exceptional. They are. Only, to judge from what Madri said to me, I ought to be applying this to my own case and that ought to tell me more. But I don't get any message that way, there's no clear-cut issue in it.'

'To coin a phrase,' he replied, 'wait and see. You may soon work this out for yourself. I did drop a hint, you know.'

2

After dinner I headed for the sundial, like a cliché murderer revisiting the scene of his crime. A discord of voices among the trees on my right resolved itself – or didn't resolve itself – into an argument between Janice and Freda Bamberger, with Mei-ling in attendance. Something about the schisms in Women's Lib. Within the few seconds it took me to pass in and out of earshot, I heard, for the first time, Janice employing four-letter words. I didn't linger.

The vista below the sundial stretched innocently downhill. I knew there wouldn't be blood on the grass, and I looked for blood. Returning, I saw Paul and David Jacks again, very much as they were last night. They were sitting on the bench where Karen sounded me out six days ago.

Paul beckoned me over. 'I didn't get a chance to congratulate you on your Grail script.'

'Thanks.' He'd had ample chance, but this was the first time he could use congratulation as an opening gambit.

'It raises possibilities for when we get going with the National Quest.'

In spite of my waning zeal for this venture, I realized it was still on, and I was still expected to help stage the Return of Arthur. With my photographer in Paul's pocket, as he appeared to be, the article might run into trouble if I refused.

'Show Geoffrey those photos,' said Paul.

I sat with them on the bench. David produced a sheet of small coloured prints and ran his finger down four of them. 'I took those last night, a few yards from where we're sitting. Here, use this.' He gave me a magnifying glass.

All four pictures showed the lawn near the sundial as it had been during my time under SP5. In each of them the flashbulb had caught a human quarry. Three were profiles of Bernard in his brief tunic and curious head-dress, walking from right to left of the camera. The other was a similar profile of someone else, unclothed, female.

David's dismal pleasure was manifest. 'These are really exciting. I could use two of them with the Rosmer-Madri stuff. "Weird companions of controversial public figures," some angle like that.'

I was still engrossed in the pictures. 'Why only one of her?'

'She went off down the slope, over there, before I was ready to take another. I looked for her afterwards but she'd gone.'

'Who is she?'

Paul raised his eyebrows. 'Why, dear Annabel of course. I was there. I wondered what she was up to.'

'But is it Annabel?'

Without a blow-up it was difficult to be certain. I got them both to concede that the hair looked too short and not dark enough, and the body looked too ample. They refused, however, to admit a margin of error. 'It can't be anyone else,' Paul insisted. 'I ought to know, oughtn't I?'

'It was dark. How close were you?'

'Close enough to recognize the way she walks. It's the hardest thing to disguise.'

I gave up and tried a different query. 'What about me, then? Where was I?'

'You? How on earth should I know?'

'But I came out of the wood, there, and crossed the lawn after her.'

'You couldn't have. We'd have seen you.'

'Here, let's get this straight. You both saw... Annabel... and then Bernard. Right?'

'Right,' they answered together.

'But not me.'

'No.'

I tackled David separately. 'You might have been busy with your camera and not noticed.'

'I suppose that's just on the cards. But Paul—'

'No, it's OK,' said Paul, with a glance that was meant to warn me. 'I understand now, it's a private joke, I'm afraid. Sorry.'

Luckily David sighted John in the distance, talking to the satanic accountant, Simon Calthrop. He darted off for more chat and pictures. Paul turned to me. 'Were you on an SP-trip?'

'Yes.'

'What happened this time?'

I could hardly tell Paul. 'It was confusing – and this business of my not crossing the lawn makes it worse. If you don't mind, I'd like to go over my notes again and see if there's an explanation.'

'Fair enough. You did see them, though, somehow. That Bernard lad, and Annabel jaybirding across the greensward.'

'I did.'

He twitched his hands nervously. 'I had an SP-trip of my own near here, once. In the temple.'

'When was that?'

'Once. No, I'll be honest. Last night. Soon after this incident of yours. There was a pill in my back pocket, it must have been there for ages, I took it on impulse.'

He wasn't being honest. The stray pill was a polite fiction dissembling his illicit supply. But obviously he had a story he couldn't hold in, he had to spill it to someone. I showed willingness to listen. Promptly he slid into the same vertiginous mood as that night in his room. The same style of talking, too. In which he digressed before he started....

'Martin sidetracked them properly this morning. Yes, yes, I won't argue, there was a lot in it, sound straight psychology – but all that sweetness and light, that stuff on being open and not exploiting or organizing – all building up to Cloud-Cuckooland under the benign smile of his proto-presences.... These Cryptocrats could teach him a thing or two about how people have to be organized in real life. Well, so could I. It's not as if he followed his own advice. He manipulates the students himself, and by keeping secrets, by not being open. They never get to be told about SP5. They don't learn where all this is coming from.'

Paul had a point, of course, but I didn't concur. I just made a non-committal sound.

'So, what about SP5 then?' he rattled on. 'You know something? Martin sees his beautiful proto-realm because he wants to. Because he has to, or he'd go round the bend. Other SP-trippers don't.'

I demurred. 'They don't all see it as he does, no. But none of them have seen anything that refutes him.'

'If you mean he's clever at stretching his theories to cover every new trip reported, then maybe, maybe. But even that didn't work with me, you know. When he heard what I saw, he wrote me off as a bad job. Even then he thought up a word for it – two words – trust Martin! Guess what was the matter with me? "Psychic allergy".'

I was wary of rousing too many memories of a phase Karen had portrayed more grimly. 'Tell me what you saw last night in the temple.'

'Oh, nothing in your line. SP5 delivers the goods for you all right. Free flights and historical pageants and naked women. I just see what's actually there, and it's no fun.'

'You mean the stuff hasn't any effect on you?'

'I didn't say that, did I? Stop talking and let me get a word in. David went off to bed. I stepped back into the temple with a torch, to check on a bit of equipment. (For the other ritual. We're putting it on tonight, did I tell you?) Then I, er, happened to find that pill, and took it, and put down the torch so that it floodlit our Horned friend above the altar. And I looked at him.'

'You'll have been through that first bit where it takes hold. What Martin calls the "plunge". Everybody has that even if it lasts only a second.'

I nodded.

'He makes out,' continued Paul, 'that it's a switch-over of consciousness from ego to protoself. You fall apart and then reassemble in the other centre. I'll tell you how it was with me, though. I fell apart, and I plunged. But I didn't reassemble.'

'After the dust had settled, *it* - reality - wasn't *me* any more. It was the Horned One. No, I didn't have Pygmalion fancies about the statue coming to life. It was the same as always. But *it was me*. Or rather it was all that was left of me. Except for a horrid conviction that this was all wrong and the real me was somewhere else. Only, there wasn't any ground for the conviction to stand on. I tried to think, and there wasn't an "I" to think. I even tried what you might call praying (which isn't my scene at all), and whatever it is that prays wasn't there to pray. The Horned One was. Steadily. He'd taken over a part of me himself. That part was limping on after a fashion. The rest of me was just agony without identity.'

His hands were trembling and the last, rather studied phrase came in a near-shriek. This was an authentic horror. Some comment was demanded, however inept. 'I do understand, up to a point. The Miserific Vision.'[5]

I don't know whether he took the allusion, and I regretted it a moment later, it was too flip and literary.

Paul hastened on. 'Martin's right in some ways. With SP5 you do see the "Inwardness of Things". But I saw through. Or rather there was a seeing-through process happening, and it was centred on the Horned One.... Traps.'

'Eh?'

'Traps. Endless traps. THEY scatter them around. We get caught in them, build religions and ways of life round them - but this showed what they actually are and what the motives are, and how THEY have power through them.'

I was losing grip on his pronouns. 'THEY. Who do you mean?'

He didn't reply to that directly, but his voice was husky with anguish. 'Have you ever had those nightmares where some meaning-less sight - even a simple everyday object - is utterly awful? It may be a face. It needn't be an ugly face, just a face, and yet if you didn't wake up you'd crack with terror.'

'I know. The myth of the Gorgon is about that. A woman once told me that the worst dream in her life was that she was staring at an electric radiator.'

'Yes, that's it. The Aztecs in Mexico had a chief god who devoured human sacrifices in thousands, and they called him Tezcatlipoca. It means "Smoking Mirror". To me that name is a whiff of hell. It's a nonsense-image out of deep nightmare.'

'So then, you were saying—?'

'Better leave this for now.' He indicated Simon, who was bearing down on us with John Rosmer.

3

'Hallo there,' said Simon.

'Everything under control?' said Paul, bouncing back into a fair semblance of professional bonhomie.

'I've given Mr Jacks a few hints about our temple ritual this evening.'

'Fine. We have every confidence in you, you'll run it most expertly. I looked the place over myself last night.'

I grasped vaguely what Paul was planning. 'Do you feel happy with this, in view of what we were just discussing?'

'As they say, when you fall off a horse, remount immediately.'

'Don't follow,' said Simon.

Paul laughed. 'I was telling Geoffrey a bad dream with the Horned One in it.'

'That could be auspicious. Incidentally,' Simon addressed me, 'I'd like to ask you about the Grail business, when you can spare a few minutes. Surely you've censored it. This belongs to the disguised paganism of the twelfth century, the religion where the priests were called devils, and William Rufus and Thomas à Becket were divine victims.[6]

'It's been argued, yes.'

'That Old Religion angle,' said Paul—'do you think we might bring in Owen and Kwame on our ritual? They've both been witches.'

'I rather doubt it. They're disillusioned.'

'Ah well. I think we've got it made anyway.' The prospect of organizing had restored Paul's aplomb. 'If this temple effort gives David a few good pictures, I believe he'll be agreeable to helping with the National Quest. He's already promised to consult a few editors and producers on launching it.'

'PAUL!' Freda's scream ripped along the lawn. She was in front of the pillars with her husband Joe, Arnold Gore, and Norman: a Cryptocratic montage.

Paul grinned. 'Sounds as if we're wanted. Excuse.' He and Simon moved off, leaving John beside me on the bench. Up to now he'd been silent.

'Are you letting it go ahead?' he asked.

'What, their ritual?'

'That, and the follow-up. They've been telling me more about this Return-of-Arthur project.'

'One thing at a time. The ritual – I'm not sure what it is myself – but the object is to provide picture material to go with my article. Well, you heard.'

'In other words it's a media sales-gimmick with no real bearing on Allhallows.'

'I suppose that's a possible description.'

'Whose article is this, yours or theirs?'

'What are you suggesting I ought to do?'

'Seems to me *you* can do only one thing. Put your foot down.'

I sighed. 'It would mean a row... and I don't want to stir up trouble. I don't feel equal to it. This week has trampled me flat. There've been too many things to cope with. It all needs mulling over in peace.'

'How much peace are you likely to have, if they press on with their National Quest?'

'I don't have to join in.'

'You're in already. It's your own work they'll be using as a scenario for the pantomime. Did you write your books for that? To supply the backing for an instant pop-Arthur? To be status symbols for Neo-Fascists to wave around – not read – at rallies on Cadbury Hill and Glastonbury Tor?'

I glanced at him, his black hair, his dark eyes, his curiously calm face. He hadn't raised his voice by a decibel.

'My books aren't sacred. They aren't even particularly important.'

'The mysteries of the island of Albion are both. You've taken on a trust by unfolding them in public. Or the trust has taken on you.'

'Are you saying I should run after that lot' (Paul and his fellow-conspirators were still in sight) 'and tell them to cancel?'

'You have no other course.'

4

I didn't run after them. I spent the rest of the afternoon in my own room, recording and scribbling as so often before, and going over my stack of notes. These are so bulky as to be almost beyond control, but I'll have to keep them. When it comes to the final write-up they'll doubtless be useful to expand the tapes.*

The work was not done without distraction. Self-caused distraction. John's firmness had shaken me. Should I seek a second opinion? Perhaps I ought to talk over last night's events with Martin (who would want to hear, after all) and see what light he could shed. Then again, though, there were deterrents. I could hardly forget that he was an analyst even if he no longer practised. What would he read into such a... such a juicy experience? No. I might be his guest, and temporarily his student and semi-colleague, I wasn't his patient yet.

Another course that occurred to me was to re-draw my circle on the floor, which had got a little scuffed over the past three days, and invoke my protoself again. I did try that, but had no sense of guidance, only a nagging certainty – as at the end of the first attempt, but prolonged, this time, in defiance of stubborn mental rejection – that I already had my answer.

Supper, in memory, is a blur. Paul told me they would be starting the temple rites at ten. 'I should warn you, Simon's fanatically punctual.' Here was my chance to flash the red light. What I did was say 'Thank you' and acquiesce. The idea babbling in my head at that point was, I think, that since a veto might annoy David Jacks enough to disrupt the article, my journalistic duty was to give them the benefit of the doubt and wait to see what their performance was like. It might even be relevant. Some such argument as this gave me an excuse to retire to my room and go on working, though with frequent pauses and vacillations.

At 9:50 I set out for the temple along that much-traversed lawn. Mentally the debate continued. My heart was pounding. Going through the pillars I met Karen coming the other way. Since the Grail affair, I hadn't spoken with her or even been near her; at least in the indisputable flesh. She was now carrying a sword. Not my Grail prop-sword either, but the real weapon from Martin's study.

* A correct anticipation, as the length of this expanded version has proved.

'They asked to borrow this for their ceremony. I got halfway there, then decided they shouldn't have it.'

'So you're bringing it back.'

A woman flourishing a real sword, not a dummy or fencing foil, can be either comic or disquieting. Karen was far from comic. Her Allhallows title 'house-warden' came back to me with a new force. I'd never seen her looking so serious – even stern – and she didn't thaw for me.

'Be careful, Geoffrey. It does matter who holds the sword.'

'I'm sure it does.'

'I suppose you're on your way to the temple yourself.'

'Yes.'

'And this is to be part of your *Globe* feature.'

'As extra colour. That's the idea at any rate.'

Her face remained rigid. 'I've no right to comment, really. You're more successful than I ever was, to be handling a *Globe* assignment at all.'

'Considering the Allhallows view of success, that's scarcely a compliment.'

'I mustn't detain you.'

She went by me, gently squeezing my arm, but without the slightest relaxation of manner. I paced on through the dusk, passing the sculp-ture (which I pushed, on impulse, to reassure myself that the man was still there), and the uncommunicative sundial. I was still balancing factors against each other, but the agitation had lessened. My pulse was normal. Karen, somehow, had calmed me. I couldn't have foretold which course I would follow. Yet my state was no longer indecision. It was knowing that a decision had already been reached without knowing what it was.

Noises were issuing from the temple, not the diffused hubbub of an audience settling, but strange wordless yells and gong-notes. Martin and John stood outside the door.

'They've been at it for some time,' said Martin.

'Paul told me ten o'clock.'

'They must have started early then.'

John raised his eyebrows. 'You weren't informed of any change?'

'No,' I confessed, 'I wasn't.'

He didn't remark on that. He didn't have to. We opened the door and went in.

The Finger and the Moon

It's hard to recall, after the event, what I did expect before it. Decadent French novels and modern horror yarns had prepared me for the would-be obscene or blasphemous. Yet Paul's PR intent surely implied it couldn't be quite like that, and it wasn't.

My first impression was of bad air, bad visibility. Greenish smoke wreathed from a bowl with a suspended lamp under it, mounted on a metal tripod. The burning chemical had a sickly odour – not the smell of incense, or cannabis – that made my head swim. The light that struggled through came from three resinous torches of the most primitive kind, one in a sconce beside the Horned One, the others held by two bearers with their backs to me.

Most of the chairs had been pushed aside. In the open centre before the altar, Simon officiated. He had put on a short surplice coloured deep indigo. His sober inconspicuous manner had dropped off him: he was twirling and leaping, tossing his arms up, shouting meaningless jargon. Some of it seemed to be addressed to a large black cat on the altar steps. Even at that juncture I wondered how they got the cat to keep still. I never found out. Perhaps with a tranquillizer.

In one role or another, every Cryptocrat was assisting. Herod sat with the gong, beating time. The Bamberger couple were at the altar. Above it the horned sculpture stood up as ever with one hand raised, the flickering light giving it an eye-cheating instability. Two chains had been attached to its lower hand. One trailed off to the altar's left, and ended in a noose lying slackly round Freda's neck. The other led to Joe, similarly posed on the right.

Both wore costumes which looked as if they'd been made (and very likely were, now I come to think of it) for a fancy-dress party which I'd rather not have been invited to. Hers, in essence, was a pinkish two-piece bathing suit. Technically it covered her more than a bikini. The top, however, had a pair of breasts printed on it. They were realistic, but tinted so as to be manifestly not her own. In itself the device was nothing new. I remember it among the commercial way-out gear of a bygone spring, when the bosom of a highly paid model spread through the land. Freda, though, had improved on it. The pubic zone of her lower garment bore a corresponding image correctly located.

For her husband of course the scope was narrower, but the shorts which he wore himself were embellished with a design recalling the well-known giant etched in the hillside chalk of Cerne Abbas.

Otherwise unclothed, he had painted himself in several areas with crude streaks and whorls of various colours. Both of them swayed and lunged and gesticulated, rattling their chains. Joe held his whip (now at last revealed) and cracked it at intervals in Freda's direction, while Herod hammered the gong and Simon younced[7].

I soon recognized one of the torch-bearers by his red hair. Norman. The other half-turned and disclosed himself to be Arnold Gore. Paul was seated in a chair by the tripod, fumes rising round him, the only person not active. David circled through the room with his small camera. His movements steered my attention to two unscrutinized figures in the shadows. Unisex in garb, but female, they were doing a little dance of their own. Animal masks hid their faces. The taller was a goat, the shorter a donkey.

The whole jamboree was so absurd, it should have been funny. What made it nasty was that it wasn't funny. Granted, in a permissive age, nobody can manage real orgies or impieties any more: still it was a failure in mere dignity that Simon, for instance, should cut his capers with that skimpy dark gown draped over an ordinary suit, like Mr Chips[8] gone mad. But no, it wasn't funny. Nor was the Bambergers' smutty cabaret.

And certainly none of this was relevant.

Simon wound up the proceedings with a litany to Satan which several joined in. I caught a few stock phrases of devil-worship, such as 'Our Father who wast in heaven'. Herod, to keep the record straight for himself, interjected 'slandered brother of the Lord Jesus'. The prayers mentioned potency and secret knowledge and 'hidden forces from the veiled world'.

Then silence. A gradual unwinding. Very slowly Simon removed his surplice, and laid it on a chair. Joe and Freda sat down on the altar steps. Neither paid any attention to the torpid cat.

Martin spoke. 'May I offer our apologies for arriving so late? As this event was staged – partly at least – in aid of the article that Geoffrey is writing, I'm sure you'll accord him the right to comment. Geoffrey?'

This was it, and it was easy beyond belief. 'Thank you, Martin. I've been watching and listening with great interest. I can't pronounce on this as a Satanist exercise. But it does concern me as part of the *Globe* feature. I'm sorry, David, but I'm not allowing it to be used.'

'Not allowing? Who's in charge of the pictures, you or me?'

'Sorry again, I know you've been to some trouble. But it's my article, and no picture of this is appearing with it.'

Arnold glowered at me, but it was still a vestigially diplomatic glower. 'Doesn't the editor decide?'

'I'm not sure how it will go if I refuse point-blank, but if necessary I will refuse.'

'Suppose it kills the article?' David protested.

'Then it does. If the *Globe* insists on using these pictures, the *Globe* won't get my script.'

'Hell. You might have told me.'

'I ... hoped the ritual would fit in as part of the story. It won't. It has nothing to do with what I came here to write about. I can't even see how it has anything to do with the National Quest idea.'

Nobody answered, nobody made a move. The dancers had unmasked and were, predictably, Janice and Mei-ling. The temple had become fetid and stuffy. Shirts were damp, foreheads glistened, everything drooped.

Martin spoke again. 'Frankly, I agree with Geoffrey. It's not for me to dictate to him. But in my own judgement this simply isn't Allhallows.'

Freda snarled: 'You don't want your precious outfit associated with anything naughty?'

It was odd to see the Bamberger sadism provoke a response in kind even from Martin. Everybody had looked at her, and instead of replying he looked at her himself. She was exposed, a shade too long for comfort, to the gaze of a mainly masculine audience. With the spell broken her costume weakened her position.

At last Martin did reply. 'That's not the point, Mrs Bamberger. Show us a Satanism we can accept as genuine and we'll exchange notes on it. One or two real diabolists have been here before now. But this! It's kid's stuff. With respect, Mr Calthrop.'

'Thank you very much, Mr Ellis,' said Simon. 'If I'm so ignorant of the Real Thing, are you so familiar with it?'

'I can tell you what it's like. Proud and sly, secretive and contemptuous, the cult of the Void and the cosmic No[9]. You lot here – why, you've been having fun. Don't let me spoil your fun. But don't expect me to buy it, or permit that fine sculpture to be dragged into it for the amusement of the public.'

Paul stumbled to his feet. Something was badly wrong with him. His wilder mood was back, worse. He'd been closest to that bowl with the chemical in it, and the fumes perhaps were toxic. At any rate he tore into Martin as if no one else had been present. In a sense no one was. The dialogue that ensued can have made no sense to most of the listeners. I caught the main gist myself, but felt that nuances were escaping me all the time. It was like picking up a newspaper correspondence when you've missed the first letters.

'You know it all, Martin? You've reached the Ipsissimus degree?'

Martin sounded tired, patient. 'We don't need to go over that again. I got far enough to find out the truth.'

'On your trips I suppose – by the technique we know of.' (Even now, Paul wouldn't utter 'SP5' among strangers. Hoarding a potent secret had become second nature to him.)

'By the technique we know of. Yes.'

Paul sneered. 'Two can play at that game. You haven't got a monopoly.'

'That's not news to me, Paul.'

'Only, I see through. You and your airy-fairy pipe-dreams of Higher Wisdom! I see where they come from. Call yourself a psychologist – why, you've forgotten even that. You daren't remember. All this proto-rigmarole you hand out to students... God, you don't KNOW, you really don't. Do I have to spell it out? Your entire proto-thing, Martin, grew up round Frances. Your wife got cancer and died and you couldn't face it, couldn't face what had happened to her. There had to be something better than this. That's all.'

It was a low blow. Martin winced, and his face grew older. Paul weaved towards him, leering. 'Though just as man to man, now, I'm not sure why you had to make it so complicated. Seems to me you've consoled yourself pretty smoothly in other ways. You and your lady house-warden! And Annabel even, dear Annabel, have you left Annabel alone? I'd need convincing.'

Martin waved him back. 'You can't expect me to talk any longer. Whatever brought this on, I suppose it's more serious than I thought. But not now. Please, not now. Excuse me.'

He threw open the temple door, and exited. So did John and I. Most of the rest, buzzing and bewildered, followed. Out on the lawn the five non-participating students had gathered, drawn by the noise. Madri too was there, though I'm not certain about her junior colleagues. Martin tried to go straight on through them. But Paul darted round in front and obstructed his path, boiling with revelations.

'Listen. You've got to face it now. Let me instruct you on our *technique*. Yes, it does show realities you'd never see otherwise. But *I* saw through, I tell you. *I* saw how the traps are laid, traps like Frances for escapists like you. Why she died like that. How you get caught up in your own fantasies... and it's all according to plan.'

'Whose plan?' said Martin quietly, in a tone of weary exasperation.

'There you go. You prove it with every word you speak. THEY've got you to blind yourself to what they are and how they're using you. I never saw your lovely proto-realm. That's their cunning, their camouflage. I saw what's behind it. The great anarchs, the Old Ones, brooding, biding. Oh yes, there is an Unseen, true enough, and you're right, we can open the gates and let it flood into us, but it's no fairy-godfather Higher Self that floods in, it's alien. If we master it... stay in control of it... but the first step is to acknowledge it, even through a cheap image like that in there' (he pointed at the temple). 'We share the power with THEM or go down.'

Until those last sentences my strongest feeling was no worse than distress. Because of his piled-up tensions, plus fumes, Paul had come unstuck. It was painful, but he'd recover. His final words altered that and made me go cold. The Satanist ritual... it was more than a PR masquerade for him. Ye gods, he meant it! Was he insane? He was still coherent, shockingly so. My mind ran back to the video-cassette sequence, and other bits of my bizarre session in his room. Looking at Paul I could almost believe he was possessed. His face was changed and he seemed bigger, more formidable; while Martin waned, older and weaker every second.

Then, from the group of students, Mrs Frobisher spoke. Her voice was agreeable, kind, a shade patronizing.

'Paul if I might just put a word in I think you're a little bit confused because you don't know what it is you've contacted you're quite right of course only you shouldn't call them Old Ones you can read about them in Scott-Elliot or Conan Doyle's novel *The Maracot Deep* they were the degenerate rulers of Atlantis sometimes called the

Black Brothers and their evil influences are still at work in the world and they're incarnate from time to time and I knew a fishmonger in Ealing whose assistant was a Black Brother I don't mean a Negro he was white and fair-haired and came from Norfolk but I picked up the strongest bad vibrations from him I've ever felt and the fishmonger said yes he knew and told me things about him and you sound rather like him now Paul, I don't mean the assistant I mean the fishmonger.'

She trailed into silence, beaming. The hush lasted a second or two. Then Madri began to laugh. Not loudly, and not at Mrs Frobisher. A deep, holy, healing chuckle. Nothing could check what she began. Steve suddenly roared, Owen exploded. Kwame (surely with a private piquancy over the Black Brothers) perceived that it was all right to laugh and did, with a splendid throaty bass. Mr Frobisher, loyal to his wife, was more subdued but got as far as a grin.

The contagion spread to John and me, and to the two unmasked girls, who fell, not reluctantly, into each other's arms. Norman and Arnold held their torches up and smiled awkwardly. So did Herod. The spurt of a flashbulb attested David Jacks's presence of mind. I've no remembrance of Simon, but through the temple door I glimpsed Joe and Freda standing below the Horned One clutching raincoats around them, Joe sheepish, Freda sour-visaged and ridiculous beyond words.

St Thomas More said it. 'The Devil, the prowde spirite, cannot endure to be mocked.'[10]

On my first Allhallows morning I'd heard Mrs Frobisher and wondered why Martin had let her come. Now I knew. His own deepest being, far down in the psychic iceberg, had foreseen and contrived and brought this good angel to him at the time when he would need her. Like other classic magicians he had battled with a rival and won. Even if, in keeping with the ironies of his doctrine, he'd prepared the victory with no consciousness of what he was doing.

Brushing past Paul, he strode off along the lawn. A great many people seemed to be drifting towards the house, joking and arguing. Martin outdistanced everybody. John and I were still fairly close behind him when someone shrieked. We turned. I saw one last memento of my evening in Paul's company – his gun. Paul had rushed after us and was pointing it in the general direction of Martin, who was well past the kinetic sculpture, caught in a gleam of light from an upstairs window. A single shot was as much as Paul had time for, the students grabbed him. His bullet hit the sculpture; its metal strips shuddered.

After that I have dazed recollections of people shouting, and Annabel running from the house, and talk of phoning for a doctor. I offered help and they assured me they could manage. It's muddled. But I do know the outcome. John and I were walking along, the same way as before, and he said: 'You certainly started something there.'

Other Scene

I

STARTED? But surely I was finishing. The article might survive or might not, there was nothing more to be done for it. My cue was to take a tactful leave and let them sort out their domestic clashes in privacy. Later when they'd cooled off, and Allhallows was less crowded, I could return and discuss my script if any. Maybe I'd stirred things up beyond my intention. But, I told John, even if part of the blame did attach to me, it wasn't in terms of 'starting' that I wanted to think.

Again I collided with the Rosmer implacability. 'You're involved. You can't quit.'

I began to protest that this was simply a job - or at least, could still be back-pedalled into that status - when an image from the previous night jumped up and hit me. All right then, one had to face facts... it wasn't a scene which SP5 would have been likely to evoke from an uninvolved subconscious. Or protoself.

So, I was involved like he said. Instant therapy then? A hint from Martin might be apt, even the didactic Martin of his last lecture. 'To find the way and keep it, you must go forward, not back. Into problems and through them.' And something about 'pressing on' and 'experiencing everything till your path is clear'. I could follow that advice, and without launching out beyond the assignment, either. I still carried a virgin Allhallows package with me, an untouched item in the assignment itself: my third SP5 pill.

It might have been more scientific to wait till daylight, so as to have a contrast with Nos. 1 and 2. However, I showed it to John and he approved. 'From all accounts, that could help you towards an answer,' he said. 'You'd better find a secluded spot, though. Any ideas?'

'Over there, in that corner where the maze is.'

'Then we'll know where to search if you don't come back. Good luck.'

A few of the students were in sight, but to judge from their interest in the bullet-scarred sculpture, the evening's uproar was still absorbing them. I slipped away into the starlit hush of the old garden, and swallowed my final dose.

2

Nothing happened.

Nothing altered.

I felt my pulse, paced up and down, looked at the constellations, then at the maze entrance. I looked at it because I wanted to look at it. There was nothing to see. I looked because I wanted to. At my first encounter with that maze, five days back, it had said *No* to me. Now it said *Yes*. I went in. There was no reason to go in. I went in because I wanted to.

Annabel's key-poem came readily to mind. As she had foreshadowed, I couldn't have read it from the piece of paper she gave me – not enough light – but no need. Right, left, left. Funny though, it wasn't actually the key-poem, it was a nursery rhyme, yet it was working just as well. Straight on. Left. Straight on. Soon I'd be at the centre. Someone or something would be waiting for me. Down steps. Up steps. I stopped a moment. Nothing to stop for. I stopped because I wanted to.

Round a corner at last, and the door in front of me. The same fumble with the stiff handle and the big latch. Through. Pools and sculpture. Not enough light for a reflection in the concave mirror, not at four paces. I took those paces, one two three four, and saw. Myself slightly enlarged... but myself in SP-vision, surrounded by the familiar aura, filling the mirror and haloing my reflected face.

Wait though, this had to be a trick. Not a true reflection. Optically it couldn't work because the proto-light isn't real light. This was a Marx-Brothers joke I must have arranged, like Groucho pretending to be Harpo's reflection when the mirror wasn't there. Or the other way round. I always identified with Groucho. Whichever I'd become now, it was fun to peer out from the pseudo-mirror (where I obviously was, now that I grasped the setup) at my own perplexed face. That fellow had had a long trudge through the maze to get to me, and here I was in my little glass island all the time. Funny too, there was no perceptible difference in size between us. He leaned towards me and I leaned towards him, playing at reflections, because I wanted to, not because I had to. I'm not sure which of us completed the Groucho-Harpo routine by walking all round the other. Anyhow we both thought it hilarious.[1]

'Define Absolute Reality!' shouted my doppelganger.

I took the Zen allusion. 'That hedge, of course.'

We burst out through a gap in it which I hadn't noticed before, into moonlight. The moon was gigantic, ten times the diameter of poor Luna, with uncharted markings. Everything was bright silver, the ground, the air, our two selves. No more auras, we were both inside an infinite aura. I was wading uphill through a field of poppies, towards a low crest which the immense white disc overhung. The companion who had my face got to the top of the crest beside me. Below us lay a beach, and a shining sea where huge dolphins played.

'It would be wisest,' said my doppelganger, 'to go to HIM first and clear up that part of it.'

His voice hadn't startled me before, but this time it did. So far as I knew, no one had conversations in the domains opened by SP5, or even heard them. If I could register that in my own mind, could be startled in my own person, then the net outcome of all that confusion in the glass must have been that my companion was now the spokes-man of Otherness.

He led the way down a cliff-path and along the sand. We both left footprints. A few hundred yards from our descent point we arrived at a cave, and Martin emerged slowly from its depths carrying a lantern. He still had the air of age which had saddened me, but now it was tranquil, its dignity reinforced by the moon-silvering of his hair....

There's a gap when I try to recollect who spoke first and what was said. Presently Martin and I were talking, that's all. It was retroactive, we *had been* talking. This wasn't a new dialogue, it was one that had been going on for days, and less intensively for years. Only, of course, it hadn't. I recalled Martin's own diary record of the first SP-trip, and recognized an effect he'd described: awareness of a different past, lived through by a different route.

Martin was leading up again to a proposition already put to me and deferred.

'...You've been at Allhallows long enough to know what I mean.'

'Yes. Mind you, I can still do that article.'

'I don't doubt it. But you know, now, it won't be the real story.'

'No, it won't. Every answer leads to more questions.'

'You see and hear things you don't understand. Right?'

'Right. You're putting it moderately.'

'But so do I,' said Martin. 'I'm not peddling a closed system. That's the sort of fallacy we must break away from. It all goes on.'

'A new chapter, you might say, in the Mysteries of Britain.'

'Exactly. And there, Geoffrey, you do most definitely come in. You're at home in the dimension of myth. I'm in it, perforce, but not at home. So I'm asking you again. Nobody's better qualified. Stay around, work with us, decide how much you accept as sound and worth developing, and write the book which I can't.'

I glanced at my double. He sat on the sidelines, mute.

'Believe me, Martin, I'm honoured. You're implying that this is where my own... vocation, if we're going to use that word... ought to lead.'

'Where it did lead, years ago. Can you be positive what's cause, what's effect? Go over the sequence of events. You dropped in on that lecture at the Free Mind Society before any of this happened. Allhallows came to me soon after. So did SP5. The rest has followed. But this Avalonian territory was more yours than mine. Perhaps I was only brought here – and perhaps I only got in on the SP5 tests – because you'd been at the lecture and a link had been forged. You were the person who could return in due time, and interpret Allhallows to the world in terms that would justify its existing at all. So it may have been allowed to exist because you'd been lined up to do the job. You, in other words, may be the reason for me.'

...I can't remember the end of that discussion, any more than the beginning. My double and I were walking along the beach. Ahead I saw a woman in a flowing white dress (most surfaces looked pale under that moon, but her dress actually was white), gliding through the shallow foam where it hissed in and out across the sand.

'But of course,' Karen was saying. 'Isn't that the natural way to look at it? Everything started after Martin met you. It hurt like hell, but we had our crisis and then it all began to add up. I think you're about due to re-enter the scene in person.'

'Would you want me around?'

'I told you, I want you in the family. "Around" or not. We'd play that by ear, wouldn't we? You'd have a room at Allhallows and whatever else you want.'

'It's odd, but this idea of my composing a popular gospel, so to speak – it first came to me through Paul, not Martin. When he was explaining that National Quest scheme.'

'I told you Paul was a bright lad.'

...My double and I were walking along the beach. Ahead I saw a woman in a flowing white dress....

'Up here.' He diverted me firmly to a flight of steps cut in the cliff face. At the top was a plateau of level ground, its sweep broken only by a hunched black protuberance like a tree-stump. This, on closer inspection, was Paul sitting in a chair. At least I think it was Paul. He had his back to the giant moon. His face was a speaking darkness.

'Don't worry, Geoffrey, you'll be welcome.'

'Could we agree to differ on some points?'

'Naturally. If you're around Allhallows much, that's what you'll be needing. Differences. A devil's advocate to raise awkward issues and keep you critical. Do you know what they taught me in my consultancy days? "Question every detail." More of you authors should study management technique.'

He had to be Paul, and yet he didn't sound altogether as he should. It was like listening to a ventriloquist's dummy.

...We were walking on the plateau. The turf underfoot was cropped short. Maybe my doppelganger would respond now?

'I seem to be getting railroaded into this. The Book of Allhallows.'

'Wouldn't you agree,' he said, 'that you're cut out for the job?'

'Possibly. But it doesn't fizz.'

'It never does till the arrow strikes.'

'Explain.'

'Up to now, all you've been doing in this place where we are is meeting yourself. The arrow has to strike from beyond you. From the country outside the contact zone – where you can't go, yet.'

'The proto-realm?'

'If you adopt Martin's terminology. I don't care for it. The realm of counterpointed Being.'

'That's rather a mouthful.'

The Finger and the Moon

My third SP-trip included an episode which I've tried to slot in without success. I can't recall any break in the sequence where it would fit. Logically it belongs here, but it branched out somehow on a time-fork.

In a good indoor light, I was reading the *Globe* supplement. The page was near the end of my article on Allhallows. It belonged, therefore, to the future. Unfortunately it bore no date. I tried to make out the picture and couldn't, it blurred. But the text was in sharp focus. It ran roughly as follows.[2]

Martin Ellis is well aware that you can't influence people much by abstract homilies on vocation, even with an exotic setting. The advice has to 'take', the recipient has to be turned on. This will happen, if it does, through some extra influence or event beyond a guru's control.

One thinks of cases in literature, such as the sea-bird that suddenly persuaded the boy Whitman he was a poet ('Now in a moment I know what I am for, I awake') or Proust's famous madeleine that released *le temps perdu*. Star graduates of Allhallows like Madri and John Rosmer testify that their new life-style had its actual birth in a key incident. Madri's did involve Ellis, but only by way of a chance remark of his which showed her how to blend poetry with Tantrism. Rosmer's was an unrelated public event at the other end of England, the Greydale electrocution scandal – or to be exact, the scandal plus a comment made on it by his then senior officer.

This outside jolt which brings an Ellis disciple into action can't be arranged. What Ellis claims, in effect, is that he sets the charge so that it will blow up when some unforeseen match lights the fuse. Although the idea is crucial, he prefers not to labour it in his lectures for fear of destroying the students' spontaneity. Apart from occasional throwaway remarks and hints (which can be tiresomely cryptic) he lets them work it out for themselves.

But as so often at Allhallows, there are wheels within wheels. Even the unforeseen, Ellis implies, doesn't really come by pure chance, because nothing does. The outside jolt which completes the treatment he has started is really set up through wire-pullings in the proto-realm. He asserts this without pretending to fix it. While preparing the ground he trusts that the proto-realm will, in its own good time, deliver.

The theory that our key accidents and encounters are in some obscure way 'planned' - even that we ourselves, in the hidden-part-of-the-iceberg sense, have a share in planning them - has wider bearings. As a practising analyst, Ellis noted that some of his patients were depressed by the debunking that traces admired human activities back to such accidents, to 'childhood trivia and rationalized compensations', as he put it himself. Hostile critics have tried to deflate Ellis's own theories by tracing them to a traumatic blow in earlier life.

Too good a psychologist to deny the facts, he has given them a new look by carrying Jung further. Proto-psychology gives fresh dimensions to cause and effect. Proust - meaning the unseen part of the Proust Binary - can plant the madeleine that will ignite his own genius. Or it can be planted for him by a 'presence'. Influences of the same sort can contrive that a Madri and a John Rosmer shall be on the spot to elicit the words that will transform them. Long-delayed and random-seeming connections 'here' may reflect instant, straightforward linkages 'there'.

Certainly Ellis carries conviction when he insists that 'what you are for' is a meaningful idea, a guideline out of neurosis and chaos. Also, when he contends that its implications are radical, making it almost the reverse of the submissive 'station in life' which Victorian moralists used to preach. The arrow from the blue does strike, whoever launches it.

Some of the challenging results are already public knowledge.

...It was no longer dark. A rapid tropical-type dawn was breaking.

'No,' said my double, 'this isn't what you'd call the real dawn. This is the sun shining at midnight. As it did for the initiates of the Great Goddess.'

He wasn't far out, my watch said 12:40. Nevertheless the sun did rise. It looked no bigger than anywhere else. For a few degrees above the world's rim it was orange, then it glared with full summer brilliance. The morning was still dewy and fresh but warming fast. We were in a broad park-like stretch of land with occasional copses. It was bounded by a wall. On the eastward side this wall was only a hundred yards or so distant - aged mellow brick, with sunflowers growing along it, and a gate.

A white horse trotted from behind bushes. Two children were mounted pillion-wise on its back. They rode parallel to the wall and then through the gate and out of sight.

'This way,' said my double, starting off in the same direction. We reached the gate and halted. Beyond, the ground fell away to another beach. No sign of the children or their horse. But on the verge of the sea-grass I saw an expected figure. Annabel was doing what might have been yoga exercises. The cut of her short garment momentarily and comically suggested a gymslip, but it was more colourful, with a curious design of wands and wreathed leaves.

'That's it,' said my double.

'Can't I go any further?'

'You wouldn't want to.'

He was quite right, I didn't. But I watched Annabel thoughtfully.

'What's the message then? Are you offering me the cult of youth as my inspiration? It's a bit shopworn.'

No answer. Her flexing legs gleamed white and elegant in the sunshine.

'Or do you mean...

'At your age? Don't be ridiculous. She is. That's it.'

...The waves, breaking long and slow. The sun glittering on the sea. Two humpbacked green islets with standing stones on them. Sea again and more islets, but always sea between and beyond, shading off horizonless into infinite blue, infinite space. A lightness and gladness no words can capture.

Ninth Day

I WAS SPRAWLED PAINFULLY on the ground. Grass was still under me, but I was at the centre of the maze, with clear sky above and a normal summer dawn breaking. The SP5 state must have passed at some point into sleep. How much had been vision and how much dream?

Stiffly I got up and went out, fastening the door behind me. That sheet of paper with the maze-solving instructions was in my pocket, unused. Reading the poem in reverse, I found my way safely back to the entrance. It was not yet five o'clock. Allhallows appeared to be at rest in spite of last night's upheaval, and so did the Cryptocratic tents. Upstairs I washed, dozed, reflected. Full sleep would not return. At last I went out again.

She was in the place where I met her with that unexplained dog, on open ground near the approach to the maze, in sight of Glastonbury Tor. No dog, however. It was a long time since we'd last spoken together. The assorted ways I'd been seeing her, in the flesh and in vision, made it tricky to hit on a correct gambit.

In sober fact it was our third early-morning meeting. 'This is getting to be a habit,' I said.

Annabel's eyes were tired. 'I lost track of you last night. Can you tell me how all that trouble started?'

We strolled along past the back of the house. I gave her a circumspect account. She asked no questions and showed no surprise.

'What about Paul?' I asked, sounding as solicitous as I could. 'How is he?'

'Asleep. We couldn't get the doctor. But Martin says they went through a lot of this before, when Paul had his other trouble. It'll pass off.'

'I'm glad to hear it.'

'Paul got calmer when they took him indoors. He lay down and I

283

sat with him.'

We'd come to the kinetic sculpture. I stopped. 'When Paul fired, you know, he hit this.' I pushed it as usual. The strips creaked and scraped, the human figure failed to appear. Offhand it was hard to diagnose what was wrong, but the bullet must have damaged some vital joint.

Annabel pushed too with the same result. 'That could make sense,' she commented.

We sat down on the bench. She was anxious to tell me something. 'When Paul staged that séance... I didn't want to.'

'I thought not.'

'It won't happen again. I mean, not like it did then.'

'My dear, it's your own business.'

'But I want you to know, and I can't tell you without telling the reason. You did realize why I performed for him.'

'I believe so.'

'Last night when I was trying to settle him... suddenly there was nothing, it wasn't there any more, not with me. Oh, not because he'd gone around acting crazy, I'm sure you understand how that wouldn't be it. But it isn't going to be the same.'

I mumbled some avuncular nonsense.

'Anyway,' she continued more brightly, 'we'll have to do some sorting out. It's a pity this happened in front of so many people. Still, the students aren't put off. They think it proves it's all real, there are forces at work here. They're right too. Poor Paul, it's a shame we should be able to, well, use him as an exhibit. That's how it's turned out all the same.'

'You expect Allhallows to carry on as before.'

'But of course. What about you, though? Martin was suggesting you might work with us on a bigger scale, after you've done your article. Write a book or something. I'd like it if you did.'

The news didn't surprise. However, I could now contemplate cool-ly what might lie ahead. Another set-to with the photographer (I was in for that whatever I did); more long talks with Martin and Karen and a convalescent Paul; further sessions with Cryptocrats, Tantrists, students; further wrestlings with doctrine; an attempt (it would have to be very cautious) to probe Paul's nightmares; and alongside it all, the need to come to terms with an insidious feeling that maybe neither the doctrine nor the nightmares mattered in detail....

'There's plenty of stuff for the article. After that – yes, Martin may have the right idea – but it's too soon to commit myself. First I've got my own sorting out to do. I'll have to go over everything I've seen and heard, and piece all my notes together. Then I can see how it looks, and decide whether I could go on further, collaborating with Martin.'

'We're all sure you could help a lot. Even Paul. I think you'd find he could make himself very useful with research or whatever, when this upset is over.'

I thanked her absently. I was struggling to express a deeper misgiving.

'You know – to speak purely as a writer, without bringing personalities in – Allhallows is difficult to get a grip on. Suppose I simply tried telling the story of this visit of mine. I came; heard lectures; met A, B and C; had some experiences that puzzle me...'

'I don't mind explaining one or two of them,' Annabel put in.

'All in good time, dear, and I'll enjoy listening. But the trouble is, I could write down all the facts and it just isn't like that. If I went on to work it up into a book, it'd be a worse problem still.

'I suggested doing the article because I thought important things might be happening here. They are. Not only at Allhallows, but in other places nearby where the same... mysteries... are active. You know; you've lived in a Glastonbury commune. Half a century from now, the life of this country may be totally different because of things that have started in Somerset during the past decade. Historians will look back and accept it.'

'I'm sure they will.'

'But how can you convey this if you're writing at the time, when you're in it yourself, so as to make it sound as important as it'll turn out to be? How can you convey what all this is about?'

'When I was over there with the communes,' said Annabel, 'we knew we were simply living another act in an enchantment that's been going on for thousands of years. I'm not sure if anybody knows what it is, but it keeps making something wonderful happen when people are giving up hope that anything will. We're part of it here too.'

(We had ceased, she and I, to be alone in a hushed morning. No one else was in sight yet, but house and camp had begun to stir.)

The Finger and the Moon

'It's a problem for the poor writer,' I replied. 'Look at a previous act in this enchantment of yours. Our old friend King Arthur. When romancers wanted to convey what the saga of Arthur was about, they had ways of doing it. They could dress him up in myths of a golden age, they could put him into prophecies, they could surround him with disguised gods and superhuman wizards and miracle-working saints. British mythology supplied all that was needed to build up the facts into what they stood for, the glory they meant in human lives. Arthur could be woven into that mythology, he could become more true by becoming more mythical, if you follow me.'

I doubted if she did. However, I plunged on.

'The trouble is, we aren't allowed to invent legends nowadays. So how can we give a modern story the same weight, the same mystique, even if we do see it as another chapter in the deep history of the island of Albion? Who'd be able to do that?'

'Maybe you,' she said.

Note

IN PORTRAYING ALLHALLOWS and its inmates I have done my best to play fair. Many of the hints dropped in the dialogue can be followed up, and will be found to have a genuine bearing on ideas and themes which the story develops. To take one obvious example, Martin cites Jung as his chief influence. A glance through some of Jung's works will shed light on aspects of Allhallows which no character actually mentions. (It would be wrong if any did.) The same is true of various references to Aleister Crowley, Robert Graves, and others.

As a rule, however, a novel should not depend – or even seem to depend – on 'required reading' outside itself. I refrain therefore from pursuing a point which could be taken as implying that this one does. Except to remove a possible source of puzzlement. Any student of magic who has read to the end, and perhaps even not as far as that, will have noticed images from the Major Trumps or Arcana of the Tarot, occurring in the main story as well as the passing allusions of the Grail Ritual. So I will state here that all twenty-two are present, some fairly openly, some disguised. The scenes where they come in reflect a consensus of expert interpretation, with a few added notions of my own. By using these well-known and potent symbols, and sometimes letting them partly shape the action, I have tried to convey nuances which could not be made explicit, for reasons given in the story itself.

Here too, though, I am anxious to avoid any impression that *The Finger and the Moon* depends on some sort of key. Hence I leave it to readers having occult interests to pick out the Tarot passages for themselves, with the assurance that they will not be missing anything vital if they fail to complete the list.

Afterword (2003)

THE FINGER AND THE MOON was not planned. Having invented the setting and the main characters, I let the story develop with only a vague idea of where it was going. The course that it took seems to me, now, to have shown an intuitive understanding which I was not clearly aware of at the time.

In the junior upheavals of the Sixties and early Seventies, as I have said in the Preface, I was already past the age to be a participant except marginally, but on the whole I applauded the rebelliousness and some of the attempted "alternative" lifestyles. A phrase that suggests my attitude then is "The more the merrier". Let there be all sorts of excitement, all sorts of fantasy, all sorts of novelty, and let the best elements have a chance to rise to the top. Some of what was happening could be seen as a promising kind of activation, breaking outworn moulds. New life could emerge.

I had cared profoundly for Glastonbury before any of it started. When Glastonbury became a focus of mystical hippiedom, my book *King Arthur's Avalon* got into a best-seller list in the alternative publication *International Times* (*IT*). My personal convictions, though different, never led me to support the local anti-hippie attacks. To a certain extent I think my sympathy was justified. Several of the long-term developments were very good, and have remained so.

That all seems a long time ago. Yet *The Finger and the Moon* still has its relevance, and not only because of the New Age. Allhallows, as I conceived it, was to be a forum for anything and everything that came under a very broad definition of magic, with Martin trying to bring coherence and direction through his own ideas, and guide his groups into new alternative courses. However, the logic of the story (so far as it had any) pushed me towards a more discriminating stance.

In the first place, I began to suspect that the magical stuff, with its SP5 accompaniments, would be unlikely to create anything truly sane and stable. The "star graduates" – Madri, Rosmer, Hoad – went their own way, and at Allhallows itself destabilization was a built-in hazard, though it might not be fatal. In the second place – and I re-emphasize what I have said in the Preface – a perception grew that these things are not always merely neutral or harmless. They can have possibilities of a very dubious kind, either in themselves or through exploitation. As the story turns out, the intelligent and manipulative Paul disintegrates briefly into a sort of diabolic possession. I am not saying anything about real evil spirits, but I am recognizing real evil, or the possibility of it.

The Finger and the Moon attracted readers who seemed to think it was true, at least in substance, and even wanted progress reports on the experimentation with SP5. It is only a story. But the facts that I found emerging as I wrote are rather more. Some of these things do have potentialities for wisdom and insight – Isaac Newton, one of the greatest scientists who ever lived, spent years studying alchemy – but they are not always free from danger to sanity and morality. Today, those who are so inclined may enthuse about the New Age and its manifestations, generally or selectively. But something that should always be present is caution.

Also – and this is a very big "also" – a sense of humour.

Notes to the Text

First Day

1   This echoes a dictum of Bertrand Russell (1872-1970): that if you say you see a cat, what you actually mean is that you see a feline patch of colour. Russell's cat reappears on page 94. This book contains other "in" jokes of the same kind. A reader may or may not pick them up; it doesn't matter.

2   Touches of genuine autobiography.

3   The Free Mind Society may seem even more archaic today than at the time of writing. However, it isn't pure fantasy. Some such group actually did sing the hymn which I quote. In the 1970s there were still people around who had known H.G. Wells (who I trust needs no introduction) and the Pankhursts (pioneers of the women's movement).

4   Herbert Spencer (1820-1903) was a Victorian philosophical writer, influenced by Darwin. He coined the phrase "survival of the fittest"; decided not to marry another author, Marian Evans, better known by her pen-name George Eliot; and wrote nine volumes of a System of Synthetic Philosophy.

5   Originally, the Glastonbury Fayre, held in 1971. It was reborn as the Glastonbury Festival, which has continued to happen on and off at the Summer Solstice, attracting over 100,000 participants. The narrator's attitude to the original event reflects my own, at the time. See Patrick Benham's book *The Avalonians*.

6   I've been told that when the finances were all completely worked out, *Man, Myth and Magic* didn't make a profit after all. It's a valuable work of reference, just the same.

7   In making Martin forecast the importance of Magic, I was on the right track, given a fairly broad definition of Magic.

But the prediction really looked beyond the 1970s, to the larger ramifications of the New Age.

8   *Oz* and *IT* (*International Times*). "Underground" or "Alternative" publications, popular in the Sixties.

9   *Doomwatch* was a BBC television series (1970-72) that drew attention, through fictional episodes, to various possibilities of disaster.

10 The ex-docker. Terry Hoad, who is mentioned again on pages 43, 67, 79 and elsewhere. He presented himself to my imagination, and I intuitively knew him to be important without understanding why.

11 An expression meaning "old-fashioned".

12 Madri voices my own view, at a time when it was fashionable to "drop out" in ways that deprived the dropper-out of credibility.

13 John Rosmer's activities reflect a hope on my part that an appreciable number of "protesters" might, sooner or later, show genuine public spirit and enterprise. I dare say some have done so, but Rosmers are rare, and I was right to see the Campaign for Nuclear Disarmament (CND) as a largely spent force that might "flare back into life" occasionally, but would never recover its early impetus.

14 An English stately home that is open to the public and offers various entertainments.

15 "DO WHAT YOU WILL" is a maxim that has occurred in several interesting contexts, with different implications. See pages 55 and 253-4.

16 "To help them with their inquiries" is a euphemism used in British journalism to refer to people whom the police are investigating. Karen is making a mild joke.

17 Curiously, when I pictured the scene, I saw the Chinese girl clearly without knowing why. Later a situation developed where a Chinese person was needed.

18 It will emerge that the four permanent staff members at Allhallows are conceived as vaguely archetypal in relation to the narrator—archetypal, that is, in terms of Jungian psychology. Martin is the Wisdom figure; Karen and Annabel are older and younger aspects of the Anima; Paul is the Shadow. But no symbolism or allegory is intended, and a reader will do better to

forget the archetypes altogether, rather than try fitting them to the characters.

19   This is the source of the title.

20   Vinoba Bhave (1895-1982) carried on some of Gandhi's reforms in Indian villages. I met him and he made the impression described.

Second Day

1   I discussed what I have called the Glastonbury Madness in *Avalonian Quest*, pages 17-19.

2   E.A. Freeman (1832-92) was a real historian, who is no longer thought of very highly, but who did make this perceptive remark about Glastonbury.

3   I have since reconsidered Arthur, in *The Discovery of King Arthur* and elsewhere, but most of this paragraph is still fairly acceptable.

4   A novelist and a dramatist, writing in the Sixties and Seventies. Arthur's "comeback" has since gone much further.

5   Not entirely intuitive. Hereford Cathedral's famous Mappa Mundi or World Map, a thirteenth-century work, has now been shown to reflect a tradition about Cadbury.

6   This is a parody (I hope, a good-humoured one) of things I had heard said about Somerset's alleged landscape-Zodiac. Even the exhortation to wear thin-soled shoes was not my own invention. There is more about the Zodiac theory on page 141.

7   A quotation from William Blake.

8   *(and elsewhere)* As mentioned in the Preface, at the time of writing it was not generally regarded as sexist to say "he" etc. for persons undefined. In this context it means "he or she", as the composition of the Allhallows group should make clear. Likewise with "Man" for humanity, on page 48 and elsewhere.

9   A wise observation, adapted from one of C.S. Lewis's stories. The original is "You are never told what *would have* happened." I don't think it is appropriate to Paul.

10   Aleister Crowley (1875-1947) was a self-styled magician and teacher of spiritual development, who liked to use the spelling "magick". He had, and deserved, an ugly reputation, but attracted disciples with his exposition of what he called "The

Law". Posthumous admirers included, it is said, the Beatles, if perhaps not for long. The characters' acquaintance with some of Crowley's ideas is quite credible.

11 "Redbrick" is a term sometimes applied to Britain's younger universities.

12 "Women's Lib" was still a current term for feminist activism.

13 Autobiographical. I did it at Cadbury with a curtain-rod, on the advice of an experienced dowser.

14 Arthur Koestler (1905-83) was the author of *Darkness at Noon* and other novels, and books on philosophical and psychological topics. I think I invented Lalkov.

15 A lot of this sort of thing is still going on, and becoming, if anything, more extravagant.

16 *Dad's Army* was a successful BBC television comedy series (1968-77) about the wartime Home Guard, still warmly remembered.

17 Autobiographical. See my book *Miracles*.

18 See my book *The Hell-Fire Clubs*.

19 Autobiographical. See *Miracles*.

20 The numerologist's success with one subject and failure with another was based on a performance I saw myself.

21 Parallels between the ancient Babylonian Creation Epic and Milton's War in Heaven are far more numerous and striking than they appear in the extracts; it was not practicable to quote either at adequate length. In *The Book of Prophecy* I have considered the paradox that Milton seems to be echoing the Creation Epic though it was not available till its discovery and translation centuries later. I introduced the passages here mainly to convey an impression of strangeness. But they relate to "knowing what I couldn't know" at the top of page 75, and they are mentioned again on page 161 with a Martin-type explanation.

Third Day

1 A Tarot image, like others in the story. See page 288.

2 The I-Ching is a Chinese method of divination which impressed Jung. See page 71.

3 "Flower Power" was a label for a hippie phenomenon of the

Sixties, associated with the slogan "Make love not war".

4   If the centre of a maze is connected with the perimeter, through whatever complications, you can get to it sooner or later by constantly turning to the right. If the centre is an "island", not connected with the perimeter, you can't.

5   Fact. In some of this page, Martin is saying more or less what I would say myself, and have said in other places. He doesn't always do that.

6   I have repeated this from time to time and found it to be an important guiding principle.

7   "Faculty X" is a term coined by Colin Wilson in *The Occult*.

8   I have heard that Kekulé's story was improved in the telling. But the instances in the following paragraph are, I believe, valid.

9   Autobiographical.

10 This is more or less what happened with my biography of Gandhi. The real incident is described in *Miracles*.

11 Angels were not a popular topic at the time of writing, but they became so during the nineties. More than thirty books about them were published in a single year.

12 David Jacks is of course fictitious, but he has touches of Donald McCullin, a most distinguished photographer with whom I once had the privilege of working.

13 Both names are derogatory. Frank Buchman (1878-1961) led a movement called Moral Rearmament. L. Ron Hubbard (1911-86) invented Scientology.

14 An "in" joke. There actually was a Canadian magazine called *First Statement*, and if you look up one of its 1944 issues, you will find an article by Martin Ellis. It was a pen-name.

15 The Grail ritual reference is factual, though the portion that finally reached the TV screen was very brief.

16 The word "protoself" was my own invention, but it is worth noting a passage in a book by Professor Robert Tocquet about a "deep region" of the mind which he associates with the feats of mathematical prodigies or "lightning calculators":

> This deep region is nothing else but the *daimon* of Socrates, the *Theos* of Plotinus, the *planetary genius* of Paracelsus, the *transcendental ego* of Novalis, the *subliminal self* of Myers, the *unknown guest* of Maeterlinck, and, according to the term

I have frequently employed, the *subconscious* or the *unconscious* of the psychists. But "unconscious" not, it would seem, because it lacks consciousness in itself, but only because our normal consciousness does not ordinarily perceive it.

I think this should all be seriously considered, up to a point, though Martin pursues it farther than I would. In portraying him, I was trying to imagine a person who would sound something like a religious teacher without teaching a religion.

17 I did once have this odd sense of inverted time, and have wondered about it in relation to prophecy.

Other-Scene I

1 I picked Serotonin up from Colin Wilson. Perhaps it isn't very relevant, but never mind.

2 The pseudonym—taken from a Spanish Inquisitor—of a well-known composer of crossword puzzles.

3 Dorothy L. Sayers was an author of detective stories regarded as classics of the genre.

4 An inversion of a well-known saying of the Canadian media theorist Marshall McLuhan (1911-80), "The medium is the message".

5 Russell's cat. See *First Day*, Note 1.

6 Ironically, there are now whole books and conferences about consciousness.

7 See *First Day*, Note 9.

8 In this SP5 "trip" and others that follow, I tried to imagine experiences appropriate to the persons undergoing them.

9 B.F. Skinner (1904-90) was a leading exponent of Behaviourist psychology. I seem to recall that he proved some point he had made by teaching pigeons to play ping-pong.

10 The bench was there at the time of writing, but was afterwards removed.

11 I was recalling two lines of Blake (from *The Marriage of Heaven and Hell*):

How do you know but ev'ry bird that cuts the airy way
Is an immense world of delight, clos'd by your senses five?

12 The theory that the terracing around the Tor forms a ritual path

in the shape of a spiral labyrinth was first worked out in detail by Geoffrey Russell, and approved as a possibility—no more than that—by Philip Rahtz, who carried out archaeological work on the Tor in 1964-6.

Fourth Day

1   A long low-cut flounced dress, as in ancient figurines of the Minoan Goddess, discovered in Crete.

2   "Mr. W.H." was the unidentified youth to whom Shakespeare addressed most of his sonnets.

3   "Steady State" and "Big Bang" were rival cosmological theories. The former is now out of favour.

4   The "population explosion" was a much-publicized issue at the time of writing.

5   George Gurdjieff (1877-1949) was a somewhat mysterious "guru" with a Russian background. He established an institute in France where, from 1922 onward, he was expounding an arduous technique of self-realization involving his own conceptions of magic.

6   "Protoself Psychology" is not meant to be taken too seriously, but it's a system that Martin might have worked out.

7   Teilhard de Chardin (1881-1955) was a Jesuit palaeontologist and theorist about evolution, whose book *The Phenomenon of Man* was widely read in the 1950s. It was approved by one eminent scientist, Julian Huxley, and attacked by another, Peter Medawar.

8   Noam Chomsky (1928-) is an American theorist of language.

9   Thomas Traherne (1636-74) was an English poet and Christian mystic.

10   To some extent this did happen at Glastonbury, for a while.

11   Roedean is an expensive upper-class English school for girls.

12   An echo of the Neo-Platonic philosopher Plotinus (c. 205-70).

13   Dr. John Dee (1527-1608) was an Elizabethan polymath who was led astray by the charlatan Edward Kelley into unfortunate activities, including an early form of Spiritualism, and wife-swapping.

14   Paul's room. The story happens when office equipment would not normally have included a computer. Paul, however, is up to date.

15 This is suggested by a passage in G.K. Chesterton's book *The Everlasting Man*. Paul would probably not have read it, but the same thought might have occurred to him, or been suggested to him by someone else.

16. This is Crowley stuff.

Fifth Day

1 Carnaby Street in London was a centre of the more trendy sort of Sixties fashion.

2 The Versailles Adventure was an experience described by two women, Charlotte Moberly and Eleanor Jourdain. They believed that during a visit to the grounds of the French royal palace of Versailles in 1901, they had strayed back in time to the eighteenth century and talked with people of that period.

3 Paul's Miltonic reading again. The parallelism of the texts, when compared in full, is a genuine mystery. I have discussed it in *The Book of Prophecy*.

4 The term "New Age" already existed at the time of writing, though it was not yet widely current.

5 Sir Oliver Lodge (1851-1940) was a physicist, and one of the few eminent scientists who ever became a convert to Spiritualism. He was undoubtedly influenced by the death of his son Raymond and the wish to believe that Raymond still lived.

6 Albert Camus (1913-60), French writer.

7 This is Martin, not myself, yet he is putting forward ideas that seem to me interesting. There is something like them in Tibetan Buddhism.

8 While astronomy certainly seems to rule out influence by planets or stars, a present-day astrologer can still talk about correlations and synchronicities. Mr. Frobisher need not be a complete fool, and Martin is not irresponsible in giving him time to address the group.

9 Autobiographical. I still have the magazine with my article and a photograph of the Indian school inspector.

10 Terry Hoad, the Catholic social worker mentioned on page 29. He never appears personally in the story, and his absence was intentional. It was clear to me, even then, that he couldn't be fit-

ted in. I conceived him as an authentic saint, and I wouldn't presume to present a saint as a fictitious character. If he had appeared,
he would have introduced a different reality, beside which much
of the Allhallows scene would have been unsubstantial. The
way in which Karen speaks of him shows her limitation in that
respect, however understanding she may be in others. Hoad, by
the way, would not have said he was in mortal sin, just like that.
He might have said, with wry amusement, that some cleric had
told him he was.

11 One of the maxims of La Rochefoucauld (1613-80).

Other-Scene II

1 My view of the original Arthur is now somewhat different, but
not radically so.
2 Visionary characters, drawn from Celtic mythology. The White
One, Gwyn-ap-Nudd, is a demigod with a home inside Glastonbury
Tor. His father Nudd—actually Nodens or Nodons—is a god
with a silver hand, whose temple at Lydney in Gloucestershire
has been excavated. A detailed discussion of these beings would
be out of place, but see also pages 194 and 204.
3 My Titaness has since found her way (with embellishments) into
the modern Glastonbury mythology. See Kathy Jones's book *The
Goddess in Glastonbury*.
4 There is a hint here at the messianic return of Arthur, but I made
use of a far earlier Celtic myth from which the motif of the sleep-
ing-and-waking king is derived.

Sixth Day

1 This sticker existed, but I don't know who was responsible for
it.
2 The turning-to-the-right method. Mentioned previously, see
Third Day, Note 4.
3 Gurdjieff. See *Fourth Day*, Note 5.
4 The Belloc-Chesterton ferment. Conversions to Catholicism
were unusually frequent in England during the inter-war period.
Two famous and versatile authors, Hilaire Belloc (1870-1953) and

G.K. Chesterton (1874-1936), were influential through most of the period. Chesterton is quoted on page 141. A convert himself, he had built up a brilliant reputation as a journalist, critic, poet and novelist before his reception into the Church in 1922, and this helped to secure a public for his Catholic writings.

5   Stevick is imaginary, but Brennan and Whyte were real writers on management problems, both of whom described experiments that cast doubt on received wisdom.

6   Poujade was a French politician who led a party in the 1950s, supposedly devoted to the interests of small traders and entrepreneurs. It faded out, and Freda would have been right to use the word "antediluvian", though it was perhaps wrong on my part to assume that she would have known about Poujade at all.

7   The myth of President Kennedy's survival was current as described, for a surprisingly long time. However, Arnold's "inside information" was not part of it.

8   The temptation of my narrator has a faint echo of the grimmer temptation of C.S. Lewis's principal character in his novel *That Hideous Strength*. I hope I would never have been tempted myself in a similar situation. As a matter of fact, I suspect that I actually was sounded out by certain residents of Los Angeles who had read *The Finger and the Moon*. But I didn't make the right responses to their overtures, and whatever their intention was, it went no further.

9   Neo-magical jargon.

10 There are reminiscences here of the oldest Merlin legends. The Welsh "Myrddin" was the original form of the name.

Seventh Day

1   Another of the more explicit Tarot images: The Hanged Man.

2   The Grail ritual was originally written for television performance, and, in part, performed. See also *Third Day*, Note 15.

3   Madri and John Rosmer, the two "star graduates", make their entry. There is a deliberate and important irony about them. As is spelt out on page 231, they do not take SP5: it is *not* the key to the Allhallows phenomenon. Even in imagination, I was never prepared to go all the way with the drug enthusiasts of the Sixties.

4   A remark made by the dramatist Arnold Wesker.

5   Rosmer's honourable gesture of protest—genuine protest, expressed in the protester's life, not mere vituperation—was perhaps fairly credible at the time of writing. Thirty years later it is less so. While I can still sympathize, it is no longer possible to see him as simply right, and he strikes me now as one of the most dated of the characters. That does not detract from the force of his intervention on page 265.

6   I am not happy that I put these words into the narrator's mouth. There is something here, but theorists like Jessie Weston seem to me to have gone too far. While the Grail theme was not approved by the Church, I would say this was because it was strange and offbeat, rather than because it was felt to be semi-pagan.

7   I leave the Grail Ritual to the reader, recalling an observation by William Blake: "The ancients consider'd what is not too explicit as the fittest for Instruction, because it rouzes the faculties to act."

Eighth Day

1   This is a summary of my book *Do What You Will*, re-issued in 2000 as *The Hell-Fire Clubs*, which I was writing concurrently with *The Finger and The Moon*. Martin is not entirely exact.

2   Martin's denunciation of western society, or something like it, could be heard more widely at the time of writing than it can now. But it is a justifiable preface to what he says about finding one's vocation and breaking free.

3   I think I coined the phrase "living differently" myself, when discussing the implications of Gandhi's career and teaching, and drawing a contrast with the mere negative "dropping out" that was popular in the Sixties.

4   Martin is too hopeful, but I don't think it was a mistake to let him express his hope.

5   The Miserific Vision is a diabolic parody of the Beatific Vision, the experience of God enjoyed in heaven, according to Christian doctrine. The actual phrase "the Miserific Vision" was coined by C.S. Lewis in *The Screwtape Letters* to mean the equivalent in hell.

6   A theory developed by Margaret Murray and Hugh Ross Williamson, no longer in favour with any appreciable number of historians.

7   The word "younce" may not be in dictionaries, but I have heard it used in Canada of the noise made by a tiresome cat—"Stop youncing!" It seems appropriate to Simon, especially as he is in some sort of communion with a cat.

8   Mr. Chips was the schoolmaster in James Hilton's bestselling novel *Goodbye Mr. Chips*, filmed in 1939, and made into a musical in 1969.

9   True of real Satanism, but I'm not sure that Martin would have had the insight.

10   Quotation from Thomas More. This too is in C.S. Lewis's *Screwtape Letters*, as a motto at the beginning.

Other-Scene III

1   A famous scene in the Marx Brothers film *Duck Soup* (1933).

2   This fairly down-to-earth summary conveys a good deal of what I would seriously invite a reader to reflect upon, whether or not in Martin's terms.

CPSIA information can be obtained
at www.ICGtesting.com
Printed in the USA
BVOW03s1826171017
497919BV00001B/9/P